Harbor of Dreams

A Novel

by Joseph A. Tringali

Calkins Harbor Publishing Company

ISBN-13: 978-0-9998698-2-6

Translation editing and cover design by
Kristen Privitera Barrett

DEDICATION

This book is dedicated to those who dare to dream

and who care enough about their dreams

to make them into reality

Lt. Col. John A. Tringali, USAF (Retired)

Delta Air Lines

Elizabeth Anne Tringali, PA-C

Tringali Vibrant Health

PREFACE

Make me over in the morning
From the rag-bag of the world!
Scraps of dream and duds of daring,
Home-brought stuff from far sea-faring,
Faded colors once so flaring,
Shreds of banners long since furled!
Hues of ash and glints of glory,
In the rag-bag of the world.

Taken from, Spring Song
by
Bliss Carman (1861–1929)

CHAPTER 1

The wheels of the Boeing 747 thudded down on the Bonita Airport runway, and a dozing Marilyn Dupré Townsend stirred uneasily on the shoulder of her husband.

"Marilyn, wake up; we're home," Jack said softly as he kissed her hair.

"I know; I'm not asleep. I just don't want the honeymoon to be over yet."

"It's not going to be over just because we're home."

"That's what they all say," she said, opening the dark eyes that he found so captivating. "But somehow I don't think Cap'n Kelly's Marina will be able to compete with Paris." She looked at him earnestly. "Jack, promise me we'll go back every year."

"That's a pretty big promise. What happened to New Orleans?"

"We can go there, too," she said, stretching as the plane rolled toward the Bonita terminal. "Let's just take all that money you've got socked away and travel for the rest of our lives."

"What about your unofficially adopted sister Jennifer Calkins and Dupré's Restaurant?" he reminded her.

"How did you know about the name change?"

"Long distance. I checked in with Rob at the office every few days while we were gone."

"You checked in with R.J.? Your law partner? You mean you were working on our honeymoon?" she demanded.

"Not at all; just checking in." he kissed her lightly. "Besides, it's all your fault. "You're the one who turned me back into a practicing lawyer, remember? We always check in. Rob will probably do the same thing when he's off with Jennifer on their honeymoon in the Fall."

The plane rolled to a stop and passengers began jamming the aisle. The first-class cabin was far larger than the Concorde which had brought them across the Atlantic, but in spite of the accommodations it seemed everyone just wanted to get off the long flight from New York to Bonita. Jennifer and R.J. were waiting to welcome them home, and it wasn't long before they were in a limo heading for Bonita Key and the marina that occupied the cove at Calkins Harbor.

"Jennifer, it was so wonderful. We greeted 1986 from the top of the Eiffel Tower. The City of Light was covered with frost, sparkling and laid out at our feet. I was so glad Jack's mother gave me her fur coat; it was freezing up there! But it was so beautiful I didn't want to come down. I can't wait to tell Papa about it," Marilyn gushed. "By the way, why isn't he here?" she asked as the driver guided the car away from the terminal.

"Oh . . . well, he went back to New Orleans . . . for a visit . . . just for a while. There really wasn't anything for him to do with the restaurant torn apart like it is," Jennifer explained as she quickly looked out the window.

"Torn apart?" What do you mean, 'torn apart'? What did you do?"

"Nothing, really. It looks a lot worse than it is."

"'Looks worse than it is?' Jennifer, what's going on?" Marilyn demanded.

"Nothing. Really, nothing. I just had the crew come back for a few small changes, that's all. We'll be ready to open in a month at the latest."

"A month? Jennifer, the restaurant was all set. We had our rehearsal party there, remember? And we've only been gone for three weeks! What could you possibly have done in such a short time?"

"Don't worry about it, Marilyn," the young blonde assured her. "A month longer, tops. And it'll be worth every penny."

"How are things at Townsend & Meacham?" Jack asked his younger partner as he tried to steer the conversation away from the subject of Dupré's and whatever disaster awaited them in Calkins Harbor.

"Fine. Great," R.J. replied. "We're moving along on the appraisals of the Calkins holdings. I think they're going to come in at somewhat more than I anticipated. And wait till I tell you about the criminal case that Judge MacIntyre assigned me to try."

"Wait a minute. Those appraisals are going to show the estate's net worth is more than twenty-five million, and you're talking about some stupid criminal case?"

"Jack, I can do the estate tax returns in my sleep, and we'll throw everything into a couple of trusts. No big deal. But let me tell you about this case . . ."

"Is it the one you told me about? The 'He was in bed with me' defense?" Jack asked patiently.

"Yeah. I believe her, Jack. I really think my guy was framed."

Jack heaved a sigh and looked out the window. Small children and inexperienced lawyers had one thing in common—they believed everything.

Marilyn tried to steer both conversations to a safer topic. "Is Jack's mother still here or did she go back to New York?" she asked Jennifer.

"No, she's not here," Jennifer assured her.

"So she's home in New York?" Jack clarified.

"No, she's not in New York," R.J. replied.

"Jennifer, what happened to Mrs. Townsend?" Marilyn insisted.

"Well, she sort of . . . that is, she . . . well, as a matter of fact . . . she went to New Orleans with your father."

"She what?" Marilyn demanded as Jack began to chuckle.

"She went to New Orleans with your father, Marilyn." R.J. repeated.

"Oh, my God!" Marilyn complained as Jack laughed louder. "And I don't see what's so funny," she added, piercing him with her look.

"Come on, Honey, take it easy. It's not like she can get pregnant or anything."

"John Townsend, shut your mouth!" Marilyn hissed, looking at the driver who was smiling broadly. She slammed shut the window to the driver's compartment. "This is not funny!" she shouted in a whisper.

"I think it's kind of neat," Jack replied. "It's like a movie . . . that movie with Sandra Dee, what was it?"

"A Summer Place," Jennifer said quickly. "Only it was the children who fell in love and ran away. I just loved that picture, didn't you, Jack?"

"Will you two stop it?" Marilyn pleaded. "This isn't a movie; this is my life."

"Well it may be your life, but your father's run off with my mother," Jack said, still chuckling at the thought.

"Jennifer, why didn't you stop them?" Marilyn demanded.

"Stop them? What was I supposed to do, stand in the doorway with a shotgun?"

"They're both adults, Marilyn," R.J. said in his fiancé's defense. "There's not much anyone can do about it."

Marilyn put her head in her hands. "Oh, my God! Another scandal involving my father!"

The big car turned into the private road to the marina. Unlike the old days when the Calkins brothers ran the place, it was now paved, as was the parking lot outside the two-story building that was destined to become Dupré's Restaurant. Although clouds of shell-rock dust no longer greeted each new arrival, the sight through the tinted windows of the limo did nothing to improve Marilyn's mood. Workers were swarming over the building that was at the moment covered in scaffolding. A new roof was being constructed and a crane was preparing to hoist a huge wooden truss into place.

"Oh, God, Jennifer, what did you do?" Marilyn said when she found her voice.

"Nothing. Really, nothing. It really does look a lot worse than it is. We didn't touch the inside hardly at all."

Marilyn put her head back on the upholstered seat. "Jack, let's go back to Paris, please," she pleaded.

"Come on, it'll be finished in a month; you're going to love it." Jennifer said as the car rolled to a stop.

"Head's up! It's the Boss Lady!" one of the workers yelled as Jennifer picked up her white hard hat from a nearby bench and tucked in her long blonde hair.

"Here, put these on," she said, handing out similar hats to her three companions. "We don't want anybody getting conked on the head around here. Insurance, you know."

The crane let out a roar and belched greasy smoke as it lifted a large truss off a nearby flatbed trailer and held it there while it momentarily swayed in the air. "All right, comin' up! Watch it up there!" Foreman Tim Gorman shouted to the men atop the scaffold.

"Isn't it the greatest thing you've ever seen?" Jennifer said, sweeping her arm around the site.

"Jennifer, how much is this costing us?" Marilyn demanded.

"Not that much! You'd be surprised. It's mostly cosmetic work."

"Cosmetic work? They're adding a roof, for heaven's sake!"

"But it isn't structural. Here, let me show you the plans." She ushered them into the first floor of the building that was still cluttered with the debris of what once had been Cap'n Kelly's Boatyard. "Look at this," Jennifer said, unrolling a set of blueprints. "The building was too plain, Marilyn; just straight concrete block and stucco. It looked a like an upside-down shoebox. We're adding a balcony with wrought iron filigree all the way around and an overhanging mansard roof. Very French, don't you think?"

"It does improve the place," Marilyn admitted, "but how much does it cost?"

"Not that much, really. Now, I haven't done anything with this area yet," Jennifer said, gesturing around the cluttered first-floor room. "I'm saving it for Phase Two; but let me show you some preliminary sketches that Jim Lacey and I have been working on." She unrolled a second set of plans. "We figure that once we outgrow the second floor, we can get rid of all the junk down here and turn this area into a bar, lounge and gift shop."

"Gift shop? Jennifer who do you think is going to be coming here, anyway?"

"Tourists, Marilyn. Tourists. Once they see this place and taste your father's cooking, they'll be breaking down our doors. Come on, let me show you what we're doing upstairs."

"Why don't Rob and I go to the boat and unload our luggage?" Jack suggested.

Marilyn looked back at him. "Don't you dare!" she said, her dark eyes flashing. "I need all the moral support I can get right now."

The upper room that had been so elegantly decorated just a few weeks earlier was now havoc personified. Tables and chairs had been piled in a heap and covered with drop-cloths while carpenters supervised by Jim Lacey put the finishing trim on new wainscoting and arched windows.

"As soon as the carpenters are out of here, the painters will put a coat of stain and varnish on the woodwork, and we'll be ready for the wallpaper." Jennifer said happily. "Really, we're just about finished."

"Jennifer, the cost?" Marilyn reminded her.

"It was nothing. All we did was poke a few extra holes in the walls and put in a couple more windows. Don't those arches just knock your socks off?"

Arlo Woodbrace popped in from somewhere and began a heated discussion with Jim Lacey who took off his hard hat and appeared to be trying to reason with him. Arlo suddenly noticed the new arrivals and ran over to them.

" 'afternoon, Commodore, Missus. Nice ta' have ya' back. We got a' couple a' things that got a' get straightened out," he began by way of a welcome.

"Take it easy, Arlo," Jim protested. "Let them get their feet back on the ground first."

"Yeah, well . . . see, we've been kind a' waitin' f'r ya' an' all."

"Thanks, Arlo. We missed you, too," Jack replied.

"Well, I didn't mean we missed ya' . . . I mean, that's not what I mean. We did miss ya', both of ya', but see . . . this here's important stuff. We got ta' have a meetin' right away."

"What kind of meeting do we have to have, Arlo?" Jack inquired dryly.

"You know, the Club. You bein' the Commodore 'r President an' everythin'."

"Arlo, will you give him a chance to catch his breath? Jim Lacey demanded.

"What am I president of, Jim? Jack asked.

Lacey's blue eyes laughed behind his wire-rimmed glasses, and his white hair seemed out of place with the energy he radiated at the moment. "Well, while you were away, the people here . . . you know, Mrs. Calkins left all of us shares in the marina."

"I know. I remember."

"Well, we had a whole lot of questions, and we sort of got together and thought it would be a good thing to have an association. And . . . well, there was no question but that you were the most qualified to be president, so we elected you."

"That's very flattering . . ." Jack began.

"I'm the Sergeant of Arms," Arlo offered.

". . . but I'm afraid I'll have to decline."

"Oh, you can't do that . . . Commodore. Les Leslie was elected vice-president and he's over in Italy with Arlo's son Dennis. If you don't take the job we'll have to start all over again."

"You must have some other officers . . ."

"I'm the Sergeant of Arms," Arlo repeated.

"Miss Dupré . . . I mean, Mrs. Townsend is the treasurer, and my . . . partner . . . Eddie Miles . . . is secretary. And that's about it."

"Me? How did I get involved in this?" Marilyn protested.

"Well, everybody knows about your background in accounting, and we didn't think you'd mind. Besides, you'll be working right alongside your husband."

"How did you get left out, Jim?" Jack asked.

"Oh, I'll be much too busy running the restaurant. I couldn't take on anything like this."

"Did you know about this?" Jack asked, turning to R.J.

"Actually, yes. But not until it was all over. Anyway, I thought I should save it for a surprise."

"Howard Garner says he's gonna' buy up everybody's shares an' toss us all out on our rears," Arlo reported. "I told ya' he was gonna' make trouble."

"The Will doesn't specify whether the shares are transferable or not," R.J. said by way of a reminder.

"I can't believe Monty Holcombe could have overlooked that," Jack observed, referring to the general counsel of the Bank of Bonita who drew up Margaret Calkins' Will.

"All right, let me get this straight," he continued. "My mother ran off to New Orleans with my father-in-law; my wife and I have been elected officers in this . . . I don't know . . . membership corporation or residents' association, I guess . . . and one of the members is threatening to sue the other members and throw us out. Anything else?"

"My business partner still hasn't told me how much these few small changes are costing us," Marilyn said, looking at Jennifer and glancing around the room.

"Anything else?" Jack repeated.

"We have an armed robbery trial coming up," R.J. said sheepishly.

"Of course: the 'He was in bed with me' defense. How could I forget that one?"

"Jennifer," Tim Gorman shouted from the top of the open stairway. "I've got to know how you want us to enclose this when we're finished."

"Be with you in a second, Tim," she called.

"My fellow Cap'n Kelly-zians," Jack announced grandly, "the Secretary of the Treasury and I are going home to unpack. Matters of State will have to wait until we are finished." He took Marilyn by the hand and the two of them headed for the stairway. "Sergeant at Arms Woodbrace," Jack called back over his shoulder, "please find someone who can play Ruffles and Flourishes for my inauguration."

"He wasn't serious, was he?" Arlo asked after they left. " 'cause maybe I could get a record 'r tape 'r somethin'."

"This isn't the kind of homecoming I had planned," Marilyn sighed as the limo crawled over the potholes in the road along the seawall.

"We'll have to talk to the Secretary of the Interior about this road," Jack suggested. "I wonder if that might be Erlene Rodgers?"

"Jack, how can you joke about this? These people are counting on us . . . on me."

Aren't you the one who's always talking about performing a task in this life?" he smiled. "Besides, it might be fun in a perverse sort of way; it'll be an experiment in self-government." The driver stopped the car next to the white trawler and opened the back door. "Come here," Jack said to his bride. "I want to show you something I couldn't show you on our wedding night in New Orleans." He walked her to the stern of the boat and gestured toward the transom where a nameboard with carved gilt letters spelled out "MARILYN" had been affixed. "She still hasn't been officially christened, but she's named after you. Do you approve?"

"She's beautiful," Marilyn replied as she leaned against him. She turned and looked at him after a moment. "Jack, if we leave right now, do you think we could cruise her all the way back to Paris?"

CHAPTER 2

"*Buona sera, Signori. Benvenuto al' Italia.*"

"What'd he say, Dennis?" Les Leslie asked his traveling companion.

"Uh . . ."

"I saidé, 'Good evening, Gentelémen. Welcome to Eetaly.'" The young bellman who had shown them to their room had dark hair and arched eyebrows that made him look permanently surprised. His olive-skinned face glowed with pride as he repeated the words in what must have been his best version of English, and he stood his ground waiting for a tip.

"Yeah, that's right. He said, 'Good evening, Gen'l'men . . .'"

Les cut Dennis Woodbrace off sharply. "I don't need ya' ta' translate f'r me when he's talkin' English, ya' ninny. Only when he's talkin' Eyetalian. I thought ya' took it in school?"

"Eef there is anything you needé, please callé me. *Mi chiamo Antonio.*"

"He's name's 'Anthony,' Les."

"I figured that out f'r myself," Les said through clenched teeth.

"Eef you wouldé like to see the City, I amé most goodé guide. I speek Eenglish muché goodé," the bellman offered.

"Yeah, well, look, Antonio," Les said, handing him a five-dollar bill, "we don't need ta' see the City."

"We're leavin' f'r Licata tamarra'," Dennis volunteered.

"So sooné?" *Ma, Signori,* you just come 'ere. Please, leté me show you somé t'ings . . . 'ere ina' Palermo."

"Look, we ain't got time. We're goin' ta' Licata on a kind a' business trip," Les said, pushing him toward the door.

"Wait a minute, Les," Dennis interrupted, "maybe he can show us where we can rent a car 'r somethin'."

Fiat automobile, Signori," Only the besté *per gli Americani."*

We don't need no car. We c'n take a train," Les protested, still edging Antonio toward the door.

The young man turned to Les. "The trainé, *Signore,* sometimesé she's a run, *e* sometimesé . . ." He finished the sentence with an exaggerated frown, a shrug, and an extended right hand that fluttered in the air like a wounded bird.

"It'd be a whole lot easier ta' find her if we had a car, Les. She might not be livin' right near the train station, ya' know."

Les looked at the younger man with an expression that was supposed to tell him to button his lip, but Dennis did not have his father's years of training around Les, and the look went right over his head.

"You are lookiné for someone, *Signori? Una donna?* A woman? I 'avea cousins in Licata who cané be most helpful."

"No, that's all right. We'll handle it," Les said as he pushed the man out of the door.

"Signore, eef you permité me, your friendé, he does not speaké *Italiano* muché goodé. I cané translate for you."

"That's all right, we'll handle it. Thanks, Antonio," Les said as he closed the door with the bellman still outside.

"Why didn't ya' let 'im help us, Les?" Dennis asked.

" 'cause I don't want everybody knowin' my business, that's why. The only reason y'r here is because y'r father told me ya' could speak Eyetalian, and I was knuckleheaded enough ta' believe 'im."

"Hey, I can talk it. I took it in high school. It's j'st that they talk it so danged fast 's all!" Dennis complained.

"An' ya' c'n read it too, right?"

"Yeah, I c'n read it," Dennis pouted.

"Good. Here's a phone book," Les replied, throwing it to him. "Read it as slow 's ya' want. Find out where we c'n rent a car tamarra'."

"Geez, I don't know . . ." Dennis said as he began paging through the book.

"What's the matter? A car was your idea. Ya' mean ya' can't read Eyetalian neither?"

"I told ya'; I c'n read it," Dennis protested. "It's just that I'm a little rusty 's all. It's gonna take me a little bit ta' kind 'a figure it out ag'in."

Well, ya' got all night," Les reminded him. "We'll get up first thing tamarra' mornin' an' hit the road. If we're gonna find 'er we might 's well get on with it."

❧ ❧ ❧

"Yoo-hoo." Eddie Miles decked out in a floral shirt and his sunbonnet was standing outside the newly-named Motor Yacht *Marilyn*, waving and trying to be noticed.

"No, it can't be anyone for us," Marilyn complained, not looking up from her unpacking. "No one could be that cruel."

"It looks like Eddie is a one-man welcoming committee," Jack observed, peeking out a portlight in their stateroom. "I'll get it," he said as he made his way up to the salon.

"Welcome home; I brought a little something for the newlyweds," Eddie's voice flowed lightly down from the salon. "Is our bride here?"

"She's unpacking below," Jack's voice said.

"Well, I don't want to intrude," Eddie said with a loud but conspiratorial whisper.

Marilyn knew it was time to face the music, and she went up into the salon.

"Here she is!" Eddie beamed when he saw "the bride."

"So nice of you to come by, Mr. Miles," Marilyn responded.

"Oh, well, we can't be so formal now, can we? Especially since we're all going to be working together."

"Yes, Jim Lacey told us about the elections," Jack said.

Eddie's eyes widened. "Isn't it exciting? You know, I've never been elected to anything, so I got some books from the Bonita library. Who knows where this might lead? Why many of our State legislators started out in local government just like us."

"The Governor's Mansion can't be far away, Eddie," Jack observed.

"Oh, now . . ." Eddie blushed, "that's all right for the likes of you, but I have my sights set lower: on the Calkins Harbor Town Council."

"You're going to run for office, Mr. Miles . . . Eddie?" Marilyn asked.

"Not right away, of course. Not until I've finished up my term here. I wouldn't want to leave you people in the lurch. But, you know, I've been thinking . . . why should those of us who have . . . a different lifestyle . . . why shouldn't we get out there and take our rightful place? Jim and I have been so happy here, we've felt so much love and acceptance from the people at Cap'n Kelly's . . . I truly feel that given the choice most other people would feel the same way." He suddenly blushed again. "Oh, I'm sorry . . . look at me, I'm making campaign speeches already."

"I think you're right, Eddie. And I'm proud of you for being willing to stand up for your convictions," Marilyn said.

Eddie Miles' smile broadened and his glowing cheeks got redder. "Well, I must be going," he said a little shyly. "I just wanted to bring over this home-baked apple pie." He handed Marilyn the covered dish he had been holding. "I probably won't be able to do much of this once my real duties take hold."

"Secretary is a full-time job," Jack agreed in a serious tone that made Marilyn cough to cover up a giggle.

"Oh, Dear, I hope you didn't catch anything in Paris," Eddie said solicitously. "I have some chamomile tea . . ."

"No, thank you . . . Eddie. I just need a little rest."

"Oh, well, if you need anything . . ." Eddie Miles blushed again. "Why don't I just run along and leave you two lovebirds to your little nest. Bye-bye," he said as he scooted out the door.

"Has this whole place gone mad? Marilyn said quietly. "The marina now has a Residents' Association, and Eddie Miles is planning to run for the Town Council?

"I think he'd be just what this town needs," Jack said. "There are enough off-beat people around here." He looked at his wife and added, "With the backing of one or two prominent people, I'll bet he could make it."

"Maybe," Marilyn responded. "But I prefer to think of extra fuel tanks. With a couple of them I'll bet <u>we</u> could make it . . . all the way to Paris."

❧ ❧ ❧

Morning in Palermo came quite a bit sooner than the American visitors expected. Les and Dennis slept right through it, and it was almost noon before either of them stirred.

"What in Blue Blazes . . . What time is it, Dennis?" Les bellowed.

"Uh . . . it's only about seven o'clock, Les."

"Seven? It can't be seven o'clock an' that bright outside. Are you sure y'r watch is workin'?"

"Yeah. I put a new bat'ry in it last month."

"But did ya' set it ahead?"

"What do ya' mean, did I set it ahead?"

"Did ya' set it ahead on the plane? The sun comes up earlier over here!"

"G'wan. The sun comes up the same time all over."

"But the time changes, ya' ninny. Did ya' set y'r watch ahead f'r the time change?"

"I guess I kind a' f'rgot about that," Dennis said, looking at the ceiling.

"Well were adrift now," Les complained, leaping out of his bed. "It must be almost noon. We went an' wasted half a day an' ain't done nothin' yet."

"Take it easy, Les," Dennis pleaded. "Why are ya' so uptight, anyways?"

"Uptight? Who's uptight? I ain't uptight. I just want ta' get this over with 's all. Now roll out a' that sack. Let's grab a quick bite an' hit the road."

Les' plan for a quick breakfast ran into its first snag when the hotel menu said *Pranzo,* and they noticed everyone else was having a large afternoon meal. The second problem was that Italians never do anything in a hurry, especially anything as important as eating. Les gulped a cup of coffee and tried to make Dennis bolt down lunch quickly in spite of a waiter who could have held down a second-front job between his visits to their table. After they made it out of the hotel, they learned that *Pranzo* is followed by a siesta from two o'clock to four, and during those hours businesses are closed and no one does anything, at least anything they are willing to talk about. And as if that weren't enough, when they finally got to the car rental place Dennis had located, Les found out that renting an automobile in a foreign country isn't just a matter of walking in and plunking down a deposit.

It was eight o'clock—the Italian supper hour—when they dragged themselves back to the hotel, exhausted and car-less.

"*Signori,* you looké muché tired," Antonio said by away of a greeting when they stepped into the lobby.

"You got that right, pal," Dennis grumbled. "Tired an' hungry, too."

"You renté *la macchina?*"

"They don't rent cars unless ya' got an international driver's license, Antonio," Les answered wearily. "We'll have ta' take th' train after all."

"Oh, no, *Signore.* You no 'ear? The trainé to Licata hasé much *problema.* Beeg *accidente.* No more trains for a' leasté *settimana.*"

"'*Settimana*'—that's seven days. He means a week, Les," Dennis put in.

"A week! What in the name a' Saint Elmo are we gonna do here f'r a week?"

"*Signori, uno momento.* Me, I cané drive muché goodé. I cané take you to Licata."

"No, that's okay . . ."

"That's the only way we're gonna get there, Les," Dennis reminded him. "Unless ya' want ta' sit around here f'r a whole week."

"All right. Okay. I'm licked," Les said, defeated at last. "Anything, just so's we get there. An' right now I could use a little a' Nelson's Blood. Ya' comin', Dennis?"

"Ya' mean a drink?" Dennis protested. "Ain't we gonna eat first?"

&

"All right, I guess we should start by calling this first regular meeting of the Cap'n Kelly's Residents' Association to order," Jack said, looking around the room at the people who had gathered in the makeshift meeting area that had been carved out of the clutter of the old first-floor showroom. "I'd like to take a minute to thank Sergeant at Arms Arlo Woodbrace for moving everything out of the way and setting up the table and chairs."

A couple of people applauded, and Arlo looked down at the floor. "All right, I suppose the first order of business should be to call on our Secretary to read his minutes of the organizational meeting." Jack was counting on Eddie to get the formality ball rolling.

"Point of Order, Mister Chairman!" Howard Garner's hand was in the air.

"Shut up, Howard!" Arlo shouted.

"Yes, Howard?" Jack asked, silencing Arlo with his hand.

"Are we using Robert's Rules of Order for this meeting?"

"We haven't decided that yet, Howard," Jack replied.

"Why don't we decide that first?" Garner demanded.

"Why don't ya' decide ta' shut up?" Arlo taunted.

"I think we can put off that decision for a little while, Howard, unless the people here feel some need to get wrapped up in rules nobody really understands." Jack's comment was met with embarrassed silence.

"All right, hearing no objection, let's have a report of the Secretary."

Eddie Miles cleared his throat and adjusted his reading glasses. "The organizational meeting of the Cap'n Kelly's Residents Association took place on January . . ."

Jack scanned the room carefully while Eddie droned on, telling most people what they already knew. They had gotten together and talked about things and elected officers, and it sounded as though they thought that meant their troubles were over. He noticed that Eddie always referred to him as "the Commodore," and was surprised at the number of times he heard that title. Apparently, every time Vice-President Les Leslie ran into a problem during the preceding three weeks, he told everyone "the Commodore" would take care of it when he got back from his honeymoon. So far, the "to do" list began with new electrical service to the docks, ran through paved roads, and ended with an enclosure for the dumpster, not to mention a few details like the possibility of cable TV. The situation was no longer funny.

". . . Respectfully submitted, Edward Miles, Secretary," Eddie concluded.

"Are there any corrections or additions to the minutes?" Jack asked. Once again, there was dead silence. "All right, hearing none, the minutes stand approved as read. Now to old business."

"Point of Order Mister Chairman!" It was Howard Garner again.

"Aw, Criminy! Just shut up, Howard!" Arlo shouted.

"He can't keep saying that to me!" Garner complained.

Arlo stood up, ready for a fight. "Yeah, who's gonna stop me?"

Jack tapped the end of his pen on the table. "All right, guys, settle down. What's your problem, Howard?"

"I think I should be recognized first."

"The Chair recognizes Howard Garner," Jack said formally.

"Thank you. I believe that before we begin dealing with business, we should have a constitution and bylaws."

"Good point. How would you like to be the chairman of that committee?" Maybe giving Howard something to do would make him feel like he was a part of things.

"How much does the job pay?" Garner asked.

"It pays the same as my job—nothing." Jack responded.

"Sorry, I can't afford it."

"We can do the bylaws," a voice called out from the back of the room. It was Nancy Neblett, sitting next to her husband, Doctor Tom. They lived on a Matthews over on the other side of the marina.

"That's the spirit," Jack said. "Doctor and Mrs. Neblett have volunteered to be the Constitution and Bylaws Committee. Now who would like to help them?"

"Can I ask a question?" This from "Sibby" Maggio who had moved aboard a very old, very beaten-up Trojan tri-cabin when he split from his wife a year ago. Sibby was a youngish good-looking guy from "up North" somewhere. He might have been in his mid-thirties, and he was one of those guys who didn't have a regular job, but was always on the very edge of making a "deal." Only God knew how he survived. Sibby had always minded his own business and never expressed an opinion, so Jack was surprised to see him raise his hand.

"I mean, as long as we all own this place, we don't have to pay no more dockage, right?"

"An' who's gonna pay f'r everything, y'r Aunt Tillie?" Arlo shouted.

"Hey, just 'cause we elected him Sergeant don't give him the right to talk to people like that," Sibby protested.

"All right, everybody calm down," Jack said, again tapping his pen for order. "You brought up a good point, Sibby. Since we're the owners, we won't be paying the Calkins family anymore.

Sibby nodded his head in agreement.

"But that doesn't mean we can live here free," Jack continued. "Obviously there are taxes to pay, and utility bills—and that's just for a start. I've heard a lot of talk about improvements. Somebody's going to have to pay for them." There was another embarrassed silence. "Unless somebody has a better suggestion, I'd like to ask our Treasurer to prepare a report on just how much money it takes to run this place, and how much each of those improvements will cost." Jack didn't have to look at her; he could feel Marilyn's cold stare. "Who would like to help her with that project?"

"I will; I'm good with numbers," Erlene volunteered.

"Me too. I'll help," bespeckled and bearded Phil Schover called out from the back row.

"All right, now we're getting somewhere," Jack said. "Let's move on . . ."

"Thanks for the assignment. It was just what I needed," Marilyn muttered as they walked back to their floating home later that night.

"Honey, you had to know you were going to get stuck with that job. If you don't teach them to have a committee, how are they going to learn how to run this place?"

"So all I have to do is amortize the taxes, establish a sinking fund for capital improvements . . ."

Jack cut her off with a kiss. "You can do it. You're smart; that's why I married you. And Doc Neblett and Nancy are really good people. We're lucky to have them on board with this."

"So what will you be doing while I'm trying to explain accounting principles to Erlene and what's-his-name?"

"Phil Schover is a sharp cookie, Marilyn. He's a self-made man who retired here from his electronics business up

North. He'll be a real asset. As for what I'll be doing, it looks like my first job will be to explain to Arlo that 'Sergeant at Arms' does not mean 'Official Shouter.'"

"And your second job?"

"Figure out what the heck to do about Howard Garner.

CHAPTER 3

Darkness came quickly to New Orleans in late January, and the foreshortened days melded into long, intimate evenings in small bistros and elegant restaurants scattered like stardust throughout the French Quarter. On Decatur Street the mellow, golden paneling of Tujague's Restaurant lent an added warmth to the room while outside a chill wind blew off the Mississippi River on the other side of the high levee.

"To another glorious day, *oui, Madame*?" Henri Dupre said as he filled Victoria Townsend's glass with a rich, ruby *Moulin a Vent.*

"I've had a wonderful time with you, Henri," she replied.

"And we are not finished. Soon Mardi Gras will come, and then you will see . . ." Words failed him. He tilted his head back and rotated a hand in the air, overcome by the images he himself had conjured up.

"I'm sure it's delightful, but we must think about getting back home."

"Home? Where is home, *ma chère?* People say, 'Home is where the heart is', no?"

"Home is where the heart is, yes," she replied as she took a sip of wine and looked at him across the table. "Where is your heart, Henri?"

"*Madame*, my heart will always be here, in *la Vieux Carré*."

"But you can't stay in the Old City," she reminded him. "You have responsibilities in Calkins Harbor. You gave your word to your daughter."

"*Oui*," he admitted soberly. "I would not hurt her . . . for any reason."

"And I have plenty to keep me busy in New York," she added.

He did not reply for a long time. Finally, he looked up at her. "Victoria, it does not have to be as you say."

She waited silently.

"You, too, could move yourself to Florida. Many people do so," he suggested.

"Henri, I have many things in New York. Investments. Committee work. Social engagements."

He stroked his hand in the air, brushing aside all the very good reasons she had for not doing what he suggested. "Happiness, *ma chère!* Do you have happiness in New York?"

"I have a . . . very full life," she answered.

"Full, yes. But is it a happy one?" he insisted, taking her hand across the table.

"I don't know," Victoria Townsend admitted. "It was happy enough, I suppose." She looked down at the table, avoiding his gaze. "At least I thought so. My life was full of rules and expectations, and I . . . did what was expected of me. I went to the schools that were chosen for me . . . had the friends I was told to have . . . married the man I was supposed to marry. People were gracious to me; those who seemed to be my friends sought out my company. I never thought about true happiness . . . the kind of happiness that comes from being free . . . being myself." She looked up and added, "I'm not even sure of who 'myself' really was. I'm afraid this is all very new to me, Henri."

"If you were to live in Florida, close by, we could continue . . ."

"Continue what? Continue this? Continue to live in a fantasy world?"

He shrugged. "If that is your wish, why not?"

"What is your wish, Henri? If you had one wish, what would it be?"

He looked at her carefully and thought for a long time. "I would only wish to be with you," he said finally.

She felt herself blushing, something she had not done in a long time; it was something she thought she was no longer capable of doing. "No other wish?" she asked. "No wish to live your life over; to avoid the mistakes, the heartaches?"

"And where then would be the . . . How you call it? The *challenge,* the excitement of life?

"You have no regrets then?"

"Regrets? Regrets I have many. The pain I caused others, that was not good; that is a debt I must someday repay. No, *ma chèri*, I have made many mistakes . . . many. But they were mine. Painful as they were, I learned from each of them. I do not think it would have been better for me to avoid them."

Victoria smiled as he topped off her glass and refilled his own. "You're not afraid . . . just a little . . . of moving away from everything you know?" she asked.

"I know life, *chèri*; I know people. Everywhere they are the same."

"I would be leaving many friends whom I know in New York," she said quietly.

"*Peut-être* I could be more to you than a friend," he suggested.

"I believe that would make me happy," she replied.

❧ ❧ ❧

In Calkins Harbor the sun rose on another day of dust and noise at Cap'n Kelly's Marina. Jack escaped early for the serenity of the Townsend & Meacham law offices, leaving Marilyn to fight her way though the scaffolding and whatever awaited her inside her own office. "Uncle" Doug Calkins, whose worst days always had been those in which he was forced to make decisions, no longer had anything to worry about: his mother's Will turned over the boatyard to its residents and left him without a job. But since he was Jennifer's uncle and an ex-officio member of the Cap'n Kelly's family, he was free to come in every day and do what he did best—peruse the newspaper and comment on the state of the world at large. Jim Lacey was hard at work getting in the way of the construction crew, and Jennifer drove up for a quick inspection before heading off for another day of her last semester at Bonita College.

Marilyn watched her get out of the yellow Cadillac she still drove and tuck her long hair into her hard hat; she was so different from the young girl who played the piano in the living room of the Magnolia Avenue house a year ago. She was standing next to Tim Gorman, the construction foreman, and gesturing up toward the unfinished Mansard roof. It looked like something was not going according to Jennifer's plan, and she was letting Tim know about it in no uncertain terms. In a moment she came through the outside door.

"It has to look old, like it's been here forever, but not ratty. Why can't they understand that?" she asked, going to the small refrigerator she had installed in a corner of the office while Marilyn was away.

"Did you ever think of staying in school for a couple more years and getting a degree in architecture?" Marilyn asked.

Jennifer opened the bottle of Perrier water in her hand. "Please! Just let me finish this year out so I can get on with my life, okay?" She put the bottle to her lips and took a sip. "So, any word from the wayward parents?"

"I don't want to talk about it," Marilyn said, fussing with papers on her desk.

"Marilyn, they are adults. Besides, what's the harm?"

"I really don't care to discuss it, Jennifer," she replied, not looking up from what she was doing.

"Okay, have it your way. But sooner or later, you're going to have to accept it."

Marilyn looked up. "I don't want to talk about it!" she said, her voice rising and tinged with anger.

"Okay! I'm leaving for class. But keep an eye on those guys. Just because I want the place to look 'old' doesn't mean they can get my materials out of other people's garbage. Okay?"

"Whatever you say," Marilyn sighed.

Jack reported to his new office with a mixture of excitement and misgiving. In one way it was nice to be back at work, but at the same time the responsibilities of an office had already begun to take hold. He could feel himself losing the luxury of mornings alone with his word processor and a cup of coffee. His first novel was with a publisher, and the second one which he had been urged to write was already being "pushed to the back burnnah" as Judge MacIntyre would say. His young partner had—foolishly, Jack thought—accepted an assigned criminal case from the

Judge, and, partners being partners, Jack found himself being drawn into it against his will.

Trials are the legal profession's Rite of Passage; R.J. needed one of his own to season him as a lawyer. Jack had warned him more than once that the problem with his career was he had begun it by assisting Jack in the successful defense of a truly innocent client. And, Jack said, innocent clients and successful criminal defenses were about as rare as snow in this part of Florida: theoretically possible but extremely unlikely. In spite of the older voice of reason that came to him from Jack's walnut-paneled office, R.J. was into the case with both feet.

"Do you have a minute?" he asked, standing in Jack's doorway.

"Sure, Rob, what's up?"

"We'll be picking a jury in front of Judge Mac in a few weeks."

Jack did not respond, nor did he comment on R.J.'s use of the senior judge's nickname.

"I was wondering . . . do you think you could sit in on one last interview with my client and his wife?"

"You mean bring them here?"

"Of course. This is our office."

"I didn't mean that," Jack said apologetically. "What I meant was, what's your guy doing out of jail? Isn't this an armed robbery?"

"While you were gone I got Mac to lower his bail enough so that he could get out if his parents put up their house for security."

"And of course they did," Jack observed.

"Well, wouldn't you?"

"*Touché.* All right, Rob, I'll sit in while you talk to them one more time. But remember what they taught you in legal ethics: if we find out they're lying, we can't let either one of them take the stand."

"And if they insist?"

"We back out and your guy gets another lawyer. No matter what happens, we can't be put into the position of suborning perjury."

R.J. stepped completely into the office and sat down in the chairs across the desk of his mentor. "Jack, what if they really, really insist on testifying?"

"What's going on, Rob? Is this scumbag lying to you or not?"

"I . . . I don't know. His wife Janney is a really sweet girl, but when I tried to pin her down about that 'he was in bed with me' story—you know, like you told me to—all she would say was she was asleep in bed with him." He looked at Jack and added quickly, "But she also says she's sure that she would have woken up if he tried to get out of bed. She says she's a very light sleeper."

"And what does the scumbag himself have to say?" Jack asked.

"He says he never left the room."

"You've deposed the other witnesses?"

"The lady next door was watering her lawn and saw him coming in at six-thirty."

"She was watering her lawn at six-thirty in the morning?"

"She's something of an eccentric," R.J. explained.

"That's an understatement!"

"My guy says she hates him because his dog has messed on her lawn a few times."

"So she's going to perjure herself and send in innocent man to prison because his dog crapped on her lawn?"

"She's really pretty eccentric," R.J. repeated.

"Look, Rob, the rules are simple: if we know someone is lying we can't allow that person to testify. Period. On the other hand, if we only suspect he—or she—is lying, we counsel them about the danger of perjury and let him—or her—make the decision. Ultimately it's up to the jury to decide who's telling the truth."

"I know. I know all that. It's just that I don't want . . ." his voice trailed off.

"You don't want to represent a scumbag," Jack said, finishing the sentence for him.

"You got it," R.J. replied.

"Welcome to the sewer, my friend. And don't say I didn't warn you!"

"Arlo, c'mere, quick!" Erlene shouted after she opened the envelope she found lying on the sole of their sailboat cockpit. She had been about to walk Tommy to the school bus stop at the entrance to the marina, but the envelope stopped her and she told him to run on ahead.

"What's a' matter?" Arlo shouted as he barreled up the companionway. "You hurt?"

"Read this!" she answered. "Howard Garner is offerin' us a thousand dollars a share f'r each a' our shares!"

Arlo snatched the paper from her hand and read it carefully. It was an open letter to the residents of Cap'n Kelly's from Howard Garner. It was true; he was offering one thousand dollars cash to anyone who was willing to sell his or her share of the marina. No questions asked. The letter said that interested takers should see him at his boat and gave a number where he could be reached for more information.

"I tol' th' Commodore he was gonna make trouble," Arlo said as he re-read the paper again and again. "I got ta' get this down ta' him right away."

"What's it mean, Arl?" Erlene complained. "Ya' think people 'r goin' ta' sell out ta' him?"

"We ain't; that's f'r sure," Arlo replied.

"Two thousand dollars, Arl; that'd be a real nice nest egg."

Arlo looked at her as if she had just spoken a blasphemy. "Y're not takin' this serious, are ya'?" he demanded. The expression on his face and the tone of his voice told her that "No" should be the appropriate answer.

"Well, I was just sayin'. . ."

"Erlene! Howard Garner is a crook! He said he was gonna buy up th' place an' throw us all out on our rears, remember?"

"Well, if he is, we might 's well get some money f'r our shares," she replied.

"I ain't even talkin' ta' ya' about this anymore," Arlo said disgustedly. "I'm gettin' dressed and then I'm headin' downtown ta' see th' Commodore." He turned and went back down the companionway without another word.

❧ ❧ ❧

Les Leslie and Dennis Woodbrace were squeezed into a Sicilian *carozza*—horsecart—the unwilling victims of a guided tour of Palermo.

" 'ere isé the famoso *Chiesa di San Giovanni degli Ermiti,*" Antonio said with a majestic sweep of his hand. "The churché isé very ol' . . . I don' know for sure 'ow muché. É whené we leave 'ere, we gonna see *la Piazza Petronia*, where there'sé beautiful *fontana,* itse', 'ow you say, 'fountainé.'"

"We don't care about no church a' hermits, Antonio, and we seen all the fountains an' piazzas we want ta' see. Now we just want ta' get on the road ta' Licata" Les demanded.

"*Signore,* I tolé you, *che mio cugino*, my cousiné, é hasé the car. *É* he'sé busy today," Antonio explained with a dramatic shrug of his shoulders. "*Domani*, tomorrow, we go to Licata *subito*—firsté t'ing, righté 'way. Now, leté me show you some more beautiful t'ings."

"C'n we get somethin' ta' eat first?" Dennis Woodbrace asked.

"Good night! Ya' just wolfed down a tub a' pasta," Les protested.

"Yeah, well ridin' around like this in th' open air makes me hungry f'r a little bite."

"I'll bite ya' myself in a minute," Les offered.

"*Signori,* we stopé for *gelato,* eh?

"That's ice cream, Les," Dennis translated.

"I know what gelata is," Les replied through clenched teeth. "All right, we'll stop f'r geleta Antonio. But tamarra' we're gettin' on the road first thing. I want ta' get this job done *pronto*. Understand?

CHAPTER 4

The shiny brass plate engraved with the names of Townsend and Meacham reflected Arlo Woodbrace's grim expression as he gingerly turned the handle of the heavy wooden door. He would have preferred to do this with Les Leslie at his side, but Les was off in Italy somewhere, and there was no time to waste. Howard Garner was up to no good; Arlo was sure of that. He was going to take over the marina, and something had to be done to stop him. Arlo took a deep breath and went inside.

"May I help you?" The well-dressed woman on the other side of the glass asked him.

"Yeah, I guess. C'n I see the Commodore f'r a minute?"

"You mean Mister Townsend?"

"Yeah, Commodore Townsend."

"One moment; I'll see if he's in. Your name is . . .?"

"Arlo. Arlo Woodbrace. I'm kind a' his neighbor. I was here one'ct."

"Of course, Mr. Woodbrace. Just have a seat. Mr. Townsend will be with you in a moment."

A few minutes later Jack himself appeared in the waiting room, and Arlo instantly felt more at ease. "Come on in, Arlo," Jack said. "What's on your mind?"

"We got a problem, Commodore; we got a big problem," Arlo began even before he sat down. "Here." He thrust the paper across the desk at Jack.

"Where did you get this? Jack asked as he read the offer.

"Erlene found it on the cockpit sole this mornin'," Arlo replied. "I tol' ya' he was gonna make trouble, Commodore."

"You also said Howard was tighter than a two-dollar watch. This says he's willing to part with some money."

"Only so's he c'n buy up th' place an' toss us out on 'r rears like he said he was gonna do."

A thousand dollars a share would be the bargain of the century if Garner could pull it off, Jack thought. Including himself and Marilyn there were twelve residents in the marina. Even in its run-down state it was probably worth half a million dollars; that came out to forty thousand a share. And if it were improved like the residents wanted it to be, the sky was literally the limit.

"Do you think anybody will take him up on it?" Jack asked.

"Well Sibby Maggio is always broke. He needs money on account a' his ex, ya' know? An' even Erlene . . ." Arlo hesitated and looked at the floor.

"What about Erlene?"

"Well even Erlene was sort a' kind a' thinkin' about it. 'course I talked 'er out of it."

If Garner managed to get someone as loyal as Erlene thinking about his offer, it could be the beginning of a real problem.

"Have you talked to Sibby?" Jack asked.

"He ain't been aroun' f'r a couple a' days. He prob'ly don't even know about it yet."

"That's good. Who else do you think might find this a pretty good offer?"

"Gosh, I don't know. That Schooner guy, I don't know much about him. He keeps to himself a lot."

"Phil Schover is too smart to fall for this," Jack said, almost to himself. "He knows those shares are worth a lot more."

Arlo's eyes widened. "They are? How much 'r they worth?"

Jack instantly regretted his outburst. He looked at Arlo and said, "They're worth a lot, Arlo. They're worth a great deal of money. But let's just keep that to ourselves for now, okay?"

"Wow. Sure. Okay. Now what 're we gonna do about Howard Garner?"

"I'm not sure right now. I'm not sure there's anything we can do about him. We need to snoop around a little bit. Think you can handle that?"

"Me? Wow! Sure!" This was great. Commodore Townsend was asking him for help! Maybe it was a good thing that Les was in Italy after all. "What do ya' want me ta' do?"

"Put the word out very quietly that I want to talk to anybody who's thinking about taking Howard up on his offer."

"Y'r gonna put the squeeze on 'im, huh?"

Jack smiled. "This isn't the movies, Arlo. Things don't work that way. Let's just say I want to make a counter-offer. You tell anyone who's interested to see me first; I'll take it from there. Okay?"

"Wow! Sure. Okay," came Arlo's eager reply.

"And Arlo, let's keep our plan a secret. I'm counting on you to not let this get out. Okay?"

"You bet, Commodore," Arlo replied as he got up to leave, overlooking the fact that Jack had not actually told him about a plan.

When he was gone, Jack leaned back in his chair and pondered the situation. He could out-bid Garner if it came to that, but he didn't care for that idea. He liked his life the way it was. Even though he had stumbled into being a "lawyer again," he and Marilyn spent many happy hours aboard the boat that he named after her. It was their private sanctuary. If Cap'n Kelly's was suddenly infected by investment fever, there was no telling where it would end, but one thing was clear: life would be unalterably changed, and that change would not be for the better.

Besides that, there was his loyalty to Margaret Calkins. She was a sharp lady, and she had—for whatever reason—attempted to create a self-governing community in which each resident had an interest. She would not have approved of the idea of people buying up shares in the marina and trading them like so many stock certificates.

Lastly, this situation might end up in a court battle, and the law is very big on the "clean hands doctrine": "one who seeks equity must do equity." Jack had to maintain a consistent position in the affair in order to protect Margaret's Will if it ever came down to an all-out legal battle over interpretation. He could hardly ask a judge to impose a limitation on the transfer of shares if Howard Garner could show that Jack himself had been attempting to buy them.

The more he thought about Garner's offer, the less sense it made. Arlo had said Howard wanted to buy up the place and throw everybody out. Why would anyone want to buy up a going concern to put it out of business? Garner had to know there were people at Cap'n Kelly's—himself included—who would never willingly sell their shares. Why start an expensive war with them? True, the marina occupied a nice piece of waterfront property, but any investor wearing the rosiest of rose-colored glasses would have to recognize that it needed a lot of work to come up to even second-class status. There were still a lot of waterfront properties on the west coast; why not go after one of them? Why didn't Garner take the other approach: sell his share and use that money as part of the capital for another parcel that he could acquire and develop with far less effort? True, he might want to buy up Cap'n Kelly's and tear it down out of spite, but that was a pretty expensive way of getting even with someone, and it raised the additional question of who could have pissed him off enough during his short time there to engender that kind of wrath. Despite his abrasive personality, Howard had never expressed any particular malice for anyone at Cap'n Kelly's.

Unless . . . unless Howard was simply a stalking horse for someone who did bear that kind of malice. Someone who had a guaranteed income and half a million dollars to throw around. Someone like Junior Calkins.

Junior had the necessary malice, and he had the necessary money. If no one stepped in, he could buy up a majority interest in the marina, "throw everybody out on their rears" and re-sell the property. Even if he didn't make a dime profit—even if he lost money—it might be worth it to him in terms of pure spiteful satisfaction. The more he thought of it, the surer Jack was that Junior was the manipulator pushing Garner's buttons, and unless other facts came to light that proved him wrong, he would operate on that theory. Now he would have to pull everyone in Cap'n Kelly's together to see how high the offer would go.

Sharon Crowley's voice on the intercom reminded him that it was time to meet R.J.'s client. Jack went to the conference room/library and found his partner with a heavy-set guy and woman whom Jack assumed must be the guy's wife who planned to testify.

The guy stood up to shake hands when Jack entered the room. His name was Chuck Laggley. His was in his late twenties or early thirties, and maybe fifty pounds overweight: the roll of flesh that bulged out over his low-slung belt was barely covered by his tee shirt. He greeted Jack with a smile that revealed bad teeth, and his unshaven face topped off his appearance that confirmed him as a loser. The woman, on the other hand, was slim and innocently attractive, with short auburn hair and a pleasant smile that make Jack wonder what she saw in the hulk by her side.

"Chuck and Janey Laggley, this is my partner, Jack Townsend," R.J. said by way of introduction. "Jack, I was just telling them that you would be co-counsel at the trial."

Great, Jack thought. The Assigned Counsel Office barely paid enough for one good trial lawyer, and R.J. just dragged in a second one. Now their firm could lose even more money.

"Heard a lot about you, Mr. Townsend," Chuck Laggley said. "Glad to hear you're gonna be representin' me."

"I'm just holding Mr. Meacham's coat on this one," Jack said quickly. "He's a darn good lawyer; you're lucky to have him."

"Yeah, well, like I said, we've been over this a hundred times. I really don't know nothin' about the robbery," Chuck explained. "See, I was workin' at th' station an' they kept cuttin' back my hours, so I told the manager if they didn't give me more hours, I'd quit."

"What is it you did there, Mr. Laggley? Jack asked, interrupting what already sounded like a too-well-rehearsed story.

"Like I said, stock shelves, do the floors, you know, stuff like that."

"Wait a minute, I thought this was a gas station?" Jack said.

"Gas station and convenience store," R.J. quickly explained.

Great. Chuck Laggley, thirty-year-old stockboy, had told off his boss and quit his job shortly before the robbery of the store.

"Anyways, like I said, a few days after I had that blow-up with the manager, the place gets knocked over, an' so now they're tryin' to pin it on me."

"And he was home in bed . . . asleep," Janney Laggley quickly added.

"And you were with him?" Jack asked her.

She looked away for a moment; either she was embarrassed by the question or she was covering for her husband. "Well of course," she said. "How else could I know he was there?"

Her answer was too defensive, and Jack tried again. "Mrs. Laggley, the State has an eyewitness who saw your husband return home at six-thirty in the morning. Both of you can't be right; either somebody is mistaken or somebody's lying."

"That lady's been after me ever since we moved in," Chuck Laggley interrupted. "She's got it in for me because my dog shit on her lawn."

Jack ignored him for the moment. "Mrs. Laggley?"

"I'm a very light sleeper," she explained. "Because of the baby. We have a baby at home. And I'm sure that I would have woken up if Chuck had gotten out of bed."

"So you were asleep?" Jack confirmed.

The woman nodded her head.

"All right now, Chuck," Jack said, turning toward her husband. "You're convinced this woman is lying about you because your dog messed up her lawn?"

"Hey, why else would she do it?"

"I don't know. Maybe you have loud parties; maybe she caught you smoking weed. You tell me."

"Like I said, I never did nothing to her."

"Could she be telling the truth?"

"Like I told you, I didn't have nothin' to do with no robbery."

"I didn't ask you that," Jack said coolly. "I asked you whether your neighbor could be telling the truth."

"All's I can think of is, she's don't like me 'cause my dog keeps shittin' on her lawn."

"A dog messing on somebody's lawn is a pretty flimsy excuse for committing perjury and putting an innocent man in prison. It's going to be damn near impossible to break her story if we use that approach. Could she be telling the truth and just be mistaken about the date?" Jack queried.

"What do you mean?" Chuck Laggley asked, leaning forward in his chair.

"Could she have seen you coming home at six-thirty in the morning on some other day, and just have gotten the date wrong?"

Laggley leaned back in his chair and thought for a long minute. "Yeah, sure, that's possible," he confirmed, nodding his head thoughtfully. "Like I said, sometimes I do go out early."

"Do you ever go out early in the morning to get the paper or a pack of cigarettes?" Jack offered.

"Sure. Yeah. All the time. Well, I mean, not all the time, but yeah, sure, I've done that."

Jack's smile was that of a comrade-in-arms. "And I guess sometimes you go out for an early breakfast just to get away all by yourself, so you can think, right?"

Chuck Laggley smiled in return. "Well, like I said, she doesn't get much sleep with the kid and all, so sometimes I just let her . . . you know." He hesitated when he realized that if he continued along that line it would not fit in with his wife's "light sleeper" story.

"But I always know when he leaves," the loyal Mrs. Laggley interjected.

"All right, let's think about that, Mrs. Laggley," Jack said, turning back to her. "Sometimes your husband does go out early in the morning. We know that because the lady next door saw him at least once. And because he's a good husband, he tries not to wake you up. Now, how do you know he didn't go out and not wake you up on the day of the robbery?"

"Well . . . I don't know what you mean . . ." Even if she wasn't stalling for time, she sure sounded like she was.

"What happened on the day of the robbery that didn't happen any other day?" Jack suggested.

"Chuck got arrested; I remember that."

"All right. What happened on the morning of the day that Chuck got arrested?"

"I didn't wake up?" she asked.

"You can't ask me; I wasn't there," Jack replied.

"Well, I didn't wake up."

"And?"

". . . and I always wake up when he goes out early, even if he thinks I don't," she added quickly. "You know. I don't get up, but I still hear him moving around and leaving and everything."

"And did you hear him moving around and leaving and everything the morning of the day he got arrested?"

"No."

"Therefore?"

"Therefore he didn't get up," she affirmed more confidently.

Jack turned to R.J. for the first time since he came in. "Any questions, Counselor?" he asked.

R.J. shook his head.

"When does the trial start?" Jack asked.

"The date hasn't been set yet, but likely within the month," R.J. responded.

"All right." Jack turned back to the Laggley's. "Folks, there's just one more thing. Perjury is a very serious crime . . . one of the few that's guaranteed to get you a view of the inside of a State prison. Judges don't take kindly to people who screw up the system by lying to them. If you're called as a witness, I want you to tell the absolute truth. Understand?"

They both nodded their heads but only Mrs. Laggley's eyes said that she took his words to heart.

"If the State Attorney asks you whether you met with us, what are you going to say?"

"Yes?" she asked.

"Yes. Of course!" Jack's voice increased as he drove the point home. "Your husband has a constitutional right to counsel. You're here exercising that right. And if the State Attorney asks you what we told you to say, what are you going to say to that?"

"That you told us to tell the absolute truth," she said, more confident of her answer this time.

"All right. I don't have anything else. Is there anything, anything at all, that we should know before the trial?"

Chuck Laggley and his wife looked at each other. She broke eye contact first and looked down at the floor. "Not a thing," he answered.

"Stay in touch with Mr. Meacham and he'll tell you when the trial is scheduled." Jack shook their hands and stayed behind lost in thought while his partner escorted them out. "What do you think?" R.J. asked when he returned to the conference room.

"She might be telling the truth; he's lying like the proverbial rug."

"Come on. You can't be sure of that in just a few minutes," R.J. protested.

Jack pursued his lips and looked intently at his young partner. "Did you see how he leaped at that suggestion about how the lady next door might have seen him on some other day?"

"You're the one who suggested it!" R.J. protested.

"And he went for it like a hungry trout taking a fly. Come on, Rob! If the lady next door is a nut, then she's a nut. If she's trying to put him in jail because his dog crapped on her lawn, then she's trying to put him in jail because his dog crapped on her lawn. If that story were true, he'd stick to it like a barnacle. What's more, he'd have the whole damn neighborhood in here backing him up. I'm sorry, my friend. He knows she saw him coming home on that fateful morning, and he's trying to come up with an explanation for her testimony. Mine was better than his, so he leaped on it."

"How about the wife?"

"That poor kid has a baby at home and a slug for a husband. She wants to believe him; more importantly, she wants to believe herself. But I've got to hand it to her; she won't lie. She could have said her husband was still asleep and that she got up because the baby was sick. She remembered the date because she made a note on the calendar to call the doctor. It would be easy enough to go home, find a calendar and write a note."

"But she couldn't say that because she didn't call the doctor. He would have a record of it," R.J. reminded him.

"She was <u>so</u> <u>upset</u> by the arrest of her loving, church-going, law-abiding husband that she forgot about calling the doctor. And, besides, the kid got better later on in the morning." Jack's explanation would have sounded completely plausible coming from Janey Laggley. "Anyway, she's not willing to go that far out on a limb for old Chuck," he continued. She's only going to say she 'always wakes up' and she did not wake up on that particular morning. You have to argue that means he didn't go out that morning. It's not a very strong argument; hell, it's full of holes. But that's as far as she'll go. Either she's a very principled young lady, or she realizes she made a mistake marrying the slug and really doesn't care if he goes to prison." Jack got up to leave. "Tell me something, partner," he added, "If she's asleep, how does she know she 'always' wakes up?"

Jack was at the conference room door before R.J. stopped him. "You tell me something, partner," he said. "What was all that business about not suborning perjury? Isn't that exactly what we're doing here?"

Jack stepped back into the room and looked at him: he was a model of righteous indignation. "I beg your pardon? We were meeting with your client and his witness. We did not tell either of them what to say. I merely pointed out certain inconsistencies in their stories, and, upon reflection, they were able to recall details they had previously overlooked or forgotten."

"But you don't believe either of them!" R.J. protested.

"I believe her. I happen to think she's mistaken, but I believe her."

"And you don't believe him."

"No."

"So how can we allow him to testify?"

"I don't know that he's lying; that's just my opinion. If I was on the jury I'd convict him in a heartbeat. But that's not my job. My job . . . or, rather, your job . . . is to present his defense to the best of your ability. You can't allow him to testify if you know he's committing perjury, but you can't stop him from testifying just because your partner thinks he's as full of crap as that dog of his."

Jack started out the door again before R.J. called him back one more time. "Jack, this business really does stink, doesn't it?"

"Welcome to the sewer, Rob," he replied with a cheery wave of his hand as he finally escaped from the conference room.

CHAPTER 5

Marilyn was hard at work late one afternoon, trying to explain to Erlene Rodgers the concept of "capital improvements." Erlene was a good worker and honest to a fault, but she said thinking too hard made her feel worse than seasick and their session was not going well.

"If we need new docks, why don't we j'st go ahead an' pay for 'em?" she demanded.

"Because they cost more than we have in the bank right now," Marilyn explained. "And even if we had all of the money, we couldn't spend it because we'd have to use it to pay our operating expenses."

Erlene looked perplexed.

"We couldn't pay for the docks all at once because we have to keep some money around to take care of things we need every day, like power for the lights and gas for the gas dock," Marilyn said, trying again.

"Can't we pay for 'em a little at a time, like on Will-Call or somethin'? My kids wouldn't have no Christmas if it wasn't f'r Will-Call."

"Okay, well, this is the same kind of thing, Erlene. With Will-Call you pay the store a little at a time, and they hold your money until you're paid up for the Christmas presents, right?"

The woman nodded her head in reply.

"But here, we want the work done now, not next Christmas, and the construction company wants to be paid when they do the work. So instead of paying the construction company a little at a time in advance, we're going to borrow all the money from the bank, pay the company now, when they do the work, and pay the bank back a little at a time."

"Ya' mean that big comp'ny won't let us pay 'em a little at a time?"

"They can't do that because they have current expenses just like we do. They have to pay their workers, and pay for materials, and pay for their power and gas for their equipment." Marilyn explained.

Erlene nodded, and Marilyn continued. "So we go to the bank for the money. Now, it's our job to figure out how to get the money to pay back the bank. We have to take the total cost of the money, which includes debt service, and divide it by the number of slips in the marina, and figure out the number of years we want to take to amortize the loan . . ."

Erlene's face began to turn green again. It was obvious Marilyn had lost her. She was about to try again when the door opened and Henri Dupré walked in. He was alone and very quiet. If she had not looked up, Marilyn might not have known he entered the room.

"Papa! What are you doing here?" she blurted out.

"I am here, no? I am not welcome?"

She got up from her desk to greet him with a hug and kiss on both cheeks. "Of course you're here and you're welcome," she said. "I just didn't know you were coming. Why didn't you call?"

"I, too, did not know I was coming. And I needed the time to think."

"Are you . . . alone?" she asked.

"I have been alone for almost twenty years, *ma fille.*"

It was the Guilt Trip, and it signaled the beginning of a conversation Marilyn and her father had had many times since Mama died. The only thing that changed was the number of years he had "been alone"; that number kept increasing like the number of burgers sold in some fast-food chain. Marilyn looked at Erlene who was watching Henri Dupré with growing interest. Cap'n Kelly's was a small community, and the comings and goings of its people provided a great deal of entertainment for those with time on their hands.

"Erlene, I'd like to spend some time with my father," Marilyn said.

"Sure, go raht ahead. I'll j'st work on these numbers here."

"Erlene!" Marilyn's dark eyes flashed as she jerked her head toward the door.

"Oh, all raht. I guess ya'll want ta' be alone. I'll go out ta' the gas dock f'r awhile."

"Thank you, Erlene."

"Don't mention it," the woman said as she closed the door.

"So, Papa, how was New Orleans?" Marilyn asked after they seated themselves in her office.

"*Très bon; très bon,*" Dupré answered noncommittally.

"Are the *beignets* as good as ever?"

Dupré's only reply was a shrug of his shoulders.

"I'll bet it was cool there in January. Not like here, right?"

The conversation stalled. There was a long silence while Marilyn tried to think of something to say other than what was on her mind. She wanted to know about Jack's mother; whether Papa had shared a hotel room with her in New Orleans, and especially whether Papa had shared a hotel room bed with her in New Orleans. This time it wasn't like those other women; now his philandering was touching her family. Papa didn't look like he wanted to reveal any information, and she was darned if she was going to bring up the subject of Victoria Townsend first. She would just sit there in silence until he said something about her. Sooner or later he would have to crack.

"Where is Mrs. Townsend?" she finally asked when she could no longer bear the silence.

"*Madame* Tousand is seated here with me, no?" he asked with a smile in his eyes.

It was the perfect *riposte*, and it set her back for a moment. It was obvious that Papa did not want to discuss the subject.

"I meant Mrs. Victoria Townsend. . . Jack's mother," Marilyn insisted.

Dupré stood up and looked out the window. "That *Madame* Tousand is in New York," he said finally.

"New York? But I thought . . . that is, I was given to understand that she went to New Orleans . . . with you."

"*Oui*, she did so," he said quietly.

"And . . .?"

Dupré turned to face his daughter. "And then she went to New York. And I am here." His voice was gruff now, almost angry. The conversation stalled again. His answer explained nothing, but it did not appear he was going to offer any more information.

"The construction is right on schedule," Marilyn said in a lame attempt to end the silence.

"*Oui,* Janifere must be *très joyeux*." He was still standing, fidgeting, pacing the room.

"Soon you'll be running your very own kitchen . . . with help, of course. Don't worry; you'll have plenty of help. I'll see to that."

"*Oui*, I gave my word."

Marilyn suddenly had a deep-down feeling of panic. "Papa, you're not thinking of . . . leaving here, are you?"

Dupré's eyebrows shot up quickly. "My word I gave to you and Janifere. How could I do such a thing?"

"I just thought . . . well, maybe you were thinking of living in New York. There are a lot of fancy restaurants there," she suggested.

"I left you once, *ma chouchoutte*; never again will I do so."

Now he was using his pet name for her and being noble. This was too much. Papa had to be up to something; she was sure of it. But she was afraid to say what was on her mind.

"Papa, you wouldn't . . . I mean . . . Victoria Townsend is my mother-in-law. She's a part of my family. You wouldn't make her do anything foolish, would you?"

"What could I make her do, *chère*?" he asked with a wide-eyed innocence that made her cringe. When she mentioned Victoria she had definitely hit a nerve.

"Loan you money, for example? Or invest in some scheme of one of your friends? Is *Monsieur* Yanni still looking for people to buy shares in that engine of his that runs on water instead of gasoline?"

Dupré waved off her suggestions with his hand. "That was finished a long time ago, *ma petite*. And yet, his idea was a good one. But I would never ask *Madame* Tousand for such a thing."

Marilyn stood up and faced him. Then what were you doing with her in New Orleans?" she demanded.

"I showed her *la Vieux Carré*, the old city. We ate well, we drank some wine . . ." he, too, was suddenly louder.

"And . . .?"

"And the rest is not your concern, *ma fille*."

"And you slept with her, didn't you, Papa?" Marilyn insisted with anger overwhelming her voice.

Dark anger flashed in his eyes, and for a brief moment he looked like he might slap her. "That, too, is not your concern!" he shouted.

"I think it is!" she shouted in reply.

"It is not!" he shouted back. He opened the door quickly. "I have taken a small *chambre* on the island; Janifere will know where to find me. I have nothing more to say to you." He went out and slammed the door.

The anger of a thousand broken promises welled up inside her. Nothing had changed. He was still the same old Henri Dupré: part dreamer and part confidence man swaddled around a molten core of Gallic passion and covered with a varnish of continental charm. And it looked like his latest conquest was her husband's mother, Victoria Townsend.

❧ ❧ ❧

Les Leslie muttered under his breath as the small car hit another pothole on the road to Licata. He and Dennis were jammed into a Fiat, a car that had a back seat barely big enough for one full-sized adult, and Antonio's cousin's idea of a mechanical air conditioner was the one crank which they passed around to roll down the windows. It was mid-morning, and the road dust mixed heavily with the warm Sicilian air that washed over them while they careened south on the narrow roadway over the arid spine of the island.

Antonio was in the front seat, helping his cousin Vincenzo to drive, he said. When Les protested the inclusion of yet another helper on their mission, Antonio explained that of course he never meant that his cousin would loan him the car <u>and</u> allow him to drive it. He would only loan him the use of the car together with himself as the operator. And Vincenzo's services came at such a modest cost no one could question his sincerity. Besides, Dennis reminded Les as they were about to leave their hotel in Palermo, Vincenzo might be useful in locating Elena when they finally arrived at their destination. There was only one hitch: Vincenzo spoke even less English than Antonio. And since Dennis' grasp of Italian hadn't improved much since their arrival, Les found himself pressed like a sardine in an undersized can, surrounded by other sardines with whom communication was sporadic at best, and guided by a frenzied Italian whose idea of driving amounted to playing connect-the-dots with every pothole and bump in the road.

"Ouch! Dang! Tell him ta' try an' avoid the holes, will ya' Antonio?" Les pleaded.

"Oh, no *Signore*. I cané no tellé Vincenzo nothingé while 'e's concentrate. We maybe have beeg *accidenté*."

"Well, we ain't gonna have no kidneys left if he keeps runnin' us inta ev'ry pothole he sees," Dennis complained.

"Cosa ha detto?" Vincenzo asked.

"Niente, niente. Porta la macchina," Antonio ordered his cousin, pushing his hand impatiently forward. He turned to the two men in the back seat. "Pretty soon, we stopé 'ave litté *tazza di caffè, e* scratché the legs, eh?"

"Scratch our legs?" What in blue blazes are ya' talkin' about?" Les demanded. "If I got a itch, I'll scratch it right here."

"*Signore,* you maké joke, eh? I meané, 'scratché the legs'; walk aroun' a littlé bit, *e* také th' air.' He moved his fingers as he spoke, imitating a pair of waking legs.

"C'n we stop at one 'a them *trattorias*?" Dennis suggested. "They got great cookies."

"Judas Priest, ya' just ate not two hours ago," Les protested. "Ya' can't be hungry; it ain't possible."

"I ain't hungry," Dennis said defensively. "I just thought it'd be kind a' nice ta' have one a' them cookies, is all. An', besides, I gotta pee."

"Well ya' better hold it 'r plan on peein' in y'r pants, 'cause we ain't gonna stop until we get ta' Licata."

"C'mon, Les," Dennis whined.

"*Signori*, please, pretty sooné we gonna come to beggé town. You see. *E* thené we we cane stopé for just a few minutze, eh?"

"We ain't stoppin'," Les repeated over Dennis' pained expression. "Tell y'r cousin ta' keep drivin' if he expects ta' get paid."

Antonio muttered something to Vincenzo who drove right through the next town. Then, a short time later—as if to protest such heartless treatment—the car stopped of its own accord. They were at the top of one of the mountains, passing through a small, nameless village that barely rated a dot on the map when the engine heaved out its life in a great sigh of steam.

"Muovati, putana di sua nona!" "Move, whore of your grandmother!" Vincenzo shouted, slamming his hand against the steering wheel and urging the small vehicle forward as if it were a horse-drawn *carozza*.

"Che succeso?" "What happened?" Antonio inquired.

"Ma, chi sacco io? U dulori ci pigiao," "How should I know? She has a pain." Vincenzo answered.

"What in blue blazes is goin' on now?" Les demanded.

"My cousiné, 'e say *che* the car she'sé sick. She gotta pain someplace."

"Cars don't get pains, ya ninny," Les shouted.

"Well I got a pain; I gotta pee!" Dennis volunteered.

"*Signori,* please, there's a smallé *trattoria* 'ere someplace. Let's have '*na tazza di caffè, e* Vincenso, he fixé the car, eh? *Non pensa a niente,* don' think about it, *che* we gonna be gone *subito.* Hokay?

"C'mon Les. Maybe they'll have a bathroom," Dennis begged.

"Okay, okay!" Les shouted. "But you tell Vincenzo that I want ta' get on the road 's quick 's possible. Like ya' said, *subito.* Understand? I want ta' be in Licata by ta'night."

Antonio said something to Vincenzo which may or may not have been an accurate translation of Les' words; there was no way to tell. Even if Dennis hadn't been completely distracted by his own desperate condition, they spoke Italian much too fast for him to comprehend. In a moment, he and Les were following Antonio down a dusty street, trying not to look as out-of-place as they felt, and hoping they would soon be on the road again and leaving wherever it was they happened to find themselves at the moment.

The village looked like it had not changed in a couple of hundred years, maybe longer: buildings with thick stone walls the color of sand surrounded a small square where four old men in black caps, white shirts and dark pants held up by suspenders, sat in the sun and played cards while black-dressed young women carried water jugs on their heads or shoulders. Across the road where the land fell away, a group of older black-clad women spread bedsheets on the ground to dry and bleach in the intense sunlight.

Antonio approached one of the men and touched his hand to the side of his forehead as if he were doffing an invisible cap while he said something in Italian. The man acknowledged him with a nod but did not take his eyes off the cards on the table. As Antonio began to speak, one of the other men slammed a card down with a tremendous flourish and shouted *"Scopa!"* and the table erupted into a furious debate in which everyone talked and no one listened. Antonio returned helplessly to Les and Dennis who by now was dancing to music generated from somewhere below his belt.

"I'mé sorry, *ma* they fighté about the cards," Antonio explained.

"Just ask 'em where we c'n go f'r a cup 'a coffee," Les demanded.

"Yeah, some place with a toilet," Dennis added.

Antonio returned to the men who by now were on their feet, engaged in a rapid-fire discussion that included grandiose gestures punctuated by much arm-waving, grimacing and eye-rolling. He entered manfully into the fray, cutting first one and then another of the men out of the general debate and engaging them in individual combat. It took a few minutes for them to realize that five were now engaged in what had begun as a private conversation of four, and they all stopped talking and looked at the interloper.

Antonio appeared not to have counted on quite so much attention; his body shrank to about two-thirds of its normal size and his shoulders shot up past his ears in a Sicilian shrug. He pointed at Les and Dennis, who was still engaged in his silent polka, and the men looked in their direction with grim-faces suspicion. Strangers did not come to this village, but what harm could there be in one gray-bearded American and his darker-skinned companion whose obvious need transcended any language? One of the men finally allowed his faced to relax into what might pass for a smile if he had teeth, and he said a few words while he pointed to a door on the other side of the square. Antonio was back in a moment with the happy news.

"Goodé news, *signori*. Theré's a little place righté 'ere, where we cane 'avé some *caffe e* waité for Vincenzo."

"Do they have a bathroom?" Dennis pleaded.

They hurried across the square, nodding their thanks to the men who had already returned to their stations around the table and picked up the game at the point where it had been so rudely interrupted.

A doorway in the building on the far side of the *piazza* opened into a single dark room with a bar along the left side. A few tables and chairs were scattered to the right, but the travelers' immediate need was for *un bagno,* and Dennis hurried toward the back in response to the owner's nodded direction. The man began brewing espresso for his unexpected customers and Les slid into one of the chairs in the cool darkness of the front room. He was stuck as sure as if he had run aground on a sand bar. There was nothing he could do but wait for a high tide named Vincenzo to get him afloat again.

CHAPTER 6

Jennifer, too, was impossibly stuck. Things never went as fast as she had been promised; this time it was the cedar shake shingles on the mansard roof. They were an unusual item in South Florida, Tim Gorman kept telling her. She understood that: unusual. But cedar shake shingles on the overhanging mansard room would have the right look, she insisted. The shingles and the wrought-iron filigree on the balcony would give Dupré's Restaurant the continental flavor that would complement its menu. No, it had to be cedar shake shingles, she had decided, and if they had to wait an extra month to get them from wherever they were made, well, then, they would just have to wait. She was explaining this latest wrinkle to Henri Dupré and Jim Lacey early one morning before leaving for class. Jim took the news with uncharacteristic patience, but Henri was inconsolable.

"*Merde!* Four weeks more! And then it will be more days after that, no? Janifere, this cannot be. Tell them they must finish *immèdiatement* . . . now."

"They can't get the cedar shingles now, Papa," she explained again. "They have to be shipped down from up North somewhere."

"Tell them to use anything!" he shouted in reply. "People come to a *restaurant* for *le cuisine*, not for the roof."

"I won't compromise my vision, Papa. I know the kind of look that I want."

"But Jenifere . . . *Chérie,* it will make *difference* not to the guests. Please, be reasonable with *les artisans*."

"The workmen will just have to wait until the materials get here, Papa. My mind is made up."

"But four weeks more!" He looked at Jim. "Lacey, there must be something you can do, no?"

"I have some contacts with the trades up in Detroit; I could make a few phone calls."

"Call them, *mon Dieu!*" He looked back at Jennifer and begged, "Janifere, please, be reasonable."

"Okay, I'll be reasonable," she said. "I want cedar shake shingles; I don't care where they come from. If you can get them here sooner than four weeks, we'll go with whatever you get. Remember: cedar shake, and they're going to be installed on a Florida roof."

"Lacey, you will try, no?" Dupré pleaded.

Marilyn had just arrived at the office. She hadn't spoken to her father since their argument, and the nausea she was experiencing at the moment made her not care if she ever spoke to anyone again. She had forced herself to eat breakfast after Jack left for court, but she could hardly keep it down on the short walk from their boat. She had never before minded the smell of diesel fuel, but this morning everything bothered her. She was sitting behind her desk; her eyes were closed and she was holding her head in her hands when Jennifer walked in.

"What's the matter?" the young woman asked. "Are you sick?"

"I must have the 24-hour flu or something," Marilyn moaned softly. "I feel terrible."

"Are you sure you're not pregnant?" Jennifer joked as she opened a cupboard, took out a banana and began peeling it.

Marilyn looked up at her. "Jennifer, don't even think about that," she said miserably. "I don't have time for it right now."

"You seem to have plenty of time for what causes it," Jennifer grinned.

"Jen, please. I really don't feel well. And do you have to eat that thing in here?"

"I'm sorry. It's only a banana."

"I know it's a banana. It smells like a banana."

Jennifer put away the half-eaten fruit and took Marilyn's hand in her own. "Hey, you really are sick, aren't you?"

"Oh, I'll be all right. I just . . ." she swallowed heavily. "I guess I'm just worn out. I need to get some rest and I'll be fine."

Jennifer looked at her intently and held a hand to her forehead. "Marilyn, are you sure you're not pregnant?" she asked seriously.

Marilyn closed her eyes and luxuriated in the feel of Jennifer's cool hand. "I can't be, Jen. I just can't."

"Well, have you been doing anything to prevent it?"

Marilyn's dark eyes flashed open. "Jennifer!"

"What?"

"You ask the most personal questions!"

"Well, have you?" Jennifer insisted.

"Okay, yes, if you must know. I've been counting the days very carefully."

"Counting the days?" The rhythm method? Marilyn, don't tell me you're not on the pill or something! Even you can't be that Catholic!"

"I'm not going to dignify that with an answer," Marilyn replied. She got up unsteadily, went over to the bookcase and began looking for something that apparently wasn't there.

"I mean, you and Jack have been going after each other like a couple of bunny rabbits! What did you think was going to happen?" Jennifer demanded.

"Jennifer, please!"

Just then Erlene walked in holding a white bag lush with translucent grease stains. "Hey, guys, th' Beach House is doin' take-out breakf'sts," she reported. "Anybody wanna split a sausage-egg-and-cheese on a bun and some hash browns?" She opened the bag and the fragrance of fried food quickly engulfed the room, overpowering even the odor of diesel fuel which previously that morning had seemed to permeate the entire marina. Marilyn suddenly lost all color in her face and she raced for the door with a mumbled "Excuse me!"

"What's the matter with her? She pregnant?" Erlene asked over the sound of Marilyn retching in the lavatory.

"Sounds like it," Jennifer replied while she nodded her head in reply.

❧ ❧ ❧

"'Mornin' Miss Dale, gen'lemen. Let's get stahted shall we? Ahr thayh any pre-trial motions?" Judge Regis Horatio MacIntyre was once again presiding over the criminal division of the circuit court of the Twenty-first Judicial Circuit of Florida. This time the case was <u>State v. Charles "Chuck" Laggley</u>, and Robert J. Meacham, Esq., of the firm of Townsend & Meacham was lead defense counsel.

"The State has no such motions, Your Honor." Assistant State Attorney Melanie Dale, one of the prosecutors who was regularly assigned to Judge MacIntyre's division, was ready to go.

"The defense has a motion *in limine*, Your Honor," R.J. said, rising from his seat next to Jack at the defense counsel's table.

"All rhaght, let's heah it, Mistah Meacham."

"Your Honor, the defense has learned that the police recovered a sneaker print from the freshly-mopped floor of the store premises, and the State intends to use it in evidence."

Judge MacIntyre was flipping through some papers on the bench and did not respond. R.J. hesitated. "Go on, Ah'm listenin'," the Judge finally said.

"Well, Your Honor, it's just that those prints could match any one of thousands of pairs of sneakers, and the fact that they match my client's sneakers is highly prejudicial."

"Mistah Meacham, evidence in a criminal trahl is always prejudicial to the defendant," Judge MacIntyre chided.

R.J. hesitated again. "Yes, of course, Your Honor. What I meant to say was that its prejudicial effect outweighs its probative value."

"That's bettah," MacIntyre responded, satisfied with R.J.'s proper restatement of his legal argument. "Miss Dale?"

"Your Honor, admittedly the sneaker print evidence is circumstantial, but that doesn't mean it has no probative value. I think the evidence should be admitted and Mr. Meacham should be allowed to argue its weight to the jury."

R.J. knew she was right; he and Jack had talked about this days ago. Still, Jack told him he had to make the motion to protect the record. If he didn't, he might well open them up to a malpractice suit or a claim of "ineffective assistance of counsel" after Chuck Laggley went down the tubes—as Jack assured R.J. he was going to do.

"Mistah Meacham, do you wish to resphand?" Judge MacIntyre asked.

"No, Your Honor. Thank you."

"Verah well. I'll deny youah motion, Mistah Meacham. You can argue the strength or weakness of that paticulah piece evidence to the jurah. Do you have any other motions?"

"No, Your Honor."

"Ahr you not seekin' to suppress the sneakahs themselves?"

"No, Your Honor. They were not seized as the result of a search."

"Verah well. Why don't you just go ahead and put youah reasons on the recoahd?"

R.J. wondered whether the judge was protecting him or the trial, and he looked a Jack who responded with an almost invisible nod.

"As I said, Your Honor, the sneakers were not seized during a search. After my client was arrested, the police went to his home where his wife let them in. They asked her if her husband owned sneakers, and she went to their closet and brought out the ones in question. She is a joint tenant of the property, and she told me that she was not coerced in any way. A suppression hearing would be a waste of the Court's time, in my opinion."

Be up front with Mac; it's the only way you'll earn his respect. Jack had pounded the lesson into his young partner.

"The Coaht appreciates youah candoah, Mistah Meacham. Is theah anything else before we bring up a jurah?"

Both sides conceded there was nothing else standing in the way of R.J.'s first trial, and the judge left the bench while the bailiff went down to the first floor for a group of prospective jurors. R.J. looked at Jack and nodded him outside.

"What do I do now?" he asked nervously.

"What do you mean, 'what you do now'? Rob, we've been over this. You're going to try to get six people who you think are favorable to your side: other robbers if you can find them; simple thieves and burglars if you can't. Melanie is going to do the same thing for her side, only she'll be looking for retired cops and top sergeants from the Marine Corps. You throw off the people you think will be most favorable to her, and she'll do the same thing to you. What's left is your jury."

"I know. I know that. But how do I just stand up there and talk to them? You make it look so easy."

"Melanie goes first, so you just pick up on what she said. Don't worry about it. You've got the knack; if you didn't, you wouldn't be my partner." Jack slapped him on the back and pushed him into the courtroom just before the jurors arrived.

The judge returned to the bench and the lawyers began a long morning of trying to get inside the heads of complete strangers. Would a teacher be more inclined to convict because she had heard so many hare-brained excuses during her career and was tired of such nonsense? Or would she be more likely to acquit because she enjoyed working with young people and wanted to see everyone get a second chance? How about the engineer? Jack said the general rule was they were good for the defense because they wanted everything proven to a mathematical certainty rather than a 'reasonable doubt' which was much less. But the engineer's position as an elder of his church worried R.J. Still, he would likely be more receptive to the argument that 'thousands of sneakers could have made that print'; R.J. decided to keep him.

On it went, guessing and second-guessing. Melanie Dale would excuse some people, and R.J. would excuse others; back and forth, throughout the morning. By 11:30 they were both out of peremptory challenges; any other challenges would have to be 'for cause' and ruled on by the judge who appeared to be in no mood for further delay. There were no more challenges; the jury was sworn. It consisted of the teacher and the engineer, plus a grandmother/housewife, an office worker, an auto mechanic, a salesclerk and a retired postal worker. Young and old, black and white, male and female, they were a cross-section of America, and they would see to it that Chuck Laggley had his day in court.

"Verah well," Judge MacIntyre intoned. "We'll take a brief recess and come back for openin' arhg'ments. Then we'll break for lunch."

The judge left the bench and R.J. motioned Jack outside again. "I'm going to hit hard on the fact that the gun was never found," he said.

"You better be goddam sure he didn't have one," Jack warned. "You might be asking for big trouble."

Jack's warning brought a final huddled conference at the defense counsel table while the courtroom was still empty.

"Chuck, I'm going to hit hard on the fact that they never found the gun that they said you . . . I mean, the robber, used."

"Hey, hit it all you want. I didn't do it, and I don't own a gun like the one they've been talkin' about."

"Are you sure, Chuck?" R.J. pleaded. "Are you absolutely, positively sure?"

"Absatively, posititely," Chuck joked. "One thousand and one percent, okay?"

R.J. looked at Jack who simply shrugged his shoulders. "I'm going with it, Jack," he said.

❧ ❧ ❧

Marilyn was back to her old self and buried in a stack of papers by the time Jennifer returned from class later in the afternoon.

"Feeling better?"

"Yes, I'm fine. I told you it was just a 24-hour bug."

"We'll see," she smiled. "I think it's more like a nine-month bug."

"Oh, Jennifer, stop! Jack and I don't have time for that right now. I'm still going over all these proposals. Look at all this stuff," she complained, sorting through the pile of papers, "docks, power lines, paving. And Jack's been in court with R.J. all day. Besides, he wants to take a cruise to Key West with the Club next month. We can worry about a family later."

"I think that little bug of yours might have other ideas," Jennifer warned. "Anyway, what are you going to do about your father?"

"What does my father have to do with this?"

"Sooner or later the two of you are going to have to kiss and make up."

"We're not angry with each other," Marilyn protested.

"Then why is he afraid to come in here?"

"I just don't happen to think it's proper for him to have an affair with my husband's mother," Marilyn said firmly. "Have a little decency . . . a little respect, for God's sake!" Her voice began to rise even before Jennifer responded.

"There's something you haven't thought about, Marilyn"

"What? What haven't I thought about?"

"Maybe they really love each other," the younger woman answered.

❧ ❧ ❧

Dennis Woodbrace's face was ashen as he came out of the small room at the back of the *trattoria.* "There's no toilet in there," he murmured to Les. "They ain't got no toilet."

"They gotta have a toilet," Les protested.

"They don't. All's they got 's a hole in th' floor an' a couple 'a size 14's in the concrete so's ya' c'n plant y'r feet an' lean back agains' th' wall . . . if ya' gotta do that kind 'a thing."

"Well, did ya' go?"

"Ya' don't see no wet marks runnin' down my pants, do ya'?" Dennis gasped. "It was use the hole 'r tie a knot in it."

"Well, that's one probl'm solved anyways," Les said.

"But what if . . . if, ya' know, I gotta . . . 'r somebody's gotta use the other . . . way?" Dennis demanded.

"Don't think about it. Antonio's gone ta' check on his cousin. Ma'be we'll be hearin' about the car in a coupl' 'a minutes."

It took a lot longer than a couple of minutes before Antonio entered the café, and when it did the corners of his mouth were turned down further than Les would have thought possible. It did not look like good news.

"I'mé sorry, *ma* Vincenzo he say *che* ther'sé beeg *problema con la* car. *La pompa,* the pumpé ché maké the water go 'rouné, she'sé broke. *E* e's gotta go to the nekesé town for a new one."

"Judas Priest, it's the water pump," Les groaned. "An' there's none here in this town?"

Antonio looked at him like he had been out in the sun too long. "*Signore,* there'sé no cars in thisé place. For sure there'sé no *pompa.*"

Les put his head in his hands. "How long's it gonna take?" he pleaded.

"Vincenzo 'e foun´é cousiné 'ere, cané take him to the nekesé town right away, *subito. Ma,* it's gonna be 'while. Maybe we gonna sleepé 'ere?" Antonio's voice made his suggestion sound like a question, even though it wasn't.

"Where in th' name 'a Saint Elmo are we gonna sleep?" Les asked. All of the fight had been drained out of him, much like the water in Vincenzo's radiator.

"*Non pensari a niente,*" don' think about it," Antonio said with a majestic wave of his hands. "Me, I'mé gonna talké *cu* the man owns thisé place, *e* we gonna stay righté 'ere."

Antonio's eyebrows were arched even higher than usual; he was clearly pleased with himself. Les was beyond caring, but Dennis was in shock.

"But they ain't got no toilet!" he protested as Antonio turned away to negotiate their accommodations.

CHAPTER 7

The fitful night Les and Dennis spent with Antonio in the trattoria was not much worse than the night Marilyn spent in bed with Jack. She might really be pregnant, she thought. Not that that was so bad. She wanted a family and she was sure—she thought—that Jack did, too. He would make a wonderful father. But ever since that day on the beach when he told her about the automobile accident that took the lives of his first wife and their son, and how he blamed himself for it—unjustly, she thought—they had not discussed the subject. She always meant to talk about it, she thought as she rolled over and tried to get comfortable, but the time never seemed right. And now she was "late" in more ways than one. She had been pretty queasy the past couple of mornings, although today had definitely been the worst. And what about Jack's plans for the coming months? What was he going to say?

"Jack, are you asleep?" she asked quietly.

"Yes. Now what are you going to do?" he joked.

"Can we talk for a minute?"

"I told you, I'm asleep," he reminded her.

She propped herself up on one elbow and turned toward him. "Do you really, really want to go to Key West with the Yacht Club?"

That got his attention and he opened his eyes. "What's the matter? Don't you want to go?"

"I don't know. It's just that I've never been on a boat trip of that length before."

"What are you going to do when we go to the Bahamas this Fall?"

"Are we going there too?" she pleaded. She fell back, exasperated; she had forgotten about the stupid Bahamas.

"What's the matter, honey?" he asked gently. "Are you all right?"

"Yes, yes, I'm fine," she said testily. "I just didn't know about all these trips."

"You'll love Key West, Marilyn," he assured her. "It's a lot like New Orleans. In fact, there's a little French pastry shop and café halfway up Duval Street. At least I hope it's still there. They make the greatest, what do you call them, *brouchettes*? It's a breakfast thing."

"*Brioches*," she said, giving the word its proper pronunciation. "*Brochette* is a way of cooking . . . fish, mostly."

"You know what I mean. These things are great. They slice the tops off rolls and fill them with spinach and poached eggs. I wish I could remember the name of the place: *Café de* something. And wait 'till you see the sunset from Mallory Square. You'll see a green flash; I guarantee it."

"But what if something comes up and we can't go?" she asked, praying that he would not repeat the menu.

"What could come up? Everything is under control at the office, and there isn't anything here that Jennifer can't handle. Is it about her wedding? Do you have to give her a shower or something? Because we'll be back in plenty of time for that."

"No, it's just . . ." her protest died away. "Never mind; I guess I'm just worrying about nothing."

"Well if you want to worry about something, worry about R.J. He still thinks Chuck Laggley is innocent. I hope he doesn't get hurt too badly when he gets hit with reality."

❧ ❧ ❧

R.J. didn't see it that way. In spite of Jack's warning, he had poured everything he had into a give-'em-hell opening statement that morning, pointing out that the police never recovered the gun which the store clerk said Chuck had pointed at her. And he had done a really good job of cross-examination, he thought. The clerk said the robber wore a ski mask and she only identified Chuck after her boss said it might have been him.

"So, you didn't say it was Chuck Laggley until after his name had been suggested to you?" R.J. asked by way of driving home that point.

"No, I don't know Chuck Laggley. He quit or something before I started working there," she had replied.

"And you never saw him before you identified him in a police line-up, isn't that right?"

"Yes, that's right," the woman admitted.

"And then, when you did identify him, you said, 'That looks like him,' isn't that right?"

"I . . . well, I don't remember exactly what I said, to be honest with you."

"So if a police officer said that you said, 'That looks like him,' he might be right, isn't that correct?"

"He might be; I guess he would be," she admitted.

"You don't remember?"

"No, I really don't remember."

All in all, it had been a great cross-examination, R.J. thought as he went over it again in the silence of the night. He had been able to show the identification of Chuck was tainted by a person who had had an argument—and, presumably, an axe to grind—with him not long before the robbery. No fingerprints were found at the scene, and, as for the sneaker print, well, he was going to argue it didn't prove anything at all except that most cheap sneakers come from the same factory. The lack of a weapon would clinch the case for the defense. R.J. closed his eyes and hoped he would dream of his first courtroom victory.

At the Magnolia Avenue house, Jennifer restlessly waited for dreams of her own. It wasn't the wedding that was bothering her; the date was set and the details were no problem. She didn't need a banquet room because she owned one, and the Yacht Club management would be only too happy to set aside a room for a rehearsal dinner for the granddaughter of "Casey" Calkins. A bridal shower would be fun, but there was little a bride needed when she was sitting atop a 25+ million-dollar trust fund. No, there was only one thing she needed right now, and he was in a bachelor apartment in Bonita, probably poring over papers for his stupid trial!

Marilyn was the one with all the passion in her life. Jack was always bringing her flowers and fawning over her. And now it looked like she was pregnant, which meant she would be getting even more attention. R.J. was okay; he was dignified, proper. He was too damn proper! What was he afraid of? The Calkins money? Jennifer punched up her pillow.

She wondered what it felt like: being pregnant, having a new life, a part of someone you love growing inside of you. R.J. should be here right now, she thought. There was no reason he couldn't have moved in after Grandma . . . passed on. He shouldn't have left her alone like this. It just wasn't fair. The more Jennifer thought about it, the angrier she became until she finally picked up the bedside telephone and dialed his number.

"Hello?" He sounded groggy; he must have been asleep, she thought.

"R.J.?" Could you come over here, please?"

"Jennifer? What's the matter?" He was wide awake now; she could almost hear his eyes pop open.

"I'm . . . I'm not feeling very well." She put enough of a tremble into her voice to make it believable.

"Are you all right?" It was a silly question, but at least he sounded like he was really worried about her.

"No, I'm not all right," she protested. "The room is spinning around . . . I just feel . . . terrible."

"I'll call an ambulance," he offered. That was R.J.: practical even in the face of an engraved invitation to a single-woman's bedroom late at night. She was beginning to think he even slept in this three-piece suit.

"No . . . please don't do that," she begged, her voice quavering a little. "I'm not . . . it's not that bad. I'm just afraid to be alone right now."

"Should I call your Uncle Doug?

Jennifer suppressed the urge to scream, but said, "R.J. can't you come over here yourself for a minute?"

"Well, I'm in the middle of a trial . . ." he hesitated for a minute. "Sure, I can stay with you for a little bit."

"I'm too dizzy to get out of bed. There's a spare key in the mailbox. Do you think you could let yourself in?"

"Of course. I'll be right over."

Jennifer hung up the phone and leaped out of bed. First, she had to actually put a key in the mailbox for him to find, and then she had to change into her sheerest, sexiest nightgown: that short blue one that tied in the front. She debated about the matching blue panties before putting them on. Leaving them off might look like too much of a set-up, and besides, she wanted to feel him slip them off her body. At the last minute she took everything off and jumped in the shower. She wanted to be squeaky clean for whatever happened tonight, and as the warm water kissed its way down her skin, she closed her eyes for a moment and dreamed that R.J. would soon be doing the same thing. She dried herself with a warm, fluffy towel and inspected her body while she applied perfume to all the secret places that R.J. had not yet explored. Finally, she applied just a hint of makeup: a little lipstick and a touch of rouge to her nipples which she had always thought were too pale. The window was open and she heard a car drive up as she slipped on the baby-dolls again and slithered between the sheets. She could hear him coming up the stairs as she arranged her long blond hair on the pillow, and barely had time to look weak and helpless before he opened the bedroom door.

"Jennifer? Are you all right?"

She couldn't believe it; he was wearing his yacht club blazer and a white shirt open at the collar. At least he left the necktie at home! "Oh . . . thanks for coming, R.J.," she replied weakly.

He quickly moved closer, sat on the bed and put a hand on her forehead. "Are you all right, Jen?" He really sounded worried.

"Yes, I'm all right . . . now that you're here." It was a stupid thing to say, like something out of an old movie, but it was all she could think of at the moment.

He began gently stroking her hair. "Jen, your hair feels . . . damp."

"It does? I guess I must have a fever."

He touched her cheek. "You don't feel warm."

She pulled down the covers so her breasts were visible under the sheer blue nightie. "Don't you think it's hot in here?" she asked quietly.

He leaned forward and put his hand under her arm. "My mother always used to check my temperature by putting her hand here," he said softly. "Do you want me to call a doctor?"

"Don't call anyone, R.J.," she whispered. "I think we can handle this ourselves."

"It's still a few months until our wedding," he reminded her.

"I know," she said. "Grandma always said to get an early start on important things."

His hand slid from under her arm to her breast as he kissed her, softly at first and then harder. Their tongues began to reach out for one another as his free hand came up to caress her other breast. In a few minutes he released her mouth and worked his way down her neck as she sighed in response.

"We shouldn't be doing this yet," he reminded her, not too forcefully, as she began to untie the front of the nightgown.

"That's right, shouldn't," she said as she opened it and he began kissing her body. She looked down at what he was doing. Her nipples were rock-hard; she needn't have bothered with the rouge.

He pulled back and looked directly into her eyes. "We really shouldn't be doing this yet," he repeated.

"R.J., please. I really want you here with me. Please." She brought her arms around his neck and pulled him down to her. His mouth found hers once more, and the brass buttons of his blazer pressed into her naked flesh. "Take off your jacket and stay awhile," she said as she slid it off him.

She watched hungrily as he stood up and shed his clothes. His body was lean and hard, and even now the excitement of having her throbbed in him. "This is what a man looks like when he's ready," she thought. No more drawings and diagrams and trying to imagine this moment. This is it, the real thing. And I want him as much as he wants me."

He sat down next to her again and slid off the top half of her lingerie. "Jennifer, I love you more than anything in the world," he said as he began to kiss his way down between her breasts and over her belly. In a few minutes she felt him tugging at the panties. She raised herself up to help him and she shivered involuntarily as he slid them down her legs. She was so glad she had decided to wear them; she wouldn't have missed that sensation for anything. Now he was between her legs, kissing the insides of her thighs and moving up to where they met. He breath came in short gasps, and when his tongue touched her, the sensation lifted her off the bed again. She began to tremble; her skin felt like burning ice and her muscles tensed as waves of pleasure shot through her. She was swept along by the feeling, every nerve in her body torn between begging for more and screaming for him to stop. He didn't stop; he egged her to higher and higher peaks, taking his time with her until she was sure she couldn't stand any more. And then the moment came. He was moving on top of her and after an exquisite moment of pain she could feel him inside her.

"Are you all right?" he whispered from somewhere close to her ear.

"I'm fine; I'm fine," she gasped in reply.

He began moving, slowly at first, and she followed him, matching his tempo and urging him on with her response.

"Are you sure you've never done this?" he gasped as their speed increased.

"I've thought about it every night since I met you," she replied between her own gasps of gratification.

He moved faster now; faster and harder. She felt the damp sweat on his back and her body begin to tense. She didn't think it was possible to feel any more pleasure, but he kept driving her on: higher, further. And suddenly she was swept over the edge; her body went rigid and a small scream escaped from her throat. With what remained of her senses she felt him stiffen on top of her. And then they sank down together, exhausted.

It was a long time before either one of them moved. "Are you sure you're all right?" he said when he recovered enough to roll off beside her.

She turned to him and smiled. "You've asked me that four times, Silly," she replied, running her hand through the hair on his chest.

He looked at her softly. "I love you, Jennifer," he said quietly.

"That sounds a lot better than asking me if I'm all right," she said, poking him with a finger. "And besides, I love you more."

"No you don't. I love you a lot more than you love me," he replied as he reached across and began fondling her breast.

"Oh, yeah? Do you love me enough to get dressed and buy me a chili dog at Vasilli's?" she demanded.

"Do you love me enough to get dressed and come with me?"

In a moment they were out of bed, laughing like children and throwing clothes at each other as they raced to see who could get dressed first. And then they were out the door and driving across the bridge to Bonita on a moonlit winter night in Southwest Florida.

❧ ❧ ❧

Not far from the Bonita bridge, Henri Dupré was making a long-distance telephone call to New York. It was very late, but he needed to hear a special voice in the loneliness of his night.

"Hello?" Her voice sounded dignified, refined. She had not been asleep; that was good. He suddenly felt like a schoolboy; he did not know how to begin the conversation.

"I have not disturbed you, *non*?" he inquired.

"Not at all, Henri. I was hoping you would call," Victoria Townsend answered from far away.

"I could not sleep." He paused, unsure of what to say next. "It is cool here now," he added lamely.

"We're having a terrible winter," she reported. "I've seldom seen so much snow in the City."

"You are well?"

"Yes. And you?"

"I am not well; I am thinking of you."

"I should hope thinking of me would be a happy thing," she chided.

"Thoughts of you, yes. But not thoughts of you when you are in New York and I am here, *ma chère*."

"You're very sweet, Henri. I told you I would surprise you for the grand opening."

"The opening is now again postponed, *ma chère*. Janifere must have a special roof."

"Oh, no!" The disappointment in her voice was very real and it gave him hope. "How much longer?"

"A month, they say. But I do not trust *les artisans*. Always they must have more time. *Peut-être* you could come before they finish?"

"I don't know, Henri. What would I use as an excuse?"

"To the Devil with excuses!" he fairly shouted. We love each other, no? Why must we bother with excuses?"

"Your daughter is married to my son, Henri," she reminded him. It would be a scandal."

"Where? Where would be this scandal? Here? Where people live on boats? Where women spend their days dressed in scraps of cloth? Here there would be a scandal?"

"Calm down, Henri."

"Please, *ma chère*. You must come. I cannot live another day unless I see you once more."

"Henri, you are too French," she scolded.

"And you are too English, no? Please. Come. Now."

"I'll call my travel agent first thing in the morning," she replied.

CHAPTER 8

Jack Townsend was more surprised than concerned when R.J. failed to show up at the office for their usual morning cup of coffee. Ordinarily, Rob Meacham was a man of regular habits, but the stress of his first trial must have unnerved him. Jack asked their secretary to give him a call and remind him they were supposed to be in Judge MacIntyre's courtroom at 9:30 sharp. There was no answer.

"Shall I try again?" Ms. Crowley asked, seeing Jack's frown.

"No, that's all right. He probably went right to court. Knowing Rob, he must have found something he wants to research. I'll probably find him holed up in the library."

"It's not like him not to call," she reminded him.

"Well, he's got a lot on his mind right now. It's his first trial."

Jack arrived alone at the courthouse and fondly recalled the days when he could almost tell who was there by checking out the cars in the parking lot. But now Bonita was being overwhelmed by the same building boom that was overtaking all of South Florida. Pretty soon there would be nothing from one coast to the other except condominiums and shopping malls.

"How are things this morning?" he asked one of the deputy sheriffs standing in the coffee shop.

Jack recognized him as one of the courthouse regulars. He had delivered prisoners from the jail and for the rest of the day he would provide backup security until he was ordered to return them to their unwanted temporary home. "Same old, same old," he responded grimly.

"Do you know if my partner Rob Meacham is here?" There was an outside chance the deputy might have noticed a young lawyer arriving at the courthouse much too early. His answer could save Jack from running all around the building.

"Sorry, don't know him."

That was part of the problem: no one knew anybody in Calusa County anymore, Jack thought as he headed for the elevator. Time was ticking away when he stopped at the law library. No, Mr. Meacham wasn't there, the librarian reported. She knew him because he was on a Bar Association committee with her. Jack asked her to remind Mr. Meacham—if he happened by—that he had an appointment with Judge MacIntyre in about ten minutes.

He took a side elevator up to the fourth floor where the criminal courts were located. R.J. wasn't in the hallway, nor was he in the courtroom. Jack glanced at his watch: eight minutes to go and Mac was a terror about being punctual. He asked the green-jacketed courtroom bailiff. "Haven't seen him yet," the man replied with a shrug, "but he better get his ass in here. Mac don't like to be kept waiting."

It was 9:28 before R.J. rushed into the courtroom. He was wearing a yacht club blazer and a white shirt open at the neck.

"Where the hell have you been?" Jack demanded in a whisper.

"Lend me your tie, will you?" R.J. said without answering Jack's question.

"Where's your tie? And did you shave this morning?"

"I'll shave a lunch time. It's a long story."

Jack looked at the bailiff who returned his glance with a wide-eyed warning, then pointed at his wristwatch and nodded toward the door. It was 9:29; Mac would be out any minute. Jack quickly took off his tie and draped it over his partner's neck. "Put this on, quick," he demanded. "I'll run over to the Prep Shop and buy a new one. You're counsel of record; start without me. If Mac asks where I am, tell him I was unavoidably detained. I'll be back in a few minutes."

"I know; I know," R.J. responded as he fiddled with Jack's tie and adjusted his collar.

Jack bolted for the door. It wouldn't do to be caught in Mac's courtroom without a necktie, and he couldn't imagine what possible excuse he might give the judge. The 'unavoidable delay' explanation was at least reasonably true, as long as he was outside the door before Mac entered the courtroom.

"Thanks, partner. I owe you," R.J. said as Jack put his hand on the doorknob.

"I'll settle for an explanation later," Jack said over his shoulder as he hurried into the hallway.

The door was still closing when he heard the bailiff's voice telling everyone to rise and announcing that the circuit court of the twenty-first judicial circuit of Florida was now in session. Rob was really on his own now, Jack thought.

The hell with him. He was the genius who came in late and half-dressed. Let him muddle through alone for a while. Nobody was there to hold Jack's hand at his first felony trial; why should Rob be different? Besides, he had done a damn good job yesterday; he might even pull this dead loser of a case out of the fire. If that happened, he deserved to bask in his own spotlight for a few minutes.

Jack went to the men's shop on Clematis Street and dawdled over the tie selection before he bought one and asked Bruce Ziegler where he could get a cup of coffee.

"Must be nice to be retired," Bruce said as he prepared to put Jack's purchase in a bag.

"Don't bother with the bag, Bruce," Jack told him. "I'm going to wear it. And I'm not retired anymore. I'm just killing a little time to teach my partner a lesson. No, make that, 'killing time to let him learn a lesson.'"

"I'm not going to guess what that's supposed to mean," Bruce responded.

"It means sometimes the best way to teach birds to fly is to kick them out of the nest," Jack shrugged.

"That can make for some pretty rough landings," the man observed.

"Yeah, but it also makes for a lot of flying birds." Jack finished the Windsor knot and headed out the door. It was a beautiful South Florida morning, the kind that makes residents so smugly satisfied when they think about all the poor bastards up North, slogging their way through an endless winter. Jack knew that Judge MacIntyre would not appreciate the trial being interrupted by him walking in during testimony. He would go in at the 10:45 mid-morning break, so he stopped at the New York Deli (why were people down here so interested in keeping their ties to 'back home'?), ordered a cup of coffee and phoned the office.

"Mr. Meacham called right after you left," Sharon Crowley reported. "He said he was running late and would meet you at court."

"Thank you. Did he bother to tell you why he didn't answer when you called him?"

"No, and I didn't ask." Ms. Crowley was a model legal secretary; she wouldn't think of asking one of the 'Partners' such a personal question. Even now she didn't dare ask Jack why he wasn't in the courtroom with R.J.

"Well, it's an interesting damn mystery," Jack observed, not expecting a reply.

"By the way, Mr. Woodbrace was in to see you right after you left," she added.

"Oh, God."

"He said to tell you the offer was up to two thousand a share. He said you would know what that means."

"I know what that means," Jack confirmed. "Anything else?"

"Your wife called."

"My wife? Marilyn?" It had been almost two months since their wedding, but the phrase still sounded new and a little strange. "What did she want?"

"She said it wasn't important. She said she would see you later."

"She probably just wanted to tell me that she loves me," Jack said.

"I wouldn't know about that," Ms. Crowley replied.

Back in Calkins Harbor, Marilyn Dupré Townsend was feeling about as rotten as she had felt every morning that week. She had never been seasick, but she heard it described and it couldn't be any worse than she felt at the moment. She dragged herself to her desk and used up what little energy she had left trying to keep her breakfast down. Whatever this malady was, it wasn't going away. Jennifer came in, later than usual, and her cheery greeting only made Marilyn feel worse.

"How's it going, Sis?"

"Go away and let me die," Marilyn replied, not opening her eyes or lifting her chin from her hand.

"Are you going to listen to me and call the doctor? Or do I have to do it for you?"

"I can't pick up the phone right now."

Jennifer moved behind the desk and hugged her. "Come on, I'll do it," she said as she picked up the receiver and dialed Dr. Greenman's number from memory. The receptionist immediately recognized her voice.

"Can I bring my sister Marilyn Townsend in for a checkup right away?" Jennifer inquired.

Like everyone else on Bonita Key, the woman was well aware of Jennifer and Marilyn's relationship and their pecking order on the social scale of the island. Dr. Greenman surely would want to do anything possible to accommodate them.

"What seems to be the problem, Miss Calkins?"

"Well, she's tired and listless, and she's having trouble keeping her breakfast down."

"How long as this been going on?"

"All week, I think." Jennifer looked down at Marilyn who nodded mutely against her body.

"Has she been sick all day?"

"No, just in the morr . . . nings," Jennifer replied in a little sing-song voice.

The receptionist chuckled. "I see. Well, it sounds like her problem really isn't in Dr. Greenman's line."

"I'm pretty sure it isn't," Jennifer said with a smile so big it came through the telephone line. "But I thought he could confirm it one way or the other and refer us to somebody else."

"Certainly. How about first thing tomorrow morning?" It was no use juggling an office full of patients just to tell a woman what she should already know, even for people as special as Jennifer Calkins and Marilyn Townsend.

"Is there anything she can do until then?"

"Oh, no! No medication of any kind! The receptionist said. "And it sounds like there won't be anything she can do after tomorrow morning, either. She'll just have to grin and bear it. Thank goodness the nausea goes away by itself in a month or two. We've all been through it."

Not all of us . . . at least not yet, Jennifer thought as she replaced the receiver.

"What did she say?" Marilyn moaned.

"We have an appointment with him first thing in the morning. I'm going to cut class and drive you there. In the meantime, you'll just have to plan on feeling sick."

"Please don't say anything to Jack," Marilyn begged.

Half a world away, Les Leslie and Dennis Woodbrace were once again squeezed into the cramped back seat of Vincenzo's *macchina.* Les had spent the better part of the morning installing a new water pump that Vincenzo and his newly-found cousin had brought by motor scooter from the closest sizable town. Needless to say, a serviceman had not accompanied it, and Vincenzo's mechanical ability appeared to be limited to kicking the tires and uttering murderous and complex Italian oaths at the helpless vehicle.

It was all behind them now. They were finally on their way again, and all was peaceful except for an occasional groan from Dennis.

"Man, I gotta get ta' a town with a toilet," he complained bitterly.

"What in blue blazes is the matter with ya' now?" Les demanded. "Didn't ya' go before we left?"

"I couldn't do this there," Dennis complained. "F'r what I gotta do I gotta kinda settle in an' get comfr'table.

"Well, ya' shoulda got comfr'table there."

"Are you kiddin'? In mid-air? Squeezed up against a wall like that? No way was anythin' gonna happen! Besides, they didn't even got no toilet paper."

"Don't ya' have any a' them liras? They ain't worth that much," Les said with a chuckle.

"It ain't funny, Les," Dennis retorted.

"Look, I'm sorry, okay?" Les said, more sympathetically this time. "But I don't think there's a place ta' stop f'r that kind a' thing between here and Licata. Leastways not any kind a' place that fits y'r specifications. You'll just have ta' hold out, unless ya' want Vincenzo ta' stop alongside the road someplace."

"I'll hold out," Dennis said grimly.

❧ ❧ ❧

"Where the heck were you?" R.J. demanded when Jack strolled into the courtroom at the mid-morning recess.

"That's funny, I asked you that first . . . and it was a couple of hours ago, remember?" the senior partner replied.

R.J. hesitated and the tips of his ears turned pink; if Jack didn't know better he would have said he'd embarrassed his young partner. "I was delayed, all right? Besides, I got here on time; what's the big problem?" he added, a little too defensively.

"No problem, Rob. And as far as where I was, I figured it was best not to walk in during testimony and annoy Mac. Anyway, I'm sure you did fine."

"The sneaker guy was on," R.J. explained. "I think I did a real good job on him."

"Is the print in evidence?"

"Yes, but I got him to admit that there might be thousands of sneakers with that tread pattern in Southwest Florida."

"Who's next?"

"The next-door neighbor; she's going to testify that she saw Chuck coming home early in the morning. Any suggestions for me on cross-examination?"

"Just what we talked about. Take her for a walk down memory lane. Ask her what she had for breakfast, where she went that particular day. Get her to admit she doesn't remember details, then argue to the jury that her testimony about seeing your client on that particular day isn't worthy of belief. You know the routine."

They had barely finished speaking when Assistant State Attorney Melanie Dale re-entered the recessed courtroom with one of the detectives at her side. She caught R.J.'s eye and dropped a large manilla envelope on her counsel table that landed with a resounding 'thud.' "Rob, can I see you for a minute?" she asked.

R.J. hesitated and looked back at Jack who turned to their client. "What do you think is in that envelope, Chuck?" Jack whispered.

'I don't know. Ya' think it might be the gun?"

"I'll be with you in a second, Melanie," R.J. said, stalling for time.

Jack put his hand to his forehead to cover his eyes while he whispered, "You told us there wasn't any gun, Chuck."

"No, I didn't. I said I didn't own a gun like the one they're talkin' about. An' I don't. I used ta' own one, but I lost it."

"Chuck, you said you never owned a gun!" R.J. demanded in a whisper of his own.

"Nu-huh. I never said that. Maybe that's what you heard, but I didn't say it."

"All right, enough of this bullshit, Chuck," Jack said in a no-nonsense whisper. "Did you have a gun or not?"

"Like I said, I used to have a gun. Okay, it was kind 'a like the one they've been talking about, but I don't have it no more. I lost it. I don't know; maybe they found it or something."

"Where did you lose it, Chuck?" R.J. demanded.

Laggley looked at him with a slick smile. "If I knew that, it wouldn't be lost, right?"

The two lawyers left him sitting at the counsel table and held a whispered conference with the prosecutor.

"I know you guys are going to be pissed, but we found the gun this morning, she reported.

"Come on, Melanie, this is a little late in the game, isn't it?" Jack said. "We finished discovery a month ago."

"I don't blame you for being upset, Jack, but I swear to you my guys just found it today. They wouldn't even have looked for it anymore, but Rob made such a big deal about it in his opening statement . . ."

"He gave them a little extra incentive?" Jack suggested.

"Something like that," she agreed.

"How do you know it's his?" R.J. demanded.

"I don't know; but it's got a letter "C" carved in the handle and they found it in a drainage canal between his house and the scene of the robbery."

"That 'C' could stand for anything," R.J. protested.

Melanie Dale looked almost apologetic. "I understand that Rob. It's like the sneaker print. But my guys went to a lot of trouble to find it. I'll give you as much time as you want to depose the officer, but I have to do everything I can to get it into evidence."

"Let's talk to the judge," Jack suggested.

Judge MacIntyre called in the court reporter and looked out the window of his chambers while the attorneys argued about whether the gun should be admitted into evidence, considering the fact that it could not be linked directly to the crime and the State had not disclosed its existence during pre-trial discovery. Finally, he spat some tobacco juice into the tin cup he kept on his desk and turned toward them.

"Ah'm reluctant to delay the trahal at this point, but Ah believe Ah have an obligation to give the State an opprahtunity to prove its case. Mistah Meacham, how many witnesses do ya'll intend to call?"

"Two, Your Honor."

"All rhagt, here's what we'll do: I'll recess this trahl until two o'clock. That'll give you boys plenty of tahm to depose the young man who found the gun. Ms. Dale, you can put him on this aftahnoon, and we'll see if you can get it into evidence. Ah'm not rulin' on that at the present tahm, you understand that, don't you Ms. Dale."

"Yes, Your Honor, that's fine," she answered.

"Once we get past that snag, you can put on the rest of youah case. That'll leave tamarhah foah the defense case, closin' ahghments and jurah instructions."

"That's a lot to do in one day, Judge," Jack observed.

"It'll be that orah we'll woahk on Sat'day; I'll not hold the jurah over the weekend" MacIntyre warned.

Mac's rulings were always final; the lawyers knew better than to protest, and they quickly walked out of his chambers.

"We'll finish by tomorrow, Jack," R.J. said as they returned to the courtroom. "Jennifer and I have plans for the weekend."

CHAPTER 9

Marilyn pretended to be asleep when Jack got up early and made his own breakfast. She felt guilty about staying in bed and justified it by telling herself she would not be able to take the smell of coffee so early in the day. Besides, it was probably his fault that she was feeling like this! She put a pillow over her head when he came back into the room.

"Hey, are you feeling all right?" he asked softly as he sat down on the queen-size bed.

"I'm just tired," she said, hoping he'd go away.

"I know I haven't been paying much attention to you, but the trial will be over today. I'm going to make reservations for the four of us at the Club tonight. Friday is their seafood night; and win or lose R.J. will need to talk about the case."

"How can you think about food so early in the morning?" she groaned from underneath her pillow.

"Aren't you going to kiss me goodbye?" he asked, picking up a corner of it and playfully peeking at her.

"No. I'm tired," she answered sullenly, hugging the pillow closer to herself.

"Too tired for a little peck?"

She pushed the pillow away for a moment, perfunctorily kissed him and then replaced it quickly.

"Does this mean the honeymoon is over?" he asked, standing up and straightening his jacket.

"We'll talk about it later," she replied from her hiding place.

She waited until she heard the car drive off before she began to drag herself out of bed. Jennifer would arrive soon to pick her up for her appointment with Dr. Greenman. How did medical people get themselves started so early in the morning, anyway? Brushing her teeth had been her big problem the last few days; if she could get past that she was pretty sure she could make it through the rest of the day. She stared at her reflection in the mirror over the sink as she slowly moved the brush up and down and tried not to gag on the taste of the toothpaste. It was a fine mess she'd gotten herself into this time.

R.J. huddled with Jack outside Judge MacIntyre's courtroom waiting to start the final day of the trial, as he silently watched the people bustle past: silk suits mingling with t-shirts and jeans. It didn't take an expert to distinguish the distracted-looking lawyers from the sometimes hardened, sometimes frightened-looking defendants and witnesses who crowded the hallway.

"They don't have a clue as to what's happening in here, do they?" he asked Jack quietly.

"A lot of them think it's a game," the older man replied. "They come to us because they think we know the rules better than they do."

"How badly do you think the gun hurt us?"

"It didn't help; that's for sure. It's another strand of circumstantial evidence. If Melanie gets enough of them together, the jury will braid them into a noose for Mr. Chuck Laggley."

"It was my fault," R.J. said bitterly. "You warned me to stay away from the gun issue unless I was absolutely sure he wasn't lying to me. I had to go a make a big point of it in that opening statement."

Jack put his hand on R.J.'s shoulder. "Hey, partner, he's the one who lied to you, remember? And you did a hell of a job on cross-examination. The jury knows the police didn't find the gun until yesterday morning, and you hammered the fact that the only thing linking it to your client is the letter 'C' on the handle. For all they know, it might stand for 'Colt.' It may work out for the best."

"What do you mean?

"The jury might get pissed off, might think the State is trying too hard to put poor old Chuck away. So far you've shown the victim's identification was tainted by the manager's suggestion; the neighbor can't remember anything except that Chuck came home early one morning; and the sneaker print could belong to just about anybody. If Chuck and Janey hold up on the witness stand and you do a gold-plated summation on reasonable doubt, you just might be able to pull this one off."

"Do you really think so?" R.J. asked.

"It's possible," Jack fibbed. "I told Sharon to make reservations for the four of us at the Club tonight," he added, knowing in his heart it would be a wake instead of a celebration.

Chuck and Janey Laggley were waiting inside the courtroom. Janey, in her trim, brown business suit and short, no-nonsense sandy hair contrasted sharply with the brooding hulk of a husband at her side. She had been front-row, center during the entire trial and no doubt would wait faithfully at home while he served the time he was sure to get in prison when the trial ended. Jack wondered about the misspent loyalty in such a relationship. What did Janey get out of this? Was a sense of 'belonging' so important to her that she was blind to Chuck's obvious faults? That bailiff called court into session, and after the jury was in place, R.J. called Janey to the witness stand.

"State your name and address for the record, please," he began.

"SaraJane Laggley, 31 Hoyt Street, Bonita," she replied, and then added, "but everybody calls me 'Janey'."

"Okay, Janey, and are you the wife of the defendant, Chuck Laggley?"

"Yes, I am."

"How long have you been married?"

"Three years."

It was the standard kind of Q and A that takes place in every courtroom in the United States. Jack had told him to keep it short. Janey was only there to look good, gain a little sympathy from the jury, and confirm that Chuck was in bed with her at the time of the robbery. That was it. If R.J. kept her on the stand too long he ran the risk of having her blurt out something that Melanie Dale would pick up on and use to the State's advantage. Jack had reminded him—several times—to fight the temptation to ask questions just for the sake of asking them. It was a mistake that many young lawyers made, he said, and it could be deadly—especially if your client was not telling the truth.

"Do you remember the morning of the day your husband was arrested?"

"Oh, yes. I do."

"Why do you remember that day?"

The rule about never asking a witness to tell you 'why' could safely be ignored. They had been over this with Janey at least a dozen times and she gave the answer that R.J. expected.

"Well, it's kind of hard to forget something as horrible as that."

Nice. She hadn't used the word 'horrible' in the office, but it was a nice touch, and sure to impress the women on the jury.

"Do you remember where Chuck was on the morning of that day?" Jack had told him to always refer to his client as 'Chuck' rather than 'the defendant.' It helped to humanize him to the jury and make him more of a real person. It would be a lot harder to convict sweet Janey's husband Chuck than it would be to convict a defendant who didn't even deserve a name of his own.

"Yes, I do," she responded, a little shyly. "He was in bed with me."

That answer wasn't quite as good. She was supposed to wait for R.J. to ask, 'Where was he?' before she answered. The way she said it might sound like she was trying to get out a canned answer too quickly.

"How do you know he was in bed with you?"

It was, of course, the ultimate question that Jack had raised at the very beginning. The jurors would have to believe that Janey 'always' woke up when Chuck left the house early. If they didn't, her story wasn't worth a damn; she would be just another young wife, either blinded by loyalty or afraid of what would happen to her and their child if her husband went prison.

"I'm a very light sleeper." She turned and looked at the women on the jury, just as R.J. had instructed her to do, and continued, "We have a baby at home, and ever since she was born I've slept with one eye open. I know when Chuck gets up even if I don't open my eyes. I'm sure he didn't get up that morning."

Perfect. The stuff about the 'baby at home' was probably technically irrelevant, but the jury had heard it, and if Melanie Dale objected and asked to have it stricken from the record she would look like the Wicked Witch of the West. Instead, gamely she sat there and gritted her teeth.

R.J. carefully led Janey through the remainder of her testimony, crafting his questions to sound like they did not imply the answers, but knowing all the time exactly what the answers would be, and taking her from one subject to the next with the ease born of endless pre-trial preparation. He was finished in exactly twenty minutes and he sat down next to Jack and waited to see how much damage Ms. Dale would do.

Melanie used the same "memory lane" gambit he had used on the neighbor lady; only it didn't work as well. Janey had much more reason to remember the 'horrible' day and its details, and, Jack thought, more reason to unconsciously fill in the gaps for the things she didn't remember. The prosecutor was getting nowhere and she knew it. She finished quickly and sat down. It was better to let Janey's testimony go unchallenged than to have her repeat it to the jury. The last witness would make or break the case: he was the defendant, Chuck Laggley.

Jennifer Calkins sat in Dr. Greenman's waiting room and paged through a year-old magazine. It was 10:00 o'clock; Marilyn had been inside for half an hour. Even though Jennifer suspected her 'problem' was not Dr. Greenman's specialty, she should have been out by now. She tossed the magazine aside and was about to pick up another one when

Marilyn walked out in a daze. Her dark brown eyes were open wide and they contrasted sharply with her skin that was noticeably pale.

"Congratulations, Jennifer. You're going to be an aunt."

Jennifer shot off her chair and hugged her, squealing with delight. "Marilyn that's wonderful! I'm so happy for you!"

"Do you really think so?"

"What do you mean? Of course I really think so!"

"I don't know. I just wish I knew how Jack is going to take this."

"Jack? Jack will be doing handsprings! Marilyn, what's the matter with you?"

"I just . . . I'll never forget the look on his face when he told me about . . . that time in the hospital; about his son. I want him to really want this baby. And besides, he had so many plans for this summer. This is going to cause a lot of changes."

"Changes? Why are you being so silly? Come on, let's go down to the courthouse. We can meet them for lunch and you can tell Jack the news."

"No, let's not do that. Let's not interrupt them when they're in court."

"Well when are you going to tell him?"

"When the time is right."

"But how can you stand it?" Jennifer squealed. "I'm so excited I want to tell him right now."

"No, Jennifer, don't you dare! This is my baby and I'm his wife. I'll tell him. But I'll do it when the time is right."

"Well, don't wait too long," Jennifer warned. "Secrets like this are hard to keep."

Chuck Laggley walked to the witness stand with a slick self-assuredness that made the hair on Jack's neck stand on end. Chuck was the kind of guy who tried hard to exude honesty, but the pained sincerity on his face was offset by the coldness in his eyes. Those eyes gave him away; they told you that Chuck's honesty was the thinnest kind of veneer—that beneath it lurked a man who was entirely capable of pointing a gun at a helpless woman and terrorizing her. R.J. took up the questioning while Jack sat back and wondered if the jury would see what he saw in Chuck's eyes.

"Where do you live, Mr. Laggley?" R.J. began.

"Like I said, 31 Hoyt Street with my wife. She was just up here."

It had started early; Chuck was already being cute with his answers. The "Like I said," was a habit of his—and an annoying one. If he tried that little weaselly smile of his, Jack was sure the jury would take him out and lynch him.

"Are you employed anywhere?"

"Well, I used to be." There was that smile. Chuck paused, then continued. "I used to have a real good job until they cut back my hours."

Why is it that people who are lying are incapable of giving one-word answers, Jack thought. They always have a desperate need to explain everything.

"Now, do you remember the day you were arrested?" R.J. asked.

"Yeah. It's pretty hard to forget a thing like that." Chuck flashed that insincere smile again, and Jack shuddered inwardly.

"Can you tell the members of the jury what you were doing that day?"

"I was home all day. Well, that is, until the police officers came and got me."

People like Chuck don't call cops 'police officers' any more than cops call people like Chuck 'gentlemen,' Jack thought. Both sides save that language for the courtroom where they apparently think it makes them sound more believable.

"All right, let's start at the beginning, Chuck." R.J. got the defense story out in a meticulous series of questions and answers; pausing at the appropriate times and glancing at his notes only infrequently. Jack was right in his assessment of his young partner: he had a knack for this sort of thing. He was a hell of a good trial lawyer.

Chuck's story was elegant in its simplicity: he was home with his wife. The End. The eye-witness victim was unfortunately mistaken, he said, as was the next-door neighbor who often saw him coming home early. Yes, those were the sneakers the police officers took. Of course Janey gave them up when asked; why shouldn't she? They had nothing to hide. Chuck himself would have given them to the officers but for the fact that he was languishing in the county jail at the time. The gun was not his, he claimed, with his trademark smile and a wide-eyed innocence that Jack was sure would sink him. And the fact that the gun had a letter 'C' on the handle was another unfortunate coincidence. It might even stand for the word 'Colt,' Chuck had suggested.

R.J. kept pushing ahead, straight as Alligator Alley through the Florida Everglades, determined to get Chuck's story out to the jury. In a very short time he got to the final 'Q and A.'

"Now, Chuck, I want you to look at this jury and tell them whether you robbed anyone at that store."

"No; absatively, positutely no. I didn't rob no one. I didn't do it."

R.J. sat down next to Jack, and Assistant State Attorney Melanie Dale jumped up like a hungry lioness who had just caught the scent of fresh blood.

"Mr. Laggley, you say the gun was a coincidence, right?"

"That's right."

"And the sneaker prints on the mopped floor, those are just a coincidence, too, aren't they?"

"Like I say, a lot of people have those kinds of sneakers."

"But the fact that you have them, that's a coincidence, too, isn't it?"

"That's right."

"Aren't those a lot of coincidences in one case?"

"Like I say, I don't know." Another fake smile. "I've never been in court before."

Jack clenched his teeth. Chuck might think he was being cute, but his answers just make him look like he was being a smart-ass, Jack thought.

Melanie, for one, was unimpressed with Chuck's performance. "The fact that your neighbor saw you coming home that morning—the morning when you were supposed to be asleep—that's another coincidence, isn't it?"

"No, she's mistaken, that's all. Like I say, she's a real nice lady, but she's just mistaken about the day."

"And the nice lady who got robbed, she's mistaken too?"

"Well, you know, they kind of told her what to say," Chuck replied.

"Oh, so it's a conspiracy. The company's out to get you, right?"

"I didn't say that. I just meant the manager told her it sounded like me, and she guess—I don't know—fixated or something. And meanwhile, like I say, after they arrested me, nobody bothered to look for nobody else."

Jack stole a glance at the jurors. They were watching Chuck intensely; if he didn't know better, he might think that some of them were buying this load of crap.

Melanie went on, trying to shred Chuck's story, and he kept coming back at her, explaining, sometimes cajoling her, until her frustration began to show. Jack had to admit that Chuck was good; when he decided on a story, he stuck with it—'fixated' on it—as Chuck would have said.

Finally, cross-examination was over. Chuck nodded politely to the jurors and returned to his seat at the counsel table. The judge declared a brief recess and asked the attorneys to meet him in his chambers.

"Theah, Ah knew we'd get through this case if Ah mentioned the possibil'ty of comin' in on Sat'day," Judge Mac said with a smile as he hand-rolled a cigarette. "Naow, how much time do y'all want for closin' ahrguments?" He passed his tongue over one edge of the paper to stick it down.

"An hour, Judge," R.J. suggested.

Judge MacIntyre lit the twisted end of the cigarette; a burning ember wafted down and made another small hole in his robe. "Ah'd suggest tharty minutes," he said, either ignoring R.J. or not hearing him. "It's been a rathah shaht trahl."

"Thirty minutes is fine for the State, Your Honor," Melanie Dale replied. "I'll do twenty and ten." Because she was representing the State, she would divide her time into an 'opening' and a 'rebuttal.' The State always got the last word.

"Thirty minutes is okay with me," R.J. parroted.

"That's fahne. Mistah Meacham, you'll make the usual motions to dismiss and so foath?"

"Yes, Your Honor. The Defense moves to dismiss on the ground that . . ."

"Youah motions ahr denied; you may appeal."

R.J. looked like he had been dropped into a swimming pool filled with ice water.

"Ah don't mean to be rude," Judge MacIntyre said with a smile, "But Ah'd like to get on with things. It's almost half-phast ten; if we begin naow, y'all can do youah ahrguments and Ah'll instruct the jurah befoah lunch. They won't need much tahm to delib'rate; we'll be out early this afternoon."

R.J. walked back into the courtroom with Jack at his side. "Is he always that abrupt?" the younger man complained. "Or is it just me?"

Jack put his hand on his shoulder. "It isn't just you; I guarantee that. I also hope that Chuck brought his toothbrush."

CHAPTER 10

Six times zones to the east it was already late afternoon when a small automobile carrying four cramped passengers wheeled into the ancient seaport of Licata on the south coast of Sicily. The town was a place of stone buildings and narrow, cobblestone streets where cars vied with donkey-drawn *carozzas*, pedestrians and chickens for a share of the roadway. Occasionally one of the streets would be interrupted by a flight of three or four stone stairs; a change in grade that required vehicles to find an alternate route but offered no impediment to humans and livestock. The choice of accommodations was simple; there was only one hotel: a three-story building with a bar/dining room on the first floor and neither an elevator nor air conditioning inside. But it had running water, and, as Les joked, the guests did not have to do the 'running.' Les took the only suite: two rooms joined by a bathroom—a bathroom with a real toilet, Dennis noted. He and Antonio carried up the luggage while Vincenzo secured the car and went off on foot, up and down the narrow byways, in search of *Licatese* cousins.

"Man, this place is a palace compared ta' where we spent last night," Dennis observed as he came out of the long-awaited lavatory and joined Les in the room they would be sharing. "Got any ideas 'bout how we should start?"

"I was just thinkin' about that," Less said quietly as he stared out the window. "How da' ya' find someone ya' left forty years ago?" He shook his head slowly. "The whole idea 's crazy."

"It ain't a very big town, Les," Dennis said as he joined the older man at the window. "Somebody'll remember 'er."

"Yeah, and if somebody remembers 'er, and if we find 'er, is she goin' ta' remember me?"

"I guess we won't know that 'till we find 'er," Dennis observed.

❧ ❧ ❧

Jack and R.J. sat alone at a table in Chef's Bistro, a place where lawyers went while sweating out jury verdicts, and R.J. once again rehashed the details of the trial.

"You gave them a brilliant summation, Rob. You highlighted the omissions in the State's case. If the jury has a problem with Chuck Laggley's defense, it's only because he is so eminently unbelievable."

"I should never have mentioned that damn gun in my opening," R.J. said bitterly. "You know, Jack, I think those cops manufactured it. I should have argued that."

"Are you crazy? You would have gotten an instant mistrial, and Mac probably would have held you in contempt. Not to mention the fact that you would have destroyed your credibility with him forever. Besides, regardless of what happens in the movies and those potboiler "crime thrillers," cops don't manufacture evidence, especially not in some crappy little robbery case no one cares about." R.J. looked at him coldly, and Jack continued, "I'm sorry Rob; I know you think this is the biggest case in the annals of American jurisprudence, but it's just a crappy little garden-variety hold-up. Try to keep it in perspective."

"You really don't think they carved the 'C' in the handle themselves?" the younger lawyer asked.

"No, I don't." R.J. turned away disgustedly and Jack continued, "It would have been stupid, Rob. And if they were going to do something stupid, why not carve 'C L' and really sink your guy?"

"Well, Mac shouldn't have let the jury see it," R.J. complained.

"You're right about that, especially since the victim couldn't identify it as being the gun he held on her. I think you may have reversible error there; you might win on appeal."

"And meanwhile Chuck Laggley sits in a prison somewhere," R.J. reminded him.

"We'll cross that bridge when we come to it. The jury hasn't even gotten into serious deliberations yet. They just finished lunch a few minutes ago. Let's wait and see what the verdict is."

R.J. pushed away the plate holding the half-eaten sandwich and Jack called for the check. They were about to face the worst part of any trial: waiting for the verdict.

"My back is killing me," R.J. complained as they walked back to the courthouse.

"Tension," Jack replied. "That's where it always gets me, too."

"So what do we do now, as if I didn't know?"

"We sit around and wait while six people good and true decide your client's fate. Back in my assistant state attorney days, one of the public defenders and I would sometimes pitch pennies against the jury box, but I wouldn't suggest doing that with Mac back in his chambers. You never know when he might decide to stroll into his courtroom, and I don't think he'd see the humor in the situation."

The 'six people good and true' were already sequestered in the jury room by the time the lawyers reached the courtroom where scenes of forced busy-work floated uneasily on a mood of heightened anticipation. The court clerk sorted papers and the bailiff rocked in a chair near the jury room, his foot pushing against the witness box while he waited for the jury foreman's knock announcing they had reached a verdict. In front of the judge's bench, the court reporter, his voice in a muffled monotone, read stenographic notes of another trial into a dictation machine, while Chuck and Janey Laggley sat in a corner and held hands. The place felt like the waiting room of an old-fashioned maternity hospital, or maybe a firehouse waiting for a third alarm to sound.

"This is the toughest part," Jack said quietly to R.J., "and the longer they're out, the worse it is for your guy."

"Are you sure?"

"That's the conventional wisdom," the older lawyer confirmed. "The thinking is that jurors find it easier to jump to a conclusion of innocence than one of guilt; they take longer to convict because they want to be absolutely sure of what they're doing. Of course, in this case . . ." He did not finish his thought.

"In this case, what?" R.J. asked.

"In this case, you gave them a hell of a lot to think about. I wouldn't be surprised if a couple of people in that room came up with your screwy "manufactured evidence" idea all by themselves. It could turn into a hell of a debate."

Time crawled slowly past, its passage made more noticeable by the lack of meaningful activity to occupy it. One o'clock became two, and moved on to three; still the warning rap did not come. By three-thirty the clerk had run out of papers to sort and was quietly reading a paperback book when Judge MacIntyre abruptly walked into the courtroom and told the bailiff to send the attorneys into his chambers.

"It must have been that fifty-dollah summation of yours, young man," he said to R.J. after Melanie Dale arrived from her office down the hall. "But it appeahs they'ah hung up in theah. Now what do you-all suggest Ah do just in case they don't come out?"

"They haven't announced they're at an impasse, have they, Your Honor?" Melanie asked quickly.

"No, Ah'm just speculatin' at the present tahm. But it's been well over two houahs on a verdict that should have taken fifteen minutes."

"I take it you didn't believe our client, Judge," Jack said with a smile.

Judge MacIntyre's eyes twinkled and he turned aside momentarily to spit into the tin cup on the corner of his desk. "Let's just say Ah've seen mah shahe of people like Mistah Laggley, and when I shake hand with anybody who talks that honest, I walk away countin' mah fingahs."

"Jack laughed. "Can I write that one down, Judge? I'd like to use it in a book."

"Long's you wraht daown whah you got it," Judge Mac said with a smile of his own. Then he continued more seriously, "Ah just want you-all to know that if they'ah not out in anothah houah, Ah'm fixin' to tell them what theah options ahr foah dinnah. They'll have to stay a lot longah befoah Ah let them say they're hung."

Jack could see his plans for a quiet six-o'clock dinner at the Yacht Club fading rapidly as the lawyers reentered the courtroom. This Chuck Laggley nonsense was getting to be a certified pain-in-the-ass. Marilyn had been acting strangely the last few days, and now R.J.'s jury appeared to be deadlocked. What else could happen to top off this week?

❧ ❧ ❧

Henri Dupré had left a message for Jennifer and she had dutifully picked him up after she returned from her class at Bonita College. Now they were sitting at the oak table in the blue and gray kitchen of the Magnolia Avenue house while he made New Orleans coffee and presented his case to her.

"Janifere, you must talk to Marilyn, please. You must make her see that my intentions toward *Madame* Tousand are . . . proper, no?"

"Don't you think it would be better for you to tell her directly, Papa?"

"How can I tell her? We cannot speak three words without shouting! Janifere, you are *une soeur* . . . a sister to her. You can speak to her. Tell her; make her understand. The feelings she has for Jon, the feelings you have for R.J., Janifere, those feelings are not only for the young."

Jennifer understood. She understood a lot more than she would have understood twenty-four hours ago, she thought. People need people, and they need people who are more than just friends. The need the warmth of the touch that comes in a quiet bedroom late at night, the thrill of possessing and being possessed. Henri might be old enough to be her father, but that didn't mean he didn't have those feelings anymore. Maybe she could see it better than Marilyn could because she wasn't really his daughter. Marilyn was blinded by the same mental myopia that made it impossible for Jennifer to imagine what had gone on behind Grandma and Grandpa's closed door.

"Will you speak to her, *chérie?* Will you tell her how we feel?"

"Papa, there's something you should know . . ." she began, before she caught herself and remembered her promise to Marilyn to keep the baby a secret—for now.

"*Oui*?"

"I . . . really think it would be best if you told her these things yourself. I'm . . . I'm sure she'll see things much differently now."

"I cannot, Janifere. I barely put my head inside the door and she is ready to cut it off, no?" he said with a chopping motion of his hand.

Jennifer suddenly had an inspiration. "That's because you're not talking to her on neutral ground, Papa. R.J. and I are having dinner with Marilyn and Jack at the Yacht Club tonight. Why don't you join us? You can say anything you like; she won't be able to make a scene there."

"I cannot speak of these things to my daughter in front of Jon and R.J.," Dupré protested.

"Don't worry. I'll shoo them away to look at the boats. But something tells me you won't have to say anything. In fact, she might have something very nice to say to you," Jennifer replied enigmatically.

❧ ❧ ❧

True to his word, Judge MacIntyre sent the bailiff into the jury room at four-thirty, but instead of dinner plans, he quickly returned with the news they were nearing a verdict. Now all of the courtroom personnel were in their places, waiting for the jurors who would occupy the six vacant chairs. Judge MacIntyre leaned back in his high-backed chair with his eyes closed; the bailiff stood close to the jury room door, leaning against the witness stand and waiting for the knock that would most likely mean the end of Chuck Laggley's freedom. Janey sat in the front row of the spectator's section, twisting a handkerchief, but the defendant himself showed no emotion. R.J. impatiently drummed his fingers on the counsel table; his stomach was tied in a knot, and the pain in his back was excruciating. He glanced at Jack who was quietly doodling on a legal pad, probably making notes for his next book.

Nothing happened for what seemed a long time, then the knock came. The bailiff opened the door and half-entered the room. The people in the courtroom heard him say a few words which were answered by a muffled reply from someone inside. In a moment he stepped back. Jack stood up, and motioned for R.J. and Chuck to do the same thing as the six somber-looking people filed into their places. One of two of them looked at Chuck Laggley after they all sat down, but their faces were grim wooden masks. The defendant and his lawyers resumed their seats.

"Ladies and Gentl'men, have you reached a vahdict?" Judge MacIntyre formally intoned.

"We have, Your Honor." It was the engineer, the one who was an elder of his church. They had elected him foreman.

"Pass the vahdict to the bailiff so that Ah may examine it."

The man handed a folded paper to the bailiff who carried it over to the judge. MacIntyre opened it and read it without a flicker of emotion. R.J. could feel his heart pounding and he tried hard to control his breathing as the judge handed the paper to the court clerk and said, "The cleahk will publish the vahdict."

Every eye in the courtroom was focused on the woman who began reading carefully from the top of the page in a high, nasal voice: "In the Circuit Court of the Twenty-first Judicial Circuit of Florida, the Honorable Regis H. MacIntyre, presiding."

R.J.'s hands felt like two blocks of ice on the counsel table. He had done the best he could for Chuck and Janey. He wondered how she would take care of herself and the baby if Chuck went to prison.

"The State of Florida, plaintiff, versus Chuck Laggley, defendant. Verdict. We the jury find the defendant, Chuck Laggley, not guilty, so say we all."

Chuck might have made a sound; R.J. didn't hear him because he had suddenly exhaled and found himself breathing again. Janey began softly crying behind them.

Judge MacIntyre rapped his gavel. "Miss Dale, do you wish the jurah polled?"

"Yes, Your Honor."

The clerk read the name of each of the jurors; each one affirmed the verdict that had just been read in the courtroom and said it was the one agreed to in the jury room. That formality over, the judge discharged them with his thanks and they left silently. Finally, the judge told the defendant to rise; Chuck, R.J. and Jack stood up.

"Chuck Laggley, the jurah havin' found you not guilty, you ahr heahbah dischahged." He rapped the gavel once and quickly left the bench. Jack looked at his watch, the one Marilyn had given him on their wedding night. It was a quarter to six; they could make it to the Club after all.

❧ ❧ ❧

Les Leslie stood at the open window of his third-floor room and looked out at the rooftops of Licata. It was almost midnight; a half moon gave the sky the color of blue-black ink and softly lit the scene below. The narrow streets were dark, the people of the town safely shuttered inside their homes. Elena might be in one of those homes, or she might not, he thought. But if she was alive, she could see that moon. If only he could hang a sign on it and tell her he was here: here where they met, here where they fell in love, and here where he left her standing on a quay when his ship pulled out. He had finally come back, forty years late, and at that moment he knew he did not have the guts to look for her.

Dennis was snoring peacefully behind him. How much like Arlo, Les thought: loyal to a fault, optimistic beyond reason. Dennis didn't see any problem at all with finding a woman left behind almost half a century ago. They would mention her name to a few people, and she would fairly pop out of the woodwork. And she would fall into Les' arms, and they would be young again, young and in love and ready to take on the whole world.

That's the way it always happened in Les' dreams, where it was always easy to find her, and always good when he did. And they always picked up right where they had left off, so long ago.

But now he had to face reality. And reality was that things like that didn't happen; at least they didn't happen to the likes of Les Leslie. Reality would kill his dream, and he didn't have the courage to live without it. He had his chance once upon a time, long ago, and he lost it. Tomorrow morning, he would put on a show for Dennis; he would make a few inquiries, talk to some people, maybe see the local priest. And then he would forget this foolish idea and go back home to Calkins Harbor, where he would live on his drydocked boat—and love the Elena who still loved him and lived with him in his heart.

CHAPTER 11

Henri Dupré arrived early at the Bonita Key Yacht Club. He was sitting in a high-backed wing chair near the fireplace, a bouquet of flowers lying on the table at this side, when Jennifer walked in with Marilyn.

"Papa!" It was Marilyn's voice. She sounded excited rather than angry. He stood up quickly, bouquet in hand. "What a wonderful surprise," she continued as she hugged him joyfully. As he looked at Jennifer over his daughter's shoulder, his face was a giant question mark. Never had a spat with Marilyn ended on such a happy note.

"Janifere asked me to come . . ." he began by way of explanation.

His daughter's smile was radiant and her eyes glowed. "I'm so glad," she said, hugging him again.

"Excuse me, Miss Calkins?" Sam DePasquale, the club manager approached Jennifer. "Mr. Meacham called. He and Commodore Townsend will be a little late. He told me to have you seated and to have the server bring a bottle of Dom Perignon to the table."

"Dom Perignon?" Jennifer asked. "How did he sound?"

"Well, I guess he sounded pretty happy," Sam replied.

Jennifer smiled as the man retreated to his office. "So it looks like you aren't the only one with good news tonight, Sis," she said to Marilyn.

"You have news?" Henri Dupré asked. "What is it, *ma chouchoutte*?"

Marilyn looked at him, the radiant glow still on her face. "I'm going to have a baby, Papa; soon you'll be *un grand-père*."

Tears suddenly welled up in the man's eyes and he clasped her to him. "Oh, *ma fille*, this is news *magnifique*." He kissed on each cheek, held her back to look at her and then did it again. "Jon is *tres joyeux*, no?

Marilyn hesitated for a moment. "Actually, I haven't told him yet," she admitted quietly.

"You have not told him? But why?"

"She's afraid a baby doesn't fit into their plans," Jennifer explained.

"Does not fit their plans? Of course it does not fit their plans!" Dupré almost shouted, shocked to his French core. "A *bébé* does not make attention to plans. A *bébé* comes when it comes! Plans are for the English!"

"This baby is half English, Papa," Marilyn said quietly.

Dupré responded with a continental shrug and a little half smile. "Love, too, does not make attention to plans, *ma chouchoutte*. Love comes when it comes."

Marilyn hugged her father and kissed him tenderly on the cheek. Words were no longer necessary and she added, "*Oui, je comprends, Papa*; I understand." She understood everything now. The passionate, swirling, physical, needful love the Greeks called *eros*: that love came when it came; and it could not be denied. Because of that love, the grand march of the human race continued. In spite of all of our puny human rules and conventions, Nature prevailed; She would not be denied. Tonight, of all nights, Marilyn, the chalice of the next generation, suddenly understood those words more than she ever understood anything in her life.

"Now come, you must sit down," the grandfather-to-be insisted. To be on your feet is not good, eh?" He took her on one arm and Jennifer on the other and escorted them to the dining room, a king among ordinary mortals.

R.J. walked in with a swagger of his own when he arrived with Jack a short time later. "Not guilty!" he announced with a flourish. The champagne is on Townsend & Meacham."

"There goes the assigned counsel fee," Jack joked as he sat down next to Marilyn and gave her a loving peck. "Hi. How are you feeling?" he asked her.

"Wonderful. I'm feeling wonderful," she replied with a curious smile.

A server took the cold champagne out of its bucket and began filling their glasses. Marilyn gently stopped him when he got to hers.

"I'm sticking with soda water tonight, thank you," she said.

"Soda water? What's wrong?" Jack said with a worried frown.

"Nothing. Nothing's wrong. I've just been under the weather for a few days and I'd like to stick to soda water for a while."

"Maybe it's a little something you picked up in Paris," Jennifer suggested with a barely-suppressed giggle.

"Paris?" Jack said. "We've been back home for over a month."

Jennifer looked at him wide-eyed. "Well . . . sometimes it takes a while for little things to develop," she said before hiding her grin with a sip from her champagne glass.

"All right, that's enough time on the medical report," R.J. demanded. "Now you're all going to have to listen to how brilliant I was in the courtroom."

"Tells us all about it, R.J.; I can't wait to hear," Marilyn said, glancing at Jennifer with a look that was supposed to say 'knock off the un-subtle hints.'

"Jack is sure it was my closing argument, aren't you, partner?" R.J. began. "I don't want to brag, but . . ."

"Go ahead and brag," Jack interrupted.

"It was good; you said so yourself, Jack. What I did, Jen, was concentrate on reasonable doubt . . ."

Marilyn sipped her soda water and listened as the two men, partners now in real life as well as in law, re-live the trial. This was not the time for her announcement, not in the middle of R.J.'s moment of glory. Hers was a private thing, a thing that need to be savored and cherished. If R.J.'s news was champagne, hers was fine aged brandy, to be opened softly, warmed gently and inhaled as it was sipped. Papa was right, of course—he was always right—babies came when then came. They didn't ask for permission, and they didn't care if they fit into their parents' plans. Jack would love the baby, she knew that; she could feel it. But she would not pop the news like a champagne cork; she would wait until they were alone and the time was right. Her father sitting beside her squeezed her hand under the table. That squeeze said it all: he was there for her. He had always been there for her, even in those horrible days when she thought he wasn't. Papa was entitled to his share of happiness, too. And so what if that meant the baby had only one set of grandparents? Stranger things had happened, especially in the magical place called Calkins Harbor.

"So, Jon, this is news *merveilleuses*, but my daughter, too, has news. Is that not so, *ma petite*?"

"What? Jack asked blankly, his mind still occupied by R.J. talk of the trial.

"Oh, I got the figures all done," Marilyn replied, squeezing her father's hand in return. "And we're right on target with the restaurant."

"Jen, hearing that verdict was the most incredible experience," R.J. continued. "And I'm sure that Chuck Laggley isn't guilty, by the way. I think the robber was a completely different person, but the cops didn't bother to follow up on anything because Chuck was so convenient."

"Rob, don't start that again, please!" Jack protested. "At least admit the guy had a good lawyer and got very, very lucky."

"Lucky? Lucky my foot! The guy happened to be innocent, and, okay, he had a very, very good lawyer," R.J. protested, mimicking Jack's words.

"Let's order," Jack suggested. "I suppose you'll want me to order crow if they have it on the menu."

"If they have it, and you feel like eating it, I won't stop you," R.J. replied, and added, "It would be the honorable thing to do, Commodore."

The friendly debate continued all throughout dinner. Marilyn exchanged glances with her father and Jennifer and watched the scene quietly through a different lens. She could see the four of them someday, sharing a picnic table on one of their adjoining homes, a squad of children surrounding them while their husbands good naturedly argued the relative merits of hamburger and sausage while cooking on an outdoor grill. She stayed in her own little world, dreaming her dreams, while time melted away.

"Marilyn, are you all right?" It was Jack's voice and it startled her for a moment.

"All right? Yes, I'm fine."

"She asked you if you wanted dessert," he said, referring to the young lady who was standing beside their table. "You hardly touched your dinner."

"Oh, uh, no, thank you."

"Coffee?" the server asked.

"No, nothing, thank you."

"Are you feeling all right?" Jack asked when the girl left. "You've been so quiet."

"Maybe you have something you want to tell us," Jennifer suggested. "If we can get R.J. to stop hogging up all of the conversation."

"No, I'm just enjoying the company," Marilyn said quietly.

"And I haven't been hogging up all of the conversation," R.J. protested.

"You most certainly have," Jennifer said haughtily. "And if you and Jack are going to talk about law, you can at least talk about my case."

"What about your case?" R.J. demanded.

"We have to get started doing worthwhile things with all of that moldy old Calkins money," she reminded him. "Scholarships, a community center," she looked knowingly at Marilyn and continued, "maybe we should build a new <u>hospital</u> <u>wing</u>."

"We can't do any of those things until the estate is settled," R.J. protested.

"Well, let's get started. Marilyn and I have a lot of important things to do. Don't we, Marilyn?"

"I have something important to do right now," she replied, pushing away from the table. "Would you like to come with me, Jen?"

As they walked away together, Jennifer whispered, "When are you going to tell him?"

"Not now. Tonight, when we're alone; I'll tell him tonight."

"But I want to see his face when you tell him."

"Jennifer, this is my baby; let me do it my way. Okay?"

By the time they returned to the table, R.J. had signed the check and everyone was ready to leave.

"Papa," Jennifer said quickly, "R.J. and I can leave you at your apartment." She smiled at R.J. and added, "We can come back later for my car."

"That's a great idea," R.J. agreed. "Maybe we could even go out to a show or something."

"Or something," Jennifer added.

"Well, it's been kind of a long week for me. I just want to go home and curl up with a book," Marilyn said.

"That's fine. You do that, Marilyn," Jennifer said, giving her a hug. "We'll talk tomorrow."

The goodbyes were all said and the cars were all gotten into, and soon Marilyn and Jack were on Beach Road heading south away from the yacht club and back to their floating home at Cap'n Kelly's Marina. The Gulf of Mexico lay quietly to their left and a half-moon reflected off the still water. She could see the deserted beach through the breaks in the sea grape that grew in the dunes alongside the road. If they saw a place to park, maybe she would tell him now, looking at the moonlight over the water.

"Jennifer's right," Jack said suddenly. "We wasted too much time with that trial. I still haven't figured out what we're going to do about Howard Garner and his offer for shares. The more I think about it, the more I'm sure that Junior Calkins is behind that whole mess. And how the hell am I supposed to stop him from buying up shares? It's a free country, and he has—or will have—the cash."

"Can't we talk about something else? Marilyn asked.

"You should be concerned about this too, you know. If Junior gets his hands on the marina, he's bound to make it pretty damn tough for you and Jennifer to open that restaurant."

"We'll think of something," she sighed. So much for moonlight reflecting off the water. She would have to tell him when they got home.

In another few minutes they were going through what passed for a 'downtown' in Calkins Harbor, then out the other side of town and down the private road that led to the marina. Their headlights picked up Arlo Woodbrace who was waiting by their boat.

"Did ya' get my message," he asked as soon as Jack got out of the car.

"Yes, I did. The offer's up to two thousand dollars a share," Jack replied.

"Yeah, well, Sibby Maggio's thinkin' a' takin' it."

"Where's Sibby?"

"On his boat. I told him you'd want ta' see 'im first."

"Marilyn," Jack said, taking her by the arm, "you go on board. I'll be right back."

"But . . ."

He kissed her lightly. "I'll be right back. I promise," he repeated as he walked away with Arlo leaving her standing alone on the dark seawall next to their white trawler.

It was almost midnight when he returned. She was in bed, trying to sleep and Jack in came in quietly as if trying not to wake her. She watched him undress in the moonlit stateroom, his body now as familiar to her as her own. Now they were truly one flesh, she thought. Their child was growing inside her this very minute.

"Is everything settled with Sibby?" she whispered after he slipped into bed beside her.

"Honey, I'm sorry. I figured it would only take a couple of minutes. How was I supposed to know the guy is a total blockhead?"

"You warned me about this," she said, putting her head on his chest.

"I did?" His voice sounded funny, more resonant with her head there.

"Our first argument, remember?" she said. The diamond engagement ring and wedding band on her finger glistened in the moonlight. "You told me law wasn't such a glamorous profession."

"I remember. You wanted me to defend Dennis Woodbrace, and you got your wish."

"You were my hero," she said.

She could hear his heart beating and she wondered about the baby inside her. Did it have a heart yet? Was it beating? When would she be able to hear that; when would she feel it kick? It was time to tell him.

"Jack?"

"Hm?"

"I'm pregnant."

He sat up suddenly. "You're what?"

"I'm pregnant. That's okay, isn't it?"

"Are you sure?"

She suddenly began to cry. "Yes, yes, I'm sure. The doctor said so."

"Why are you crying?"

"You had so many plans . . ."

"The hell with the plans!" he almost shouted. "Are you all right?"

She was really crying now. "Yes, yes, I'm fine!"

"Is the baby all right?"

"Yes, the baby is fine," she said through her tears.

"So why are you crying?"

"I don't know," she said, her voice getting louder through her tears.

"Well, stop it! Stop crying!" he insisted.

"Now I can't stop crying!" she shouted.

He was suddenly sitting on her side of their bed, comforting her, stroking her hair. "Come on," he said gently, "you're probably hungry. You hardly touched your dinner tonight. Let's go into the galley and I'll make you a grilled cheese sandwich."

"Yuck, no. All that gooey cheese," she sniffled. "I couldn't handle that."

"Okay, how about tomato soup with the cheap round crackers they used to give you when you were in the convent?"

She began to smile while she sniffled. "I wasn't in the convent; I was in a school." She wiped her eyes on the bedsheet and added, "Besides, they're better than those tasteless cardboard 'water' things your mother raves about. Why do rich people love them so much, anyway?" It was their private joke; she mentioned the thin expensive crackers every time the subject of 'rich people' came up.

"You leave my mother out of this," he said. "She didn't knock you up!"

"No, but her son did," she said, sniffling and smiling now.

"That's right, and he's going to take care of you. Now what do you want? How about a hot fudge sundae? With extra strawberries?"

"Nothing. Really. I just want to go to sleep. It's the best thing for the baby."

They got back between the sheets. She nestled in beside him and closed her eyes. Nothing happened. She was suddenly wide awake. And starving. And it was all his fault for putting that stupid sundae idea in her head.

"Jack?"

"Hm?"

"A hot fudge sundae would go down awfully well right now."

"Vasilli's is open all night," he reminded her.

"Let's go."

It was a beautiful drive across the bridge. The moonlight combined with the glow of Bonita illuminated the scattered clouds in the near, sub-tropic night sky and the palm trees stood out in dark outline against the shimmering light on the water. Most of the stores on the mainland were closed, but traffic was as heavy as it always was after the snowbirds arrived.

Vasilli's Restaurant was an orange and yellow tabernacle of home-cooked fast food. The interior was decorated with artificial grape clusters and even more artificial Mediterranean statues, and it was 'home' if you were lucky enough to know your way around the late-night hangouts of Bonita. The parking lot was jammed, and the place was a flurry of activity. Marilyn wondered whether they would even be able to get a table, but the problem was solved when she saw Jennifer and R.J. sitting in a booth.

"What are you two doing here?" Marilyn laughed as she and Jack slid, uninvited, into the two open places.

Jennifer's jaw dropped. "We're just out getting a midnight snack," she said when she recovered her voice.

Bernice, Vasilli's grandmotherly, blond, gravelly-voiced waitress who knew all of the regulars by name, took a pencil out of her hair and a pad out of her apron and asked, "What'll it be, Marilyn?"

"A hot fudge sundae," Marilyn replied. "Lots of hot fudge and extra strawberries and whipped cream. And can you put a cherry on the top?"

"Sounds like somebody's pregnant," Bernice croaked. It seemed Jennifer had been spreading the word. "Just iced tea for you, right Pa? Gotta start saving up for college," she said to Jack who nodded in reply. Bernice looked at Jennifer and R.J. "Your chili dogs will be right up," she said as she turned and walked away.

Jack began to chuckle quietly. "Chili dogs," he said to R.J. "Late for court. So that's what's going on!"

Marilyn looked at her husband quizzically. He turned to her and repeated, "Midnight chili dogs? Late for work in the morning? Forgetting to wear something? Remember those times?" Her eyes lit up and she began to laugh with him. In a moment neither of them could stop and they laughed until tears came to their eyes.

"What is it? What's so funny?" Jennifer demanded.

"Chili dogs," Marilyn blurted out before she again collapsed in laughter.

Jack began to tell their little secret. "When Marilyn and I first started . . ."

". . . living on the boat," Marilyn quickly interrupted, afraid of how graphic his explanation might become.

"Well, sometimes we would get hungry after . . ." he continued.

". . . after . . . late at night . . . after watching the news and stuff," she said, again taking over the conversation.

"Right, after . . . the news and stuff. And we'd always come here for chili dogs," Jack finished the story as they held hands and laughed again.

"You'd better be careful, Jennifer, Marilyn warned, blushing. Something in those chili dogs makes women crave hot fudge sundaes."

CHAPTER 12

Early morning in Licata found Dennis Woodbrace seated at a table in the hotel's first-floor dining room with Antonio and his cousin Vincenzo. The windows on either side of the open front door framed a street scene that was just beginning to come alive with the traffic of the town. Peddlers with *carozzas*, hand-led donkeys and simple pushcarts sold everything from milk to hardware, while black-garbed women began to sweep the walkways in front of the stone buildings. An old man carried a folding chair out of a doorway across the street and set it up next to two others that were already occupied. He and his companions prepared themselves to sit in the sun and hold a discourse on the problems of the day.

"*Vogliamo trovare Elena Russo*," Dennis repeated in heavily-accented Italian. "Pretty good, huh, Antonio?"

"Goodé, *Signore*, you starté speaké *Italiano* muché goodé."

"We want to find Elena Russo: *Volemo trovare Elena Russo.* Heck, there's nothin' to this. I'll bet we find her before lunch."

"It's been longé time *Signore, e* sometimes thingsé change."

"Yeah, well, it looks like nothin's changed around here for a while," Dennis said, glancing around at the gray plaster walls and the dingy, gray-green painted woodwork while they waited for Less to join them. "I can't figure out what's holdin' up Les. You'd think he'd want ta' get things goin' right away."

Antonio shrugged his shoulders. "Sometimesé whené peoplé geté close to thingsé, they geté . . . *Come si dice?* . . . How you say it? . . . *i piedi fredi.*

"Cold feet? G'wan, if there's one thing Les ain't got it's cold feet. He's been waiting for today all his life."

Antonio shrugged again and took a sip of his Italian coffee. Dennis couldn't understand how he and Vincenzo could drink the stuff; it tasted like road tar. Of course, the 'American' coffee in front of him wasn't much better. It was just a half-cup of the same gunk with hot water added: watery road tar. A dark-haired, sloe-eyed girl brought a tray of *biscotti* to the table; at least he could dunk a few of them and maybe sweeten up the murky liquid. Italians made great cookies, but they had a lot to learn about coffee. The girl smiled at him and slowly walked away, her hips moving like a well-oiled doorknob.

"You better watché outé, *Signore*; she maké beegé eyes for you," Antonio warned.

"G'wan." Dennis turned away, suddenly aware the men were looking at him as he watched her receding form.

"Italiano women, *Signore,* they noté liké *gli Americani.* They no pické you hupé; you gotta maké the firsté move."

"Cut it out, Antonio." Dennis forgot to take his cookie out of the coffee and the soggy part fell into the cup with a plunk. "Now look what ya' made me do," he complained.

Les arrived just in the nick of time and joined his three traveling companions at the table. He was wearing a sport coat over a knit shirt, open at the collar, and he smelled of recently-applied after shave lotion.

"Woah! Looks like somebody's goin' courtin'," Dennis said, happy to have a different victim to pick on at the breakfast table.

"C'n never tell who'll ya' might run inta' right?" We might get lucky right away.

"*Per favore, volgliamo trovare Elena Russo,*" Dennis repeated. "Not bad, huh, Les?"

"Yeah, not bad," Les agreed. "But are ya' goin' ta' understand 'em when anybody says anything back to ya'?"

The sloe-eyed girl came back with a cup of ersatz American coffee for Les. Her skin was the color of mocha, and her body moved like a velvet machine under her loose, nondescript dress. This time she practically stared at Dennis before she returned to the kitchen.

"*Ma, cosa sta cercando, chista*?"

"Vincenzo's askiné me what she'sé lookiné for," Antonio translated for his cousin.

"Why don't he ask her?" Dennis complained, feeling like a target again.

"Vincenzo thinksé he knows what she'sé lookiné for. Me, I know, too. Ma it'sé noté for us. She'sé lookiné for *'nu Americano.*"

"C'mon, let's get out a' here, Les. We got a lot a' ground to cover," Dennis muttered.

Les said they should divide their forces: he would stick with Antonio, and Dennis—who had at least some knowledge of the language—would pair up with Vincenzo. They would canvas the town and meet back at the hotel for *pranzo* to compare notes. Dennis was grateful for the excuse to get away from both the ribbing and the girl, and he left quickly with Vincenzo in tow, walking down the narrow street repeating "*Volgliamo trovare Elena Russo,*" as if it was some kind of mantra. As soon as they were out the door, Les leaned back and called for a second cup of coffee.

"*Ma, Signore*, we no gonna looké for Elena?" Antonio's eyebrows arched even higher than their normal permanently-surprised level.

"Yeah, sure. In a minute, Antonio. We got all day," Les assured him.

The sloe-eyed girl brought another tray of *biscotti* and more coffee. She did not give Antonio a second glance, and Les must have been too old for her, even if he was American.

"Ma, you alla timé in so beegé 'urry," Antonio protested as Les sipped what they called coffee in this place. "*E* nowé, *quando* we 'ere, you sité down *e mangiamo biscotti*."

"What kind a' nuts are these on top a' this one? Do ya' know?" Les asked, seemingly oblivious to Antonio's protests.

Antonio turned away in disgust; now he was sure all Americans were crazy.

Les didn't care. Antonio was being paid for this trip, as was his cousin Vincenzo. Dennis' inability to communicate cut off any possibility that he might stumble onto a clue, and, besides, no Sicilian in his right mind would answer questions posed by a stranger. The four of them could hang around Licata for a day or two, and then return to Palermo and home: the trip a grand but hopeless gesture to what might have been.

Les fished some lire out of his pocket, paid the girl and walked out into the street. The sun was up and the air was slightly cool: just right for a jacket. He took a deep breath; it would be nice to spend a couple of days here. Across the street, three old men sat in front of a barber shop with the ubiquitous red and white pole that proclaimed the trade of the shopkeeper. Maybe he would get a haircut.

"*Signore,* we go now, hokay?" Antonio was at his elbow, urging him onward.

"I think I'll get a haircut first, Antonio," Les replied.

"*É cazzo!*" Antonio proclaimed in disgust. "You no wanna findé nobody. You justé gonna wasté timé!"

Les ignored the comment and went directly across the street to where the men were seated. The shop had a single barber's chair, badly in need of upholstery, with marble armrests and a well-worn shiny footrest. A marble counter along one brown wall held an assortment of bottles filled with a rainbow of liquids that gave the room its only color. Above them, a stained and dusty mirror reflected Les' image and the image of one of the old men who had vacated his outdoor seat and was walking in behind him. The man said something in Italian, directed him to the chair, and drew a worn sheet around him. In a moment the other two men entered, carrying their chairs in from the sidewalk with Antonio and the third chair close behind. Apparently, the arrival of a paying customer was no reason to interrupt the men's daily discourse.

The conversation flowed around the room while the barber flicked his scissors at Les' thick gray hair and bushy beard. The men were too polite—or maybe too Sicilian—to come right out and ask Antonio what he and Les were doing in their town, but that didn't stop Antonio from attempting to finish what they had set out to do. They had gone through a lot of trouble to get here, and even if Les did have *i piedi fredi,* Antonio had no intention of returning to Palermo empty-handed.

"*Cerchiamo Elena Russo,* We're searching for Elena Russo," he said during a break in the conversation, using the Sicilian dialect that came naturally to him. The barber and one of the other men frowned and shrugged in response, but the third man—the one who looked to be the oldest of the three—began to chuckle.

Antonio appeared startled by his reaction. "*Vosia le conosce Elena Russo*? Thou knows Elena Russo?" he asked, using the respectful form of 'you' that is required by a Sicilian custom when speaking to an older person. His eyebrows were again at the top of his forehead as he asked the question.

"*Si*, the man said, still chuckling through several missing teeth. "*Ma non si chiama Elena Russo. Ora si chiama la Contessa Falconara*. Yes. But now she is not called Elena Russo. Now she is called the Contessa Falconara."

If the Good Lord did not have the foresight to have attached Antonio's eyebrows firmly to his olive skin, they would have flown off the top of his head. "*Cosa ha detto*? What did you say?" he asked, unable to believe what the man said. There had to be some mistake.

"Elena Russo," the man repeated, chuckling and nodding, "*Ora si chiama la Contessa Falconara*."

"What in blue blazes is goin' on, Antonio?" Les asked from the barber's chair. "What's all that talk about Elena?"

"*Signore*, theresé musté be somé mistaké 'ere. Thisé man 'e say *ché* 'e know Elena Russo. Ma thisé Elena Russo she'sé *contessa*." As he spoke, Antonio's hands moved faster than those of a slick magician at a county fair.

Les suddenly leaned forward, much to the surprise of the barber who nearly took off a piece of his ear. "What in the name a' St. Elmo is he talkin' about?" Les thundered. "Elena's no *contessa*. She's just a regular kid; her father used ta' own a shoe store; he was the mayor 'r somethin', that's all."

Antonio was engaged in a rapid-fire conversation with the old man even before Les finished talking. Hands flew wildly while the old man nodded often and continued his toothless chuckle. "There'sé no mistaké, *Signore*." Antonio reported to

Les. " 'er father wasé Dominc Russo, *e* 'esé used to gotta store; *e* 'er aunt, *Adriana*, she no goté marriage, *e* she still livé 'ere. Thisé man 'e knowsé the 'ole *famiglia*."

"But Elena's no *contessa*," Les protested, pushing away the barber whose scissors continued to clip the air with a life of their own. Antonio wasn't listening; his attention was taken up by the toothless man again who continued to rattle on in Italian. Les jumped out of the barber's chair and grabbed Antonio's shoulder. "What's he sayin' now?" he demanded.

" 'e say *ché* after the War, Elena's father 'e maké 'er marriage *cu* the *Counté Falconara. Ma* 'esé muché ol, *e* 'e die. Now Elena she'sé *la* Contessa Falconara."

Les' face was as white as the sheet that still hung around his neck, and Antonio vacated his folding chair and slid it under him. "*Signore*, you feelé goodé?" he asked solicitously.

Les took up a position sitting eyeball-to-eyeball with the old man, watching every tic of his brown, leathery face. "Tell 'im ta' say it again, Antonio. Real slow so's I c'n get it." Once more Antonio said something in Italian, and the man responded, looking directly at Les and punctuating each carefully spoken word with a movement of his hand. "*Elena Russo ora é la Contessa Falconara*." The man was chuckling again as if he had revealed a private joke, but there was no deception in his eyes.

Les leaned back on the rickety chair. "Well, that's that," he muttered softly.

Antonio continued to converse with the old man, but Les was no longer listening. He stared straight ahead and his eyes glazed over.

"Signore, you gonna be hokay?" Antonio said, shaking him by the shoulder when he finished his conversation. The mané 'e say *ché il Castello Falconara* isé no too far fromé 'ere. Vincenzo 'e cané drivé us or we cané geté *una carozza*."

Les stared straight ahead, his eyes blank. "An' she lives in a castle," he muttered, nodding his head as if he were watching the final nail being driven into his own coffin.

Antonio shrugged his shoulders. "*Ma* sure, ifé she'sé *la contessa*, she musté gotta live *nel castello*."

Les looked up at Antonio for the first time. "Thank these gen'lemen for me, will ya', Antonio. I'm goin' back ta' the hotel."

"*Ma Signore*, you no finishé the 'aircutté," Antonio protested.

"I ain't gonna need no haircut," Les replied as he handed Antonio a stack of *lire*, tore off the sheet and went out the door.

"*Tutti Americani sono pazzi*. All Americans are crazy," the barber said disgustedly as Antonio paid him and ran after his employer.

At noontime, Dennis, Antonio and Vincenzo gathered around the table where they had shared *biscotti* that morning. The dark-haired girl brought out *un piatto* of pasta with thin red tomato sauce, meatballs, *braciole*, and a bottle of red wine. Les was not with them. He had gone directly to his room and remained barricaded in it for the rest of the morning. He would not open up even when Dennis returned and said that he had to use the bathroom. "Go through the other side," Les had shouted defiantly when Dennis pleaded with him through the locked door.

"Your friendé, 'esé *pazzo*, crazy," Antonio said, whirling his hand around in the air next to his head. "Firsté 'e wanna findé Elena, *e* now, whené almosté we findé 'er, 'esé locké 'imself insidé 'isé room. 'esé got *i piedi freddi* for sure." Antonio twirled a healthy portion of pasta around his fork, using a spoon as a backstop, and devoured it in a single mouthful, while Vincenzo took a swallow of wine and nodded sagely; he knew a case of *piedi freddi* when he saw one.

The girl stood off to one side and giggled while Dennis tried to twirl the spaghetti on his fork like Antonio did, but either he didn't have the knack for it or the trick didn't work for lefties like himself. He ended up cutting the strands with the side of his fork and shoveling them into his mouth. "Well, I'll tell ya' what we're gonna do," he said between mouthfuls of pasta. "We're gonna have Vincenzo drive us out there, and we're gonna find Elena ourselves, and then we're gonna tell her that Les is here.

"Your friendé, maybe he no liké *che* we puté our nose *na* hisé businessé," Antonio said taking a big gulp of the warm, red wine.

Dennis tried to do the same and he almost choked. He couldn't understand how these people could drink wine without putting ice in it. "Yeah, well, I figure we're the ones who were crammed in that car for two days an' got our kidneys busted out on them potholes, an' we're the ones who slept on chairs in that place with no toilet. I figure that kind 'a makes it our business, too."

"*Cosa ha detto*? What did he say?" Vincenzo asked, twirling his spaghetti. Dennis noticed that he didn't have any trouble with it, either. Antonio said something in Italian as Vincenzo put the wrapped pasta into his mouth and nodded. He swallowed quickly, picked up his glass and held it toward Dennis. "*Bravo. Salute!*" he said.

It was almost four o'clock before they could begin their expedition. Antonio assured him that it was unheard-of to travel during siesta time, and even if they got to the *castello*, there would be no way of getting inside until the inhabitants roused themselves. Les was still locked inside his third-floor room and only grunted when Dennis told him they were going to do some sightseeing.

Castello Falconara was a squat pile of orange/brown stone and masonry on a narrow neck of land jutting out into the blue-green water of the Mediterranean Sea. It was a hunkering mastiff of a castle, its entrance was an open maw facing the land, and its hindquarters rose behind it, teased by the ocean. Dennis could not begin to guess who built the place, but it was a real castle all right, and somewhere inside of it—if they were lucky—they would find the woman who once was Elena Russo. Vincenzo parked his machina outside the huge stone arch that faced the land and the three of them, Dennis, Antonio and Vincenzo, walked under the massive portcullis and hoped that whatever held it in place for the past centuries would continue to do so for a few more minutes.

The outer courtyard was silent and empty. Small outbuildings here and there along the yellow-brown walls stood with their doors carelessly open; the sandy dirt in front of them was undisturbed. Nothing moved in the late afternoon Sicilian sun as the men searched in vain for some sign of human habitation. Another gate and another portcullis opened to a courtyard beyond the first one, and Dennis headed for it.

"*Signore*, thisé private *properita*," Antonio reminded him.

"Yeah, but do ya' see a doorbell anywheres?" Dennis asked as he walked through the second gate into the inner courtyard.

It was an area much like the first: old, yellow-brown stone walls enclosing an area of unkempt sandy dirt. Only this time the courtyard ended at a building faced with windows and a few stone steps leading up to a massive wooden door. An automobile, it's finish covered with a fine layer of sandy dust, sat near the building; it was the first indication that someone might actually be living in the place. Dennis lifted a wrought-iron knocker and banged it a couple of times before the door squeaked open and an ancient woman appeared. Her face was a mass of wrinkles and long white hair hung past her shoulders. She held one gnarled hand on the door, blocking his entrance.

Dennis was so startled by the woman's appearance that he could not remember what he was supposed to say and only managed to stammer out, "Elena Russo?" hoping to God this was not her.

The woman spat out some Italian words at him. They were fast and bitter, and he had no idea of what they meant. Antonio quickly interceded, and in a moment Dennis was enveloped in a torrent of rapid-fire Italian. It appeared the crone would have nothing to do with whatever Antonio was saying. She shouted something and was about to slam the door when Dennis intervened with his foot.

"*Vogliamo trovare Elena Russo*," he said forcefully, suddenly remembering the phrase he practiced. The woman would not listen and she pushed against the massive door. "*Elena Russo*! "*Vogliamo trovare Elena Russo*! Ouch! She's breakin' my foot!" Dennis shouted.

Antonio and Vincenzo threw themselves against the door, and it swung open in spite of the woman. Without really intending to be, they suddenly found themselves inside a two-story marble foyer with an enormous chandelier, a white marble staircase and an old woman who was screaming Italian curses at them while Antonio tried to calm her and explain their purpose.

Before they could get things straightened out, another woman appeared, standing on the marble stairs. She appeared to be much younger than the first woman, perhaps fifty or so. She was dressed in a long, high-buttoned black dress and her gray hair was stylishly swept up at the sides. "*Maruzza*! *Basta!* Enough!" she called imperiously from the staircase. The old woman immediately stopped her tirade and looked up at her. "You must excuse my servant," the woman on the stairs said in cool, slightly-accented English, "but we were not expecting visitors today."

"*Volemo trovare . . .*" Dennis began before he realized the woman could understand English. "We're lookin' for Elena Russo. Are you . . . Do you know her?"

"Yes. I am Elena Russo," the woman replied. "Perhaps you would be so kind as to tell me why you have broken into my home."

CHAPTER 13

On a quiet Florida Saturday morning aboard the Motor Yacht *Marilyn*, Jack Townsend telephoned New York for the second time in six months with unexpected news for his mother.

"Are you sitting down?" he asked after they exchanged the usual greetings.

"What have you done now?" It was her standard question to her maverick only child.

"You're going to be a grandma," he replied.

"John, that's wonderful!" she gushed. "How is Marilyn?"

"She's fine; a little sick, but fine. I'll give her your love."

"That won't be necessary. I'll see her myself day after tomorrow."

"What?"

"I'll be seeing you day after tomorrow."

"What?" he repeated, the surprise in his voice was unmistakable—and unhidden.

"I'm coming down for an extended visit. After all, I really should get to know my new daughter-in-law. Especially now that she's expecting my grandchild."

"But . . . what about your social engagements?" he stammered. "Isn't the St. Paul's Guild dinner-dance coming up around Valentine's day?"

"Oh, John, that party is always so boring," she responded. "And the winter here never seems to end. I can't wait to get down there and soak up some of your Florida sunshine."

"How . . . how long will you be staying?"

"I don't know," she replied. "I'll just 'play it by ear.' *C'est la vie.*"

"Mother, that doesn't sound like you," he complained.

"Well it is, John. You can make a reservation for me at that same hotel as last time and have a limousine waiting at the airport. Is that better?"

"At least that sounds like you," he agreed.

"I'll ignore your last remark for the sake of family harmony," she chided him before sending love and kisses to Marilyn and hanging up the phone.

Jack was lost in thought when he put down the receiver. "What's going on?" Marilyn asked as she came out of the stateroom wearing one of his shirts and flopped down beside him on the couch. She began playing with the hair over his ear.

"Hey, be careful sitting down like that!" he protested. "You don't want to shake anything loose."

"Jack," she said patiently, "you can't shake a baby loose. Stop coddling me!"

"Well, just the same, don't be jiggling around too much. As for what's going on, my mother's coming down for an extended visit."

Marilyn got up and started for the galley before she noticed that something was very different this morning. "Hey, I'm not sick!" she declared. "In fact, I'm feeling wonderful!" she added, running her hands up through her hair. "Maybe it was that hot fudge sundae. Isn't this great?"

She plucked an apple out of the 'fridge, took a big, crunchy bite and returned to the salon where she purposely crashed down on the couch next to her husband, started playing with the hair over his ear again and added, "Let's make love."

"Marilyn! You're going to be a mother!"

"You should know," she said, chewing a mouthful of apple. "So, how long is an 'extended visit'?"

"I don't know how long an 'extended visit' is, but I hope she doesn't think she's coming down here to show you how to change diapers."

Marilyn kissed him on the cheek. "I'll bet your mother never changed a diaper," she teased. "She always had a nanny for that."

Before they could get any more amorous, Jack spotted Arlo Woodbrace and Erlene Rodgers coming down the road next to the trawler. They looked like they had something on their minds.

"What's going on, Arlo?" he asked, opening the salon door.

"Mind if we come aboard, Commodore?" Arlo replied.

Jack let out a mental sigh; it seemed Arlo and Erlene had a habit of calling early, especially on weekends. At least this time they would not be surprised by the presence of a partially-clothed Marilyn Dupré.

"'Mornin', Commodore; 'mornin' Missus," Arlo said respectfully as he and Erlene entered the salon.

"We gotta talk, Commodore," Erlene said, getting right to the point. "Howard Garner offered me an' Arl five thousand dollars apiece f'r our shares. That'd make a real nice down payment on a house."

Not only did they have a habit of calling early on weekends, it seemed Arlo and Erlene always brought bad news with them. "When did the price go up?" Jack inquired.

"Erlene went over ta' talk ta' him," Arlo protested. "I told her he was a crook."

"That's ten thousand dollars, Commodore. That might not seem like much ta' you-all, but it's a whole lot ta' us."

"I told her, 'Don't go over there, Erlene,' but she wouldn't listen. She went right over there an' went nose ta' nose with him, and he came up with extra money f'r both of us." Arlo wasn't exactly sure whether he was supposed to be angry at Erlene or proud of her, so he settled for a little of both. Jack couldn't help muttering, "Damn!" and Arlo, apparently sensing the Commodore's displeasure, quickly added, "I told ya' not ta' go over there, Erlene!"

"Well somebody had ta' do somethin'," Erlene shot back. "An' besides, I didn't sign nothin'; it was only talk." It sounded like they were about to continue an argument that had begun somewhere else; it was an eventuality to be avoided at all costs.

"All right, wait a minute, folks," Jack said, holding up a conciliatory hand while Marilyn headed for the galley to put on a pot of coffee and get out of the line of fire. "Why is this offer so important right now, Erlene?"

The Gas Girl looked perplexed for a minute. "Well, it's a whole lot a' money," she repeated.

Arlo was about to say something, but Jack cut him off. "I agree it's a lot of money, but what are you going to do with it right now?"

"Well . . ." Actually, Erlene did have a plan but she didn't want to reveal too much of it all at once. "I was kind of thinking it'd be kind a' nice ta' get us a house . . . someday."

"You're not going to be able to do that with ten thousand dollars. Houses cost a lot more than that," Jack observed.

"No, but it'd make a good down payment," she shot back, her voice firm. Erlene was ready to fight for her planned nest.

"But you couldn't afford the payments if Arlo was paying slip fees for the boat," Jack suggested.

Erlene backed off for a moment. She had an answer for that, but she didn't want to mention it right now. Jack waited. "Well, no. I guess Arl'd have ta' kind a' give up the boat," she admitted quietly.

Arlo Woodbrace looked like someone had knifed him in the gut. "Give up the boat? Now wait a minute, Erlene. Ya' never said nothin' about givin' up the boat! If I'd a' knowed that . . ."

Jack calmed Arlo down with a pat on his shoulder. "All right, listen, Erlene," he said quietly, I think those shares are worth a lot more money than Howard Garner is offering right now. And I think if you hold out he'll go quite a bit higher. Now, I have clients who will pay you a thousand dollars more than Howard's best offer, whatever it is, but I want to get the best deal for you that I can, understand?"

Erlene nodded her head. This was starting to sound like the kind of stuff that made her feel worse than seasick, but she trusted the Commodore.

"All I'm asking is that you keep our conversation quiet, and tell me what Howard is offering. When we think he's as high as he'll go, my clients will step in and give each of you a thousand dollars more than he's offering for your shares. Is that a deal?"

Erlene nodded again. "Yeah, sure," she agreed.

"That's a great deal; we can't lose," Arlo agreed. If the Commodore could pull off something like that, maybe he could figure out how Arlo and Erlene could get a house <u>and</u> keep the boat.

Marilyn reappeared with a tray holding four cups and a pot of coffee. "Would you care to join us?" she asked.

"Oh, no, thanks," Erlene replied. "An' you shouldn't be doin' all that in your condition an' all." It sounded like

Jennifer had been working overtime spreading the word. "We'll just go on an' leave you-all to y'rselves." She and Arlo headed for the door and let themselves out quickly.

"Those people really know how to mess up a weekend morning," Marilyn said, putting the tray down on the salon table. "So are you going to tell me the name of your top secret clients?"

"You already know them," he said. "They're us."

At the Magnolia Avenue house, Jennifer Calkins awoke with the delicious sensation of R.J.'s warm body next to hers. So what if they had started this part of their lives a few months early? She could never get enough of this. And it wasn't just the physical lovemaking; it was everything: the way he breathed softly in the night, the way he moved next to her, and sometimes the way he grew, innocently, while he slept, without willing it or even knowing it was happening. She drew herself up onto her elbow and looked at him closely: the strong, masculine nose and the beckoning cleft in his chin. His dark hair framed a face an artist might have painted, she thought, and the soft hair on his chest barely covered the muscles that almost rippled even has he slept. She ran her hand over his chest, and he opened his eyes and smiled.

"Lady, if you're not buying, don't touch the merchandise," he teased.

She grabbed the hair and tugged gently. "I'm buying," she said. "But if you don't keep going to the gym every day, you won't have anything to sell."

"You haven't been giving me much time off," he said as he kissed her good morning.

She kissed him back. "Okay, we're both going there today for an hour," she said as she climbed on top of him. "We're going to have a real workout.

He moved his hands around her back. "Here or at the gym?" he asked.

"Both," she answered as she kissed him again.

❧ ❧ ❧

A day later, Henri Dupré switched on the television set that had been his only companion in recent weeks, and he re-cleaned his already spotless one-room apartment. Victoria Townsend would be arriving soon. It was a pity that she had to see him living in such a small place, but a man did what he had to do.

He had always lived life one step ahead of the bill collectors. Success was always on the horizon, always just a little beyond his grasp. Even now, he assured himself, his accommodations were only temporary; once the restaurant was opened, he would find something more suitable and be able to entertain Victoria properly.

And yet, although he never thought about it, and might not have appreciated the idea if he had, strained circumstances had taught Henri Dupré a valuable lesson: that all one really needed to live well in this life was an appreciation of life itself. No matter how much money a man had, it could not buy a moonlight walk on the beach with a special lady, or the satisfaction that came from preparing an intimate dinner for a loved one. Such things, which were without price, had been the only pleasures that Henri could ever afford.

"You just go ahead and put your cheese in now, and turn on the food processor," the woman said from the small television set.

"*Certainement*, if you wish to glue up wallpaper," Heni added, without looking at the screen.

"And then pour it out into a pan . . ."

"And you will destroy a perfectly good pan," Henri retorted.

"And bake for about thirty to forty minutes . . ."

"Until it is so hard, not even the rats will eat it, eh?" Henri shouted at the screen. The woman had gotten his attention, and he watched in disbelief as she popped her concoction into one half of a double-oven and immediately removed the finished product from the other side.

"And *Voila!* It's done," she said, smiling at the camera.

"*Voila? Voila*? You have the audacity to speak French?" Henri shouted at the screen. "You call yourself a cook? You are not a cook, you are an *imbécile*!"

"Tune in next week . . ."

"Next week?" Henri shouted at the screen. "Anyone who eats such *merde* will be dead next week!"

A knock at the door interrupted his tirade, and he jerked it open in a fury, startling poor Jennifer out of her wits.

"Papa! Is everything all right?"

"All right?" he shouted. "No, it is not all right. That stupid woman will poison the whole town if she is not stopped!"

"What woman? Where?" Jennifer said, picking up the phone to call the sheriff's office.

"That . . . *imbécile* on the *télévision.* She calls herself a cook. She is an assassin."

Jennifer heaved a sigh of relief, put down the receiver and turned toward the set just in time to see the logo of Miami Public Television appear on the screen. "Oh, that's just one of those cooking shows, Papa," she assured Henri. They're becoming all the rage now."

"That is not cooking, Janifere. What that woman was doing was not making food; it was a crime. Something must be done to stop her," he protested.

And something must be done to get you out of this cramped apartment before you go stir crazy, she thought. Papa needed something to do, and Dupré's restaurant needed some pre-opening exposure. An idea flashed thorough her mind, and even as she thought it, she congratulated herself on a brilliant plan.

"You're right, Papa. And the real crime is we're getting programs like this all the way from Miami. Something has to be done right here. Let's take a ride over to the Bonita television station. I have a wonderful idea.

❦ ❦ ❦

On the other side of the Atlantic, Les Leslie was in this room on the third floor of the hotel, disgustedly throwing clothes into a suitcase.

"But we ain't found Elena yet, Les," Dennis Woodbrace protested.

"That's right, and we ain't gonna find 'er neither," Les replied as he rolled up a shirt and slammed it into the open overnight bag. "Are them two guys finished packin' yet?"

"I guess they went out," Dennis replied.

"Went out! What in the name a' Hades d' ya' mean, they went out?"

"Went out; you know, like they left the buildin'."

"Left the buildin'!" Les shouted. "What d' ya' mean they left the buildin'?"

"Geez, I don't know" Dennis whined defensively. "Antonio said they had ta' go out an' say goodbye ta' their cousin 'r somethin'."

"Well, pack y'r stuff; I want ta' get out a' here 's soon 's they get back."

"But I thought you had a lead on 'er," Dennis protested.

"What d' you know about that?" Les shot back angrily.

"Nothin'. I don't know nothin'. It's just that I thought you said you got a lead, 'r maybe Antonio said it."

"We don't have no lead. Period. We looked f'r her, an' she's gone, an' that's that."

"Les . . ."

"Look, Dennis, I told ya' before, this here's my business, an' I don't want people knowin' my business. So if it's all the same to you, just Butt Out!"

"Les, I know ya' think it's y'r business . . ."

"Well it is my business!" Les shouted.

"No, it ain't!" Dennis was surprised to find that he was shouting, too.

"It damn well is!" Les' face was beet red, and Dennis had never heard him use a real cuss word like 'damn', even when they had to sleep on chairs in that little town with no toilet.

"All right, ya' might as well know the truth," Dennis shouted back, expecting the older man to punch him any minute. "The truth is, while you were holed up here, Antonio and Vincenzo and me went out and found 'er. We went over to that castle, Les, an' she's livin' there, just like that old guy told you she was."

Les grabbed him by the shirt and slammed him up against the wall. "How'd you know about that?" he demanded through clenched teeth with his face inches away from Dennis.

"Antonio told me," Dennis said, getting ready to be hit. "An' I'll tell ya' somethin' else. I talked to 'er. An' she does remember ya, Les. An' she wants to see ya'. She's waitin' there for ya' right now."

Les' shoulders sagged. He released the younger man and turned away. "Well, she's gonna be disappointed," he said quietly.

"Why? Why can't ya' just go there an' talk to 'er?" Dennis demanded.

Les faced him again; this time his eyes were moist. "Look at me, Dennis," he said softly, all the fight gone out of him. "Take a good look. What d' ya' see?"

"I see Les Leslie," Dennis answered, befuddled.

"Ya' see a fifty-nine-year-old swabbo. Ya' see a guy who's never really finished a job in his whole life. You're lookin' at a guy who lives in a drydocked boat, Dennis; a guy who took one wrong turn somewhere an' wasted forty years a' his life an' accomplished nothin'. An' ya' expect that guy ta' go up ta' some castle an' talk ta' a contessa, 'cause they said some things ta' each other when they was kids? This ain't the movies, Dennis; things like that don't happen."

"Y'r wrong, Les. I know what y'r sayin' an' y'r wrong. 'cause what I'm lookin' at is a guy who's been a good friend ta' a whole lot a' people; a guy who's always treated people fair an' square. I'm lookin' at a guy who always put everybody else's jobs ahead a' his own," Dennis continued, trying to talk over the lump that was forming in his throat. "An' I figure it's time f'r a guy like that ta' catch a break."

They were interrupted by a knock at the door. "Get it, will ya'?" Les said as he turned to continue packing.

"It can't. I gotta go to the bathroom," Dennis replied, heading for the other door.

"I paid f'r his trip an' he can't even open th' door," the older man muttered as he crossed the room himself. That was another knock; whoever it was must be in a hurry.

Les pulled the door open and saw a woman with upswept gray hair. She was dressed in a high-collar black dress accented by a black pearl necklace, and she looked at him with the same hazel eyes he had not seen in forty years.

"So, *Cecile*," she asked in a soft, regal voice, "once again you were going to leave me without saying 'goodbye'?"

Les Leslie's voice caught in his throat. He couldn't breathe for a minute. And when he did, he managed to gasp out only a single word, "Elena."

CHAPTER 14

Janey Laggley was waiting in the hall when Jack opened the office Monday morning. The office lights were still off; although Sharon Crowley was an excellent legal secretary, she didn't do Monday mornings very well, and R.J. had been coming in late, no doubt worn out from too many late-night chili dogs.

"What can I do for you, Janey?" Jack asked as he went around turning on the switches for the lights and the copier and the word processors and all of the other gadgets that had become the life-blood of a modern 1986 law office.

"Nothing . . . well, I'd like to see Mr. Meacham for a minute, if that's all right."

"Rob has been getting in a little late the past few days," Jack warned. "Can I get you a cup of coffee or something?"

"No, thank you. I'll just sit here and read a magazine if that's all right," the woman said quietly, as if she was afraid that Jack might throw her out.

"Suit yourself, he replied before being distracted by the telephone. He picked it up at Sharon Crowley's desk; it was an appraiser, and he wanted to speak with R.J. Another day had begun in the law office of Townsend & Meacham.

Ms. Crowley came in a few minutes later, full of apologies, as Jack finished writing out a message slip and ceremoniously slipping it into R.J.'s box while he looked at her.

"I'm going to have a cup of coffee," he announced. "Janey, are you sure you won't join me?" he asked through the window that separated the secretary's area from the waiting room.

"Well, all right, if you don't mind," the shy young woman replied.

"Ms. Crowley will bring it out to you," he said, smiling at his secretary. Sharon didn't mind doing the coffee routine for her bosses, but she hated doing it for clients. She said it made her feel like a waitress. It was her penalty for coming in late this morning.

He was in his office contemplating the mail over coffee when Jennifer bounced in, looking as bright and sparkling as freshly-poured soda water with Key Lime. "What brings you here?' he asked, while she hugged him and kissed his cheek.

"R.J. and I are going to pick out our invitations. Isn't that exciting?"

"So where is he?"

"There was some girl waiting to see him. She's in his office with the door closed." Jennifer's innocent young face was an open book, and her expression read that she did not like that situation.

"Don't worry, Jenny. She's a client, and lawyers are impervious to that kind of temptation, especially in the first year of marriage."

"Oh, I'm not worried," she said, still frowning. "Besides, I wanted to talk to you alone, anyway." She sat on the corner of his desk, a place where Marilyn usually perched, and Jack wondered if she had gotten a few tips from her 'sister.'

"You know, Jack, I'm really happy I have you for a brother-in-law, she said seriously.

"Well, I'm happy I have you for a sister-in-law," he replied, not bothering to point out that she and Marilyn were not really related.

She got up and waltzed around the office, checking out his diplomas. "I mean, you just <u>know</u> so much and everything."

"Rob has the same kind of diplomas," Jack reminded her.

"Oh, I'm not taking anything away from R.J.; he's great. But you have so much experience, and you've done so many things: I mean, Commodore of the Yacht Club and everything."

"Rob will get his turn," Jack assured her. This was getting uncomfortable. Jennifer's coquettishness was a little too transparent. She wanted something.

"And look at this," she gushed, fingering one of the framed documents on his office wall, "you even have a Coast Guard license. That means you can run a commercial boat, right?"

"Carry passengers for hire; but only six of them," he corrected her. "And I only took the exam for fun because a friend of mine needed an extra student to fill out a class he was teaching."

"I'll bet you even got a hundred on the exam," she said, returning to her perch on the corner of his desk.

"Just on two of the five parts. Jennifer, what is this all about?

"About? What makes you think it's about anything? Can't I just visit?"

"Jen, obviously you are here for a purpose. What is it?"

"You know the restaurant is almost finished. They just have to throw a few shingles on that special roof."

"It's going to take a lot more shingles than a few," he observed drily.

"And I was thinking . . ." Here it comes, he thought. When Jennifer thinks about something, it means a big project is in the works. "I was thinking," she continued, "wouldn't it be something if we could start up the old *Margaret* and take her out for a private party before the opening?"

"Jennifer, that boat hasn't moved in over twenty years."

"Maybe we could have the boats from the Yacht Club join us in a parade around the entire island. We could have the *Margaret* represent us. Think of the publicity!"

"Think of the publicity if the boat sinks," he warned.

"Grandma would be so proud, wouldn't she? You know the boat was named after her. You'd be at the helm in your commodore's uniform, and Marilyn and I could dress up in costumes from the Twenties. We'll get a uniform for R.J., and I'll bet even Arlo and Erlene would come. Wouldn't it be fun?"

"It would be an enormous amount of work, Jen."

"It wouldn't be work for you, Jack," she said, melting him with her liquid blue eyes. "You love boats. Think of the challenge! If anybody can do it, you can!"

R.J. saved him from a commitment by bursting into the room looking a little pale. "Jack, something's come up. Can I talk to you?" He glanced at Jennifer and added, "In private?"

"What's the problem?" the senior partner asked.

"It's a major problem about a client."

"I guess that means I'm supposed to leave," Jennifer frowned.

"Jen, I'm sorry," R.J. responded, taking her arm and leading her to the door. "I need to talk to Jack. Alone. You go on without me. I'm sure that whatever you pick out will be perfect. I'll catch up with you later, okay?"

She gave him a little peck on the lips. Okay, but that doesn't mean I like it."

Jennifer left and R.J. quickly closed the office door. "She lied, Jack. She committed perjury."

"Who lied?"

"Janey. Janey Laggley. She lied on the witness stand. She committed perjury. And I allowed it to happen."

"Wait a minute; sit down, Rob."

"Don't you understand? She committed a very serious crime and I let it happen. And now I know about it. What am I supposed to do now?" he asked as he paced back and forth in front of Jack's desk.

"Goddammit, will you sit down for a minute?" Jack shouted.

R.J. suddenly looked at him, shocked by the tone of his voice as much as by his language. He sat down dejectedly.

"All right, let's take it from the top," Jack said in a much calmer voice. "First of all, you didn't allow anything to happen. We went over this in detail before the trial. I told you I wasn't sure I believed her, but without any evidence that she was lying, there was no way you could prevent her from taking the stand on behalf of her husband."

"Yes, but now . . ."

Jack held up his hand and continued. "Secondly, at no time did you or anyone in this office tell her what to say. In fact, we both specifically warned them to tell the truth, period. Whatever she did, she did it on her own."

"Well, she committed perjury," R.J. replied, his voice trembling with rage. "That moron bastard husband of hers convinced her that it was her fault he got arrested; because she gave the police his sneakers. He kept pounding that into her head, telling her that she was sending him to prison."

"And?"

"And I guess she just cracked. That story she told in the courtroom was a total lie. She did hear him get up that morning. He got up early and went out, and then he came back around six-thirty. She was awake the whole time."

"Okay, so what are you going to do about it?"

"I'm going to call the State Attorney's Office, of course. I'm ethically bound."

"You're ethically bound to reveal the confidences of a client? That's a switch."

"She's not our client, Jack. You know that."

"She's our client's wife, and you received this information in the course of that relationship. And if you could call the State Attorney's Office, what do think they would do?"

R.J. didn't answer.

"I'll tell you what they would do: nothing. They can't try Chuck Laggley again; that would be double jeopardy," Jack continued. "Do you think they're going to want to prosecute a young woman with a baby; send her to prison for trying to help her husband? Wait 'till they hear you're coming over with that story; people will be hiding under desks and jumping into broom closets to avoid you."

Jack stopped for a moment while R.J. contemplated that picture. He switched to a 'law professor' mode and continued. "And then there's the little *corpus delicti* problem. Janey can't be convicted based only on her own statement; there has to be some independent evidence that a crime occurred. Do you really think Chuck Laggley is going to come in and testify that he knew Janey was awake the whole time?

"So what am I supposed to do about it?" R.J. asked bitterly.

"You're supposed to forget it," Jack answered quietly. "You learn a lesson from it and you move on. And you never, ever talk about it to anyone but me."

"And this great system of justice we've taken an oath to serve gets screwed, right?"

"No, I didn't say that. It is a great system, Rob, but it's not a perfect system. If you're going to work in it you have to accept that. We do the best we can. We do as much as we can do. And we have to believe there's a Somebody with a capital 'S' who takes over when we finish. Nobody gets away with anything. Believe me, everything gets sorted out in the end."

"So I just do nothing."

"You press on, Rob. You do the best you can and you press on."

"I'm beginning to hate this profession," R.J. said as he got up and went to the door."

"Stick around," Jack said as he opened it. "You ain't seen nothin' yet!"

❧ ❧ ❧

Across the ocean, Les Leslie and Elena talked far into that first night. He called for her the next morning as he promised he would, and he escorted her to church even though *Maruzza* protested vehemently and bit her fingers when they were leaving the *castello.*

The church was dedicated to Saint Anthony, Elena told him, the patron saint of the town. Les didn't care much about things like patron saints, but he would have gone anywhere with her, and he dutifully took his place by her side and did his best to stand up and sit down and kneel when everybody else did. And after Mass was over, she took him to a side room filled with many candles and statues. The walls and ceiling were black with soot in there, and all he could figure was she was making it worse by lighting another candle, but he reached into his pocket and pulled out some money and put it into a slot in the wall while she knelt and prayed some more. He stood there and watched her, kneeling in her black dress, her gray hair demurely covered by a black shawl and her face lit by candlelight. She looked perfect, like one of the statues, and he wondered what she was praying for.

They spent much of that day together, walking around the town and talking. People would sort of bow a little when they recognized her, and when they had *pranzo* at the hotel the owner served them himself and wouldn't let the regular girl near them. Vincenzo drove them back to the *castello* after that, but Elena would not permit Les to leave until he promised—solemnly promised on her prayerbook—that he would come back the next day. And she made him promise something else. He would gladly have cut off his right arm for her, but she didn't ask for that much. It was only some hair that need to be sacrificed for her. And so, on Monday morning when Les Leslie walked out of the same barbershop where he had first learned about her, he was beardless for the first time in many years. He ran his hand over the bare skin of his face and tried to get used to a whole lot of new sensations. And he tried to make sense of what was happening to him.

It was early afternoon before Les led Dennis on a tour around the walls of *Castello Falconara*. "Anybody who'd try to put this place back together'd have his gunnels under water in no time flat," he complained as his eyes scoured the broken stones on the battlements. "Look up there," he said, grabbing Dennis' arm and pointing at a parapet. "There's stones up there that 'r hangin' by hairs from that barbershop."

"Man, do ya' know what she could do with this place?" Dennis replied. "This could be the greatest tourist attraction since Disney World. It's a real castle, Les, with a beach around three sides. Do you know how much people 'd pay to stay here?"

"What in blazes are ya' talkin' about? The lady's a countess; she don't need ta' make 'er house inta' a hotel."

"How da' you know? An' it don't have ta' be a hotel. Just clean it up and give tours of the place!"

"She don't need the money, Dennis."

"Who's talkin' about her? Do you know what a place like this could do f'r the whole town? There'd be tourists . . . you couldn't keep 'em away, Les. An' those people got ta' eat someplace, an' they got ta' sleep, an' . . ."

"An' they got ta' use toilets, right?" Les chuckled.

"Yeah, what's wrong with that? What's wrong with givin' this whole town a shot in the arm? So what if she don't need the money? There's a whole lot a' people here who do."

Les' eyes twinkle. "Like that gal at the hotel?"

"Yeah, like Maria."

"Oh, so now she's got a name, does she?" Les chuckled, his newly-discovered face breaking into a dimpled smile.

"Yeah, well, I've been talkin' to 'er," Dennis muttered defensively. "She's been helping me with my Italian."

Les put a hand on the younger man's shoulder. "Dennis, my boy," he said, "seems ta' me the first thing we better do is get Elena's car runnin'. I doubt if the cousins c'n stay around here much longer. An' then I guess we better make a list a' things around here that need fixin'; after that we'll get down ta' fixin' 'em. I never planned on bein' a handyman f'r a castle, but if that's what the lady needs, then I guess that's what I'm goin' ta' be."

A white limousine containing Marilyn Dupré Townsend and her father stopped at Jack's office to pick him up on the way to the airport. Mrs. Victoria Townsend was arriving for a stay of unknown duration, and she would, of course, be greeted in the way to which she was so well accustomed. The plane was scheduled to arrive at five o'clock, and Marilyn, bless her, had already made dinner reservations for four at the Yacht Club. Jack did not believe for a moment that his mother's visit had anything to do with Marilyn's pregnancy. Victoria could only be coming to town because of Henri Dupré. Jack hadn't objected when his mother took off for New Orleans with Marilyn's father after the wedding. A little casual fling, a shipboard romance, never hurt anyone. It was good for the circulation. But this visit, this was something else. His mother was not supposed to behave like this. She was fun-loving, yes, but in a proper New York kind of way. She never ignored social responsibilities like the St. Paul's Guild, and she never responded with a devil-may-care '*C'est la vie*' when asked about her plans.

Henri Dupré, the apparent cause of all this trouble, sat across from Jack in the limo, a bouquet of flowers on the seat beside him. He was unusually silent as the car drove through the City of Bonita and turned onto the airport road.

"You're awfully quiet, Papa." Marilyn's voice intruded on Jack's thoughts as well as those of his father.

"I am thinking of many things, *ma chouchoutte*."

"Such as?"

What he was thinking he could not say, because Jennifer had sworn him to secrecy. Even if she had not done so, what could he tell his daughter? That his visit to a television station had made him feel like a small child? That he, a man who had weathered more than sixty years of the storms of life, had been overwhelmed by the lights and cables and the young men who moved among them with such confidence? And, worst of all, that Jennifer—who looked upon him as a father—was counting on him to do something he feared was beyond his ability. Henri Dupré could say none of those things.

"I am thinking of *les artisans*, and when they will complete this roof affair so we can open *le restaurant*, no?" He lied not very convincingly, Jack thought.

"Maybe it's best that we all have some time off," Marilyn suggested. "It will give me a chance to rest a little, and you will have time to show Victoria around the area. There are a lot of interesting places just up the coast from here.

The driver left them at the door and pulled into the designated limo area to await the arrival of their guest. Inside the terminal, they faced the typical airport madhouse scene that was so common in Florida during the late winter months: pale people dressed in heavy coats, smiling and kissing 'hello' here, while bronze people in pastel colors and carrying similar heavy coats kissed 'goodbye' there. Wheelchairs were everywhere, their withered occupants determined to have a few more weeks in the Florida sun, and bored limousine drivers held up placards with the names of people they had never met as they waited to introduce their charges to paradise.

Victoria Townsend was one of the first people off the plane—it was one of the many advantages of flying first class—and, as was her custom, she carried nothing but a small purse and a mink coat over her arm. Before Jack offered to take it from her, Henri Dupré elbowed him out of the way and stepped forward, flowers in hand. "*Madame* Tousand," he said gallantly, "these flowers tremble when they look upon you. If they were a thousand times lovelier they could not compare with your beauty."

Dupré bowed and kissed her hand, as years melted off Victoria's face. "*Enchanté, Madame*," he said passionately.

Jack said nothing. He didn't at all like the direction things were taking.

CHAPTER 15

Jack Townsend was angry. It was another Monday morning at the Law Offices of Townsend & Meacham, and Sharon Crowley was late again. R.J. was probably still in Jennifer's bedroom, doing whatever it was they had been doing lately, and the telephone was going crazy. His mother had been in town for three weeks, and she showed no sign of leaving. He had a good mind to put all four lines on hold, walk out the door and spend the rest of his life cruising the Caribbean with his wife—who, by the way—was busy planning the imminent grand opening of Dupré's, the money-sucking restaurant project that had so far catered one—count it one—party: their own.

"I'm really sorry, Mr. Townsend," Sharon gasped as she came through the door. "I couldn't get my car started."

Hers had to be the most unique automobile on planet Earth; it failed to start only on Monday mornings. "Sharon, we're going to have to do something . . ."

"Excuse me. Townsend and Meacham," she said into a telephone whose annoying beep couldn't have been better timed.

". . . that car." He finished the sentence while turning around and talking to the air as he walked into his office.

"Mr. Townsend, would you like a cup of coffee? And Mr. Woodbrace is here to see you." It was Sharon's voice on the intercom a few minutes later. The coffee was a nice touch; her way of saying she was sorry for another late morning. Now what the hell did Arlo want on this already miserable Monday morning?

"Yes, thank you. And send him in."

"He did it again, Commodore. Now he's offerin' everybody ten thousand dollars a share." The words started even before Arlo sat down. "An' I'm sure Sibby Maggio's goin' ta' take it; he tol' me so himself."

This would be a very good time to tell everybody to drop dead, Jack thought. Forget about the investment in Dupré's; they could get aboard the boat and cruise away from the whole damn thing. If Marilyn and Jennifer wanted a restaurant so badly they could jolly well buy one somewhere and give it to Henri, and his mother could be the waitress. Let Howard Garner win, the bastard. Let him buy the whole damn marina and turn it over to Junior Calkins and bulldoze the whole damn place into the water.

"Commodore? Howard Garner's offerin' ten thousand dollars a share an' Sibby Maggio's gonna sell out."

"I heard you, Arlo. I was just thinking . . ." Except that would mean Junior had won. What would Casey have to say about that? And Margaret? Here he was, preaching to Rob about truth and justice, about everything being sorted out in the end. Was he seriously considering running from a fight with Junior?

"What . . . what were you thikin'?"

"It's time to pay Mr. Garner a little visit, Arlo."

"All right! Now we're goin' ta' put the squeeze on 'im, right?" Arlo replied as he pounded his fist on Jack's desk.

Sharon Crowley knocked and came in with two steaming mugs of coffee. "I wasn't sure how Mr. Woodbrace wanted his," she said, as she placed them on coasters on Jack's desk, "but I can go back for cream and sugar."

"Thank you, Sharon," Jack said, patting her hand, "I really appreciate your thoughtfulness. But at the moment we have to go over to Calkins Harbor and take care of a problem. When Mr. Meacham comes in, tell him I'll be back shortly."

Arlo had his own car, so Jack drove back across the bridge alone. That was good; he needed time to cool down and think out his strategy for approaching Howard Garner. This was definitely the worst way: going to the other guy's turf. But he could hardly expect Garner to accept an invitation to come to the office. So all right, if the fight was to be on the other guy's field, Jack would have to use overwhelming force. Knock him on his ass and get out quick. The longer the conversation lasted, the more psychological edge Jack would lose.

The two cars pulled up alongside Garner's Chris-Craft. Howard was outside talking to Sibby Maggio. That was good. It looked like Sibby's deal wasn't final yet, and it also meant Jack wouldn't have to ask Garner for 'permission to come aboard'—something that would be a definite psychological disadvantage.

"Good morning, Howard," Jack said as he got out of his car. "Do you have a minute?"

"Sibby and I were just going aboard to conclude a little business deal," Garner replied. "You'll have to get in line."

"I wouldn't do it if I were you, Sibby," Jack said, speaking directly to Maggio. "At least not until you hear what I have to say."

"If you have anything to say, say it, 'Commodore'." Garner spoke the word with just enough of a sneer in his voice to make Jack want to put both hands around his throat and choke the life out of him.

"All right," Jack said, turning to Howard Garner. "Let's get it out in the open. I know what you're doing, Howard; and I know Junior Calkins is behind it." Truthfully, it was another example of a 'fact not in evidence,' but Garner didn't protest, which meant Jack was right. "I don't know yet if you're his partner or his shill," Jack continued. Garner's eyes shifted for a second. It was a sign of weakness and Jack took another stab. "But knowing Junior, I'd say he's just using you. You're not valuable enough to be his partner." Again, Garner did not respond and Jack guessed he had scored two direct hits.

"I know Junior has five hundred thousand dollars coming from Margaret's estate," Jack went on, "and he knows I have the same. What I don't know is how much he managed to embezzle out of the marina over the years, and if he saved any of it. We've all heard rumors about his gambling." Actually, he hadn't heard any such rumor, and it was likely Garner hadn't heard it either, but it suddenly gave him something to think about. It might be his position wasn't as strong as Junior led him to believe, and his eyes shifted again.

"I'm getting tired of all this nonsense, Howard," Jack continued. "It's time we get to the bottom line. Besides Marilyn and me, there are ten residents of this marina. Go back and tell your boss that as of right now Jack Townsend is offering one hundred thousand dollars a share to anybody who wants to sell out—including you, Howard."

Arlo made a noise that sounded like somebody punched him in the stomach, and Sibby Maggio muttered, "Holy Christ!"

"You're not serious," Howard Garner sneered. His pupils were really moving now, dancing back and forth between Jack, Arlo and Sibby.

"Would you like a certified check, or would you prefer cash? Jack's expression was very serious and his voice was dead calm. "Go back and tell Junior. If he wants to up my ante, that's fine. My wife and I are expecting our first child; we'll be happy to sell our shares to him if he makes an offer of, shall we say, two hundred fifty thousand? That's for both of us, of course."

Jack turned and got into his car before Garner could say another word. He made a three-point turn on the narrow roadway and peeled his tires on the dirt as he drove the short distance to the marina office. Now he was really angry, more at himself than anyone else. Blasting Howard Garner like that was a stupid thing to do. He had no real evidence that Junior Calkins was actually behind the takeover plot; Garner might be operating on his own. If he was, Jack had just committed a whole lot more money than was necessary to accomplish his purpose.

Marilyn was in her office standing next to the bookcase; she looked surprised when he walked in. "Is anything wrong?" she asked with that special look that comes to mothers when danger threatens.

"I just offered a million dollars of our money to buy the outstanding shares of this place."

Her mouth opened but she didn't say anything for a second. "Oh, Jack, not now," she said when she recovered enough to find her voice. "Not with the baby coming and the restaurant . . ."

"Okay, I'm sorry," he almost shouted, angry for allowing his gonads rather than his head do the talking for him. "I was just so damn sick of hearing about those damn offers!"

"What if Junior doesn't top your offer?" she asked quietly.

"What if Junior isn't even behind it?" he replied.

"You mean you don't know?" she suddenly looked pale.

"Not for sure, I don't."

"Oh, Jack!" She turned away from him and asked, "How many people know about this?"

"Arlo Woodbrace and Sibby Maggio were standing right there; that means everybody knows about it by now. And before you ask the next question, I'm sure it would be considered a legally binding offer, valid until I withdraw it."

She turned quickly and looked at him. "Withdraw it. Right now, before anyone accepts," she pleaded.

"No."

"For me. Please!"

"I'm not going to let that bastard screw up Margaret's wishes. He's not going to get this place, Marilyn."

"But you don't even know if Junior's behind it!" she shouted.

"No, but we'll find out real soon," he replied curtly.

"Jack, please!"

"I'm going to the office. I need to call our broker and make some unusual arrangements at the bank." He went to her and caressed her face. "Don't worry, I can handle this."

Across the Bonita bridge, Henri Dupré was not faring any better as he sweated under the television studio lights and tried once more to speak the lines other people had written for him.

"'allo, my friends, I am . . . my name is Henri Dupré. And today I will teach you to make something . . . something . . . *speciale*. It is *un* . . ."

The young director in the control booth of Bonita Public Television dropped his face into his hands and groaned, "Why don't I just go out and kill myself?"

"He's not that bad," the female producer sitting next to him assured him. "And he's getting better."

"Another five hundred takes and he might have that opening memorized. And then we can work on getting rid of that deer-in-the-headlights look."

"What do you care? You're not paying for the tape," the producer reminded him.

"I care because my name is on this thing," the man shouted. "I'm trying to build a reputation, and I'm not going to do it by putting out this kind of crap!"

"Well, we're trying to build a television station," she shot back. "And we'll be able to do that when Jennifer Calkins sets up a Foundation and we get a big chunk of that money. So just keep taping until he gets it right. And don't hurt his feelings. I want him to be happy with us. Jennifer Calkins introduced him as her adopted father."

The young director groaned again, then he leaned forward and hit the switch that allowed him to speak into the studio. "Cut. That was very good, Henri, but we'll have to try it again. We had a . . . little problem up here. Do that line again, please. And just relax, okay? We're all friends here."

❧ ❧ ❧

At the *Castello Falconara,* Les Leslie and Dennis Woodbrace had spent weeks cleaning up the courtyards, cutting underbrush from around the walls, and dealing with workmen they hired to put up scaffolding and begin repairing the walls. And about the only thing they'd accomplished was a noticeable improvement in Dennis' Italian-language skills and his appreciation of Sicilian culture. Les had many talents, but stonemasonry was not one of them; for that they needed professional help—and although hiring professional workmen in Licata was pretty easy, getting them to work was an entirely different matter.

"Where in blazes is everybody ta'day?" Les demanded as he looked up at the abandoned scaffolding.

"Feast of St. Joseph," Dennis replied as he ran out the door and headed for the *contessa's* car that was parked, clean and shiny, in the courtyard. "Everybody's at the *fiesta*."

"What in thunder does St. Joseph have to do with us?"

"He's the patron saint a' carpenters, Les," Dennis said in a tone that implied he was speaking to a child.

"All right, I'll bite. He's the patron saint a' carpenters, and . . ."

"And carpenters don't work on his feast day. That's why me an' Maria are goin' ta' the *fiesta*."

"Look, Les said through clenched teeth, I know I'm just a' ignorant American, but I got ta' tell ya' somethin', Dennis." He pointed up to the empty scaffolds and shouted, "Them wasn't carpenters up there yesterday; them was stonemasons."

Dennis shook his head sadly. Now he felt sure he was speaking to a child. "You can't expect the masons to work when the carpenters are at the *fiesta*," Dennis sighed, trying to explain the obvious. "Americans just don't understand."

"Dennis, now I got ta' ast ya' a question: What in the name a' Saint Elmo do ya' think <u>you</u> are?"

"Hey, Les, you know what they say, 'When in Rome do what the Romans do.'"

"All right so everybody's at the *fiesta*. That's another day gone. They'll all be hung over tamarra', so nothin' 'ill get started until ten o'clock. An' then there's the four-hour siesta, and another day is shot ta' blazes. An' while we're on the subject a' days, what was them two days off last week?"

"That was a strike," Dennis explained, for the umpteenth time while he rolled his eyes. "The bus drivers in *Napoli*."

"Yeah, right. The bus drivers in Naples were on strike so nobody worked down here at the bottom a' Sicily."

"Hey, the workers got ta' stick ta'gether, Les. It's nothin' personal. Anyways, I'll see ya'; I got ta' pick up Maria. Elena said I could take the car."

"That's a *Maserati Quatroporte*, ya ninny," Les shouted, pleasantly astounded by the pronunciation that tumbled out of his non-Italian mouth. "Be careful with it!"

"Don't worry. Nobody in that town'd even think a' touchin' the *Contessa's* car," Dennis replied as he got in, started the engine and drove away.

Les figured he could either stand there in the sun and watch nothing happening or he could go inside. He disgustedly climbed the marble staircase to the second floor where Elena sat, doing needlepoint in a bright sitting room. She was dressed in black, as always, but the cool smile on her face was anything but somber.

"This job'll never get done," he said, trying to find a way to say what needed to be said.

She did not look up from her needlepoint. "*Cecile*," she said with the same contented smile, "the *castello* has been here for five hundred years. It will not fall down if the work is not finished today."

"I'd like to get it finished before I have ta' go."

She looked up from the busywork in her hands and her smile faded. "Go? What do you mean, go?"

"I goin' ta' have ta' go back ta' America one a' these days, Elena. My time here is about up. If I stay much longer I'll have ta' get a visa."

"You do not have to go; you can get a visa and stay right here until your work is finished." She went back to her needlepoint; her face was firm now, the face of a *contessa* who had spoken, and once she had spoken expected to have her way.

"The work will never be finished, Elena."

"If that is God's will, then it is His will that you will get a visa and never leave," she replied with a satisfied smile. God Himself had settled the matter for her.

"I can't get a visa an' stay here, Elena. I've got some things that got ta' . . . be done in America first."

"You cannot go. I will not allow it. You can get a visa. My *avvocato* will take care of everything. You can stay right here."

"I can't, Elena," he pleaded. "I have ta' go back an' take care a' . . . somethin'."

She got up and went to where he was standing. *Cecile*, what is wrong? Is it because I am a widow? And I must remain a widow? Is that what is troubling you? I told you: I cannot change that; the people in this town expect it of me."

Her eyes would not leave his and he ran the tips of his fingers lightly over her cheek. "It's not that; it isn't you, Elena. These past few weeks, I've been happier just bein' around you than I ever thought I would be again in my life."

There was fear in her eyes now. She no longer looked like a contessa; she looked like the helpless girl his buddies described, waiting on the quay while their ship pulled out, all those many years ago. "I will not let you go, *Cecile*. You left me once and it took a whole lifetime for you to return. If you leave me again, you will never come back."

"I'll come back, Elena. I promise," he said as he put his arms around her, comforting her.

She hugged him close, trying to force her will into his body. "You said that before. The last time. And see how long it took," she said with her head against his chest.

He stroked her hair softly. "But I came back, didn't I?"

"Forty years!" she cried, looking up and him, her eyes pleading. "It took forty years for you to come back. I cannot wait another forty years."

"It's different this time, Elena. There's nothin' holdin' me. I know where you are. You know where I am. We can be t'gether any time we want."

She looked into his eyes. "We are together now. Even if I am a widow and people expect me to die as a widow, still we are together. Why must you leave me?"

"What is it? Are you in some kind of trouble? Is it money? Tell me, I will help you," she begged, looking into his eyes.

"No, it's nothin' like that. It's somethin' . . . There's only one guy who might be able . . . Trust me. Please. Just this once." He suddenly realized they were standing incredibly close, closer than they had stood since he returned to Licata and found her. Here lips were inches from his; he could kiss her . . . she looked like she wanted him to kiss her.

Les Leslie turned away from the woman in the black dress. There was something he needed to do in America before he could say the words he was thinking.

❧ ❧ ❧

Jack Townsend spent much of the afternoon on the telephone, behind the closed door of his office. He had left strict instructions not to be disturbed—by anyone. He left early, and R.J. did what any sensible partner and brother-in-law would do: he called Marilyn and asked if everything was all right. It wasn't; but it wasn't anything the family couldn't handle. Jack just had to learn how to ask for help; how not to be so pig-headedly independent all the time. He picked up Jennifer and the two of them were waiting with Marilyn aboard the motor yacht that bore her name when Jack got home carrying his attaché case.

"What's going on?" Jack asked, hoping he wasn't as trapped as he appeared to be.

"Jennifer and R.J. just came over for a little family dinner," Marilyn explained. "I'm trying out a new recipe."

The hell with that 'new recipe' nonsense; R.J. went straight to the point. "We're not going to let you do it, Jack, at least not alone."

"Thanks, but I'm the one who shot off my mouth. This is my fight."

"It's our fight as much as it is yours," Jennifer said. "And together we have a lot more ammunition."

"So what do you want to do? Offer those ungrateful bastards a million dollars each for their shares? I already offered them twice the market value; I'm surprised they're not lined up outside right now."

"Jack, whatever it takes, Jennifer and I are in it with you," R.J. said. "We'll buy them all out and share everything equally."

"We're a family, brother-in-law dear," Jennifer reminded him. "That's what families do."

"It's not the money," Jack said, trying to explain his feelings. "I know we can out-bid Howard Garner whether or not Junior is behind him. So we end up owning another piece of Bonita Key. So what? That's not the point."

"All right then, what is the point?" Marilyn demanded.

"The point is, your grandmother, Margaret Calkins, had a vision for this place. I think she wanted to leave behind a . . . well, maybe 'family' isn't the right word, but it's something like that. That's why she left the marina to the people who were living here when she died. You know how involved she was in our lives." He turned to Marilyn. "Do you really think we met by accident? Margaret knew me better than I knew myself. She knew I'd fall for you the minute I saw you, and she was right." He looked at Jennifer. "And how about sending you to the bank to get a loan you didn't need? To the trust department, remember?" He looked at R.J. "Where there just happened to be an extraordinarily handsome, eligible young bachelor with a law degree? Was that just a coincidence?"

"You think Grandma wanted everyone in the boatyard to be . . . one big happy family?" Jennifer wondered if maybe Jack had been working too hard.

"I don't know, Jen. But I think she knew a lot more about the people here than she let on, and I think she genuinely cared for them. And I think she wanted them to look out for each other, just like she looked out for us." Jack's eyes met everyone in the room and he added, almost in a whisper, "I know she didn't want them to sell out and forget about her . . . and Casey Calkins."

There was nothing more to say. The silence that followed was broken only by Arlo Woodbrace's voice asking permission to come aboard.

"Emergency meetin', Commodore," he reported. "Everybody's gettin' ta'gether in the main buildin'." He looked down, shuffled one foot a couple of times and added, "I moved some a' the stuff and set up a table and some chairs just like last time . . . if that's all right."

"That's fine, Arlo. What time?"

"Eight o'clock."

"We'll be there," Jack replied. He closed the salon door, turned to his law partner and added, in Judge MacIntyre's voice, "Naow Ah've got to give a fifty dollah summation."

CHAPTER 16

At eight o'clock sharp, Jack, Marilyn, Jennifer and R.J. met with the members of the unofficial Cap'n Kelly's Residents Association for what Jack thought might be the last time. He had no idea what he was going to say to these people. In fact, he wasn't sure he wanted to say anything at all. The family had discussed Jack's idea over a quiet dinner, and R.J. might very well be right: Margaret Calkins' vision—if she had a vision—could be nothing more than the romantic dream of a dying woman who wanted to preserve a way of life that was dying with her. Even if Jack was right about her dream, it could be the forces of consumerism and self-interest were so strong in the rapidly-changing world of mid-Eighties 'yuppies' and VCR's that her dream had no chance of becoming a reality.

"I guess we're all here," he began tentatively, as he stood up behind the head table. Years of trial practice made it impossible for him to speak sitting down.

Howard Garner was sitting at the back of the room with his arms folded across this chest and his legs stretched out in front of him. "What are they doing here?" he demanded, with an arrogant nod in the direction of Jennifer and R.J. "They're not residents!"

"Mr. Meacham is my lawyer; he's representing me," Jack said coolly. "Ms. Calkins is one of the owners of this building—and you're all here because she and my wife are gracious enough to allow you to use it. Does anyone want to object to her presence?"

Everyone except Howard Garner looked down at the floor. "Let's get down to business; I've got things to do," he said. It was pretty clear that he was at least the local driving force behind the insurrection.

"That's a good idea," Jack agreed. "Let's really get down to business, Howard. Are you going to make an offer for the outstanding shares of the marina, or are you going to shut up?" It was no use trying to be polite anymore. Only one of them was going to leave the meeting voluntarily.

Howard Garner glared at him. "I'm here to accept your offer, unless you're going to weasel out of it. I accept it right now." It sounded like Howard and Company—if there was an 'and company'—thought they were calling a bluff. Or maybe it was Howard, acting alone, who was throwing in the towel. All that remained to be seen was how many others would follow his lead, and how expensive the night would become.

"Fine. I thought you might. I didn't think you would trust a check so I brought cash." Jack picked up his attaché case and opened it on the table. It was full of money: neatly stacked hundred-dollar bills. "Step up here, sign the bill of sale and this general release, and it's all yours."

"You mean right now?" Garner's eyeballs were moving again; he should really see a doctor about that nervous condition.

"Right now, Howard. It's all yours." Jack picked up a few of the bundles, and dropped them, one by one, back into the case. "Ten hundreds in each stack, and one hundred stacks.

All neatly wrapped and certified by the bank. Pretty, aren't they?"

The bluff had been called, and the cards were on the table. Garner looked like he didn't expect it to happen, or to happen that quickly. Everyone in the room had stopped breathing while the confrontation continued.

"Howard? It's your money, Howard. You can even have the briefcase; I have several more."

Garner unfolded his arms and strutted to the table. Their eyes locked as Jack handed him a pen and said, "First the paperwork. My lawyer wants everything to be nice and legal." Garner signed the documents, slammed the attaché case shut and grabbed it off the table. "Our business is concluded," Jack said. "Now have your boat out of here by midnight."

"Midnight? You mean tonight?"

Jack looked at his watch. "That gives you a little less than four hours."

"How am I supposed to move my boat out in four hours?"

"I'd say that's your problem," Jack smiled.

"That's not fair!" Garner shouted. "Where am I supposed to go with it in four hours?"

"You can go to hell with it for all I care!" Jack shouted back. Nobody moved. R.J. thought the tension in the room was worse than any trial could ever be. Jack lowered his voice and continued, "As of this moment, I own the slip that is occupied by your boat. I want it out, and if it's not out by midnight, I'll have it towed out. You don't belong here anymore, Howard. You never did belong here. I'm giving you four hours out of the goodness of my heart; after midnight you're a trespasser. Now take your money and get the hell out of here."

Howard Garner wrapped both arms around the attaché case, turned and walked out. Arlo got up to open the door for him and was rudely brushed aside. The room was absolutely silent. Arlo returned to his seat, leaned forward with his arms on his knees and stared at the floor; some of the women rummaged in their purses and a couple of the men looked at the ceiling. Tension hung in the air like humidity after a Florida thunderstorm.

"Before we go any further, I'd like to say something," Jack began quietly. "I made an offer today, and I stand by my word. Anyone who wants to accept can do so right now." He glanced at Marilyn and hoped she understood before he smiled and added, "I don't have any more cash to hand out but I won't tell anybody else to be out by midnight."

"But let me tell you why I think you shouldn't accept that offer," he continued. "In the first place, it's not a very good offer. There are twelve shares. Once we get our new docks in and the roads paved, and when that restaurant finally opens and it's the kind of success I know it will be . . ." he looked at Marilyn again, ". . . this marina is going to be worth a lot more than a million dollars." He looked around the room; everyone's eyes were on him. "What I'm saying is, the value is here, folks, right under our feet. We're standing on it and it can only appreciate if we all work together."

He hesitated a minute and then added, in a much milder tone. "And there's something else. Margaret Calkins left this property to all of us. She was a very special lady. She had a profound influence on my life and on the lives of at least three other people in this room." He looked at Marilyn, then over at Jennifer and R.J. "She left me some money, but, more importantly, she left me a family. I owe her something for that." His voice cracked noticeably; he paused for a second, then continued. "What I owe her is to see her dream carried out." He paused again, and added, "I suspect Mrs. Calkins touched the life of everybody in this room in one way or another, and I think she left this place to all of us so we could stay here and keep looking after each other the way she looked after us when she was here in person." The room was silent except for a small sniffle; Jennifer was crying and R.J. had his arm around her. "Well, I didn't mean to get this emotional, Jack apologized, "but, the thing is, money wasn't important to Margaret. People were important. I think we should keep that in mind before we do anything foolish here tonight."

Jack sat down. The only sound in the room was Jennifer sniffing back a tear. Suddenly Erlene Rodgers stood up.

"There's somethin' I gotta say, Erlene began. "Nobody knows about this, not even you, Arl," she said as she glanced at Arlo who was staring up at her. "Miz Calkins made me promise ta' never tell nobody, but, well, she's gone now an' I gotta tell it." Erlene looked around the room and continued, "My girl Faith started at Bonita College this year. She's doin' real good, but that place costs a lot more'n you think, with tuition an' books an' her dorm an' all. I guess Miz Calkins knew I could never afford it, even with Faith workin' an' gettin' student loans. One day before she went in the hospital she called me and asked me ta' stop by her house. An' when I got there, she hands me a bankbook with Faith's name on it and enough money in it ta' pay f'r the whole four years. 'Don't tell nobody about this,' she said ta' me. 'It's just our little secret; kind 'a like a scholarship, okay?"' Erlene looked over at Arlo who gazed at her with amazement: she was actually on her feet, a strong woman speaking to an audience. "Ya' know, Arl," she continued, I don't need no house. I kind 'a like it here. I'd like ta' stay an' see how it all works out."

Erlene sat down to a silent room, and it was a few heartbeats before Sibby Maggio stood up. "Look, I don't want to get teary-eyed or nothing," he began, "but you might as well know, Miss Calkins, that I haven't been paying for my slip, not exactly. When I came here your grandmother, she knew I was going through a tough time, being separated from Babe and everything. She used to send Les Leslie over every month with an envelope so I could pay the rent to her sons and have a little left over for my two girls. And then when she got real sick, she sent word that I should go see her at home. When I got there, she handed me a stack of cash on the que-tee and told me to put it away and use it when I needed it. That's what I've been doing; I've pretty much been paying this place with her money. Anyway, I guess if I sell out and my wife hears about all the money, I'll be in court in about two shakes, right Commodore?"

"In one shake, Sibby. You can count on it," Jack confirmed.

"Yeah, that's what I thought. So, I've been thinking it over, and like Erlene said, I kind of like it here. Why rock the boat? If you'll excuse the expression."

There was another long silence before Nancy Neblett raised her hand. "Nance', don't tell me you have a story, too? Jack asked.

"I think we're going to find out we all have stories about Mrs. Calkins. "Why don't we get off these horrible folding chairs and go over to our Matthews? I'll put on some tea and coffee, and we can tell them over there."

"I just baked a pineapple upside-down cake," Erlene added. "I'll bring it on over."

The room dissolved in a general scraping of chairs and a great sigh of relief as everyone headed for the door, happy that the crisis was over. For the time being at least, they didn't have to choose between money and happiness.

"It looks like you won, Commodore," Marilyn whispered to Jack has they followed the small crowd to the Neblett's boat. "Should I tell them about the time I crashed into you and you ended up massaging my foot?"

"It's one of the many family stories we're about to hear," he assured her. "And I didn't win; Margaret won. I just did my job for her."

❧ ❧ ❧

Henri Dupré and Victoria Townsend shared a small table in the place Marilyn had recommended. The Beach House appeared to be an unlikely setting for fine *cuisine*, but she assured her father that the food was expertly prepared and modestly priced. Henri had been there several times before Victoria had arrived, and found it to be so. He concluded the chef was one who prepared meals for the pleasure of the art rather than the money it could bring him. That man had an appreciation of life, Henri told Victoria while they shared a carafe of *vin ordinaire*. The Beach House did not serve bottled wines, which was a great pity. Henri refilled Victoria's glass and observed the vintage was pleasant, yet unmemorable but for the fact that it was sipped while admiring a beautiful woman.

"Do you always know the right thing to say, Henri?" she asked as she raised the refilled glass to her lips and the candlelight from the glass lamp reflected in her eyes.

"I do not know always the right thing to say, *ma chère*," Henri assured her, thinking about the growing disaster at the television station. "Sometimes I cannot even say the right thing when it is written for me. But you are a woman of beauty that is most rare; any man would be a fool who does not say so."

She sighed and found herself almost blushing, something she was sure she had forgotten how to do. "Isn't it curious," she said, "in all my travels I've never met anyone quite like you."

"Like me? I am a simple man," he protested.

"No, Henri," she laughed. "You are French."

It was clear she was falling in love with him. What woman would not? Henri's ability to attract women had been both the blessing and the curse of his life. How could he tell her that he was not worthy of such love? He was about to become a failure. The innate talent, the charm that had always carried him through the difficult times, failed him whenever that miserable director called for action. And Jennifer, what of her? She looked on him as a father: one who could do anything; one who was invincible. He could not tell her that this idea of hers to make a television program was impossible. He could barely speak much less cook when he was standing alone under the lights and looking into the unblinking cyclops eye of the camera. Thoughts of his imminent failure—of humiliation—crowded his mind and darkened his mood. His silence was interrupted when a waitress dressed rather casually in a tee shirt and jeans brought their dinners to the table. The plates were presented in the manner of *haute cuisine*: entrees placed on them with a sense of design, and sauces poured to delight the eye as well as the palate. Once again Henri Dupré marveled out loud at the unknown *maestro* who labored to bring forth such creations to people who for the most part did not appear to appreciate his handiwork.

"There are many unappreciated people in this world, Henri," Victoria Townsend responded. "Most of them don't know they are unappreciated. They only find out when someone like you comes along and tells them they are. And very often it's too late and there's nothing they can do about it."

Henri looked into her soft gray eyes, so unlike other eyes he had known in a time so long ago that it seemed to be another life. He picked up his glass and held it toward her. "Then, *ma chère,*" he said quietly, let us drink to those who can do something about it, no?"

The black Maserati sedan with the Falconara crest painted on the doors sped westward through the Sicilian hills toward Palermo and the airplane that would take Les Leslie home. As usual, Dennis was at the wheel; his lack of an Italian driver's license forgotten or ignored for the moment. It didn't matter; there were no *carabinieri* on the island foolish enough to stop the vehicle, especially with the *Contessa* herself in the back seat.

"You promise me you will come back in one month," she reminded Les for the hundredth time since they left the *castello.*

"I promise, Elena. Don't you trust me?" he pleaded.

"No, I do not trust you," she replied, arrogantly turning her head away from him. "I trusted you once, and look at the years it cost me. Listen to me, *Cecile*: if you do not come back in one month, I will come to America for you. I should come right now."

"No, Elena, please. I have ta' take care a' this thing alone. All right?"

Elena sighed heavily; it was the sigh of someone who has lost the argument and knows it. "It is not all right, *Cecile.* I only agreed because you insist. She looked at him carefully. "You think I am a foolish woman? I am not a foolish woman, *Cecile.* I gave you my heart when I was sixteen years old. Many things have changed since then, but my heart has not changed."

"Elena, when I was here the first time . . . a lot happened ta' me after that. My life changed a lot, too, an' . . . well things didn't go so good for me."

She stroked her hand against the side of his bare face. "What happened to you, *Cecile?* Why will you not tell me?"

He smiled and said, "Well, I didn't become a Count f'r one thing."

"Is that what is bothering you? That I am a *contessa*? It was not my wish to be a *contessa*." She took his hand in hers, looked in his eyes and added, "We should have lived our own lives, *Cecile;* we should have done what we wanted to do." She hesitated and turned her face aside to look out the window, but as the Sicilian landscape flashed by, she could not see how to recapture the lost years. "It is too late for that now," she added sadly. "But it is not too late for us to be together in a small way, in a way that will not make people talk."

The narrow road took them over hills that were beginning to awaken, turning from yellow-brown to green. Here and there farmers plowed as their fathers' grandfathers had done, working the fields behind horses or mules, the smell of freshly-turned earth stirring memories buried deep in their genes. In the vast, uncultivated areas between plowed earth, shepherds tended to sheep and goats on land that was too steep or too rocky for anything Sicilians considered more useful.

Palermo was much larger than Licata. The traffic increased both in volume and in tempo as they got closer to the city, and the kamikaze recklessness of the drivers grew proportionally. The *Falconara* crest would not protect them here; its talismanic powers remained behind in Licata along with the quiet way of life that Les—and Dennis—had come to appreciate.

"Look out, will ya'!" Les shouted from the back seat as another driver did his best imitation of a dive-bomber.

"Hey, I'm doin' okay," Dennis responded as he swerved to avoid a couple on a motor scooter who appeared to be bent on their own destruction.

"Look out for that truck!" Les shouted pointing to an AGIP gasoline tanker that jumped out of nowhere and entered a traffic roundabout inches ahead of them.

"I know what I'm doin', Les," Dennis assured him.

"*Cecile,* let the young man drive. I trust him," Elena added.

Remarkably enough, although they saw hundreds of near-misses, they did not witness a single collision. It was a tribute either to superb Italian reflexes, loud horns, or the Saint Christopher medals that were more common than spare tires in their cars.

The city itself was a curious amalgam of wide boulevards and ancient, grimy stone buildings that appeared to have been there since time began. Fountains sprouted everywhere in the small parks and traffic circles, frequently serving as *al fresco* horse troughs. At one of them, a woman who looked like she could have been *Maruzza's* twin filled a bottle for her family's table with water streaming from one of a fountain's many spigots, while a horse harnessed to a *carozza* drank contentedly from the other side of the wide, circular base.

They found the airport road after only three stops for directions, a sure sign that Dennis' language skills had improved enormously, and soon they were at the nondescript terminal. It was the moment Les had been dreading.

"Take a hike, will ya' Dennis?" he said after the young driver ceremoniously pulled into a "No Parking" area. Les turned to Elena. Don't come inside; I hate goodbyes," he added softly.

"We do not say 'goodbye' *Cecile*. Here we say *'arrivederci'*. It means 'farewell until we meet again."

"Elena, I've never been good with words; I can't say all them fancy things."

"You do not have to say fancy things to me. What I want to hear is not a fancy thing; it is a simple thing."

He held her tightly and whispered, "I love you, Elena; I've loved you all my life. You kept me alive in ways you don't even know about. I have ta' leave ya' right now, just for a little while. But then I'll come back, and I'll never leave y'r side again. Never." And then he kissed her. He kissed her for a long, long time. And it was every bit as good as it had been forty years ago.

CHAPTER 17

It was a much better morning at the offices of Townsend & Meacham: for one thing, everyone had gotten in on time, and for another, Jack Townsend didn't have a blessed thing to do. The insurrection at the marina had been quelled, an appellate brief had been filed in a zoning matter—the case was a referral from another law firm—and two major real estate deals were on hold pending appraisals from the bank. In short, not a single client demanded or needed immediate attention. Jack could spend his entire day writing; working on the second book he kept promising his agent he would finish.

The early-morning quiet was shattered by a commotion in the waiting room that soon exploded into Jack's office. Junior Calkins came charging through the door followed by an apologetic Sharon Crowley.

"I'm sorry, Mr. Townsend, I couldn't stop him . . ."

"You listen to me, Mr. Lawyer-man," Junior snarled through his ever-present cigar as his spittle sprayed Jack's desk, "you and me are gonna settle things once and for all."

"It's all right, Sharon," Jack said as he waved her out. She left the room unwillingly, looking back over her shoulder as if she should do something. "Junior there's no smoking in the office," Jack said without standing up.

Junior's face was the color of raw steak. "You're a real comic, aren't you?" he snarled. "Real funny." He took the sloppy cigar-end out of his mouth and said sarcastically, "Aw, you don't have an ashtray. How about I use this?" He crushed the burning cigar into the center of Jack's walnut desk. "Is that okay?"

Jack would not allow himself the luxury of doing anything foolish like punching his lights out. People like Junior were on every street corner, and ever since the Supreme Court had allowed lawyers to advertise a dozen years earlier, the word 'lawsuit' was on everyone's mind. Jack looked at his tormentor coldly and said, "Why don't you say what you came to say and get the hell out of here?"

"Oh, listen!" Junior mocked, "Mr. Lawyer-man can use bad words and everything! Look at me! I'm so scared I'm gonna wet my pants!" He sneered an ugly, malicious sneer and said, "Here's what I'm gonna say, Mr. Lawyer-funny-man: you've been a pain in my ass for a long time. I'm gonna see to it that you're not a pain there anymore. I'm gonna be right behind you, watching every step you make. The minute you slip, you're not gonna be a lawyer anymore, and you're not gonna be funny. And if I'm real lucky, you won't even be alive."

Jack looked at him quietly without moving out of his chair. "Junior," he said quietly, "a long time ago your father wanted to have you wrapped in anchor chain and dropped into the ocean. One of the great regrets of my life is that I talked him out of it."

The door bust open a second time. Suddenly R.J. was in the room with them and Sharon was hovering just outside. "Is everything okay in here?" R.J. asked.

"Everything's fine, Rob. Mr. Calkins was just leaving. Weren't you, Junior?"

Junior Calkins had a long-standing debt to settle with R.J. Meacham. He incurred it the day he punched his daughter Jennifer in the face before she and R.J. were engaged, and the debt was foremost on R.J.'s mind. It had been accruing interest, compounding daily, ever since that fateful day, and R.J. would be only too happy to settle up now by taking it out of Junior's hide. The sneering coward took one look at R.J.'s face and the taunt muscles under his dress shirt and apparently decided he might get better terms some other time; he brushed past the younger man and hurried out the door.

"What was that all about? As if I didn't know," R.J. asked when Junior was gone.

"I guess it proves he was the one behind the takeover bid, and when Howard Garner saw cold hard cash he resigned as Junior's shill," Jack observed.

R.J. looked at the cigar butt and ugly scar in the middle of Jack's desk. "Want me to call the Sheriff's Office? I'm sure Bear Harper would be happy to arrest him."

Jack shook his head. "He's not worth the trouble, Rob." He turned to Sharon and said, "Ms. Crowley, call Sutherland's and see if they can send someone over right away for a repair job. I'm going to the marina to check on my wife."

"Want me to come?" R.J. asked.

Jack shook his head again. Somebody has to mind the store. I'll check on the house, too. On second thought, maybe it would be best for you to call Bear. Tell him we only want to report an incident; we don't want anyone arrested . . . at least not yet. I don't think Junior's nuts enough to do anything rash, but it wouldn't hurt to have a few extra patrols out on the island for a while." He got up to leave and then added, almost as an afterthought, "And Rob, let's not tell the girls about this. There's no use getting them upset.

The Commodore's law office wasn't the only place in town that echoed with raised voices that morning. At the Bonita Public Television station, Henri Dupré was at the end of his endurance, attempting to fit himself into someone else's idea of what he should be. He tried not to stare into the camera lens had become a terrifying glass eye, and he began once more, "'Allo, my friends, my name . . . I am Henri Dupré, and I wish to . . . today I will create for you . . ."

"Cut!" The director's voice boomed from everywhere and nowhere at the same time. "Natural, Henri," the man coaxed, "Try to relax and sound natural. We have to get through the opening if we're ever going to get to the cooking part."

"*Natural!*" Dupré shouted to his unseen tormentor. "Who can be *natural* here, with these lights in my face? And how can I cook? This is not a kitchen! The food I cannot smell! Nothing is real!"

"It's a set, Henri," the director's voice replied. "We talked about this, remember?"

"I do not care how you call it!" Dupré shouted back. "It is not a kitchen! How can I cook the food if I cannot smell it?"

"You're not going to cook anything, Henri," the disembodied voice droned. The finished product will be hidden in the oven. You'll just mix the ingredients and put them in there, and after we cut away, you'll pull out the finished creation."

"But this is not cooking!" Dupré shouted. "This is madness! This is for *imbéciles!*"

"That's the way we do it, Henri," the director's voice assured him."

"No! That is the way you do it!" Dupré replied. "This is the way I do it!" With that he threw a sauté pan at the disconnected double oven. The glass shattered behind him as he walked off the set.

Back at Cap'n Kelly's Marina, the workmen had finished putting on the Mansard roof and were taking down the scaffolds that encased the building. Marilyn retreated into her office and tried to block out the noise of wooden planks and steel uprights being dropped to the ground. Things were nearly ready—finally—and unless Jennifer got another bright new idea, all that remained was for them to hire a staff and schedule a grand opening.

"Can I come in?" Erlene asked as she poked her head in the outside door.

"Erlene! Come in quick before something falls on you!" Marilyn shouted.

"That's all right; they're workin' on the other side of the buildin' now." A plank hit the ground with a hollow 'thunk' right behind her. She jumped in and added, "Maybe it would be a better idea ta' come in."

"Ah was just wonderin'", she continued when she was safely inside the office, "if ya'll have made any decisions about the gift shop?"

"Gift shop?" Marilyn felt like she was coming in to the middle of someone else's conversation.

"Jennifer's been takin' about openin' the gift shop," the Gas Girl confirmed, "an' I just wanted ta' get my bid in early.

I'd be real good at runnin' it, and it would be a whole lot better than sittin' out on the gas dock all day."

Marilyn felt like her jaw had been shot full of Novocain: it refused to move even though she wanted to say something. Finally, she managed to blurt out, "Well, she did mention something about a gift shop, Erlene, but it wasn't anything definite."

"That ain't the way she sounded ta' me. She was tellin' me an' Eddie Miles about it the other day, and she sounded real sure of herself."

Marilyn had to agree with the Gas Girl on that score. Jennifer always sounded sure of herself. "I'll talk to Jennifer as soon as she gets here," Marilyn promised, thinking they would indeed have a lot to talk about.

"I'd sure appreciate it," Erlene replied. "I sure would like ta' get off that gas dock an' get me an inside job with air conditionin'."

Arlo Woodbrace was just hanging out at the marina when Jack drove in that morning. Arlo was a born helper, but the workmen who were swarming over the main building made it clear that his help was neither wanted nor needed. With Les off in Italy somewhere, Arlo didn't have much to keep himself busy. He couldn't even go back to his boat because of the fight he had with Erlene earlier when she said she was sick of seeing him mope around all day. He really needed something to do and he jumped at the chance when Commodore Jack Townsend called to him from his car.

"What's going on, Arlo?" Jack asked.

"Nothin'; nothin' much." He wondered why the Commodore was home from the office so early, but even Arlo would not ask that question.

"I got tired of sitting around the office," Jack declared, almost as if he could read Arlo's mind. "How'd you like to help me with a little project?"

"Wow! Yeah, sure, Commodore. What 're we doin'?"

"Jennifer wants to get the *Margaret* underway for the grand opening. Think we can handle it?"

Arlo's mouth dropped open. That was more than a 'little project.' The *Margaret* hadn't been moved in a lot of years. She probably couldn't move; probably silted right into the bottom. "Yeah, sure, I guess," Arlo answered lamely. "I mean, I guess we c'n do it. I guess."

"I'm going to change into some work clothes," Jack continued. "Why don't you meet me aboard the *Margaret* in a couple of minutes?"

"Yeah, sure, I guess," Arlo repeated, wondering if maybe the Commodore had slipped a couple of his mental gears.

Jack drove off to his home on the *Marilyn*, and Arlo walked to the corner of the marina where the *Margaret* waited with the helpless resignation of all old derelicts. Most boats didn't die all at once, Arlo thought. Boats were a lot like people: when they stopped being upgraded, stopped being renewed, that's when they stopped being useful; and that was when all too often many of them went off into a corner somewhere, and life ebbed away from them a little at a time, day by day, until nothing was left.

The first thing you noticed about *Margaret* was she was old. Real old. So old she was made of wood instead of steel, which was really strange for a commercial boat. She must have been pretty old when Cap'n Calkins bought her 'way back when. Arlo never paid much attention to her before, but now he examined her carefully from the security of the seawall. *Margaret's* pilot house was small and canted forward at what her builder must have thought was a rakish angle. Her bow was nowhere near as high as modern shrimp boats, and on her aft deck the rusted derricks that once lifted her nets and made her a proud, working member of the community, held only useless shreds of rigging. Orange rust stains trickled down her weathered hull; whoever built her probably used iron fastenings. The stains meant they were rusting away underneath her weathered paint; some might even be completely gone. If Arlo and the Commodore managed to get her engines started—which was a very big 'if'—the vibration would probably shake her planks loose and she'd go down in pieces right there in her slip.

"What's the matter? You worried?"

"Huh? No, I mean, yeah. I guess." Arlo had been lost in thought and hadn't heard the Commodore walk up behind him.

"Come on, let's go aboard," Jack said as he slapped Arlo on the back. "There's nothing like banging on an old engine to make you forget your troubles."

They stepped gingerly onto the old deck and walked around to the port side before they found a hatch that looked like it might lead down into an engine room. Jack handed Arlo one of the two flashlights he had brought, and started down the old ladder.

"Be careful. There's no tellin' what's down there," Arlo warned as Jack descended into the murky darkness.

A few dirty portlights let in barely enough light to make out the outlines of the room. Jack switched on his flashlight while he was still on the ladder; the floorboards looked dry and reasonably solid, and there were no furry animals crawling around the place. He let himself down and called for Arlo to follow.

"Wow, look at this place," Arlo said when he joined Jack. Their combined flashlights pierced the darkness and exposed a small room that was dominated by two massive greasy-black engines; everything else around them was painted bilge gray. In a far corner a small workbench stood mute sentinel; it was littered with tools where their long-ago master had left them, and they waited in vain for a return that never came.

"I never seen engines like this," Arlo said, playing his light over one of the huge machines that reached the level of his knees.

"Packard Straight Eights," I think," Jack replied. "Casey must have had her repowered. Why the hell would he use gasoline engines?" he asked rhetorically.

"Prob'ly got 'em cheap," Arlo suggested. He had never met Cap'n Calkins, but tales of his parsimony were legendary.

"I guess," Jack agreed as he hunched down for a closer look at one of the cast iron blocks. "Six-volt electrical system, too. Where the hell are we going to find batteries?"

"Maybe we should just tell Jennifer we can't get 'er goin'," Arlo suggested.

Jack looked up at him. "This is family, Arlo. You don't give up that easily when you're doing something for family. Let's get those portlights open and let some air in here; then we'll string up a few extension cords and lights and see if we can get the shafts to turn. At least that'll be a start." He looked around the dispirited room and added, "You know, I'm getting a good feeling about this boat. I'll bet we can get her going again."

Arlo Woodbrace looked at Commodore Jack Townsend carefully. Now he was almost sure the Commodore had slipped a gear, but he dutifully went up the ladder to round up some extension cords while Jack went to work on getting the long-shut portlights reopened.

Arlo had fished a couple of fifty-foot extension cords and two extension lights out of his storage locker and was on his way back to the *Margaret* when he noticed a stranger poking around on the drydocked *Elena*. "Hey!" he shouted. "Hey, you! What d'ya' think y'r doin' up there?"

A vaguely familiar face looked down at him. The guy looked so much like Les Leslie he could have been his younger brother, only Les' didn't have a brother as far as Arlo knew. And this guy was clean-shaven and had a dimple on one side. "Just checkin' over my boat, if ya' don't mind," the stranger said, using Les' voice.

"Les? Is that you?"

"Who in thunder would it be? Y'r Aunt Fannie?" Les climbed down the ladder from *Elena's* deck, shook Arlo's hand warmly and then suddenly embraced him in a bear hug. "It's good ta' see ya', Arl. It's real good ta' see ya'."

"It's good ta' see you too, I guess," Arlo replied, unused to both the clean face and the display of emotion from his usually cantankerous friend. Suddenly the questions tumbled out of him. "How'd ya' get here? Did ya' find her? Where's Dennis?"

"Took a cab from the airport; I guess nobody saw me come in with that hullabaloo goin' on out front. An' yea, I found her. An' Dennis is still over there, supervisin' . . . Arl, ya' ain't gonna believe me when I tell ya'. She's a countess an' she lives in a castle." He suddenly noticed the orange and yellow wires slung around Arlo's arms, and added, "What are ya' doin'?"

"Huh?"

"With them wires? What are ya' doin'?"

"Oh! Me an' the Commodore are gettin' the old *Margaret* goin' again. She lives in a castle?"

"Dennis is over there now, overseein' the guys we hired ta' fix up the place. Where's the Commodore? I gotta talk ta' him."

"Dennis? My son, Dennis? He's supervisin' at the castle? Arlo couldn't believe it.

"That's what I said. Where's the Commodore? Over on the *Margaret*?"

"Yeah. Ya' mean like Dennis is in charge a' them guys?"

"What guys?"

"The guys fixin' up the castle!"

"'a course he's in charge of them," Les insisted. He hired most of 'em. That kid's got a good head on his shoulders; knows how ta' talk ta' people, too. Leastways he does when he ain't in town takin' lessons from Maria. And ya' should hear some a' the ideas he's come up with. I don't think Elena will ever let him come back here."

"Who's Maria?"

"This is a long story, Arl. Let's go find the Commodore; I don't want ta' have to tell it more'n onec't."

❧ ❧ ❧

Henri Dupré was unusually quiet during dinner that night with Victoria Townsend. They were at the Yacht Club—guests of Townsend & Meacham, as usual. That idea bothered him even more than the idea of his own inability to carry out Jennifer's television idea. He had many things in his life, but he had never been a kept man. And now, with more than sixty years to his name, and the restaurant opening delayed again, he was on the verge of becoming one.

"You barely said a word all through dinner. A penny for your thoughts, Henri," Victoria said as she watched him finish another one too many glasses of wine.

"You would be over-charged, *ma chère,*" he warned her.

"Would you like to tell me what's troubling you?"

"There is no trouble. Only I am thinking."

"About . . . ?"

He looked at her, his dark eyes smoldering with an anger she had never seen in them. "About nothing," he said, almost harshly.

Victoria's eyes flash back defiantly and Dupré knew instantly that he was outgunned. "Forgive me, ma *chère*," he said with what was supposed to be an ingratiating smile. "I have not been myself; I know it. I am thinking of too many things when only I should think of you."

The words were right, but the Gallic charm was missing. It was as if Victoria knew the secret of the magician's trick, and because she knew it she could no longer be mesmerized by the performance.

"They say familiarity breeds contempt. Perhaps we've been seeing too much of each other," she suggested.

Henri Dupré did not respond, and they finished dinner in a chilled silence.

CHAPTER 18

Marilyn spent a restless night thinking about gift shops, suppliers, sales taxes and employee withholding. She couldn't get comfortable no matter how much she tossed and turned and fluffed her pillow. Jennifer always leaped into things without looking at all of the consequences. This time it was no different. It was all very well to be on the right path and have faith in the outcome, but business decisions needed to be made a little more carefully. She managed to corner Jennifer when the younger woman stopped by the office the next morning before going on to Bonita College.

"Jennifer, Erlene was in here yesterday asking about a gift shop . . ."

"Isn't it a great idea, Marilyn?" Jennifer gushed. "We would be giving jobs to people who need them, and taking care of our customers at the same time. I just know we'll make a big profit."

"Jen, we don't have a gift shop," Marilyn protested when she could get a word in.

"I know, I meant to talk to you about that; really I did. But I've been so busy with school and the wedding and everything."

"You haven't done a thing about your wedding except pick out invitations. And I'm hosting the bridal shower, remember?"

Jennifer's eyes widened. "Well, I've been <u>thinking</u> about the guest list," she protested. And that takes a lot of time. Besides, there's so little money involved in the shop it's not worth talking about."

"How much?"

"Nothing, really," Jennifer explained.

"How much, in American dollars, is 'nothing'?"

"Tim Gorman said probably around fifty. No more than seventy-five at the most," Jennifer said, throwing her hands in the air.

"Seventy-five thousand dollars! To remodel a room full of junk into a gift shop?" Marilyn protested.

"It's not that simple. They have to update the electrical service, and bring the place up to code for plumbing."

"What does plumbing have to do with a gift shop?" Marilyn almost shouted.

"Well as long as they were remodeling, I told them to turn part of it into a bar and lounge, you know, so the people who are going upstairs for dinner will have a place to wait for their tables."

"Jennifer," Marilyn sighed, "we haven't served the first dinner yet. This whole thing could be a colossal failure."

Jennifer looked at her with a mixture of shock and disbelief. "Are you kidding? With your father's cooking and the view from up there . . ."

"I know, I know," Marilyn said quickly, interrupting the speech she had heard a thousand times. "'It's impossible for it to fail.' Jennifer, you'd better understand something: any business can fail. I'm not going to invest thousands more of Jack's money into this thing until it's actually open and showing a profit!"

"I already signed the contract," Jennifer said haughtily."

"You what? We're partners. You can't just sign without consulting me!"

"Well, I did; so, sue me."

"All right, fine, Jennifer. You can own the gift shop, and the bar and the lounge and whatever big idea you think up next. We'll just be partners in the restaurant." Marilyn demanded, putting a stop to this nonsense.

"I signed your name to it, too," Jennifer added quickly.

"You can't do that!" Marilyn shot back. "That's forgery!"

"No, it isn't," Jennifer protested. "Not if my only intent was to bind our partnership. We're general partners and I can bind both of us. R.J. said so."

"He knows about this?"

"Not exactly; not yet. I just got to talking to him about legal stuff one night."

"Jennifer, we just can't do it. We can't risk any more money," Marilyn pleaded.

"Why not? We've got a lot more!"

"That's not the point . . ."

"Well, what is the point, Marilyn? I thought we were supposed to do some good with that money. So we create a few jobs for some people who live right here at our marina. That's doing some good, isn't it? And besides . . ." Jennifer pulled out all the stops, turning away and sniffling . . . "I'm having my wedding reception up there." She looked at Marilyn and her lip quivered a little. "Yours was at the Yacht Club and it was so nice. I don't want to walk up some dumb old outside stairway in my wedding dress. And I can't very well walk through that greasy dump inside wearing white! And we had to do it sooner or later. I thought you'd be proud of me because I saved us so much time and money by keeping the workmen right here, working on the job."

Marilyn put her arms around the younger woman and said, "Jennifer, you'll have a beautiful wedding, I promise. And you won't be walking through any greasy dump. We'll build a grand staircase inside the building if you want one. I was just a little . . . shocked, that's all."

"Can we have an elevator, too? We need one to meet the building code."

"Well, I guess if that's the law," Marilyn said, still stroking the younger woman's hair.

Jennifer suddenly looked at her watch. "Oh, my God! Look at the time! I'll be late for class!" she said, her tears suddenly dry. "We can talk about the details later, okay? The workmen are starting inside today."

Jennifer bolted out the door and Marilyn felt a little like what Les Leslie would have called 'snookered'.

Early the next morning, Les gingerly opened the door to the offices of Townsend & Meacham. He was alone, and much too early for his appointment, but that couldn't be helped. He had to leave early if he was going to sneak out of the marina before Arlo got home from his night job and started asking a million questions or—worse yet—tagging along. The waiting room's dark, wood-paneled walls were set off with an oriental rug and the leather chairs. By now the brass lamps and tables covered with boating magazines were all familiar objects, but they did not make him feel at home. Unlike his previous visits to the Commodore's office to talk about the goings-on of at the marina, Les was about to disclose the convolutions of his own life, and that thought gave him an empty feeling in the pit of his stomach. His dreams of Elena had never ended like this, sitting in a lawyer's office, trying to undo deeds that had been done long ago; trying to make sense of things that had never made much sense in the first place. He would not be here today if it were not for her. It was easier to leave the past in the past, where the calming oil of time smoothed out the troubled waters of his life. But Elena wanted him to be with her, and he wanted it too—wanted it more than he had ever wanted anything in a life that had twisted and turned through the years. That meant legal papers; and it meant dredging up muck that had been buried long ago. And that meant talking to a lawyer.

"Mr. Leslie?" The young lady, Sharon Crowley, was talking to him through the window that separated her office from the waiting room. "You're a little early."

"Yeah, I, uh . . . I didn't have nowhere ta' go," Les answered apologetically.

"Mr. Townsend isn't in yet. Can I get you a cup of coffee?"

"No, that's all right," Les said automatically, not wanting to put her to any trouble.

"Are you sure?"

Maybe refusing wouldn't be considered polite, so he changed his mind in a show of cooperation. "Yeah, okay, if it's handy."

A man came in with a couple of toolboxes. He said he was there to repair a desk, and the girl showed him inside before she brought Les a coffee mug decorated with a trawler on one side and the code flags 'Tango' and 'Mike' on the other. 'T & M'—it was a nice, nautical touch, he thought.

"Problem?" he asked, blowing on the coffee and nodding in the direction of the door the man had gone through.

"Mr. Townsend had a little accident with his desk yesterday. Sutherland's sent a man over to take care of it," she answered off-handedly, before returning to her own world behind the window.

She wasn't unfriendly, just businesslike; the way Les figured you were supposed to be in places like this. Polite, coffee, no idle chit-chat, no lollygagging around. Not like it was at Cap'n Kelly's where a question like, 'Problem?' might start up a half-day discussion with numerous opinions and several offers to lend a hand. It was the difference between the marina and this office; between home and the hard edge of the law where people's lives were broken and dissected. The difference made him even more uncomfortable, and he flipped through a magazine without really looking at its pages, trying to get his mind off the reason for his appointment.

Jack and R.J. came in a short time later, in the middle of a conversation and looking like they weren't expecting to find him on their doorstep. "You'd be the perfect District Justice for Phi Alpha Delta fraternity, Rob," Jack was telling his younger partner. "Traveling around the State, talking to law students. You're still young enough to relate to them. You'd be great at the job." The Commodore stopped talking when he noticed Les sitting there in the waiting room. "Hi, Les. You're here pretty early," he said as he extended his hand.

"Yeah, well, I figured I might's well get it over with," Les Leslie said, shaking hands all around.

"Mr. Townsend, Jim Sember is in your office taking care of your desk," Sharon Crowley warned through her window.

"Then I guess we're assigned to the library," Jack replied.

"I'll bring your coffee in there," Sharon offered.

"Want me to sit in?" R.J. suggested.

"Les?" It was Jack, asking their client for his consent. Les Leslie looked around uncertainly for a second. He didn't want his problem blabbed all over town. Still, R.J. was a lawyer, and the Commodore's partner, and that meant the

Commodore trusted him. And two heads were better than one, especially when the problem was forty years old.

"Yeah, sure; that'd be okay," Les agreed. "Two heads'r better than one, right?"

"Make that two coffees, please, Sharon," R.J. said as the three men left the waiting room.

It took a few minutes for them to get comfortable in the library and they made a bunch of useless small talk around the big conference table before the girl came in with two matching coffee mugs. She didn't bother with extra cream and sugar. Les figured she knew how her bosses liked their coffee. Once she left it room it was time to get down to business.

Jack took a sip of coffee and asked, "How can we help you, Les?"

Les liked that approach. It sounded like something somebody at Cap'n Kelly's would say. "First off," he said, "I don't want his done for nothin'. I expect ta' pay, same's anybody else."

"We charge up to two hundred dollars per hour, depending on the complexity of the case," Jack said casually. That's per lawyer. Right now, you're talking to two."

Jumpin' sea snails! No wonder they could have leather chairs and brass lamps all over the place!

Jack smiled and added, "Of course, you get the 'family discount.'"

"What might that be?" Les inquired, hoping the clock hadn't already started to run.

"Why don't you tell us the problem and let us worry about that?" R.J. replied, exchanging a smile with his partner across the corner of the table.

Les hunched forward with his arms on his knees. He rubbed his hands together as if he were warming them before a fire and he looked down at the floor. "See, this happened a long time ago," he began. "An' I never thought much about it. I mean, I never figured it'd come up anymore, ya' know?" He looked up, back and forth between the two lawyers for reassurance.

"Some problems go away by themselves, Les, and some don't," Jack said.

"Yeah, well, this 'un didn't. See, Elena wants me ta' get a visa and stay over there in Italy. But I can't get a visa, leastways, I don't think I can, because . . ." He looked down at the floor again. "Because I was convicted of a crime . . . a real, bad, bad crime. A long time ago, back during the War."

There was a long silence before Jack asked, "What kind of crime, Les?"

The man moved his head just enough to look Jack in the eyes and said, "Treason."

"Treason?" R.J. said. "During a war you can be shot for that. Firing squad, isn't it?"

"Many's a time I wished they'd a shot me," Les replied, looking at him. "But instead I spent ten years in Leavenworth." He lowered his head again and added, "It was a kinda deal they worked our f'r me." The man became silent again and his brows knotted under this thick mat of steel and black hair.

"Who were 'they,' Les? Who worked out that deal?" Maybe you should start at the beginning.

"Yeah, I guess I should start at the beginnin'," Les said, sinking back into his chair. "See it was 'way back when I met her. I was just a kid when I joined the Navy, seventeen years old an' fresh off the farm from Eldorado, Illinois. A year 'r so later, I thought I knew everythin'. I was over there in Italy—Licata. An' the first time I saw Elena . . ." He looked back and forth between Jack and R.J. "Well, you fellas know what that's like, I guess."

"She was on her way ta' church with her family, see? And I followed 'em right inta' the church. I wasn't her religion 'r nothin', but I sat down in one a' the pews and bluffed my way through it, just by watchin' everybody else while I was lookin' at her. After a couple a' weeks a' doin' that, I tried ta' talk to her. Well, her mother and her aunt was with her, and they didn't care f'r that at all. They gave me a real good goin' over in Eye-talian, an' shooed me off.

"I figured I was scuppered good and proper, so I went back ta' the ship ta' try an' figure out how I could get ta' meet her. A couple a' days later the Skipper sends for me. I couldn't figure what the Old Man wanted, but I reported like the book says ta' do, and when I got ta' his quarters, there was Elena standin' there with a fella the Old Man says is her father. Well, ya' c'n guess I knew I was hard up in a clinch, and I stood ready ta' take whatever they was gonna hand out ta' me f'r talkin' ta' the girl. Next thing I know, the fella . . . her father . . . starts talkin' ta' me in English, well, ya' know, a sort a' broken-up English, and he's apologizin' ta' me, and tells me his wife an' his sister was way outta line f'r hollerin' at me like that. Says he wants me ta' come over f'r dinner so's he c'n make it up ta' me." Les took a deep breath, put his hand to his mouth and looked away at the library door. It was a painful memory.

"What did your captain have to say about that?" R.J. asked.

"Oh, the Old Man," Les continued, looking back at them across the table, "the Old Man was happy as a pig in stink. Elena's father was the mayor a' the town 'r somethin', and our orders was we was supposed ta' be good neighbors."

"So, anyways, I went off ta' their place that very night, an' ate with 'em. The mother and the aunt gave me the Jack Nastyface all night, but her father, he was Prince Charmin'. And me an' Elena looked at each other across the table." Les half smiled now, remembering the night. He took a deep breath and continued.

"After dinner, the father says we're all goin' ta' take a walk, and Elena an' the two women, they walk on ahead while the father walks with me and we talk about stuff."

"What kind of 'stuff', Les?" Jack asked, suspecting now where this story was going.

"I'm gettin' ta' that," he replied, sensing the point of Jack's question. "It was nothin', just chewin the fat, ya know? An' when we got back ta' their place, he invites me ta' come back again."

"And you went back," R.J. concluded.

"Darn right, I did." Les looked right at him and added, "Wouldn't you?" He turned to Jack and continued his story. "I was invited back a whole lotta times, and whenever I went it was the same thing: supper an' then a nice long walk. An' talk."

Les paused again, almost as if he wanted to be interrupted, but no one spoke. This was his story, and he would have to tell it. After a few moments he added, "Well, ya' c'n see where this headin', I guess. After a while he starts astin' me some questions: 'Where's this ship goin'? When's that one pullin' out?', that kinda thing.

"And you answered him," R.J. suggested.

"No, I didn't," Les almost shouted; then in a calmer tone he added, "At least not 'till they told me to."

"Why don't you tell us that part," Jack suggested.

The man took a deep breath and continued, "Well, I was young, but I wasn't stupid. I went back ta' the Old Man an' I told him. 'Skipper,' I says, 'There's somethin' funny goin' on over there.' And I told him everythin' same's I'm tellin' you."

"What happened, Les?" Jack asked.

"The Old Man said he had a good friend in Naval Intelligence; somebody he'd gone ta' the Academy with. He called that fella an' had Elena's father checked out. Sure enough, Dominic Russo was a collaborator. He had been workin' f'r the Germans 'r anybody else who could do him some good." Les paused to let the full impact of that statement sink in.

"Well, this fella from Intelligence—this friend a' the Old Man—comes over personally and goes ta' work on me. 'This is a great opportunity,' he said; told me how it was my duty to my country ta' see it through. He even talked a' makin' me an officer, lieutenant maybe; even said I might end the war as a light commander." Les smiled a wry smile and added, "An' the next thing I know, he's givin' me bogus information ta' pass along."

"Your captain knew about this?" R.J. asked.

"Sure he did; he was sittin' right there in the room when they cooked it up."

"But there were no written orders," Jack guessed.

Les leaned on his arms and looked at the floor again. "No, there was no written orders. They was gonna test me out first; see how I did. They didn't think about orders, I guess, an' neither did I. All's I could think about was them gold stripes an' how they'd impress Elena."

The room was silent again before he continued. "Anyways, the way them deals work, ya' can't give 'em information that's completely bad 'r they'll know somethin's up. So ya' tell 'em stuff that's almost right. Either it's a little bit late, 'r a little too early, 'r ya' got the time right, but the headin' a' the ship is wrong. Always just a little bit off."

"Somebody was telling you what to tell her father?" R.J. asked.

"The fella from Intelligence. Only he wasn't very intelligent, I guess."

"What happened, Les?" Jack asked.

"They give me somethin' ta' pass along about a troopship goin' up the boot a' Italy. This stuff was the real McCoy, dead-on perfect: time, destination, everything. They was gonna let the ship put out ta' sea, and then call 'er back f'r some reason. It was supposed ta' get me in tight with Dominic Russo, an' then the Intelligence fella would transfer me ta' his unit, maybe as an ensign." Les looked down at the floor again and said nothing.

"But somebody forgot to give the order, and the ship never got the message to turn back," Jack suggested.

"A whole lotta good men died because a' me," Les added, never looking up from the floor.

"It wasn't your fault," R.J. protested. "How could they blame you?

Les looked up and his eyes locked on Jack. "Shit rolls downhill, right? Jack said quietly.

"In the Navy it rolls ta' the lowest deck, Commodore," Les added.

"So you took the heat for someone else's mistake," the older lawyer said.

Les looked back and forth between Jack and R.J., pleading his cause. "Who'd a' believed me? There was no orders! They give me a Jack-strop lawyer who said I'd be shot if I didn't cooperate. So I did what he told me ta' do, and I shipped out in the brig. An' it was another ten years before I saw the outside of them walls at Leavenworth." He hesitated for a moment before his eyes met Jack's again, and he added, "An' after I got out, I went ta' sea again, sailin' on any bucket a' bolts under any flag that'd have me. And I never looked back until now." He put his hand to his mouth and looked away, but there was no hiding the moisture in his eyes.

"Did Elena know what her father was doing?" R.J. asked quietly.

"No!" Les shouted in reply. "She didn't know nothin'!" He looked embarrassed by his outburst and added, quietly, "Leastways I never told her nothin'." He shook his head and added, "An' I don't want her ta' know nothin' even now. An' if gettin' me squared away means she has ta' find out, I'll just thank ya', pay ya' f'r y'r time, an' f'rget the whole thing." Les ran his hand across where his beard used to be and said, "And there's somethin' else: if I don't get squared away an' get back ta' her in a month, Elena said she would come here ta' check up on me." He looked directly at Jack and added, "Still think ya' want ta' sign up f'r this voyage, Commodore?"

CHAPTER 19

"Mrs. Townsend? What do you want us to do with all the stuff out here?" Tim Gorman, the construction foreman was standing in the doorway that led to the main floor of the old showroom.

"Didn't Jennifer tell you?" She should have known it was a silly question. Jennifer never bothered with details.

Tim Gorman almost laughed. "She said to check with you," he said, still smiling. He had been on the receiving end of that line many times while he and his crew turned the top floor of the old marina building into an upscale French restaurant. It was nice to have someone else on the spot for a change. "We've got to get all this stuff out of here before we can get to work. Do you want me to just order a dumpster and have my guys throw everything out?" he suggested.

"Throw it out?" Marilyn protested. "Aren't all those things worth something?

"I guess they are if somebody wants them," Gorman replied, "but as far as I'm concerned it's just a lot of junk that's in our way. We have to get it out of here."

"Well, we're not going to throw everything away, that's for sure!" Marilyn had seen enough money spent on

Jennifer's big restaurant idea, and millions or no millions, she wasn't about to waste any more of it. If Erlene wanted an inside job, she could start right now. The men could move everything out of the first floor and Erlene could inventory the items. They would sell them, even if they had to sell at fire-sale prices. Somebody needed to inject some common business sense into this operation.

"Where would you like us to put everything?" Tim repeated, still waiting for an answer.

That was the problem. Renting a warehouse would cost a fortune, and trucking all that stuff over to it would add to the expense. They needed a building close by; next door would be ideal.

"Mrs. Townsend?" the foreman was waiting for an answer.

"Where can we get a tent, Tim?"

"Excuse me?"

"A tent. We're going to put one up in the parking lot. Have your crew move everything into it, and then we're going to have the biggest marine equipment sale Bonita has ever seen."

❧ ❧ ❧

Back at the offices of Townsend & Meacham, Les Leslie had told his story in all its detail and had been shown out with the promise that something would be done. The question facing Jack and R.J. was what that 'something' would be.

"Damn it! How could they have done that to him!" R.J. exploded after Les was safely gone. He slammed a nearby book down on the library table in disgust.

"Hey, take it easy," Jack said. "We don't need any more damaged furniture around here."

"How can you sit there so calmly? Doesn't something like this just rip your guts out?"

"Sure it does, if it's true."

"You don't think Les is lying too, do you?"

"Not consciously, Rob. But he might be selectively remembering things. Forty years is a long time to carry around that kind of baggage."

"Not Les. He can't be lying."

"Selectively remembering," Jack repeated. "Do you remember your Latin from prep school?"

R.J. laughed. "Most people don't go to prep school, Jack. We have to deal with things called high schools."

"It took us a whole year to translate Cesar's Commentaries," Jack continued. "I only remember two things: 'Gaul is divided into three parts,' and 'Men easily believe that which they wish to believe.' Knowing about Gaul's parts has never done a damn thing for me, but that second idea . . . the one about people easily believing the things they want to believe . . . I've seen that a work a whole lot of times in his business."

"You think that's what's going on here? It can't be, Jack," R.J. protested. "A guy like Les; he's a total straight-shooter. He'd never do anything like that."

"Maybe not intentionally, but, I don't know . . . A guy is eighteen, nineteen years old, away from home, lonely, has the hots for a girl. I don't know what that guy would do." Jack looked at his younger partner. "But it looks like we're going to have to find out."

"Where do we start?" R.J. asked.

"Damned if I know."

R.J. laughed again. "What do you mean, 'Damned if I know'? You're the senior partner; you're supposed to know everything."

"Yeah, well, let's not let it get out that I don't," Jack replied. "Anyway, let's start with our notes. Sharon can type them up when we're finished. We have the name of the ship and the captain, and Les had some idea of the name of the Intelligence officer."

"Tuesberry or Tudberry," R.J. said, looking at his yellow legal pad.

"One of the guys at the Club was telling me about how he looked up the war record of a relative of his when he was in Washington. He was either at the Navy Department or the Smithsonian."

"My guess would be the Navy Department," R.J. suggested.

"Me too. Why don't you get on the phone with them, Rob. Tell them we're lawyers trying to locate a Navy veteran. See if they have any current information on any of the names we have."

"What if they ask me 'Why'?"

"We're trying to straighten some records out for a client; he's a veteran and he has some money coming from an estate."

"What do you think our chances are of getting this finished in a month?" R.J. asked.

"Are you kidding? We better get ready for a visit from a real, live *contessa*."

❧ ❧ ❧

Henri Dupré sat and stewed in his too-small apartment—that, too, was paid for by his son-in-law. He was caught in a trap of his own making, and he could see no way out of it as he waited for his visitor. Jennifer had not yet learned of his outburst at the television station, and he could not tell her without admitting that he was a fool; he was incompetent and unable to perform a task which she thought was so very simple. He could not speak to Victoria about it; to do so would be to admit to her, too, that he did not have the talent that came so easily to other people—even those who could not pronounce '*soufflé*,' much less create one. There was only one person he might speak to about such things, and even that would not be easy.

A sharp knock at the door called him out of his reverie. This discussion would be difficult, and for a brief moment he thought about pretending he was not home. But that would solve nothing. And besides, Dupré had been the one who called the man who was knocking. He took a deep breath and opened the door. Jim Lacey was standing in the hallway.

"Lacey, *mon ami*, come in. Come into my humble *pensione*," Henri Dupré said grandly.

Jim Lacey looked warily at the man he always suspected would someday elbow him out of the restaurant he had built. "I came over as soon as you called," he said, still standing outside the door. "You sounded pretty upset."

"Please, Lacey, come inside," Henri Dupré insisted. "We must talk. We must get to know one another, oui?"

Jim Lacey walked in with all the trepidation of the fly who enters the spider's living room.

"Do you care of coffee?" Dupré asked. "It is fresh made, and I will add some cognac."

"Thanks, but I can't have the caffeine. Heart problem, you know."

"*Très bien*, then we will drink the cognac without the coffee. It is better that way," Dupré smiled.

"Well, okay, but just one," Lacey agreed.

They sat at the small kitchen table. Dupré downed his drink quickly, steeling himself up for his confession. And while he poured himself a second glass—and downed that one as well—he told Jim Lacey the whole sordid story of Jennifer's grand idea, and the aborted television show; the endless rehearsals that never went right, and how ignorant the people there made him feel, always putting words in his mouth that came out wrong; and mostly how foolish he had been to listen to Jennifer in the first place.

"It sounds like a real mess," Lacey agreed when Dupré finally finished spewing out the story.

"It is a mess *terrible*," Dupré confirmed.

"Well, what do you expect me to do about it?" Lacey asked, pouring himself a second cognac and refilling Henri's glass for a third time.

"You know people, Lacey," Dupré pleaded. They respect you; they listen to you. You are able to do many things. I have seen you do them. And Janifere, too, listens to you. Do something now. Tell them this is all foolishness. Make them from me go away."

"Maybe you should think about this, Henri," Jim Lacey suggested, toying with an idea of his own. "It would be a hell of a way to advertise the place."

"But I cannot do it, Lacey," Dupré protested. "One does not teach new tricks to an old dog."

❧ ❧ ❧

Across the Atlantic, Elena Russo, the *Contessa Falconara*, sat in a sunlit room and busied herself with needlepoint while she recalled the twists and turns in the path that had been her life. Cecil Leslie had not changed, she thought. Even as a young man there had been a certain quiet dignity about him, about the way he kept his own counsel. He was not like the boys of her village who she sometimes overheard bragging about their strength or bravery or prowess with the opposite sex.

Things had been hard for her family during the war. The Germans occupied her town when she was fourteen and ripe as a pomegranate. She saw the way the soldiers looked at her; it frightened and thrilled her at the same time. At first her father forbade her from leaving the house, but then, as time went on, things improved. Her father made friends with those who were in power. He was able to get more food for their family, as well as for other people who came to him for help. He helped those people, and—Sicilian to the core—they devoted themselves to him. After a while even the soldiers greeted her, politely and, it seemed, a little respectfully. It was her first brush with the sort of fame that causes people to be recognized by strangers, and that, too, thrilled her in a way she did not understand.

And then one day American airplanes began flying over the town, carrying huge bombs that would rain death out of the sky, and she often heard a sound like far-off thunder, a sound which she knew was not thunder. The dogs of the town would bark only when the American planes—the ones with the bombs—were coming. At those times she would hide in the basement with her mother and they would listen to the sound like thunder overhead.

Not long after that the Germans began to leave the area. She often saw her parents whispering together when they thought she did not see them. Her father's brow was frequently furrowed, and her mother sometimes cried for no reason, but Elena secretly hoped the Americans would come soon and bring freedom to the people.

And they came. The Americans. Her father, as before, bowed and smiled to the new conquerors. He made himself useful to them as well, while he protected the people who had become fiercely loyal to his family. Before long, things returned to normal. He was once again respected and the people came to him for what favors he could provide. And then she met *Cecile*. She saw him, tall and straight in his uniform, when he followed her to church with her mother and her aunt *Adriana*. She prayed all though Mass that he would speak to her that day, but her prayer went unanswered. It took many more weeks before he approached her, and then her two chaperones chased him away. It was only when she appealed to her father that she got her wish; then *Cecile* would come to their house, and eat with them, and stroll with them in the evenings. As time went on, her father permitted *Cecile* more liberties, and once he even walked with her alone and held her hand. He kissed her that day; it was her first kiss. He told her that he would come for her when the War ended, and they promised that day they would marry each other.

But *Cecile* left without saying a word, and he did not even write to her. Her heart was broken. She thought she would die, and even thought of taking her own life. Her father told her the American was not good enough for her, that her destiny was to become royalty. He told her that she had to be strong, that she must do what had to be done for the sake of the family.

And so, Elena Russo, just short of her eighteenth birthday, found herself married to the Count *Falconara*, a man more than twice her age. She moved into the castle where one of the servant women took her under her wing. Elena was a good wife to the Count. She read many books and watched how the older women behaved, but she heard whispers over the years: whispers about her father. When his name was mentioned, men said things with their eyes and a hand movement that looked like they were curling mustaches. Her husband, the Count, would not discuss such matters with her: they were not the things of women, he assured her. And in the dark of night, when he told her he loved her and would protect her, Elena prayed her rosary and resigned herself to a barren marriage and unanswered questions.

The *Contessa Falconara* put down her needlepoint. She had not thought of these things for a long time. Now she rose from her chair and looked out at the blue-green water of the Mediterranean Sea. It had been fourteen years since the Count died, and ten since her father joined him; she had waited long enough for answers.

"*Dennis!*" she shouted as she swept out of the room and down the marble stairs to the entrance hall.

Maruzza came scurrying out of the kitchen: loyal Maruzza. Her name meant "Little Mary" and although she had grown smaller over the years, her strength never failed when she was protecting her mistress and the Falconara name.

"*Che è successo?*" "What happened?" Maruzza demanded.

The *Contessa* wanted her automobile, and the young man, Dennis, who would drive it for her. She was going to see her father's sister.

"*Vengo io,*" "I'm coming," Maruzza said, taking off her apron.

No, the *Contessa* told her, this was a family matter. She would speak with her aunt alone.

Maruzza was still insisting the *Contessa* could not leave the castle without a proper chaperone when Dennis appeared. "What's up?" he asked, ignoring the Italian diatribe that spewed from Maruzza whenever she saw him.

"You will take me to see my aunt, Adriana Russo," she announced, over Maruzza's continuing protest.

"Sure. Right now?" the young man replied.

"Now. There is a matter of some importance which I must discuss with her," the *Contessa* said as Dennis raced ahead of her to open the door.

In another moment they were in the shiny, back Maserati sedan, heading toward town. The time had come for an explanation.

Marilyn Dupré Townsend had mixed emotions about meeting her mother-in-law for lunch at the Bonita Key Yacht Club. On the one hand, it was nice to get an invitation from Jack's mother, but on the other, she had to admit the society matron from New York intimidated her no matter how pleasant Victoria tried to be. It was silly, of course. After all, Marilyn was a 'Mrs. Townsend' too, but somehow she didn't feel like one whenever Victoria was around. At those times she felt more like she did when the principal, Sister Hubert, came through the Sainte Anne's dormitory on her weekly inspection tours: she just wanted not to be noticed.

"Well, Marilyn, this is lovely, isn't it?" Victoria said after Sam DePasquale welcomed them and personally escorted them to a cozy table for two.

"Yes, it is," the newer Mrs. Townsend replied, wondering what she was doing here and what they could possibly find to discuss over lunch.

"We so seldom get to speak privately. How are you feeling?" Victoria asked.

"Fine, thank you."

"And the baby?"

Marilyn brightened at that. "Oh, everything is fine. The doctor said I might even feel it kick pretty soon."

"You be sure to let me know when that happens, won't you?" Victoria reminded her.

Marilyn assured her she would. The server came to take their drink order, mercifully interrupting the conversation that was going nowhere. Marilyn asked for soda water; the senior Mrs. Townsend ordered Scotch—her usual Blue Label brand that the Club had begun to stock at her request. There was a long pause before the conversation picked up again. Finally, Victoria Townsend said, "Marilyn, you know, I don't have many close friends here . . ."

"Oh, I'm sure everyone at the Club thinks very highly of you," the younger woman interrupted.

"Yes, well, that is not exactly what I had in mind," Victoria said. I'm afraid there is no one I can speak to . . . well, to find out what other people are thinking."

It was a very strange thing to say. Marilyn did not know how to respond, and the confusion must have shown on her face.

"What I mean to say," Victoria continued, "is that I don't have any close friends to tell me if . . . well, if I perhaps inadvertently hurt someone's feelings."

"Oh, I'm sure you'd never to anything like that," Marilyn said quickly.

"We all do things like that, sooner or later," Victoria said, taking a sip of the drink the server placed in front of her. "And when we do, we have to rely on those who are close to us to tell us about it and give us an opportunity to . . . make amends."

"You certainly haven't done anything like that to Jack or me," Marilyn assured her.

Victoria Townsend looked at her daughter-in-law and took another sip of Scotch. "I was speaking of your father, Marilyn."

Marilyn's eyes widened. She hoped they weren't going to discuss anything too . . . personal!

"Henri has become rather . . . distant in the last few days, and I've begun to wonder if it's my fault," Victoria said.

"I . . . I can't imagine anything," Marilyn began, still hoping whatever the problem was it did not relate to the bedroom. "Has there been any change in . . . anything . . . you do?" It seemed 'girl talk' was no respecter of age or social position in this situation. Apparently, she and her mother-in-law were equals in this matter and she tried to inquire into the details—as politely as possible, of course.

"We've had some wonderful evenings here," Victoria responded, either missing the implications of the question or ignoring them. "But lately he's become rather moody." She leaned forward as if she were about to reveal a secret. "I'll tell you frankly, Marilyn, your father is the reason I came to Florida. I hope I haven't done anything to . . . hurt his feelings."

"Why don't I speak with him," Marilyn suggested. "I'll find out what's going on, and I'll give you a full report."

"That's what I was hoping you would say," Victoria Townsend replied. "Now, let's enjoy lunch."

CHAPTER 20

Marilyn cuddled close to her husband in the stateroom of the trawler yacht that bore her name, and, as usual, worried about everything.

As soon as he learned about the baby, Jack had gone out and hired an architect, and even now their new home was being constructed next door to the Calkins family home. Not that that was a problem; it would be nice to have Jennifer nearby, especially with a newborn baby. Marilyn had somehow always known that would happen, but it meant leaving the *Marilyn* all alone in the marina. Marilyn had come to think of the vessel as a part of herself, and she already worried, in a strange way, about the inevitable day when they would have to leave her and return only for occasional visits.

She worried, too, about her father and Victoria Townsend. Victoria said that her father had been acting strangely cold and aloof. That was not like Papa; something must be wrong. It wasn't as though she could begin probing into his life—if, indeed, that was the problem. It was going to be another sleepless night.

"Jack?"

"Hmmm?

"Are you asleep?"

"Not anymore."

"You're going to have to have a talk with my father."

"About what?" Jack yawned. He was beginning to hate these late-night bedroom conversations.

"You're going to have to find out what's bothering him."

"I didn't know anything was bothering him," Jack said, rolling over and hoping to ignore whatever it was Marilyn was talking about.

"Your mother told me he's been acting strange; kind of distant or something. She thinks she may have somehow hurt his feelings and she wants me to find out what's wrong."

"So find out. He's your father."

"I can't talk to Papa about anything like that. It's a male thing. You'll have to do it."

Jack yawned again and pulled the comforter closer to his chin. "Forget it, Marilyn. I'm not about to get involved in my mother's love life. Besides, it's probably for the best."

She pulled away from him and propped herself up on one arm. "How can you say it's for the best?"

Jack yawned. "Well, you know, my mother is all tied up with her society friends, and your father is . . ." he yawned again, ". . . well, he's your father."

"What's that supposed to mean?" Marilyn shot back defensively.

"Well, it's just that they're . . ." Jack opened his eyes and hesitated. He suddenly realized he was up to his knees in conversational hot water, and the water was getting deeper—and hotter.

". . . from two different worlds. Go on, say it," Marilyn demanded, sitting up fully.

Jack was wide awake; as wide awake as if he had awakened in the middle of an unpredicted storm and found his boat dragging her anchor onto a lee shore. He sat up, too, and tried to get the rapidly deteriorating situation under control. "Honey, the fact is, they're from . . . different cultures. I don't think they have all that much in common," he said as he gently stroked her arm.

"Don't you 'Honey' me!" she said as she pulled away and stood up. "You think my father's not good enough for your mother, don't you? He's all right to run off with to New Orleans for a fling, but no one for her to get serious about, right?" she shouted.

"I didn't say that," he replied, his own voice rising a little.

"That's what you meant! Go on, say it!" she demanded, "'They're from two different worlds.'"

"Well, they are from two different worlds," he said with an exasperated tone in his voice. He was standing now, too, and trying to point out that he was only stating the obvious.

"Then we must be from two different worlds too," she demanded.

"Well, aren't we?" It seemed perfectly obvious to him that they were.

"How dare you speak to me like that!" she shouted. "Now! Now when I'm carrying your baby!"

"Wait a minute! How did the baby get involved in this?

"You don't know? You don't know that you just insulted me and your child?"

"What are you talking about, he asked, going around to where she was standing next to her side of the bed. "I only said . . ."

"Don't say it!" she shouted. "Don't say it again!"

"What? That we're from different backgrounds? But it's true. We are."

"That's it! Get out! I'm not sleeping with any man who thinks I'm beneath him."

"Marilyn, what are you talking about?"

"Get out!" she shouted, pushing him away.

"Marilyn, please, don't get upset. It's not good for you right now," he said, trying to calm her.

"You don't care about me; you don't care about our baby."

"I do care," he said as he tried to stroke her hair.

"No, you don't," she insisted, pulling away from him. "Just go away. Leave me alone."

"Marilyn, you're just upset because your hormones are out of balance or something."

She picked up a pillow and hit him with it as hard as she could. "My hormones!" she shouted. "My hormones are fine! Get out of here! Go away! Leave me alone!"

He put his arms around her, more forcefully this time. "I'm not leaving you alone when you're upset like this. Now settle down. I love you very much . . ."

"No you don't," she repeated, trying not-very-hard to push him away. "You think I'm just some poor little match girl who was lucky enough to marry a rich lawyer."

"I didn't know you sold matches in the convent," he said, kissing her forehead. "I thought they just made you pray all the time." He began kissing the side of her face, working his way down below her ear.

"Don't make fun of me. And it was a school, not a convent."

"I always get those confused," he whispered as he kissed her ear. Then he held her at arm's length, looked in her eyes and said, "And you're not a poor match girl; you're a professional woman. You have more degrees than I have, and you're my wife and my friend. And I love you."

"I don't know what's wrong with me," she said quietly as she shook her head. I don't know why I'm so upset. I just worry so much about everything," she sighed, leaning against him, enjoying the warmth of his touch.

"You're just . . . going through some changes, that's all," he said, gently caressing her. "Everything will be all right."

"Will you talk to Papa?"

"I'll talk to Papa. Everything is going to be just fine."

"Do we have any ice cream in the freezer?" she sighed. "I'm starving."

Jennifer and R.J. sat on the porch of the Magnolia Avenue home looking for shooting stars in the springtime sky. It had been months since Grandma Calkins went to her final reward. It was a reward, people said, that was assured because of her many acts of kindness—most of which were just now coming to light. As Jennifer sat on the porch swing with her head on R.J.'s shoulder, she kept thinking about that day prior to Marilyn's wedding when Father Valencia showed her around St. Peter's Church, and told her about her grandfather's anonymous generosity, both to the priest's own parish and to Rabbi Frankel over on the mainland in Bonita. She thought, too, about Jack Townsend's impassioned plea that awful night when Howard Garner tried to convince everyone to sell out and destroy everything her grandparents had worked for. More and more she was seeing her own life and the lives of the people around her as an irresistible continuum, as inexorable as the tides that ebbed and flowed through Calkins Harbor every day. She had control of the Calkins fortune now, but she was just another link in a chain that could bring both love and hatred, happiness and sorrow, to her grandparents' beloved town. It was what Grandma would have called a 'path,' and sure enough, doors kept opening as fast as Jennifer could get to them.

"R.J., there's more to this than a restaurant, you know," she said quietly.

"Excuse me?"

She turned and looked at him, her blue eyes reflecting the light from inside the house. "There's more to this than a restaurant or a boatyard or an old fishing boat. We have a responsibility for these people's lives."

"You can't adopt the whole town, Jen, even if the estate works out to be thirty million dollars."

"No, not like that; of course not," she said soberly. "But we have to put that money to work, making this a better place. And you're right, it has to be the whole town, not just the boatyard."

"Jen, I didn't mean . . ."

"Face it, R.J., Calkins Harbor is a dump."

"Well, it's quaint," he protested.

"Mount Dora is quaint. Calkins Harbor is a dump," she insisted. "But we can make Calkins Harbor into a place like Mount Dora. We could re-do the whole town."

"Jennifer you can't buy the whole town. And besides, you can't save people from themselves. If you really want to change things, you have to lead people and make them want to follow you."

"So how am I supposed to lead these old shellbacks into wanting to do anything with this dump?" she asked sullenly, returning her head to his shoulder.

"You have to be creative. You're already starting out with a charitable foundation. You could expand that idea to give low-interest loans to people who agree to fix up their property. Attach conditions so they're only eligible if they do it according to certain specifications," R.J. suggested. "Start with the area around the marina. You have a restaurant and you're talking about restoring your grandfather's old boat. Maybe we could come up with some kind of attraction to tie everything together. Some kind of event that would encourage people to have pride in their town.

Jennifer was no longer listening; her mind was racing faster than one of the meteors that shot across the late-night sky. She sat up and looked directly at him again.

"Like a boat parade around the entire island," she said.

"Boat parades are pretty common in Florida, Jen."

"Not if they end up in the harbor with a big celebration; not if they have some kind of visiting dignitary; somebody really unique."

"The Governor? We might be able to arrange that."

"No, no. Somebody really unique," she insisted. She leaned back on his shoulder and added, "And that idea of yours about giving people interest-free loans for fixing up their property, that's brilliant."

"Wait a minute. I didn't say interest-free," he protested.

But she wasn't listening again. "We could really get something started here, R.J.," she said. "We could really put this town on the map."

❧ ❧ ❧

At Cap'n Kelly's Marina, Arlo Woodbrace kissed Erlene goodbye and set off for his midnight-to-eight shift at the Solid Waste Authority. It wasn't so bad. He had been on that shift at the S.W.A. so long that he didn't remember what it was like to sleep though the whole night. All of his friends were there, too; the guys who would stop at the Anchor Bar outside of Bonita before heading home after the sun rose. They were a kind of brotherhood, those late-night workers, just like the people at Cap'n Kelly's, and Arlo guessed that if he ever got a day job he would miss them in a peculiar sort of way.

He hadn't gone a dozen steps before he noticed the lights on in Les' boat. She was still perched up there on her keel, high and dry and out of the water, balanced on the two-by-sixes and concrete blocks he helped Les put into place years ago. Les never used to work late, especially not back in the old days when he lived aboard on the sneak. But Junior Calkins was gone now, and Arlo guessed that Les didn't care anymore whether anyone knew he was living up there or not. The boat was lit up brighter than a Christmas tree in the dark lot of the marina and, as Arlo got closer he could hear the sound of a radio coming through one of the open portlights. He had a whole hour to kill before his shift started, and it didn't hurt to be neighborly, so he climbed up the rickety ladder to the rear deck and asked if he could come aboard.

"Huh? Yeah, sure, Arl. Ya' kinda startled me there f'r a minute," Les replied. "Just don't step where I'm workin'." He was on his knees, concentrating, laying down caulk in the seams between the teak boards of the deck.

"What're ya' doin'?" Arlo replied from his perch on the ladder. It wasn't really a question; it was perfectly obvious that Les was laying down caulk: the kind of nasty, tedious job that Les usually avoided. Additional feet anywhere on the deck would not help the situation.

"Got ta' get 'er done, Arl," Les replied, not looking up from his work. "This here job's been goin' on way too long."

"Yeah, well, I mean, what's the rush? You don't usually work on 'er at night."

Les didn't stop what he was doing. He wasn't about to be drawn into a conversation and a Pepsi or a coffee, like in the old days. "Comes a time when ya' got ta' move on with y'r life, Arl. I kinda think that time's about here f'r me."

It was a completely unsatisfactory explanation, but Les didn't look like he wanted to continue the conversation, and he sure as heck wasn't going to encourage Arlo to step aboard. "Yeah, well, I gotta get ta' work," Arlo offered.

"See ya', Arl," Les said, working the caulk gun down another one of the seams.

"See ya'," Arlo replied as he backed this way down the ladder. Things sure were changing around Cap'n Kelly's.

❧ ❧ ❧

Six hours to the east, dawn was creeping relentlessly into the morning sky. The *Contessa Falconara* had slept fitfully, troubled by the weight of sins that already had been assessed against other souls. Her visit to her father's sister opened old wounds, gave new life to old fears that until now had been shuttered in an almost forgotten corner of her girlhood.

It was not so much what Adriana Russo had said, but rather what she did not say when Elena confronted her with suspicions she had nurtured from a lifetime of overheard whispers. "Slut!" her aunt had called her. "*Putana* -- Whore!" No one spoke like that to a *contessa*—not even an aunt; especially not an aunt. It could mean only one thing: that her suspicions were true; that her father was wicked and he was responsible for some great evil that had befallen an innocent man. And, she believed, that innocent man was the American boy she fell in love with so many years ago.

"Your father gave you a life!" her aunt had screamed at her in Italian. "He made you a *contessa*!"

"My father stole my life!" Elena Russo shouted back. "He bartered me into an arranged marriage to feed his own arrogance. Now tell me, what other lives besides mine did he destroy?"

"Slut! Whore!" her aunt had shouted again. "You should get down on your knees and thank my brother . . . and me, too . . . for making you such a life."

Forty years of doubt crystalized into a single moment of recognition and Elena Russo, the *Contessa Falconara*, knew she would never breach the wall of silence in her hometown. She looked at the older woman with the icy stare she had learned from her husband the Count. "Yes, I am a *contessa*," she said coldly. "And a *contessa* kneels only to the King . . . and to God. Now listen to me, Adriana Russo. One way or another, I will learn what I need to know. But from today forward you are no longer my aunt. You are a bitter old woman with terrible sins on your soul; sins for which you will someday pay dearly. And I have only pity for you."

Elena had re-lived every moment of that argument over and over through the lonely night. Now it was morning; too late to try again for the comfort of sleep, but not too late to right a wrong she still did not fully comprehend.

Her mind was made up. She swept into the room where Dennis Woodbrace was sleeping. "*Dennis!* Come on, get up!" she demanded.

"Huh? What's goin' on," the young man was startled into wakefulness and quickly covered himself with the bedclothes.

"Come on, get up," the *contessa* demanded again. You must drive me to church right away, *subito*. And then you will drive me to Palermo.

"Palermo?" Dennis protested. "What are you talkin' about? What time is it?"

"It is almost six o'clock. Now get up. First we will go to Mass, and then we must go to Palermo, to the airport."

"The airport? Where are we going?'

"Never mind where I am going. You are staying here. Now get up."

Later that morning Maruzza muttered a prayer loud enough for her mistress to hear while she packed the *contessa's* black dresses and shawls for this disgraceful act. She prayed the late Count would avert his heavenly eyes from such foolishness; that he would forgive his wife this terrible sin. For a woman, a widow, to travel alone, halfway around the world was disgrace enough, but to go to a place where a man from her past now lived and surely waited for her was beyond all decency. People would talk; the family name would be disgraced forever. Elena, the last of the Falconara's, would stain her sainted husband's name with an indelible blemish.

"*Basta, Maruzza*," the Contessa finally demanded. She was not about to be harassed by a half-mad servant woman whom she only kept on out of charity. The old-world customs that defined everything and everyone around a *contessa* had done nothing for Elena Russo but force her to live a life of enduring loneliness. She was closer to her sixtieth year than her fiftieth, and it was time for customs to be damned! What she was about to do was not illegal or even immoral. If the people of the town were so poor they needed to discuss the details of her life for their amusement, then so be it. She would give them that amusement. But whether they were amused or not, she was going to America . . . alone!

CHAPTER 21

Early that same morning, Jack Townsend was about to keep an appointment to have breakfast with his mother her at her hotel. Regardless of his promise to Marilyn, he was not about to do anything to smooth over Victoria's silly romance with Henri Dupré. They were obviously unsuited for each other, and the sooner his mother saw that and returned home to New York, the better it would be for everyone—especially Jack.

Victoria Townsend was already at a table when Jack entered the hotel's dining room, and the scene gave him a momentary feeling of uneasiness. All the intervening years had been swept away for an instant, and he was again at the family's summer home in Saratoga, with the sun streaming in through the windows and the gardeners manicuring the wide, green lawn outside.

"Good morning, Mother," Jack said, as he kissed her proffered cheek. "Did you sleep well?"

"I slept abominably, thank you," she replied. "Now will you please tell me what this is all about?"

"Why does having breakfast with you have to be about anything?" he smiled.

"John, you couldn't wait to get out of the house and race off to Cornell instead of going to Columbia like your father and grandfather. And after you graduated you ran off to Florida to make your own way instead of settling down to a nice Wall Street practice. I find it hard to believe that you've suddenly developed an abiding interest in my company."

"Now, Mother, let's be fair . . ."

"Out with it, John."

The server interrupted by pouring coffee for Jack and leaving a fresh pot of tea for his mother. After he was gone, Jack crossed his arms on the table and said, "All right, the problem is Henri Dupré."

"Did he send you on this mission, or was it his daughter?"

"Neither, really. Look, Mother, I don't know what's going on between the two of you, and I don't want to know."

"How gallant of you," Victoria interrupted.

"But the fact is, you and Henri are from . . . well, you're from two different worlds."

"Please don't sing it, John. It's much too early."

"What I'm trying to say is, you and Henri have completely different backgrounds, and I think it would be better for both of you if you just cool things with him before someone gets hurt."

"How kind of you to think of me. And your advice about 'cooling things,' does that apply to you and Marilyn as well?"

"Mother, don't change the subject."

"I am not changing the subject. Marilyn is Henri's daughter; she and you are from the same different backgrounds, as you put it. Perhaps you, too, should 'cool things'. But, of course, it's a little late for that, don't you think?"

"Now, Mother don't start. That's an entirely different situation."

"Why? Why is it different?"

Jack leaned back in his chair, exasperated. "Because it obviously is," he said.

"Because in your relationship the male is the wealthy Townsend and the female is the humble French Creole, is that the difference?"

"Mother, this is not personal."

"Is that the difference, John?" Victoria Townsend demanded.

"All right, maybe that is the difference," he conceded. "Maybe it isn't fair, but society accepts certain things about men and not about women."

"What 'things' are those, John?" his mother asked, sipping her tea. "I've never heard it put quite that way."

"Look," Jack said, his voice beginning to rise, "You know perfectly well that a man can support a woman without anybody raising an eyebrow. It doesn't work the other way around. Henri might be a perfectly nice guy to have a drink with or even to run off to New Orleans with for a week or two, but you can't get serious about him. How do you think he'd fit in with your friends back in New York?

"I don't think I'll be going back to New York."

"What?"

"I'm beginning to like Florida, and I've grown very fond of Bonita Key. I think I shall stay right here."

"You can't do that! How about the St. Paul's Guild? And your committee work? You can't just abandon those people!" Jack looked at her intently and added, "And what would The Governor say?"

"I don't know what my grandfather would say, John. You once told me that you moved to Florida because you got tired of trying to figure out what he would say. Well, now it's my turn. I don't know how many years I have left on this planet, but I intend to live them for myself." She picked up her teacup again and looked at her son over the top of it. "I trust that does not shock your sense of propriety, but if it does, then, as the locals say, 'That's tough!'"

"All right, fine!" he said loud enough to turn a few heads in the dining room. Then he lowered his voice and added, "Maybe it's your turn to find out what it's like to be broke, too."

"And what is <u>that</u> supposed to mean?" Victoria Townsend demanded.

"It means that Henri Dupré is a proud man. He's lived life on his own terms for a long time. He's not going to tolerate you picking up the check forever. What are you going to do then? I'll tell you one thing: you can forget about the racing season at Saratoga. And the thousand-dollar-a-plate charity balls? Forget them, too. He comes from a different way of life, Mother. Are you willing to make those changes? Do you know what Madame Dupré used to do? Jack demanded. "She was the waitress in their café. And sometimes the dishwasher, too. Can you see yourself doing that?" Jack glanced at his watch. "I have to get to work," he added. "Work. It's something some of us do on a regular basis."

He stood up to leave. "John, Dear," Victoria Townsend said quietly, "thank you for this little chat. It's been very enlightening."

❧ ❧ ❧

It was not quite noon when the telephone rang in the marina office. Marilyn picked up the receiver and heard the overseas operator ask if she was willing to accept a collect call from Dennis Woodbrace in Palermo, Italy.

"Miss Dupré . . . I mean, Mrs. Townsend? It's Dennis . . . Dennis Woodbrace. Listen, I'm sorry ta' bother ya' an' everythin', but I gotta talk ta' Les Leslie right away," the tinny voice said.

"He isn't here in the office, Dennis," Marilyn shouted although it obviously was not necessary to do so.

"Yeah, well, c'n ya' get 'im or somethin'? It's real important that I talk ta' him right away," Dennis pleaded.

Marilyn fumed at the thought of putting down the receiver while overseas telephone charges continued to mount, but Dennis' voice sounded urgent, and—of course—Les Leslie had no telephone on his drydocked boat. The line would have to remain open while she hurried outside to fetch him.

Les ran for the office as soon as he got word. "Dennis? What's goin' on?" he bellowed after he grabbed the receiver off Marilyn's desk.

"Ya' better get ready, 'cause she's comin' over," the tinny voice said.

"What d'ya' mean? Who's comin' over?"

"Who d'ya' think I mean? Elena. We're in Palermo an' she just got on the plane," the far-off voice responded.

"She can't be gettin' on a plane!" Les bellowed. "She said she'd give me a month!"

"Yeah, well, I guess she changed her mind. *La donna é mobile*, Les."

"What in the name a' St. Elmo is that supposed ta' mean?"

"That's what she said ta' me when I reminded her that she promised ta' wait f'r a month."

"Ya' gotta stop 'er Dennis. I ain't ready yet. I ain't got *Elena's* bottom caulked 'r painted," Les shouted, suddenly shifting to a discussion of the wooden *Elena* sitting on her keel in the dirt while he ticked off the list of projects still undone. "An' 'er cabin, well, I just ain't ready f'r visitors yet, especially not Elena," he added, shifting back to the human Elena.

"Well, there's no stoppin' 'er, 'cause the plane just took off," Dennis replied.

"Why didn't ya' call me before? Maybe I could a' talked her out of this!" Les demanded bitterly.

"Call ya' before? She wouldn't let me out of 'er sight. First chancet I got was when she got on the plane. Anyways, she's goin' through Rome and then Miami. She won't get ta' Bonita 'ill late ta'night, y'r time."

"Ta'night! How in blue blazes am I supposed ta' get 'er ready by ta'night?" Les demanded, referring again to the *Elena* that was already at the marina.

"I don't know, Les. But ya' better figure out somethin' 'cause she's on 'er way," Dennis said before he hung up.

Les' face was ashen as he put the phone down on Marilyn's desk and sat in a nearby chair. He was supposed to have another few weeks; now she would be arriving in less than twelve hours.

"Is something wrong, Les? Marilyn inquired.

"She's comin' ta'night," he said, gasping like he had just run a marathon.

"Who's coming?" Marilyn asked, hoping it was not who it appeared to be.

"Elena." He was breathing hard and looking around in a panic like either he needed a place to hide or expected to see her standing right there in the room.

"The Countess? She's coming here? To the boatyard?"

"Be here ta'night." He looked at Marilyn. "What am I gonna do?"

"I'll call my mother-in-law," Marilyn suggested. "If anyone on this island knows how to entertain royalty, she's the one."

Sibby Maggio, dressed in jeans and an oily tee-shirt, was drenched with sweat as he knelt down in the heat of the Margaret's engine room and told himself for the hundredth time that he should not have gotten involved in this project. He wasn't even sure how he had been sucked in, except that everyone around the marina was starting to pitch in with things that needed to be done, and one day without thinking too much about it, he mentioned to Commodore Jack Townsend that he once owned a garage up North and had worked on engines since high school. And when Jack asked him if he knew anything about Packard engines, Sibby bragged—in front of Jim Lacey—that he could take one apart with his eyes closed.

So there he was, in the sweaty, steamy bowels of an ancient boat, taking apart an engine and handing the parts to Jim, who—after all, since he wouldn't have a restaurant to manage until Jennifer decided the building was finished—had appointed himself Sibby's helper.

Sibby took of the head-bolts of the port side engine, and with Jim's help slid aside the heavy cast iron head that normally covered the cylinders. He took the extension light Jim offered and began looking into each exposed cylinder, exposing the tops of the pistons.

"No reason why these shouldn't move," he mumbled as he knelt next to the engine. "No rust; they don't look froze up."

"So why didn't the shaft turn when you tried it?" Jim asked.

"Don't know yet," Sibby retorted as he opened his old standby—a can of Marvel Mystery Oil—and began pouring it into the cylinders. "But if we keep takin' pieces off, we'll find out pretty quick."

"Are you going to be able to put it back together if we do? Jim asked.

Sibby looked up and wiped his dripping brow with the back of his hand, smearing a streak of oil across his forehead in the process. He glared his response. The question didn't deserve an answer. These guys at the marina were all alike; figured he didn't know how to use his hands just because he had decided to live off his wits. At the moment he was working on his latest get-rich-quick scheme of finding sunken treasure out in the Gulf of Mexico. All he needed to do was find the right partners and bring them together in the right deal where they would put up the money. "Listen," he said to Jim Lacey, "I said I could take one of these apart with my eyes closed, and I meant it."

"I'm sure you can," Lacey teased. "I was just asking if you could put one together again with your eyes open."

Sibby might have said something, might have even told the smartass to get the hell out of there and he would get the old Packard running without anyone's help, but before he could speak, a familiar voice called down the engine room hatch.

"*Mes amis*, you are down there, no?"

"We are down here, yes, Henri," Jim Lacey responded as Dupré began to make his way down the ladder.

Christ, it was just was they needed: another body taking up space in a room that was crowded with a workbench, batteries and two Straight Eights. And Dupré knew less about engines than Lacey did; he'd probably want to start cooking down there.

"Lacey, you have taken care of our small difficulty, *oui*?" Dupré asked as he squeezed in next to Jim to get a better view over Sibby's shoulder. All they needed now was to have Arlo Woodbrace drop by, Sibby thought; they could deal up a little poker right here in the engine room.

"Look, fellas, it's getting' a little tight in here . . ." Sibby began.

"Not yet, Henri," Lacey said quickly, ignoring Sibby's suggestion. "I've been helping Sibby. Why don't you give us a hand?"

"I know nothing of such things," Dupré protested. At least he got that right, Sibby thought.

"Sibby will show us what to do," Jim Lacey assured him.

Sibby wanted to tell them to get the hell out of the way, but the two guys were really trying to help, and, well, they were doing their best. No use hurting their feelings.

"All right, this is an old shade-tree mechanic trick I got from my Dad," Sibby explained. "Let's put a pipe wrench on the driveshaft. You guys try to turn it, real easy. I'll tap on the pistons with a block of wood and a hammer, while my old buddy Mystery Oil works its way down. Maybe we can get her to move."

The two men squeezed themselves over to the end of the engine where Jim Lacey fixed a pipe wrench into place on the shaft. "Now take it easy," Sibby instructed. "We don't want nobody gettin' hurt, and we don't want nothin' to break, either." They looked at him and nodded and Sibby nodded in return.

The mechanics-in-training grunted against the wrench, and a few moments later, with Sibby gently but firmly banging on the pistons the driveshaft began to move, inch by inch. Sibby called a halt and the men relaxed to catch their breath.

"Well, Henri," Jim Lacey observed, laughing, and wiping sweat off his glasses with his shirt. "It seems that old dogs can learn new tricks after all!"

On the other side of the marina, Les Leslie joined by his old pal Arlo Woodbrace, was driven into a flurry of activity by the anticipated arrival of Countess Elena. He was picking up the paint cans, scraps of wood and assorted litter that had accumulated around the not-yet-waterborne *Elena* over the past years. The boat wasn't ready, of course, and no amount of picking-up was going to make her ready, but Les had to do something, and at the moment 'something' meant getting the place picked up. At least Elena wouldn't see her namesake surround by the boatyard detritus that gravitates to a drydocked boat as surely as stardust is drawn into a black hole.

"She shouldn't be doin' this ta' me, Arl," Les said as he tossed an empty varnish can into a nearby barrel and heard it disappear with a satisfying 'Clang!'

"Yeah, well, I don't think ya' c'n get 'er finished before she gets here," Arlo replied, trying to balance an armload of wood scraps as he headed toward a pile near his own boat. An' Erlene ain't gonna like me takin' this stuff home."

"It's only temporary, Arl," Les protested. "We'll get a dumpster in here ta'marra' an' have it all hauled away."

"So why're we doin' this?" Arlo protested again. "She ain't gonna be gettin' here until late ta'night, an' she ain't gonna have time ta' come down here an' see this stuff."

Les stopped his frenetic movement for a minute and looked exasperatedly at his companion. "I told ya', I don't want her knowin' that I've been livin' in a drydocked boat!"

Arlo pointed at *Elena*, sitting high and dry on her keel. "Les," he said, "that boat ain't gonna make it inta' the water by ta'marra' mornin'."

"I know she ain't gonna make it inta' the water by ta'marra' mornin'," Les exploded. "But leastways I want ta' make the place look presentable. Maybe she'll think *Elena's* only been out a' the water for a couple a' weeks."

"A couple a' weeks? Les, have ya' taken a good look at 'er? Not even a landlubber'd believe that! She ain't been caulked; her hull ain't been painted . . ."

"I know what ain't been done! Now just keep pickin' up out here while I go aboard 'n' start on the inside. We got ta' get 'er lookin' like somethin' before Elena gets here!"

❧ ❧ ❧

Victoria Townsend was an island of calm in the freshening gale of activity in and around Cap'n Kelly's that was being caused by the anticipated arrival of an Italian countess. "Dear, it's just a title," she assured Marilyn when she arrived at her daughter-in-law's office in response to a desperate plea for help. "Besides, the Italian government doesn't recognize its royalty anymore."

"But she lives in a castle!" Marilyn protested.

"Yes, well, I would be much more impressed if I knew the castle had indoor plumbing and central heat. On the whole, I've found castles to be rather drafty, nasty places; quite good for the tourist trade, but rather lacking in creature comforts.

"Well what are we going to do with her? How are we going to keep her busy?"

"Marilyn, entertaining royalty is just like entertaining anyone else: you feed them little sandwiches with the crusts cut off and introduce them to people whom they'll never see again."

"Do you think we could get the Governor to come down for Tallahassee?"

Before Victoria could answer, the door opened and Jack walked in, on his way home from working on a case that was more related to the royal visit than anyone knew at that moment. He looked at Marilyn, and then at his mother. The office at Cap'n Kelly's was not a place that she ordinarily visited. Marilyn blurted out the news.

"The Countess is coming!"

"Excuse me?"

"Elena, the *Contessa Falconara*," Victoria Townsend explained. "She's arriving tonight. We'll have to meet her at the airport with a welcoming committee."

"You can welcome her after you see me off. Rob and I are flying to Washington tonight," Jack responded.

"Washington? Jack, you can't go; not tonight!" Marilyn protested.

"I have to. It's important," he replied.

"Can't R.J. handle whatever it is on his own?" Marilyn asked.

"May I remind you, Commodore, that you are what amounts to the Head of State for this community, and you have certain responsibilities?" his mother added icily. "And I think Mr. Leslie will need a lot more moral support than Arlo Woodbrace can supply."

"Well, we're only going up there to get some information," Jack said. "I suppose Rob could do it without me, if both of you think it's so important.

"One never knows what visiting royalty might expect," Victoria observed. "I've reserved a very nice suite for her at my hotel, but she is still entitled to some sort of official welcome."

Jack picked up the telephone and began calling Jennifer's house. It was where he would most likely find his young partner. Rob would have to fly up to Washington alone.

CHAPTER 22

Les Leslie didn't care much for the fact that what looked like most of Cap'n Kelly's was with him at the Bonita airport waiting for the last flight to arrive from Miami. The problem was, that phone call from Dennis was kind of like shooting a flare gun into a bucket of gasoline: in no time flat the whole marina was ablaze with the news that Les' old girlfriend—the woman fate had made into a countess—was on her way to their shore. And everybody couldn't wait to get a gander at her.

Les didn't mind Commodore Townsend and his Missus so much; in fact, it was kind of nice having them there to hold him up, if you could understand that. And Jennifer Calkins, she was okay, too. She and the Commodore and Marilyn had been at the airport seeing off R.J. who had gone to Washington to work on Les' problem. But there was a whole fleet of other folks at the airport that night, starting with Arlo Woodbrace who had stayed home from his job; and Erlene Rodgers, dressed in her Sunday best; and the Commodore's mother and Frenchy Dupré; and even Sibby Maggio who was becoming a lot more neighborly than he used to be; and Jim Lacey and Eddie Miles, who was standing there holding a fresh-baked pie. Well, the pie was a nice thought, Les had to admit. But there was just too darn much hullabaloo about Elena coming to town. For a guy like Les, who had spent his whole life keeping quiet about his business, it was a lot more attention than he could handle.

Les retreated to the airport coffee shop with Commodore Jack Townsend while the others cooled their heels in the waiting area. "Don't mind tellin' ya' I'd just 's soon be here alone," Les muttered to Jack as the girl behind the counter poured their coffee.

"We'll be happy to leave, Les," Jack offered. "We certainly wouldn't want to do anything to embarrass you."

"Oh, no; it's nothin' like that, Commodore," Les apologized. "Nothin' against you and the Missus, an' Miss Jennifer, too. It's all the rest a' them. I just wanted ta' kind a' keep this whole thing quiet, 's all."

"That's not an easy thing to do when you're living at a place like Cap'n Kelly's," Jack reminded him.

"Yeah, well, see, the thing is," Les continued, blowing on his coffee and taking a sip, "where I'm livin' 's kinda the problem. Elena . . . well, she's a . . . ya' know, she lives in that castle. What's she gonna think when she finds out my digs is a drydocked boat?"

"If she cares about you Les, it shouldn't matter where you live. Should it?"

Les looked at Jack carefully and said, "Maybe that was okay f'r you, Commodore, but see, a guy like me, well, I ain't got too much ta' show f'r my life."

"You better take a look around, Les," Jack replied. "Margaret Calkins used to say that in the end, people are all that really matters. You have an airport full of friends—that's what you have to show for your life. These people didn't come all the way out to the airport at midnight just out of curiosity."

"Wouldn't be too sure a' that," Les muttered. "An' I wonder what they'll think if things don't work out with Mr. R.J. goin' ta' Washington."

"They'll think what they always thought: that you're a darn nice guy." Jack put his hand on the older man's shoulder. "And Les," he added, "things will work out. They always do. Sometimes they don't work out the way we plan, but they always work out."

"Even if you an' Mr. R.J. find them records, 'r if ya' find the guys, ya' don't think they're gonna tell the truth now, do ya'?"

"I don't know what we're going to find, or where we're going to find it, but I do know things will be a lot easier if we can confirm your story. Now why don't we go sit in the waiting area with the rest of the folks? Elena will be here any minute."

It was almost the end of the tourist season, and the airport waiting room was deserted by South Florida standards. People who were in the Sunshine State to escape winter had been settled in for months; the few lonely souls who arrived late at night in early April almost always did so for reasons other than fun and sun. The marina residents who made up the self-appointed welcoming committee were scattered in groups of two and three around the nearly empty room. Les made a beeline for Arlo Woodbrace who, although he could be a pain in the neck sometimes, at least provided the kind of homey security that Les needed at the moment. Jack paid for the coffee and got some hot chocolate to take to Marilyn.

"Is anything wrong?" she asked quietly as he handed her the cup.

"Les needed a little shot of self-confidence," Jack replied. "He was having an attack of 'I'm-not-good-enough-for-her.'"

"There seems to be a lot of that going around," Marilyn said. She nodded in the direction of her father who, instead of sitting with Jack's mother, had formed an unlikely alliance with Sibby Maggio and Jim Lacey.

"All's not well on the road to love," Jack observed.

Marilyn looked up at him with her dark, knowing eyes. "You know, I've been thinking a lot about Grandma," she said softly. She smiled and repeated Margaret Calkins' words of long ago, "Everything happens for the best."

Jack turned away, afraid she would see the guilty look on his face for trying to derail the love affair of his mother and Marilyn's father. If things really were meant to 'work out.' And, he wondered, if things really did 'happen for the best,' was his interference helping or hindering that goal.

On the other side of the room, Sibby Maggio was expounding on the state of the *Margaret's* engines while his companions gave him their full attention.

"A couple of days and those shafts'll be turnin' like I dipped 'em in butter," he bragged. "Then once we get the heads back on, and get her new batteries installed, we'll fire her up."

"Isn't that taking a pretty big chance?" Jim Lacey asked. "Those engines haven't been started in years. What if one of them blows up or something?"

Sibby shrugged shoulders. He had one hand in his pocket and flipped the other one out in front of him with an extended thumb and forefinger. "How else you gonna do it?" he asked. "Unless you think we're gonna move that boat by turning the shafts by hand. Sooner or later, we're gonna have to put fuel in her tanks and hit that starter switch."

"I don't know," Lacey countered. "That first spark . . ."

"Ah, g'wan," Sibby guffawed. "I'll tell you what," he said, thumping Jim's chest, "when we get ready, you guys go up on deck wearin' life preservers, and I'll stay down in the engine room alone, how's that? Only I want somebody to take a pitcher of you guys so I can show it to my wife."

"Your wife?" Lacey asked. "When did you start talking to her again?"

Sibby suddenly looked a little sheepish. "Well, you know, the other night I took her some money, and I was tellin' her about what's goin' on at the place, and I said I was helpin' out a little bit. No big deal." He shoved his hand back into his pocket and turned toward the dark windows overlooking the runway. "When's that plane gettin' here, anyway?" he muttered to the glass.

In another corner, Victoria Townsend tried to appear interested as Erlene Rodgers and Eddie Miles discussed the items they would stock in their still-to-be-constructed gift shop. It was not the kind of conversation that was likely to hold her attention. Most of their problems were imagined, she thought, revolving as they did around what kind of cheap trinkets they would pass off on hapless visitors.

"Everytime I go anywheres, I always get me somethin' with the name a' the place on it," Erlene said. "It'd be kinda nice ta' have things that say "Cap'n Kelly's Marina 'r somethin' like that."

"And a gift shop would give the people of the town a place to sell their crafts," Eddie Miles suggested. "We could even sponsor an arts and crafts fair of some kind."

Like Sibby Maggio, Victoria Townsend turned her attention to the darkness outside the window. Arts and crafts fairs were not her idea of social adventure. Even a deserted runway was more interesting than such twaddle. What a shame that Calkins Harbor—that the whole island of Bonita Key—didn't have a real social event like the racing season at Saratoga with its parties and balls. They had done so many good things for the community. And talk of work! The planning, the coordinating, deciding on worthwhile charities;

Victoria Townsend knew that kind of work very well. It was the kind of work that could transform a community–and she had done it all her life. An event like that would be a worthwhile outlet for her energy as well as her talent. And it always began same way: with someone's dream.

Jennifer sat alone nearby, paging through one of her ever-present bridal magazines, and Victoria struck up a conversation.

"You know, Jennifer, it's a shame Calkins Harbor doesn't have some kind of focal point for a social season," she began.

"I'm sorry?" Jennifer wasn't paying attention at the moment; her head was filled with bridal gowns and reception parties.

"Some sort of gala event. Saratoga has its racing season; New Orleans has its Mardi Gras. Even up in Tampa they have that pirate thing. What do they call it? Gasparilla Festival? It's too bad Calkins Harbor doesn't do something like that."

Jennifer has flipped through her magazine to photographs of a European wedding where the bride and groom arrived in a horse and carriage and the guests dined outdoors on the lawn of an ancient estate. Her hand suddenly stopped turning the pages. She sat very still for a few seconds, and then looked at Victoria Townsend with an intense expression. "Mrs. Townsend, what did you say?"

"I only observed that most tourist destinations have a social season with a special event, much like Mardi Gras or the races at Saratoga."

"And we need something like that here in Calkins Harbor," Jennifer added.

"It's a shame something like that doesn't exist here," Victoria Townsend confirmed.

Jennifer took her hand and said, "Come with me, Mrs. Townsend," she said, taking her to where Jack and Marilyn were waiting. "That's a great idea!"

"Marilyn, your mother-in-law has a terrific idea," Jennifer gushed.

"Please, Jen, not another idea. I don't have the time or energy for any more ideas."

"No, listen. You'll love this. It's perfect. In fact, it's the kind of thing you've always wanted."

"Jennifer, whatever do you mean?" Victoria demanded. "What perfect idea do I have?"

"Marilyn, do you remember telling me about Mardi Gras in New Orleans," Jennifer continued excitedly. "How it all started because some Russian count came to visit? That's why the colors are green and gold and purple, because they were the colors of his royal house, right?"

Marilyn nodded. "The Grand Duke Alexis, but that story about the colors is just a legend; I have no idea if it's true."

Jennifer's blue eyes widened. "Well, we're being visited by an Italian countess, aren't we?"

"Oh, that's silly," Marilyn protested. "It's not the same thing at all."

"It isn't? I'm getting married, aren't I? And a *contessa's* coming to visit?"

"Jennifer! Are you suggesting we turn your wedding into some kind of street festival?" Marilyn demanded.

"What would Grandma and Grandpa do if they were here?" Jennifer demanded. "They'd want me to have a big wedding so they could invite all their friends. Well, guess what? It turns out their friends are just about everybody in town! And half of Bonita, too! So, we'll invite everybody!" she said grandly. As she talked Jennifer's face took on the same excited, wonderful expression she had long ago, when she first told her grandmother her idea about creating a restaurant on the second floor of the marina building; it was the same expression she wore at the church the morning of Marilyn's wedding when she announced she wanted to call the place 'Dupré's.' It was a sure sign that opposition was useless.

"The whole town?" Marilyn protested. "Where would we put them?"

"You already solved that problem with that wonderful tent in the parking lot!"

"Jennifer! You can't get married in a tent! I won't allow it!" Marilyn said, suddenly treating the younger woman as some kind of wayward child.

"Why not?" Jennifer demanded. Her eyes suddenly lit up even more and she gasped. "And, oh my God! I just thought of something else! That tent is red and white, isn't it? What are the colors of the Italian flag?

"Red, white and green," Victoria Townsend interjected, warming to the idea.

"So, we'll decorate it with green banners, and we'll decorate the tables in red, white and green. And the bridesmaids will wear green dresses with white sashes of some kind—and carry bouquets of red carnations. The colors of our visitor's royal house, just like Mardi Gras. Marilyn, is Grandma trying to tell us something or what?" Jennifer demanded.

"Jennifer, get ahold of yourself. Settle down," Marilyn said. "The tent is red and white because that's the one the company happened to deliver, and now it's filled up with the junk Tim Gorman's crew took out of the first floor . . ."

"I've attended many perfectly proper garden weddings in tents," Victoria Townsend interjected. "And red, white and green are lovely colors." Jennifer had hit on just the kind of social event Victoria had in mind.

"See? It's great, Marilyn. This is a harbor, so R.J. and I can't drive up in a carriage like that couple in the magazine. We'll arrive aboard the *Margaret.* We'll start our own tradition, a big social event right here in Calkins Harbor! And then we'll celebrate it every year with a boat parade and a festival where we'll decorate everything in red, white and green. This is the best, absolutely the best idea I've ever had! Ever!"

"Jennifer, do you have any idea of how many people you're talking . . ."

"And wouldn't Grandpa be impressed? You know, he used to call me his Princess. This would really be a tribute to him, wouldn't it?" Jennifer blushed and added, "I mean, you know, Grandpa was kind of like the king around here and . . . well, the town is named after him and everything."

Marilyn smiled. "All right, settle down, Your Highness. Let's think about this."

"Then we'll at least think about it?"

"Jennifer, whenever you start thinking about things, we start spending lots of money," Marilyn reminded her.

"It's for the good of the town, Marilyn. It's really for the town."

"She's right about that, Dear," Victoria said. "Something like this could be the shot in the arm this town needs." She turned to Jennifer and added, "Jennifer, I think you have a perfectly marvelous idea."

"You do? You can't be serious!" Marilyn protested. Her mother-in-law did not seem to be the kind of person who went in for street festivals and tents.

"It would certainly attract visitors, and that would be good for your restaurant."

"See? I told you, Marilyn," Jennifer added. "It will be good for business, and we'll make oodles of money. Does that satisfy you? Come on, Marilyn; please say 'yes'."

"Surely the two of you can't be serious about this!" Marilyn protested.

'You know, Honey, it's not such a crazy idea," Jack interjected thoughtfully. "We do have a visiting dignitary of sorts, and Jennifer's wedding is coming up in a few months. Some pretty big traditions have been built on far fewer facts."

"I think all of you have gone mad," Marilyn insisted. "It's completely impractical."

"Of course it is, Dear," Victoria replied. "That's what makes it such a wonderful idea."

The announcement of an arriving flight cut off further conversation. Everyone's attention turned to the window and in a minute or two a gleaming jet lumbered out of the darkness; the lights of the terminal reflecting off its silver skin as it nosed toward the building. A member of the ground crew raised two lighted wands over his head; the engines died and two men pushed a stairway up to the door. In the waiting area, Les Leslie licked the tips of his fingers and slicked the sides of his hair while Arlo Woodbrace helped him straighten the lapels of his sport coat. Marilyn self-consciously brushed off her dress; Eddie Miles poked at the wax paper covering his pie. Even Sibby Maggio made sure his shirt was properly tucked in.

The aircraft door opened and passengers began making their way down the ramp. First came two tired-looking businessmen, their outfits wearily rumpled; they were probably returning from a long day of putting together another South Florida development deal on the State's east coast. Next came a youngish couple, dressed in comfortable sport clothes and carrying tennis rackets; they might be coming to Bonita to visit family or friends, temporarily escaping from the growing congestion of Miami. Finally, a small woman appeared. Her still-youthful face contrasted sharply with her clothing. She was dressed completely in black; a matching black shawl covered her formally-coifed hair that looked unabashedly gray. Her outfit blended into the darkness beyond the mirrored skin of the airplane; it was impossible to make out any other details of her appearance even in the bright light that washed down from atop the terminal building.

"That's her! That's Elena! Les Leslie shouted to no one in particular.

Jennifer's jaw dropped. "That's our countess?" she whispered to Marilyn.

CHAPTER 23

Arlo Woodbrace had been right about one thing: it would be many hours before Countess Elena got around to visiting her namesake at the marina. By the time the welcomes were said, the pie presented and the luggage collected, it was well after one o'clock in the morning and everyone, especially the *Contessa,* could only think of getting a good night's rest.

Victoria Townsend took command of the situation and whisked Elena off in her rented Lincoln to the suite she had reserved for her. They breakfasted much later that morning in the hotel dining room where the *Contessa* turned a number of heads in her black-on-black outfit.

"I am surprised by the heat of the day. It is not yet noon, and already it is hot," she said as she sat across from Victoria who was wearing a *hauté couture* summer dress set off by her jewelry. They had a table looking out over the Gulf of Mexico, and the sun shone brightly off the shimmering sand where some barely-clad young people were hard at work playing volleyball.

"Welcome to Florida, *Contessa,*" Victoria responded. "You'll find a great many things are different here.

The Countess looked around the room at the other guests who quickly averted their eyes when she caught sight of them staring at her. "Do they always wear such extravagant colors? And white shoes?

"People come here to escape convention, *Contessa*," Victoria Townsend explained, sipping her tea.

"In my country we cannot . . . how did you put it? . . . escape from convention. There, always, we think first of what other people will say."

"There are places in my country where that is true as well," Victoria replied, "and I'm afraid I used to be one of the people who did a lot of the 'saying.'" She paused for a moment, smiled a little wistfully and added, "But I'm beginning to learn that life is happier if one lives it with an open heart." She patted Elena's hand across the table. "Besides, there isn't much one can say when we're all doing the same thing."

Countess Elena looked around the dining room again. At one of the tables a man in a green polo shirt and yellow pants was laughing with a tanned, bejeweled woman who was dressed in white tennis shorts and a print blouse. "I must confess my dress makes me feel a little . . . out of place," she said quietly.

"Tell me, *Contessa*, have you ever thought of wearing anything a little less . . . formal?" Victoria inquired.

Elena smiled. "I am afraid in my country, life is very strict. My position does not allow me to be less . . . formal," she sighed.

"Perhaps not in your country, but this is America, my dear," Victoria said with a conspiratorial smile. "And it is Florida to boot. There are some wonderful shops in Bonita. I believe their frocks will be more in keeping with the ambiance of Captain Kelly's than the duds you and I are accustomed to wearing."

Elena laughed. "'Duds.' That sounds like something Cecilé would say. His words have so much color, sometimes I do not know what he is saying."

"'Scraps of dream and duds of daring,' a great poet once wrote in his ode to life's renewal," Victoria reminisced, thinking of a favorite poem that meant more to her now than it ever had in the past. "The courtiers of Bonita will make us both feel a lot less out of place around here. What do you say we go shopping after breakfast? And speaking of color, *Contessa*," she added, emphasizing Elena's title, "it seems you have the only gray head in this room. It's time for both of us to make some changes."

Elena looked around the room again and took a deep breath of the heady air of freedom. A sly smile crept over her face, and she wagged a finger between herself and her conspiring breakfast companion. "Mrs. Townsend, I think you are about to make me do something the people in my town will say is very wicked."

Victoria Townsend picked up her teacup, winked her eye in reply and said, "My friends call me 'Vicki', Elena."

❧ ❧ ❧

Robert J. Meacham, Attorney at Law, woke up that morning alone for the first time in several weeks. He was in a hotel room in a gray and drizzly Washington, D.C., without the comforting warmth of his fiancée at his side or the support of his partner waiting at their office. There was nothing for him to do but grab a quick breakfast, make his way out onto the wet sidewalk and catch a cab to the Department of the Navy.

Law school hadn't prepared him for this, he thought, as the garish yellow vehicles sped by, already full of early-morning occupants hurrying to do—or possibly undo—the business of government. He waved a folded-up newspaper, and told himself that lawyers were supposed to be people who played starring rules in courtrooms; people who wielded power behind the scenes of mega-million-dollar deals. No one told him about standing out in the rain and getting splashed by cabs, or warned him about dreary hours spent sifting among old records, helping a powerless client thread his way through an uncaring and unforgiving bureaucracy. And yet, Jack had assured him, that was what most of the law was: hard, frustrating work with occasional bright spots thrown in—the times when everything worked out right.

It was raining harder, and his shoes were already soaked by the time a battered yellow and red vehicle pulled up next to him. He jumped in quickly, grateful for any shelter, and tried to ignore the smoke coming from the cabby's dangling cigarette.

He checked R.J. out in the rear-view mirror, and squinted one eye as the smoke wafted past it. "Where ya' goin'?" the man said without removing the butt that appeared to be glued to his lower lip.

"Navy Department," R.J. responded, trying to sound confident and businesslike as the cab pulled away from the curb. He hoped the ride would be a short one.

"Which one?"

R.J. hesitated. "United States Navy," he replied, wondering if there were other naval offices in our nation's capital.

"C'mon, pal, it's too early for this. Which Navy Department are you lookin' for? Human Resources? International Programs? Hazmat? Which one?" the driver demanded as he began to weave his way through the morning traffic.

"You mean there's more than one Navy Department building?"

The wipers beat out a steady rhythm on the rain-splattered windshield and the driver looked at him in the rear-view mirror without bothering to slow down. "Mister, there's prob'ly a dozen Navy Department buildings in Washington. You must have some idea of where you're going."

"No, I guess I don't," R.J. admitted. "I'm trying to track down a Navy veteran."

"You sure you don't want the Veterans Administration?" the driver suggested.

R.J. hadn't thought of that, but he was not about to admit it to the cabdriver. Still, the man seemed to know his way around Washington, in more than just a geographic sense. And whatever he knew, it was obviously a lot more than R.J. knew.

"I'm trying to get some information on someone who retired from the Navy thirty or forty years ago. Where do you suggest I start?"

"I'd start with the V.A.," the driver offered, "but I don't think they'll give you much information."

"That would be a shame," R.J., replied, testing out the cover story Jack had suggested. "I'm trying to settle an estate, and this guy's got quite a bit of money coming."

"In that case they'll probably be glad to help you out," the cabby agreed. "Let me take you to the V.A.; you can start there. You got lots of time, right?"

"Yeah, right: lots of time," R.J. responded helplessly.

❧ ❧ ❧

Back in sunny Florida, Jennifer Calkins was sitting across from Marilyn Dupré Townsend who was attempting to reconcile the marina's financial statement.

"I've been thinking about our festival," she began.

"What festival is that?" Marilyn said without looking up.

"You know, my wedding festival. We talked about it last night. You thought it was a great idea."

That got Marilyn's attention. "Jennifer, if you're referring to your Mardi-Gras-in-Calkins-Harbor idea, I remember saying it was completely impractical."

"Oh, that's what you're supposed to say," Jennifer complained. "You're the practical one; that's why Grandma picked you. But I could tell you really liked it. I know you, Marilyn. And besides your mother-in-law and Jack both think it's a fabulous idea."

Marilyn returned to her books. "Jennifer, it's totally impractical."

"Anyway, I've been thinking," the young blonde continued, not missing a beat, "R.J. and I can't both arrive on the *Margaret*, because he's not supposed to see me until the wedding, right? So he'll have to be on the island already, waiting for his princess." She thought for a moment and settled the issue with herself. "The 'Bride coming to the Island' is a much better way to start the tradition. It's so romantic, isn't it?"

Marilyn looked up again. "What are you talking about, the 'bride coming to the island'?"

Aboard the *Margaret*. In the boat parade. Didn't you hear anything I said last night?"

"I don't recall anything about you being in a parade," Marilyn countered, wondering if she really had missed something or if she was just witnessing another case of Jennifer's brain being in idea-overdrive.

"Marilyn, we agreed we would do it like Mardi Gras. Remember? Didn't you once tell me the queen arrives by boat early in the day?"

"Jen, Mardi Gras has been going on for hundreds of years. You're not about to create an instant tourist attraction in Calkins Harbor."

"No, of course not," Jennifer agreed. "That's why we have to get the story straight now, and plan on doing this every year, for at least the next twenty years or so . . . you know, until it takes on a life of its own. We'll have to figure out a way of picking out a new Princess every year, too. It's going to be a lot of work, Marilyn, but we can handle it."

There it was again: Jennifer's famous 'we.' It was the same 'we' that had made Marilyn a part of the Calkins family; the same 'we' that made her a partner in the restaurant. Marilyn had to smile in spite of herself. "You're not going to give up on this, are you?"

"Give up? Give up on what?" Jennifer asked, wide-eyed, as if that were the most ludicrous suggestion in the world.

"Then I guess we'd better get started," Marilyn sighed, closing her ledger. "What are 'we' going to call this festival?"

"I don't know, but I'll come up with something. It has to be something very catchy, but it has to be romantic. I'll have to think about that."

The conversation was interrupted by Les Leslie who entered the marina office for what seemed the fifth time that day. Marilyn already knew what he wanted. "She hasn't called, and I don't know where she is," she said before Les could ask the question.

"Yeah, I hate ta' be a pain," Les apologized, "but, see, it's not like Elena ta' take off like this."

"Les, the clerk at the hotel told me she and my mother-in-law left around noon to go shopping. I'm sure everything is just fine."

"But, see, she don't need ta' go shoppin'," Les protested. "She's already got everythin' she needs . . ."

"Les, a woman never has everything she needs," Jennifer said. "Especially when she has a shopping companion."

"Yeah, but, see, she's a wida', an' over there . . ."

He was interrupted by the arrival of a white Lincoln carrying two women who got out laughing and barged into the office with armloads of shopping bags. One of the ladies was Victoria Townsend. She was wearing a dark blue knit shirt, white shorts and tennis shoes without socks. The other lady had on a red-and-white checkered blouse that looked like it had come off the table of an Italian restaurant. She had long pants: faded blue jeans with holes in them. And she didn't have gray hair. It was dark; as dark as it had been when she was young and living in a small Sicilian town before she became a countess.

"So, *Cecile*," the blue-jeaned woman said, "Do you approve of my new 'duds'?" She laughed and said, "Look at this! These are called jeans, and they have holes in them! I had such faded and torn clothes during the War, and I was ashamed to wear them!" She laughed again and added, "Today we pay more for the holes!"

"Elena?"

"My friend Vicki took me to see her American courtiers, the *Contessa* explained. "She said the clothes I brought from Licata were not suitable for Florida."

"Your hair?" Less was still in shock.

"You like it?" she asked, flipping the free-hanging style with the back of her hand. No one in America is old, Cecilé. Today I did not see one gray-haired woman."

"But the people in your town . . ."

"The people in my town," Elena protested with a snort. "The people in my town should see *Signore* Jordache when they want new duds. *Andiamo, eh*? It is time to show me the boat that carries my name."

Elena took Les by the arm and escorted him out of the office. Jennifer's mouth was still agape when the door closed behind them.

"Is that our countess?" she demanded for the second time in two days.

❧ ❧ ❧

On the *Margaret*, Sibby Maggio was alone in the engine room, and alone was how he liked it. No offense to his volunteer helpers, but the truth was they spent most of their time getting in the way. Sure, an extra pair of hands never hurt; to hold this or that while Sibby applied the muscle. But Jim Lacey and Frenchy Dupré spent too much time talking to each other about some kind of secret deal they had going instead of paying attention to the job.

Sibby grunted as he slid the cast-iron head block of the port side engine back and began to replace it. "Damn!" The exclamation burst out when one of the head bolts slipped between his fingers and rolled into the bilge under the engine.

"Christ, how the hell am I going to get that?" he muttered as he got down on all fours and tried to squeeze a hand under the massive engine block.

"Sibby? You down there?"

"Yeah, I'm here," he shouted, not lifting his head. He sat up when he realized who was calling him. "Babe? That you?" he shouted.

"Is it safe to come down there?" his wife replied.

Sibby got to his feet quickly. "Jesus, yeah, wait a minute," he said as he looked around for a rag to wipe the grease off his hands. She was already halfway down the ladder. She had great legs, he thought, and the best . . . the best rear-end he had ever seen.

"So this is where you been hanging out?" the separated Mrs. Maggio observed when she got down.

"Yeah, this is it," Sibby replied, suddenly feeling kind of uncomfortable. "Why didn't you tell me you were comin'?"

"I wanted to surprise you; you've been talking about this place so much." She hesitated. "And I wanted to say 'thanks' for that money. I spent most of it on the girls."

"Aw, Babe, that was supposed to be for your birthday."

"Birthdays come and go, Sibby. The girls needed new clothes," she said, raising her voice defensively. She was suddenly ashamed of the way she said it, so she smiled and added, "Besides, I didn't say I spent all of it on them."

Damn, she had a killer smile.

"So where are your friends?" she asked.

"Don't know. Don't care. They mostly get in the way down here."

"Not like me, huh?" she smiled again. "I used to hand you stuff before you asked for it."

"Yeah," he acknowledged, "even though I didn't want you working in a garage."

"What kind of engines are these, anyway?" she asked as she stepped around him and checked out his work.

"Packard straight eights." Turning around like that gave him a chance to wipe off his hands a little more, and he looked around for something.

"Don't use your pants, okay?" she said, reading his mind. "Here's a clean rag." She tossed it to him over her shoulder. "Didn't you used to own a Packard?"

"You remember that one, huh, Babe?" he said as wiped his hands. "That's where we first . . ."

"I remember," she said, cutting off the subject. "So, how's it going?"

"It was going a lot better before I dropped that goddam bolt."

"Sibby, you don't have to swear. Where'd you drop it?"

"There, under the engine."

"Down here?" she asked as she dropped to her knees and slid her hand under the massive block.

"Babe, you're gonna get all dirty!"

"What, I never stuck my hands in grease before? What a mess! Wait a minute, I think I got it." She withdrew her hand covered with oily goo and clutching the wayward bolt. "This it?"

"That's it!" he exclaimed. Babe, you saved my life."

"You got something to clean up with down here, right?" she asked.

"I got a complete shower on my boat," he offered. "It's kinda small, but it's cozy."

"I'll bet it is," she replied. "I think I'd rather stay down here . . . unless you want to come over for dinner tonight."

"Dinner?" he asked. "You mean it?"

"Just dinner, Sibby," she said. "You haven't seen the girls in a while and I'll make your favorite: lasagna."

"Dinner would be great, Babe. Just dinner," he repeated.

"All right, so we'll see you around what? Six?" she said, wiping her hands on the same rag he had used.

"I'll be there," he confirmed.

She tossed him the rag and he watched her as she started back up the ladder. Damn, she still had a very fine ass.

❧ ❧ ❧

Jim Lacey poked at the salad Eddie Miles placed on their dinner table. "Where's the dressing?" he demanded. "You know I like lots of salad dressing."

"I put in all that you're allowed," his life partner assured him.

"Well, it must have gone through in a rowboat," Lacey groused.

Eddie did not answer, and they ate in silence for a few minutes. Finally, he asked, "Are you going to help him?"

Jim didn't need a name to know their discussion was turning to Henri Dupré. "I don't see what I can do about it, Eddie. He's scared stiff of those people down at the television station."

"I remember the Jim Lacey I knew in college," Eddie recalled. "He used to read all those books about Cecil B. DeMille and Frank Capra. He was going to be a movie director, you know."

"That was a long time ago," Lacey said ruefully.

"I remember you running around with that hand-held camera, making films of campus activities. They showed them in the Student Union during Winter Weekend."

"It was a foolish childhood dream," Jim Lacey insisted.

"Eddie Miles reached across the table and took his friend's hand. "Was it, Jim?" he asked softly. "You might have lived that dream if your father hadn't passed on; if you hadn't been forced to quit school and help your Mom in the restaurant."

"You helped too," he reminded Eddie, squeezing his hand in return.

"Yes, I was anxious to be with you, so I put my dreams of radio aside and pitched in with you."

"Me, slinging hash; you waiting on tables, being nice to people who didn't deserve a smile from your pretty lips," Jim said bitterly.

"We made a go of it," Eddie said.

"Yes, we did," Jim agreed. "We made a good go of it."

They were both quiet for a while, and then Eddie said softly, "You know, James, everyone else around here seems to be getting a second chance at their dreams. It wouldn't be fair if we didn't get ours, too."

"Life isn't fair, Edward."

"I'm not so sure about that," Eddie replied. "Maybe it doesn't seem fair in the short term; but over the long haul I've found life to be very fair indeed."

"Well, anyway, it's too late for us," Jim Lacey said.

"It's never too late," his life partner insisted, squeezing his hand again. "You're a good man, Jim Lacey. You'd be a better one of you took care of yourself and didn't gripe so much, but you're a good man all the same. You deserve a second chance at your dream as much as anybody . . . anybody including me. Now eat your salad. And when you talk to those people at the television station tomorrow, remember you can catch more flies with honey than you can with vinegar."

"This salad could use a little of that honey and vinegar," he said, poking at the greens in front of him. "And maybe some mayonnaise, too."

CHAPTER 24

Later that week, Victoria Townsend and Elena Russo found themselves at the Magnolia Avenue house for a tea party. When they arrived, they were surprised to find they were the only guests. After appropriate small talk in the living room, their young hostess asked them to join her around a dining room table covered with starched linen and laid out with Grandma's china and silver.

"My Grandmother used to serve tea to Marilyn and me on Wednesday afternoons," Jennifer explained, pouring tea as she had so often seen Margaret Calkins do. "She said afternoon tea is what separated us from the unwashed."

Victoria Townsend smiled; it amused her to watch the new doyenne of Calkins Harbor as she took her first steps into the ways of society. Jennifer's innocent awkwardness reminded Victoria of herself, and how she felt many years ago before she began thinking about the real meaning of life.

"I'm afraid if Vicki and I continue to clean *Cecile's* boat, we will soon join the unwashed," the *Contessa* said.

Jennifer almost blushed. "Oh, I didn't mean . . . I wasn't referring to either one of you," she stammered.

"I'm sure Elena didn't think you did, Sweetheart," Victoria reassured her. "She only meant that scrubbing the interior of Mr. Leslie's boat has been a new experience for us."

"Of course, the two of you aren't used to working like that," Jennifer agreed.

"Perhaps Vicki is not," the *Contessa* replied, smiling at Victoria, "but when I was a young girl I spent many such hours in my father's shoe store."

"Oh, I didn't mean . . ." Jennifer's voice dropped off in a flurry of confusion. She picked up a dish of chocolate éclairs and began passing it, but her polite offer was lost when she knocked over her teacup. "Oh, no! What have I done now?" she cried as she began sopping up the spilled tea.

Victoria stopped her. "Jennifer! Don't use a linen napkin! In fact, don't do anything. I'll get some cold water before the stain sets." She hurried into the kitchen and an instant later she and the Countess were laboring over both the tablecloth and the napkin.

"I'm sorry. I guess I'm not very good at this," Jennifer said, looking as if she were about to cry.

"You're doing just fine, Sweetie," Victoria assured her. "Afternoon teas take a little practice." She looked up from what she was doing and added, "But perhaps you wouldn't be so nervous if you just came right out and told us what's on your mind."

"What makes you think . . ."

Jennifer's protest was cut off by Countess Elena. "Jennifer, when women come together like this, it is to make plans for things we will later allow our men to believe they thought of for themselves. Is that not so, Vicki?"

The still-uncrowned matriarch of what was the beginning of Calkins Harbor society heaved a sigh of relief and the room relaxed with her.

"Well," Jennifer began, brushing the cup aside and leaning forward on the table, "I wanted to talk to the two of you about my festival idea."

"A festival? Here?" the Countess asked.

"The idea came to Jennifer while we were waiting for you at the airport, Elena," Victoria explained. "I think it's a rather good one. Go on, Dear, explain it to her."

"You know how festivals are a big tourist attraction, like Mardi Gras? Well, Mardi Gras got started because a Russian nobleman was visiting New Orleans. And you're a noblewoman, well, I mean, you have a royal title and everything, and I'm getting married in September. I thought we would have a festival based on an Italian noblewoman welcoming me to this island for my wedding, and then we could have a festival. We could start our own tradition, with a boat parade and a party for the whole town . . . and it would be good for business, too."

The *Contessa* looked like she might be considering the idea. At least she wasn't showing any signs of rejecting it out of hand, and Jennifer quickly added something that might be a problem. "Of course, you would have to stay here for a few months . . ."

The former Elena Russo waved off that objection with her hand. "Vicki has arranged for some very nice rooms for me at the hotel; I am quite comfortable." There was a long pause while she thought over the rest of the idea. Finally, she said, "So, you wish to make a big *sposafesta*?"

"A what?"

"A *sposafesta*. A . . . how do you say it? A bridal feast. A party for your wedding."

"How do you pronounce that again?" Jennifer asked.

"In my town they say '*sposafesta*.' *Sposa* is a bride, and *festa*, of course, means feast. But, Jennifer, it is only their dialect. I am not sure if it is a real word. It is just something that people put together."

"It doesn't have to mean anything," Jennifer said as her excitement began to ignite the room. "What does Mardi Gras mean? Or Super Bowl? It just has to sound like it means something. In fact, it's better if it doesn't mean anything; then we can tell people what it means and make up our own tradition around it!" "*Sposafesta*," Jennifer repeated, carefully rolling the word around in her mouth. "*Sposafesta!*" She drew her hand across an unseen billboard and added, "Painted in green letters on a red and white background with an exclamation point . . . and underlined with a sort of slash '*Sposafesta!*' Can't you just see it?" she asked excitedly. "Written with a brush in a kind of painted scrawl . . . almost like graffiti. That's what I've been waiting for. That's the name we need: ***Sposafesta!***

"It certainly does have a ring to it, and I do love your ideas," Victoria said, bitten by the young woman's infectious energy. "I don't want to throw cold water on this one, but festivals like Mardi Gras involve much more than just a name."

"Of course. That's why the two of you are here!" Jennifer exclaimed. "Who knows more about creating an Italian festival? With the two of you on our team we're unstoppable!"

"Jennifer, you move too fast. I do not know what it is you expect of me," Elena said.

"I expect you to be who you are: the Italian countess, of course!" Jennifer blurted out. "We can't do this without you!"

Victoria Townsend sat back in her chair and smiled wistfully. "I think we can make *Sposafesta* the highlight of the Bonita social calendar. What do you say, *Contessa*?"

The Italian countess stood up, extended her arms and royally bowed her assent. Jennifer Calkins banged a silver spoon on the table as she had seen her grandmother do whenever an idea had been born at her Magnolia Avenue tea parties.

"Then it's unanimous," Jennifer decreed. "September 6, 1986, will be our first annual *Sposafesta*!"

Sharon Crowley's voice on the intercom startled Jack out of his reverie, thinking about the tidal wave of change that was sweeping over what had been his private refuge. Les Leslie without a beard, and a countess in torn jeans cleaning his boat, and his mother wearing shorts and volunteering to help her. Where would it all end? It was almost a relief to hear his secretary say, "Mr. Meacham is on the line for you." At least that sounded normal.

"Rob, how's it going?" Jack almost shouted with relief.

"Going? It's going rotten, thank you. Do you know that it does nothing but rain up here in April?"

"I'm sure that's not true, Rob. Washington is supposed to have some very nice weather. Think of the cherry blossoms."

"It rained for two days. Today it stopped but I still haven't seen the sun."

"Okay, you didn't call to give me the weather report."

"No, I called to tell you I've finally found the records of Les' court martial. I also found some nice people who have taken pity on me and are helping me out. In other words, I'm beginning . . . just beginning . . . to get somewhere."

"That's great. When will you be home?"

"Probably a couple more days. I'll give you the bad news first: if that Tuesberry or Tudbury guy ever existed, he wasn't mentioned in the proceedings, at least not in what I've seen so far. And Jack, get this: here's why I'm calling you. There was no trial. Les pled guilty. And he was represented by a lawyer . . . a Lieutenant Davisson; Lieutenant Byron C. Davisson."

"Why does that name sound so familiar?"

"I'm not sure, but I think I know him from Bar meetings. If you check our copy of the Florida Bar Directory, I think you'll find he's a judge down in the next circuit."

"Hold on a minute," Jack said as he hit the "Hold" button and headed for the library. He picked up that phone as he was flipping through the directory pages.

"What circuit did you say?"

"The one that's south of us. It's the twenty-fourth, isn't it?"

Jack ran his finger down the list of names. "Damn! You're right, Rob! Hon. Byron C. Davisson. His office is in the Cypress County Courthouse. That's practically next door to us."

"How's that for a coincidence? It proves we're on a mission, Jack. The doors are opening!"

"We're on the right path, anyway," Jack agreed. "Let's hope those doors open when we get to them."

"We can't miss! The way things are breaking now, we'll have this little problem cleared up in no time!"

They ended the conversation with R.J. on high hopes, mostly built on the progress he made after days of frustration. Jack wasn't so sure. Finding out about Byron Davisson cut two ways: it meant the truth might be a lot easier to find—right in the next county in fact. It also meant that Les had a real lawyer at his court martial, not some officer thrown into the arena to make it look like a fair trial. It was no longer the kind of kangaroo court that Les had described.

The problem needed some careful thought, and Jack always thought better when he was doing something else. It was late enough in the afternoon for the senior partner to make an executive decision without feeling guilty about it, so he buzzed Sharon Crowley and told her he was leaving for the day. With any kind of luck, she would wait at least fifteen minutes before she put the phones on "hold" and followed him out the door.

Sibby Maggio looked lovingly at the port side engine. She was clean as a whistle. Damn, he did good work, he thought. Now it was time to begin work on her sister on the starboard side. He was laying his tools out as carefully as a surgeon preparing for an operation when he was interrupted by Jack Townsend descending the ladder into Sibby's private domain—the *Margaret's* engine room.

"What are you doing down here?" Jack demanded.

"That's funny. I was just gonna ask you. You said you wanted to get this tub moving, didn't you?"

"I'm sorry, Sibby. I didn't expect anybody to be down here," Jack replied sheepishly. He looked down and noticed that although the starboard side engine was its old grimy self and surrounded by nothing but tools, the port engine was incredibly clean. If he didn't know it was ancient, he would have said 'new.'

"Hey, you been working down here?" Jack asked.

"Christ, you really know how to make a guy feel good, you know that? Of course I've been working. The pig over there is completely rebuilt." He pointed to the starboard engine at his feet. "I'll have this one done in another week or so."

"Sibby, I am really impressed," Jack said, running his hand over the finished port side engine. "When you said you used to own a place . . ." Jack broke off. That was no way to say what he was thinking without insulting the man again.

"You figured I was some kind of grease monkey, right?"

"Will this thing run as good as it looks?" Jack asked, trying to change the subject.

"Stand back, Commodore." Sibby hit a starter switch and the engine instantly turned over. "Put a little gas in her tanks, that baby'll be humming."

Jack looked at the marina's hustler and deal-maker in a whole new light. "I'm impressed, Sibby," he repeated. "I'm really impressed."

"Take a look at the carburetor. I rebuilt it myself," Sibby said, the pride of accomplishment obvious in his voice.

"Where did you get the parts?" Jack asked, still awed by the man's hidden talent. "And the batteries. Aren't they six-volts?"

"Six-volts and not easy to find, let me tell you. As for the parts, I've been shelling out of my own pocket. Don't worry, I kept a list. I figured sooner or later somebody would ask and I'd get my money back."

"Get your money back my ass!" Jack exclaimed. "You need to be paid for all this work!"

"Forget it, Commodore!" the man said, suddenly putting up defenses. "I'm just helping out like everybody else around here. I gave up the grease monkey routine."

"Sibby, this may be none of my business, but what's the big hang up about 'grease monkey'? You're obviously a very good mechanic. Why do you have a problem with that?"

"The problem is, I want to go to work in a coat and tie . . . just like you."

"Let me tell you, that's not all it's cracked up to be. Ask Rob Meacham when he gets back."

"You know, Commodore, it's funny. You guys who do it, you all say the same thing: it's not all it's cracked up to be.

But let your daughters want to marry somebody who doesn't wear a coat and tie . . . that's a whole 'nother story."

Jack nodded his understanding. There was a lot more to this than was being said in the engine room. "Sibby, how much time have you spent down here so far?"

"I told you, I've been keeping a list."

"You said you've been keeping a list of parts. How much of your time have you spent down here? Your <u>time</u>, Sibby?"

"I don't know," he shrugged. He never thought about working on engines in terms of time. "You know, I do it when I feel like it; sometimes even at night I'll get an idea and come down to try something out."

"Time, Sibby. How much time? Twenty hours? Thirty? Forty?"

Sibby shrugged. "I don't know; four, five, six hours a day. A week, maybe a week and a half. You know how it is: you get into things and you just keep on truckin'."

"All right, forty hours. How does that sound?"

"Forty hours sounds about right."

"Forty hours at fifty dollars an hour. I'll have Marilyn cut you a check for two thousand dollars. You can pick it up tonight."

"Naw, naw, man. I see what you're tryin' to do. You're tryin' to suck me in. That's not gonna happen, Commodore. I'm doin' this for fun, okay? My goal is a coat and tie."

"Dammit, Sibby, you have a talent here that few people have. Why do you refuse to use it?"

"Talent, huh? Okay, so answer my question: would you let your daughter marry a guy like me?"

"The owner of 'Maggio Marine Services'? Why not?" Jack answered.

"Don't go there, Commodore," Sibby replied. "That dream died a long time ago in Ohio. Only it didn't have the word 'marine' in it. It was a funky little gas station, but it was ours and we did okay, until we got wiped out when 'big oil' put up their place across the street. We came down here in a trailer . . . a travel trailer . . . the four of us. We lived in it for months until Babe found a job and I was able to pick up a few deals. And you know what her parents said? They said, 'We told you he'd never be nothin' but a grease monkey!' They said, 'We told you not to marry that guy!' That was it, man, 'We told you so.'"

Jack nodded. He heard the same story many times in his career. The names and places changed; the people and the problems were always the same. "Okay, so you hit a bump in the road . . . it was a hard bump," he said. "But that's no reason to give up on your dream. Thanks to Margaret Calkins you now have a very big asset. And you have friends who are willing to back you up."

"So why don't I just sell my big asset and buy that coat and tie?"

"Better yet, why don't you do what you're good at doing and live your dream? Why don't you work at something you enjoy? I'll set up a company for you; we'll even find an office for you around here somewhere. Jack patted him on the shoulder, smiled and added, "You can show up in a coat and tie if you like . . . as long as you keep your fun clothes in your office closet."

"I can't even balance a checkbook, man!"

"There are a lot of people around here who can do that. They'll help you get started and once you're on your feet you might even hire one of them. They'll be working for you . . . doing the things you can't do, or don't want to do."

Sibby turned away, squatted down and began rummaging through his toolbox. "Oh, man, you are giving me a bad headache, Commodore."

"Good! Maybe that means you're finally thinking."

Sibby looked up at him. "Maybe I am."

"Then I'll get out of your way," Jack said as he headed for the ladder. "That check will be waiting for you in the office. And don't forget to add in the cost of the parts!"

That evening, Jim Lacey faced Henri Dupré's apartment door and took a deep breath. He couldn't believe how easy it had been to talk to the people at the public television station. All he had done was mention his college experience and throw around a few phrases like 'dolly shot' and 'voice over' and they accepted him. They must really be desperate, he thought. So the first part of his plan had worked. Now he looked at the locked door and prepared himself to do what the Great DeMille would have done—lie to his star; lie to him and flatter him. He knocked once and Henri opened the door immediately.

Jim Lacey hung his head and shook it sadly. "Let's have one of those drinks, Henri."

"Lacey! What is the trouble? What happened?"

"It's no good, Henri," Jim said, brushing past him and going straight for the cognac bottle and two glasses. "They won't let you out of the contract that Jennifer signed. They said you're a vital part of the whole thing."

"But this is madness, Lacey," Dupré protested. "Why me? It is *impossible*! I cannot do it! I cannot perform for those people!"

"They did make one concession," Jim said, sipping his brandy and pouring a second one for Henri. "They agreed to change the format and give you a new director."

"Who will they put over my head now?"

"Me."

"You?"

"Me."

"But what do you know of such things?"

"I did quite a bit of it in college," Jim Lacey replied rather nonchalantly.

"College? Not a *restaurant*?"

"Before the restaurant business," Jim shrugged. "I did a lot of it. You know, 'dolly shots,' 'hand helds,' 'voice overs.' It's really pretty simple stuff. Almost boring in fact."

"We would be working together?" Dupré asked, warming to the idea.

"Very closely together."

"And Janifere? She will not know about my . . ." He hesitated, unable to mouth the word 'failure.'

"She won't know a thing. As far as anybody is concerned, the television people have decided to change the format for artistic purposes."

"No looking into a *camera*? No speaking? No *memorization*?"

"Dolly shots and hand-held-over-the-shoulder stuff in the kitchen with voice-over added later. Pretty basic stuff, really. As far as looking into the camera, you won't even <u>see</u> the camera."

Henri Dupré's mouth turned down in a scowl and he rubbed his hand over his chin. "This I could do," he said thoughtfully. He downed the remains of his second cognac and nodded. "*Bon!* This I could do."

Jim Lacey refilled the two glasses and they made a toast to success. He hadn't told Henri the exact truth, of course; but then he hadn't told his producer the exact truth either. He left out the parts about leaving college after his junior year, and never having fully completed a project or a degree. He wondered how DeMille would have handled this. He wondered how he was going to deliver on his promises. And most of all he wondered how he would handle his lifelong dream of being a Director at this stage of his life.

CHAPTER 25

When the airliner reached cruising altitude and leveled off, R.J. tilted back his first-class seat for the return trip to Bonita. He gratefully sipped the Scotch the attendant brought him and continued the unwinding process he had begun in the airport lounge. He wasn't the kind of person who drank alone—ordinarily. But he had spent a grueling week in Washington, crashing headlong into the bureaucracy and the bureaucrats who seemed to be intent on frustrating the people who paid their salaries. He had wasted an entire day at the Veterans' Administration, bouncing from one comatose chair-warmer to another, trying to find a place to begin his search. After being talked-down-to by countless clerks who never had last names, and always sent him somewhere else, he gave up on the cabdriver's suggestion and headed for the Navy Department where his instinct told him to go in the first place. There he found more delays: old records had been archived and it would take 'a day or so' to get them. But at least the records existed, and when they arrived they supplied him with the name of Les' commanding officer: Guthrie Westenbok. By the end of the week, R.J. was familiar enough with office procedures and friendly enough with the staff to learn that Westenbok had reached the rank of captain before retiring to Tucson, Arizona. But try as he might, R.J. could not locate 'Tuesberry' or 'Tudbury', the man from Naval Intelligence. If he existed, he had disappeared. After a week of fast-food lunches and lonely dinners, R.J. had packed it in.

Doubts were creeping into his mind and chipping away at what once had been an absolute certainty. He had seen so many layers of government and read through so many records that it was almost impossible to believe that anything like the spy mission Les had described could happen without something—anything—being put in writing. And it was even more difficult to believe that an innocent man like Les could have gone off to prison for ten years without someone—anyone—coming forward and exonerating him. Maybe Jack had read the situation properly; maybe Les was the victim of his own memory—of "easily believing the things he wanted to believe," as Jack had once quoted from his days in prep school. There was no way to know other than by getting back to work and digging deeper. And then what?

He thought of the day a million years ago on Jack's boat when he begged for a chance to become what he called 'a real lawyer,' and how Jack had warned him about the perils of swimming in what he called a sewer. Now, with his career barely underway, he learned to his horror that he had already represented one client who committed outright perjury, and he was about to uncover the secrets of another one—secrets that might be better left secret. Now he understood how his chosen profession took its toll on its practitioners. Searching out the truth on a daily basis was a lot more complicated than it looked in the movies. It might not be such a good thing after all.

❧ ❧ ❧

"Rob, you did a fantastic job. Really great," Jack said when he arrived at the office the next day.

"How can you say that?" R.J. demanded. "I didn't find Tuesberry or Tudbury or anybody from Naval Intelligence. Not even a mention of them."

"You found Davisson and Westenbok. They must know something," Jack replied.

"Big deal! Neither one of them did anything for Les forty years ago. Why should they help him now?"

"Who knows? Times change . . . things happen. Besides, why are you so negative? You were hell-bent-for-leather when you left."

R.J. leaned back in his chair and stared at the ceiling. "Jack," he asked thoughtfully, "what if this whole thing turns out to be nothing more than what you said? What if it's just Les' memory playing tricks on him?"

"Would it be better for him to know the truth, or for him to spend the rest of his life believing he was the victim of a nefarious plot?" Jack asked rhetorically.

"Are we supposed to make those decisions? Who gave us that kind of authority?"

"There are no easy answers in this business, Rob. There are only easy questions. As for decisions, let's not make any until we at least talk to Judge Davisson."

"When do you want to do that?"

"I called him last week after you called me. I thought we could take a ride down there later today . . . take him out to lunch or something."

"Does he know why we're coming?"

"I mentioned the name 'Les Leslie' and said we would bring a notarized release so he could speak with us. Frankly, it didn't seem to make much of an impression. We'll just have to wait and see if he remembers anything at all."

❧ ❧ ❧

In another part of town, Jim Lacey was having a private meeting of his own with Victoria Townsend in a corner of her hotel dining room. "Well, Mr. Lacey, it's a pleasure to be having breakfast with you, but you must have other reasons for driving across the Bonita Key bridge."

"It's about Henri Dupré," Jim began.

"Is anything wrong? Is he ill?" she asked, the concern clearly showing on her face.

"No, nothing like that. It's about the disaster at the television station," Jim began.

"Disaster?" Victoria seemed really upset. "I'm not aware of any disaster! Was it on the news?"

Jim assured her it wasn't a physical kind of disaster, it was a looming disaster of a personality. He told her the whole story of Jennifer's idea for a television program, and the contract with the station, and the pressure it had put on the man who was supposed to be their star.

"I see," Victoria said, sipping her tea and nodding. "So Henri tried it and he failed?"

"I hate to use that word," Jim smiled. "but he did smash one of their ovens before storming off their set."

"I'm certain Henri hates the word 'failure' more than you do," she replied. "But I can't see what I can do about it."

"You can be his co-star."

Victoria looked at him intently. "What is your role in this Mr. Lacey?"

"Well . . . frankly, I'm the new director."

"I see. Do you have any experience in that field?"

"Not much," Jim Lacey admitted, "But, fortunately, Henri doesn't need much direction."

"What does he need, if I may ask?"

"Henri needs to be turned loose; he needs to be in a real kitchen, not an artificial set in a cold studio. He needs to be surrounded by real people. Most of all he needs someone who appreciates him. I believe that 'someone' is you. You can make him a success."

"How?"

"Just by being there . . . by being part of his audience. It's no secret how he feels about you. I think you feel the same way about him. What he needs is your approval . . . all right, I'll say it . . . your adulation. He needs you and a small audience . . . very small for now . . . so that he can perform. Once he has that, Henri's personality will take over. I'm sure of it."

"And your job will be?" Victoria asked.

"When that happens, my job will be to hold on and enjoy the ride," Jim joked. "Now let me tell you my idea for opening the program." He quickly sketched out his ideas for her, and while she listened to his excited description, she understood why Henri had been acting so distant. Jennifer had unknowingly thrown him into an area where he had no friends—a cold, empty studio where his magnetic Gallic personality had no effect. His growing isolation had nothing at all to do with her. It was caused by his own fear of failure—and the fact that he had come so close to having to admit it. She and Jim Lacey would not allow that to happen again, but they had to do it gently. They understood Henri could not be pushed, but with the right touch—a gentle touch—he could be led.

Back in her office in Cap'n Kelly's Marina, Marilyn Dupré Townsend sighed with relief. She finally had things under control. The financial statements for the marina were complete, and the work on the first floor of the restaurant was underway. When the bank recognized the Residents' Association and came through with a loan, they could hire contractors to improve the docks and the electrical system and pave the roads. With any luck, the marina would be in A-1 shape just about the time the baby was due—just about the time they would be moving into their new home next to the Calkins home on Magnolia Avenue. "That's great," she mumbled out loud, "just when things will be looking good around here, we'll be living somewhere else!" And not only would they be missing out on the fun of liveaboard life, they would have to leave their beloved *Marilyn* which she had come to think of as a living, breathing part of herself.

The telephone jarred her out of what could have turned into a blue funk. "This is Dan Getty over at VSP Marketing," a man's voice said. "Is Miss Calkins there?"

"No, I'm afraid she isn't," Marilyn replied. "I'm her sister. May I help you?"

"I'd like her to approve the artwork for these *Sposafesta* banners before we run all hundred of them."

"Excuse me, what was that?"

"S-p-o-s-a-f-e-s-t-a," the man spelled out. "You know, she wants that paintbrush graffiti effect with the slash and the exclamation point? I think we've done a perfect job with the artwork, but she needs to approve it before we run them."

"I'm sorry, Mr. Getty, but you'll need to see her for that approval."

"Well, have her call me as soon as she gets in, okay? I'd like to get this job out of the way so we can use our equipment for other things."

"I'll certainly do that Mr. Getty . . . Oh, and Mr. Getty?"

"Yes?"

"How much do these banners cost?"

"I gave her a great deal because she plans to order a lot more of them. These are only fifty dollars each. Of course, that includes the mounting bracket."

"I'll be sure to speak to her as soon as she comes in," Marilyn promised.

❧ ❧ ❧

Lunchtime found Jack and R.J. at a table with Circuit Judge Byron C. Davisson in a restaurant across from the Cypress County Courthouse.

"I'm glad you fellows could meet me today," the Judge began. "I've got a jury trial beginning tomorrow that will probably go for a week, and then two more backed up after that."

"We appreciate your time, Judge," Jack assured him. "We'll try to make this as brief as possible."

"I have to tell you honestly, Mr. Townsend," Judge Davisson continued, "I've been turning that name over in my mind ever since you called. I don't remember anyone named 'Les Leslie.'"

"His real name is 'Cecil,' your honor," R.J. added.

"Mr. Townsend said that, but it didn't help at all."

"It was a very big case," your honor," R.J. argued.

"No doubt it was for him," Davisson replied. "But you know how it is, after a while you just can't remember all the names and the people. 'Cecil' or 'Les'; no matter what you call him, I honestly don't remember the case. You say he was charged with treason?"

"That's right," R.J. replied.

"And I got him a plea to ten years?"

"That you did, Judge." Jack confirmed.

The Judge shook his head. "I don't remember it, Mr. Townsend. I know that may sound strange, but a lot of cases have gone under my bridge in the past four decades and more."

"I don't doubt that for a minute, Judge." Jack agreed.

"Do you think you might have some notes or something?" R.J. asked.

Again, the judge shook his head. "Mr. Meacham, that was so long ago that I still considered Indiana my home. I moved to Florida after that . . . first to Miami and then again over here to the Gulf Coast something like twenty years ago. Even if I had kept notes, I guarantee you they wouldn't have survived two major moves and house-cleanings that accompanied them."

"We understand, Judge. A lot of time and a lot of miles have gone by," Jack agreed, thinking of his own checkered life in Florida.

"I'll tell you this, though," Judge Davisson continued. "I may have been young back in those days, but I can't see myself pleading a man guilty if he didn't do something. And from the little bit you've told me, that's what it sounds like: your guy . . . our guy . . . did something. He was involved someway, somehow. I wouldn't have had a hand in sending him off for ten years if I wasn't convinced of that."

"I hope you're wrong, Judge," Jack said.

"I hope I'm wrong too, Jack," the Judge replied. "But I doubt it; I really doubt it."

"Well," Jack sighed, "I guess it's going to take a trip to Arizona to find out."

Noon at Dupré's, the still-unopened-but-not-unoccupied restaurant, found Chef Dupré, Victoria Townsend, Jim Lacey, a young woman television producer and two workmen quickly recruited from Tim Gormley's crew, sitting around a table sharing a bottle of wine. Things were progressing nicely until two men with hand-held cameras, a fellow with a microphone on a boom, and some guys with lights and cables began to scurry around them.

Henri suddenly got a bad case of nerves. "Lacey, *mon Dieu*, my hairs are straight?" he asked, combing the sides of his head with moistened fingertips.

"Don't bother, Henri," Jim said casually. "They're not filming anything today. They're just here to take light readings and check camera angles." He turned to one of the camera men and said, "You guys aren't taping, are you?"

"Pal, they didn't give us any tape," the man behind the lens assured him. "With luck we'll do some taping next month . . . maybe."

"All this, for tests?" Dupré said with a raised eyebrow.

Jim Lacey leaned in close and whispered, "Union rules, you know."

"*Oui, il syndicat*," Dupré nodded. No more needed to be said on the subject.

"Let's have another bottle of wine," Jim said, opening a lush red and pouring all around. "If we have to sit here and be lighting dummies, at least we can enjoy ourselves."

The talk moved freely around the table with Henri expounding on life, love, and—of course—food and cooking. When Jim saw Henri was sufficiently relaxed, he suggested they all move into the kitchen so the 'technicians' could complete their lighting measurements in there.

"What's on the menu, Chef Dupré?" Jim asked when the five members of his hand-picked audience surrounded him in the kitchen. Henri looked around and was surprised to see shrimp, oysters, rice—in fact, all of the ingredients for one of his favorite quick dishes.

"*Ah, bien*," the Chef replied. "We begin with something simple but filling, eh? *Le Bouillabaisse* of my home in *la Vieux Carré*, the French Quarter. It is called *Gombo Creole*, but in English they say it back to front: 'Creole Gumbo,' eh?" He laughed and finished the wine in his glass. Jim quickly refilled it.

Down on the first-floor construction site, the heady scent of onions lovingly sautéed with a hint of garlic, aromatic spices, tomatoes and fish stock began wafting over Tim Gorman's crew while the men took their noontime break, sitting on odd piles of lumber and opening their lunch boxes.

"Man, what's he cookin' up there?" one of them asked no one in particular.

"An' how come Jerry and Pete are gettin' a taste and not us?"

"They happened to be doing nothing when Jim Lacey said he needed two guys to fill in, okay?" Tim Gorman said, mad at himself for not volunteering.

"I wonder if he's handin' out samples?" the first man said.

"It's a TV show; there aren't any samples," Tim assured them.

"Yeah, well, he's gotta be doin' somethin' with what he's cookin'. Let's go ask him for a taste."

Before Tim could stop them, his crew was trooping up the outside stairway. One of them stuck his head in the kitchen door and asked, "Hey, Chef, any samples for us?"

Henri laughed heartily. "Of course, *mes amis*! Always there is plenty here!" He turned to the young producer. "Young lady, please, put out some plates and spoons for my friends. Lacey! We need more shrimp, more oysters, a piece of fish or two, and more rice, *sil vous plaît*. Sit down, *mes amis*," he shouted to Tim Gorman's crew, and you as well, he said, pointing to the sound man and guys with the cables. “It is my delight for me to prepare your food!”

CHAPTER 26

A blazing Arizona sun baked the Tucson International Airport parking lot as Jack and R.J. ran the rental car's air conditioner before attempting to get inside.

"Brother, I thought Florida was hot," R.J. complained as he stood next to the open driver's side door.

"And have you ever seen so much brown?" Jack asked. "I guess they don't know about grass out here. Do you have the map?"

"I'm ready, I know exactly how to get there."

"Don't get us lost, Rob," Jack warned.

"Hey, you're talking to a guy who found his way around Washington, D.C. for a whole week," R.J. reminded him.

"Washington has cabs," Jack replied. "And it isn't surrounded by desert."

A forty-minute drive brought them to Sun Valley Gardens, a sprawling subdivision of squat, look-alike homes laid out on flat, monotonous streets. There were cacti everywhere, but few trees and even fewer lawns. Many of the residents had conceded defeat to the ever-present rocks and sand of the desert landscape. Once inside the community, it took only a few minutes to find the home of retired Captain

Guthrie Westenbok. They left the car parked on the street and rang the doorbell. An old man with rheumy blue eyes came to the door. He was wearing a sleeveless undershirt and nondescript pants.

"Captain Westenbok? My name is Jack Townsend," Jack said, extending his hand toward the still-closed screen door. "This is my partner Rob Meacham."

The old man didn't move to open the screen, and after a long moment Jack lowered his hand.

"It isn't 'Captain' anymore," the man said. "It's Guthrie. Or Gus. Take your choice."

"We represent one of your men: a fellow by the name of Les Leslie," Jack explained.

The old man's eyes seemed to get even more liquid. His jaw set tight and he said nothing.

"May we come in for a minute? It's pretty hot out here," R.J. joked.

"I always knew sooner or later somebody like you two guys would show up," the old man said. He turned and walked away from the screen, leaving the inner door open. The two lawyers took it as a grudging invitation and followed Westenbok into his living room.

The only light came from a television set against the far wall and a crack where the cheap polyester-lined draperies failed to come together and allowed in a brilliant sliver of the scorching desert sun. The air was heavy with the smell of stale cigarette smoke and once Jack's eyes adjusted to the darkness he noticed that the walls that might once have been beige had declined to a stained, yellowish, nicotine brown.

Gus had seated himself in a recliner. A wobbly metal TV table at his right held a stack of magazines, a remote-control unit and an over-full ashtray. He held his jaw tight as he stared straight ahead at the television's offering of a game show, but it was obvious he wasn't watching it. Jack and R.J. sat down on a couch along one wall.

"Captain, we're private attorneys," Jack began. "We don't work for the government."

Guthrie Westenbok did not reply. Jack decided to wait him out. At least he hadn't asked them to leave.

A last the old man looked at Jack. "Still goes by 'Les,' does he? You know that's not his real name."

"It's 'Cecil'," Jack replied with a smile. "I guess that's why he goes by 'Les.' He needs your help, Gus."

"I didn't help him forty years ago. What makes him think I'll help him now?"

It was the first hint that Captain Guthrie Westenbok, U.S.N. (Ret.) knew what they were doing in his house. It was also the first hint that whatever he knew had been gnawing at him for forty long years. "He doesn't think anything, Gus," Jack explained. "He doesn't even know we've found you. I thought it would be best to keep this between ourselves for now."

"Would you fellas like some coffee? She's out right now," Gus said, vaguely referring to a woman who might be his wife, "but there's always coffee in the pot."

"No, thanks. We just had some," R.J. said, trying to avoid contact with anything as intimate as a cup in the grimy house.

Jack overruled him. "Coffee would be fine."

The old man hoisted himself out of his chair and made his way to the kitchen with Jack and R.J. at his heels. When he got there he went directly for an open pack of cigarettes on the table and lit one while Jack nodded R.J. toward the coffee maker on the counter. The old man took a drag on the cigarette and coughed violently. "The cups are over there," he said to R.J., nodding toward one of the cupboards with eyes that had grown even more watery during his coughing spell. He sat down heavily and took another drag, looking at Jack across the table.

"If you're going to tell me they're bad for me, don't bother. I've got lung cancer. Doctor says I've got anywhere from six to sixteen months. It's a little late to give them up now."

"There's treatment," R.J. offered.

"Chemo. Radiation. Not for me," the man replied. "Just makes you sick before you die, and you still end up dead." He looked at R.J. then turned to Jack. "Were either of you fellas ever in a war?"

R.J. shook his head and Jack said, "No, sorry."

"Don't be sorry." Gus coughed again. "Those of us who were there . . . the things we saw . . . the things we did . . . we made up our minds about dying then. What is it that Shakespeare calls it? 'A necessary end'? Besides, it's too late for me."

R.J. poured three cups of coffee while Jack tried to steer the conversation back to the purpose of their visit. "It isn't too late to help Les," he suggested.

"He was a good kid," the old Captain replied. "A little too good, maybe. Too green. Or maybe too naïve." He looked directly at Jack and said, "You can't always believe everyone in this life, Mr. Townsend." It was the first indication the Captain remembered either of their names, and he said the words in a tone of voice that spoke of a bitter lesson.

Jack remained silent, sensing there was no need for further encouragement. Gus wanted to tell his story now; he needed to unburden his soul. All they had to do was give him time.

"Did you know Lieutenant Commander Tuesberry?" R.J. asked quietly, hoping to get the story started.

"Tutbury," the Captain corrected him. "Eugene Tutbury. 'Tut' to those of us who liked him, 'King Tut' to those who

. . . well, to those who liked him less. Tut had the kind of personality that could charm the skin off a snake . . . or the pants off any young lady he happened to fancy. There were many times I watched him turn on that charm and escort some sweet young thing out to his car." The retired captain paused and shook his head silently. "But it didn't mean anything . . . he was just fooling around with girls. I never thought he'd do it to a friend."

Gus lifted his nicotine stained fingers to his mouth and took another deep drag on his cigarette. He coughed again and continued, "We roomed together at the Academy . . . all four years. Tut was smart as a whip . . . never had to open a book. He pulled me through with him." He looked at Jack and said, "You have to understand that. I never would have made it through without Tut's help." Jack nodded. Law school had been bad enough, he thought.

"We graduated together, Class of 1934. I don't know how he did it, but Tut somehow got us assigned to the same ship for our first cruise. He wasn't much of a sailor, so later, once the War started, he talked his way into Naval Intelligence. I never knew how he did that either. But they wanted officers, especially Academy grads, and I guess Tut told them what they wanted to hear. He was very good at that."

"What about Les Leslie, Captain? Jack asked gently.

Gus nodded, took another drag on his cigarette, coughed a little and went on. "Your . . . I guess he's your client?"

Jack nodded his response.

"He was seeing some Italian girl. After a while he came to me and told me something fishy was going on with the girl's father."

"Les told you about his suspicions," R.J. said, confirming the fact.

Gus nodded again. "Well, it sounded to me like we might be on to a spy, or at least a collaborator. So I called Tut. I figured I'd do him a favor. I owed him a lot, and . . . well . . . maybe he could do something for me one day. That's how it's supposed to work, right?" The old man looked at Jack with a wry smile and said, "Tut was aboard my ship before the week was out."

"Did he have orders to do what he did?" Jack asked quietly.

"I didn't ask him then. You don't ask a chum for orders, do you, Counselor? But later, when it got going deeper, I . . . I did ask him then."

"And he said?" R.J. asked.

"'No problem!' It was always 'no problem' with King Tut."

"I don't suppose he showed them to you?" Jack inquired.

The old man looked at Jack with his watery blue eyes and silently shook his head. "Maybe I should have pressed him more; maybe I should have stood up to him, told him he wasn't talking to one of my men without me seeing something in writing. Maybe I should have done a lot of things, but I didn't."

"And when the troopship went down?" R.J. said.

The old captain's voice grew hoarse and he whispered, "That's when he told me he was working completely on his own."

"Who screwed up, Captain?" Jack asked in a whisper of his own.

The old man looked directly at him again. "Tut did. He was in bed with some chippie when he should have been giving the order to turn that ship around. I guess it just slipped his mind."

The only sound in the house was the babble of the television set in the other room. The raucous laughter of the studio audience provided a gruesome counterpoint to the dying captain's story.

"Where is Lieutenant Commander Tutbury now?" R.J. asked through lips that were almost too dry to talk.

"Commander," the dying captain said. "He made full commander, and he's dead. By his own hand. He blew his brains out in Rio de Janeiro in 1954 . . . ten years to the day after that ship went down . . . and while that poor boy still sat in prison."

"Couldn't you have done something about Les then?" R.J. asked quietly.

"Did you ever try to get Navy records changed, Counselor?" Gus demanded. "And what was I going to tell them, that I stood by and watched while an innocent man got convicted? So I could save my friend? The years were gone . . . that was finished. I made a few inquiries, found out the boy was going to be out of prison soon. Tut was dead. I still had a career. Was I supposed to throw myself on the same pyre?" The old man's voice had been rising. He looked back and forth between the lawyers and he almost shouted, "What good would it have done?" before he collapsed in a fit of coughing.

Jack waited until the man recovered, and then said softly, "It would have served the cause of justice, Captain."

Guthrie Westenbok looked at him and replied, "I'll be getting my justice soon enough."

"We have to see that Les gets his," Jack said firmly. "We can do it quietly, but he's entitled to the return of his good name."

The old man nodded. "Quietly or not, that's the story, Counselor. And it's the truth. How's it go? 'The truth, the whole truth and nothing but the truth, so help me God'?"

Jack nodded. "That's how it goes, all right."

"Well you better get started on whatever it is you have to do, because you won't have me around to tell it much longer."

Jack stood up. "We'll have to take a sworn statement to preserve your testimony. I'll make arrangements to get a court reporter out here."

Gus Westenbok looked up at him. "She'll be out of the house around this time tomorrow," he said, again referring to the absent woman. "She doesn't know about this. She thinks I was a hero. But I hid the truth, and because of me an innocent man got hurt. That makes me the worst kind of coward."

Jack offered his hand and the man took it. "We'll do our best to keep her out of it, Captain," Jack promised quietly. "We don't want to hurt anyone. We're just trying to straighten things out."

❧ ❧ ❧

Once again R.J. took the wheel and drove back toward the airport where they would find a hotel for the night. They would have to return another day with a court reporter for a sworn statement. Jack was in the passenger seat with his head back and eyes closed, and neither of them broke the silence for a long time. Finally, Jack spoke.

"Rob, about the coffee: don't refuse an offer of food when you're a guest. An offer like that is some kind of Biblical thing. Book of Genesis, I think."

R.J.'s thoughts weren't about coffee. "All of those men died because King Tut was busy getting laid," he said bitterly.

"The men at Balaclava died because somebody misunderstood an order," Jack replied. He opened his eyes and saw his younger partner looking back at him. "Balaclava. The Charge of the Light Brigade. Remember?"

"That was just a poem," R.J. reminded him.

"No it wasn't. It really happened. The poem came later," Jack said.

"Well, it's different."

"Is it?" Jack asked. "Why? Why is it different? Because it happened a hundred years ago instead of forty? Or is it different because those men were British and the men Tut killed were Americans?" R.J. did not respond. Jack closed his eyes again, laid his head back and continued, almost speaking to himself, "Or is it because the men of the Light Brigade died in the sunshine, in a gallant charge, with gleaming sabers and flags flying and horses under them, while our poor bastards drowned in some dark, stinking troopship? They're all equally dead, Rob; killed by the stupidity of war."

"Why did you tell Westenbok we'd keep it quiet? He doesn't deserve anything from us . . . from Les."

"I don't know what he deserves," Jack answered. "He'll be meeting the final Judge before too long. Let Him figure that out. As for me, I'd prefer to solve Les' problem without causing any more pain . . . if that's possible."

"How?"

"I don't know yet, but I'm sure it's going to take another trip to Washington when we get back home."

"Can we take a few days off?" R.J. pleaded. "I'm getting pretty tired of lonely restaurant meals."

"Don't worry," Jack laughed, slapping his leg. "This time you'll have me to keep you company."

"I'd still like a few days off if you don't mind," R.J. groused.

CHAPTER 27

Whether Jack minded it or not, R.J. was not in the office for the next two days, and he came in late and left very early for a few more after that. He was a partner, not an employee—Jack had made that clear from the first day of their handshake agreement—so he made an executive decision and gave himself a little R & R.

Jennifer, too, was making herself scarce. No doubt she was spending 'quality time' with R.J., Marilyn thought, and that was just fine. Uncle Doug went into his office with his newspaper every morning, and only interrupted her when he told he was going out to lunch. He always invited her, and when she politely declined—as she always did—he always asked if he could bring something back for her. Even though she politely declined that offer as well, he always returned with a piece of fresh-baked pie, or cookies, or her most serious addiction: peanut crusted doughnuts. "Got to take care of our little mother," he would say when he put the bag down on her desk before disappearing to the adjoining office to watch afternoon television.

It was peaceful. It was pleasant. It was almost boring, until the afternoon that Jennifer burst in full of her usual excitement and enthusiasm.

"Marilyn, quick, you've got to see this!" she said as soon as she opened the connecting door from Doug Calkins' office.

"Jennifer! Somebody from VSP Marketing called twice. They said we're paying them $5,000 for banners! What's going on?"

"Right, they want me to approve the artwork," Jennifer explained. "I'll do it on my way back from class tomorrow!"

"Jennifer, five thousand dollars!" Marilyn insisted.

"Pocket money . . . chump change when you see this! Come in here right now!"

It was impossible to argue with her, so Marilyn moved into the adjoining office and into one of the available chairs while Uncle Doug tilted his back and listened while Jennifer made an announcement.

"I'm going to show the two of you my top-secret project that's going to make our marina famous nationwide . . . maybe even worldwide." She popped a VCR tape into the machine, perched on the edge of a desk and waited.

The logo of the Bonita Public Television station appeared, and a voice that sounded a lot like Eddie Miles said . . .

"And now, from the famous Dupré's restaurant in Calkins Harbor, Florida, join us with Chef Henri Dupré . . ."

Marilyn said, "Jennifer, what is this?"

"Shhh," came the answer.

The next shot was of Marilyn's father, sitting around a table, drinking wine with some friends. "You know, *mes amis*," he proclaimed, sounding like he was slightly into his cups, "to be happy in this life you need three things: good food, good wine, and the love of a beautiful woman."

At that he looked at the lady next to him—Victoria Townsend—who smiled back, winked an eye, lifted a glass to him and sipped from it.

"Good wine," Henri continued, looking around the table, "ah, good wine you can buy. The love of a beautiful woman" he nodded in Victoria's direction, "that you must find for yourself."

He looked across the table in the direction of the camera again, and held up what was now a half-full wine glass. "But for good food, *mes amis* . . . for good food you must come into my kitchen."

Henri got up, looking as comfortable as he would have at home, and the people at the table followed him into his inner sanctum while another "title shot" appeared on the screen and Eddie Miles' voice invited viewers to, 'Come Into My Kitchen starring Chef Henri Dupré.'

Once there Eddie's off-camera voice asked. "What's on the menu tonight, Chef?" and after a moment's hesitation, Marilyn's father said, "'*Ah, bon*.' We begin with something simple but filling, eh? *Le Bouillabaisse* of my home in *la Vieux Carré*, the French Quarter . . ."

This was another one of Jennifer's ideas, Marilyn thought, and it could only be going in one direction—BIG! She shuddered at the thought of what might be coming, but in spite of herself she couldn't take her eyes off the screen. Her father was a born performer and someone at a TV station understood that well enough to turn him loose. The rest of the program consisted of Chef Dupré doing what he did best—cooking—while voice-overs explained what was going on. Chef Dupré interrupted with occasional live outbursts like "*Merde*! More oysters I asked for, and my friend Lacey brings me scallops!" He held a few up. "These they are oysters?" Now he was playing directly to the camera. "So, *j'ai pas vraiment d'choix*, we have no other choice, with more seasoning into the pot they go! Our guests are hungry! For them we make a small change and create something new! *Viva la différence!*"

The video ended with people enjoying his cuisine while the Chef circulated among their tables, joking and pouring more wine, while a voice Marilyn clearly recognized as belonging to Eddie Miles invited viewers to "Tune in next week . . ."

Uncle Doug laughed and clapped, "That was great, Jenny! Just great!"

Marilyn sat in shocked silence. Finally, she asked, "What are you going to do with this, Jennifer?" She hesitated and added, hopefully, "It's some kind of school project, right?"

"School project? Are you kidding? This is the pilot for our new series, 'Come Into My Kitchen' filmed right here at Dupré's Restaurant," Jennifer said.

"New series?" Marilyn asked weakly.

"The station signed us up for thirteen episodes. They plan to start running the program the first week of June!"

"The first week of June? Jennifer, how are you . . . what are . . . who's going to do all this work?"

"The same people who did it last time: Jim Lacey will direct; the station will supply the technical crew . . . for now, at least; Eddie Miles will do the voice overs . . . did you know he did that stuff in college by the way? . . . and, of course, your mother-in-law because Jim says your father can't perform without her in the audience. And I'm sure your father knows thirteen recipes."

"You're going to pull all this together in six weeks?" Marilyn protested.

"Jim will. He's already working on it. If they start broadcasting the first week of June, the first season will end just before *Sposafesta*. Isn't that cool?"

The magic word brought Marilyn to her senses—and her feet. "*Sposafesta*? Jennifer . . . what is that?"

The festival, Marilyn . . . my wedding; arriving aboard the *Margaret*; we talked about this," Jennifer replied, and added, "Marilyn, honey, are you feeling all right?"

"Five thousand dollars for banners?"

"We have to decorate the town, of course."

"We can't spend any more money until this place generates some income!" Marilyn shouted.

"All right, please, calm down. Think of the baby, okay? Just be calm. I might as well tell you I made a few, little, teeny-tiny changes in my plans for the first floor."

Marilyn collapsed back into her chair. "Tell me," she said weakly.

"With this TV thing going, we can't waste all that space with just a bar and lounge and these offices. I told Tim Gorman to gut the whole place. I showed him my plans and he said there would be no problem getting it finished before September."

"Gut the whole place?" Doug Calkins protested. "Where's my office going to be?"

"I'll get to that in a minute, Uncle Doug."

"Please don't say the tent," Marilyn said as she held her head in her hands.

"No, not the tent of course, Silly! The tent will be cleaned up and we'll get it ready for the wedding ceremony. Erlene Rodgers did a great job of selling most of that junk, and we'll give away or throw way the rest of it. As for these offices, I've already arranged to have a double-wide in here next week."

"A trailer?" Doug and Marilyn both protested.

"A double-wide. They do it all the time when people rebuild commercial property and need to keep the business going. It has rooms for offices, and a new, clean lavatory, and even a kitchen and conference room. In fact, it's a lot better than the dump we're working out of at the moment."

Marilyn put her head back and closed her eyes. "What's going to happen to this dump?" she whispered.

"Okay, let me show you these sketches," Jennifer said, opening the pad that seldom left her side. "See, here, where the offices are now, will be the bar and lounge area. Notice that the windows behind the bar are these . . ." she gestured toward the office windows that looked out on the marina ". . . we can't afford to waste that view. Tim's going to dig down and lower the area behind the bar so the guests who are being served will have an unobstructed view. Now here, along the far wall, will be the staircase going up to the second floor . . . with an elevator in the corner, of course. It's in the same place where the old stairway was, but going in the other direction . . . so it's no big deal, Tim says."

As she spoke and sketched the details, Doug Calkins was caught up in Jennifer's excitement and began asking questions. "Well, it's going to leave a lot of wasted space under the stairway, isn't it?"

"Very good, Uncle Doug," she replied, but that's where we'll put the control booth."

"Control booth?" Marilyn sighed, without opening her eyes.

"Of course . . . for the television studio. See, the wall at the far end will have two stages, one in each corner. Your father's side . . . over here on the left, across from the control booth, of course, will have working appliances and its own elevator to bring food and equipment down from the kitchen above. The other stage . . ."

"There's another stage?" Marilyn asked.

"We'll have an audience sitting at these tables on the main floor . . ."

"Audience on the main floor?"

"You know, dinner-theater style. They'll be here one or two nights a week to see the live broadcast of 'Come Into My Kitchen.' Once we get them in that habit, we can't just let the space go to waste the rest of the week . . . can we?"

"No, of course not," Uncle Doug agreed.

"So we'll bring in local acts. We'll pack the place every night. Jim's even thinking about doing a second kind of local show, something like 'Live from Dupré's' or something like that."

"But how will you separate this area from the bar?" Doug Calkins asked, pointing to Jennifer's sketch.

"Yes, that's a problem," Jennifer agreed. "Tim Gorman and I are working on that. I wanted it to be glass with sliding doors, but Tim doesn't think that will block the sound. We might have to go with a solid wall halfway up, and double glass windows above, and maybe French doors. We'll see."

Marilyn stood up unsteadily. "Jennifer . . . Uncle Doug . . . I'm not feeling very well. I'm going home now."

"You poor thing!" Jennifer said. "Shall I come with you? We can talk more about my idea there."

"No!" Marilyn suddenly lowered her voice. "No, thank you, Jennifer. You have some wonderful ideas. But we've talked enough for now. Explain the rest to Uncle Doug. I just need to rest, okay?"

"You poor Honey," Jennifer said, going to her and stroking her hair. "Have a little faith. Everything will work out all right. You'll see."

❧ ❧ ❧

Jack Townsend had become accustomed to seeing many strange things at Cap'n Kelly's, but the one thing he never expected to see was his mother's Lincoln parked next to his trawler yacht when he got home from the office.

Marilyn and Victoria Townsend were sitting at the dinette and quietly drinking tea.

"Is everything okay here?" Jack asked, still not sure of what was happening.

"Yes, Dear, it's just fine," his mother said. "I was just visiting and sharing a cup of tea with my grandchild's mother if you don't mind."

"Jennifer's turning the first floor into a TV studio," Marilyn reported morosely.

"Oh, that," Jack said, as he put down his briefcase and headed for the bar. "It seems they weren't spending all that time off in the bedroom after all," he said as he made himself a drink. "Mother, would you care for a Scotch?"

"No thank you, Dear. I'm driving."

"I wish they had spent all that time in the bedroom. At least she wouldn't be spending more money!" Marilyn said.

Jack brought his glass to the table where he sat down and looked at Marilyn. "And you're worried about it," he said.

"Of course I'm worried about it!" Marilyn groused. "She's spending money like . . . like it's water or something."

"Marilyn, she has plenty of it."

"That's not the point! Just because she has those millions doesn't mean she should throw them away. If she has to do something spectacular, she can set up a Foundation and give out scholarships to Bonita College or something."

"She'll get around to that, Dear," Victoria assured her. "Right now she's just having fun."

"And I'll tell you something . . ." Jack added . . . "now don't get upset, all right? Just be calm. Think Zen. The fact is, I think Jennifer has a darn good idea."

"What?"

"I saw the show. Rob brought a tape in to the office today. It's really quite good."

"I'm so glad to hear that," Victoria put it. "I can't wait to see it. It was so much fun making it."

"I think you're both mad," Marilyn said, looking from one to the other. "Think of the expense!"

"Think of the people it will draw to Dupré's. When that show is a hit . . ." Jack began.

"It isn't a hit yet!" Marilyn reminded him.

"It will be Dear. Your father's personality is . . . very . . . magnetic. The show will be quite an attraction." She looked at her watch and said, "Well, I must be going. Henri and I are meeting Elena and Les for dinner." She got up and kissed Marilyn on the cheek.

"I'll walk you to your car," Jack said, as he opened the salon door for her.

When they got outside, he took Victoria's arm and stopped her for a moment. "Mother, I'd appreciate it if you would look in on Marilyn for the next couple of days. Sometimes she just . . . worries too much. She grew up that way, but there's no need for it now. Explain that to her."

"Where will you be?" Victoria asked.

"Rob and I have to fly up to Washington. We may be gone for a few days."

"Washington? Is there anything I can do to . . . help?"

"I only wish you could. We're going up to the Navy Department to . . . to take care of a matter for a client. Back in the good old days, I'm sure you or Dad could have done it with a telephone call, but things aren't like that anymore. Now the world is filled with faceless bureaucrats hiding behind stacks of regulations. We'll just have to slog our way through."

He opened the car door, kissed her cheek and added, "Please look in on Marilyn, okay? There's nothing for her to worry about. Even if she tries, Jennifer won't be able to spend all of the Calkins money."

CHAPTER 28

Late one afternoon, Jack and R.J. were in Washington, where they were ushered into the office of one of several Assistants to the Deputy Undersecretary of the Navy, a pleasant enough young woman whose sole function appeared to be to prevent anyone from moving further up the chain of command. She smiled at them from behind round horn-rimmed glasses, her trim uniform and white blouse complementing her short brunette hair. On the whole, Lieutenant Monica Qayona presented a very attractive, professional, and absolutely immoveable appearance.

"I thought we were meeting with the Undersecretary," Jack said, trying not to show his pique at being handed off to someone who was God-knew-how-many layers down in the Washington bureaucracy.

"Yes, well, I'm afraid he's unavailable at the moment. He turned this file over to his Deputy, and, since I am assigned to all legal matters, I'm afraid you're stuck with me."

"You're a JAG officer," Jack said.

"Yes, that's right," she confirmed. "On assignment here for the moment. I'll be handling this file."

"This isn't a just a file," R.J. protested. "We're trying to clear a man's name."

"Yes, well, that's a legal issue, isn't it? And because of that the file was assigned to me."

"My partner was just attempting to point out that this is a rather serious matter. It's not a simple request for VA benefits; it could easily turn into a rather nasty lawsuit."

"Mr. Townsend, I can assure you that I handle many serious matters for the Department," Lt. Qayona said with a frozen, horn-rimmed smile.

"I didn't mean to imply you didn't," Jack apologized.

"And I'm sure we can handle this file through our regular channels," she continued. It was becoming increasingly evident that the conversation was going to go where the Lieutenant wanted it to go: exactly nowhere.

"Lt. Qayona, our firm corresponded at some length with your Department as soon as this matter came to our attention," Jack continued.

"Yes, I have all of the letters, and I can assure you I've read the entire file," she said, interrupting him.

He continued speaking with as much composure as he could muster, although that was becoming difficult. "We laid out our position very carefully. We even supplied the Department with a copy of Captain Westenbok's deposition which, by the way, we didn't have to do and which might even be detrimental to our client if we have to resort to legal action. And we were absolutely assured before flying up here that we would be meeting with the Office of the Undersecretary of the Navy."

"I am a member of that office," Mr. Townsend she said, sharply. "I explained that the Undersecretary himself is unavailable. He gave the file to the Deputy, who in turn assigned it to me. I am a lawyer, just like the two of you, and I am quite capable . . ."

"I'm not questioning your capability," Jack interrupted. "I am questioning your authority."

The conversation was heating up. Apparently, one did not question Lt. Qayona's authority. "I can quite assure you I have sufficient authority to handle this file through our regular channels."

"But this isn't a 'file,'" R.J. burst out. "And we're up to our ears with 'regular channels. We represent an innocent man . . ."

"A man who alleges he's innocent," Lt. Qayona shot back at him.

"He's an innocent man," Jack insisted, "an innocent man who was wrongly convicted of treason, and spent ten years in a federal prison. And we have a dying retired naval captain who knows the whole stinking truth. Is the Department going to rectify matters, or are we going to haul the whole mess out in public before a District Judge?"

"Mr. Townsend, I'm threatened with lawsuits every day. We have a very efficient legal staff. One more case won't change our statistics very much if at all."

R.J. suddenly got to his feet. "Is that all we are, files and statistics?" he shouted. "Don't you care about an innocent man? What the hell kind of place is this?"

"Mr. Meacham, if you can't control yourself, I'll be forced to call Security."

Jack stood up and put a hand on his partner. "Don't bother to call Security, Lieutenant. We're leaving. I can see this entire trip was a waste of time. We'll file our papers in the Southern District Court when we get home. That's when the media will get ahold of the story and the avalanche will be on its way to the desk of the Undersecretary . . . or maybe higher. That might get your attention. Sorry to have troubled you."

He pushed R.J. toward the door and made a move to follow him out, but the mention of 'media' got Lt. Qayona's attention. She stood up behind her desk.

"Mr. Townsend, wait a minute. I'm sure that you, as a lawyer with many years of experience, can appreciate that these things take time."

Her tone was almost conciliatory, but Jack wasn't buying it.

"Let's go, Rob. Maybe we can catch a late flight."

"Mr. Townsend, please," the Legal Assistant to the Deputy Undersecretary continued, "I'm sure you of all people can appreciate the fact that we can't go around changing records without performing a thorough investigation."

"We've already performed a thorough investigation, Lieutenant," R.J. said quietly. "I sent you copies."

"A thorough investigation of our own," the woman continued as she sat down again. She took off her glasses and ran a hand across her forehead. If nothing else, these two guys were giving her a hell of a headache. She put her glasses back on, looked up at them and said, "I'm not saying we can't do anything . . . or that we won't do anything. It's just that these things take time."

Jack and R.J. returned to their seats across from her. "Time is something we don't have," Jack said quietly. "We have an innocent man with a horrific story; we have enormous damages; we have files full of documents and a sworn statement from an important witness who's dying. The only thing we don't have is time."

The young woman shook her head. "Well, I'm afraid that's the best I can do."

"We understand, Lt. Qayona," Jack said. He stood up again and added, "It seems we have nothing more to discuss, but thanks for taking the time to see us."

The interview was over when the door suddenly opened and a short, grizzled old man walked in unannounced. With the neatly slicked-back steel-gray hair that had become his trademark, and the weathered features that had been the subject of so many caricatures, Hollis R. Overton, the senior senator from Oklahoma could hardly be mistaken for a tourist, and Lt. Qayona shot to her feet.

"I heard there was a Townsend in the building," said the Senator in a raspy Midwestern twang, "and I wanted to be sure it wasn't Portner Townsend, returned from the grave to have another go at me." He stuck out his hand. "How 'ya doing, John? It's been a few years, but you haven't gotten old enough for me not to recognize you. How's your mother?"

"Fine, Senator."

The Senator made himself comfortable in one of the chairs, and Jack and R.J. followed his lead.

"Does she still keep horses up there at Saratoga?"

Jack sighed. If only she would, he thought. There was no telling what mischief she was getting into with Henri Dupré at the moment. "Actually, she's talking about moving to Florida, Senator. I don't know what her plans are for the farm."

The old man's eyes lit up. "I'll be retiring at the end of this term. I'll need to have a little chat with her." He sighed, wistfully. "I need to get back to the soil, John. A couple of those horses would be just what the doctor ordered." He turned to the young 'Legal-Assistant-to' who was still standing behind her desk. "Young lady, do you have any idea who you're talking to here?"

"Well, Senator, Mr. Townsend is an attorney . . ."

"No, of course you don't," Senator Overton shot back, cutting her off in mid-sentence. "Nobody knows anybody around here anymore. The whole place has been taken over by a bunch of do-nothing pencil-necks . . . people with rule books and spreadsheets tucked in fancy briefcases; people who've never seen the inside of a soup kitchen or held off a banker at a farm foreclosure." He looked at Jack and shook his head sadly. "That's why I'm getting out, John. I'm going back to Oklahoma where life is real."

Senator Overton turned to the hapless Lt. Qayona again. "Why don't you sit down, young lady, and stop skittering around like a heifer that's about to get branded. And since you don't know this fella, let me give you a history lesson. If it wasn't for his father and a couple of others like him, there might not be a United States Navy today . . . and no young assistant deputies to deputy assistants, either."

He looked at Jack and nodded toward R.J. "Is he ours or theirs?"

"He's ours," Jack assured him.

The Senator settled into his chair a little more and turned to the Legal Assistant to the Deputy Undersecretary, a woman who was young enough to be his granddaughter and continued.

"I came to Congress in '46, riding the wave of victory and full of high ideals. I was ready to singlehandedly take apart every war machine we had and turn it into scrap metal. Portner Townsend was . . . well, I guess he was supposed to be a lobbyist in those days. He claimed he was representing the steel companies, and during my first term as a Congressman, I guess I believed that. But I suspected there was more to his story and as the years went on . . . Let's just say it became pretty clear who he was working for." He paused, and caught the woman's eyes. "He was working for us."

"Portner had a way of analyzing things," the Senator continued. "He could spot problems. He would bring people together and get them talking, and he could tell you before they could where the sticking points would be. He started talking about Korea before any of us knew where the hell it was. When the time came . . . and he said it would come . . . we were ready." Senator Overton hesitated and corrected himself, "Well, at least we weren't as unready as we would have been if Portner hadn't been around Washington, working on a bunch of us."

He looked at Jack. "You probably don't remember, but your mother threw some wonderful parties at Saratoga."

"I remember you riding the horses," Jack replied.

"Fresh out of Oklahoma. I couldn't believe that New York society people knew anything about horses. After that first party was when I really started listening to your father. I figured if his wife knew that much about horses, he just might know something about his business, too. Now, tell me, what brings you to Washington? And why didn't you call me before you came here? You now, I should be mad at you for that!"

"Well, Senator . . . I didn't want to . . ."

"You didn't want use any influence. Wanted to do it on your own. What the hell's the matter with you, John? Didn't they teach you better than that?" The Senator looked at R.J. "You his client?"

"No, sir, I'm his law partner."

"Well, you have my sincere sympathy." He stuck out his hand and R.J. shook it. "I'm Holly Overton," he said.

"Yes, sir, I know, sir. I'm Rob Meacham."

"Your partner here was always doing things on his own. Sailing homemade boats on that farm pond instead of doing his piano lessons. Damn near drove his mother crazy!"

"Well, she's getting back at him now," R.J. reported with a smile.

"Is she? I'm glad to hear that. Makes me think there's hope for me." He turned to Jack. "Are you going to tell me why you're here or not?"

"It's a long story, Senator."

"They all are. Is it something your father would be proud to know you have a hand in?"

"Very much so."

"All right, what are you doing for supper?"

Jack and R.J. exchanged a look that was not lost on the Legal Assistant to the Deputy Undersecretary of the Navy.

Holly Overton looked at his watch. "I've got a meeting with the Whip in ten minutes." He looked up at Jack. "Stop by my office and give my girl the name of your hotel. She'll arrange for a car pick to you up. There's a new steakhouse in town that claims to be as good as those back home. I doubt it, but we'll see. How's seven o'clock sound?"

Jack nodded his approval.

"That'll give us time for a couple of Blue Labels before we eat." He turned to R.J. and added, "That's another thing I learned from his mother."

The Senator stood up to leave, and everyone else did the same. "We'll talk later." He turned to the woman standing behind her desk.

"Lieutenant . . . I'm sorry, what was your name again?"

"Qayona, sir."

"Yes, Lt. Qayona. Sorry. Tell whoever you need to tell that I'll be meeting the Secretary of the Navy in his office at 9:00 o'clock tomorrow morning."

"I'm . . . I'm not sure the Secretary will be available, Senator."

"You tell whoever you're supposed to tell that the Chairman of the Senate Armed Services Committee will be there at 9:00 a.m. I think the Secretary will be available."

Holly Overton shook hands with Jack and R.J., nodded to the woman standing behind the desk and left the room.

"I guess I'll be working late tonight, Mr. Townsend," Lt. Qayona said.

"Being a lawyer is not an easy life, Lt. Qayona," Jack said. He pointed to the JAG insignia on her sleeve and said, "Remember, 'The mills of the gods grind exceedingly fine . . .'"

"'They grind slowly but they grind exceedingly fine,'" she smiled slightly as she finished the quotation. "You're one of the few people I've met who recognize our JAG Corps insignia. You must be a Navy man."

"No, sorry, just the Commodore of a yacht club," Jack admitted. "But I hang around boats a lot."

"Well . . . Commodore . . . thank you for recognizing the insignia for what it is . . . rather than what some of the people around here call it."

Jack took her hand and smiled back. "My heart is always with the Navy," he assured her. "I hope we can speed up those grindstones."

❧ ❧ ❧

The late Spring weather was comfortable and Jack suggested they walk for a while. R.J. agreed, and they pushed along in silence for a few blocks while late afternoon traffic was piling up at every intersection and busses were spewing darkening clouds into the thickening air. There was a mounting urgency as the first waves of office workers left their jobs and tried to accomplish scores of domestic chores before they got home to a quick dinner, television and bedtime. Then they would have to get up the next day and do it all over again.

"How many Lt. Qayona's are on those buses, do you think?" Jack said to no one in particular. "You know . . . keep the paperwork moving, never make a decision, pass the file off to someone else." He turned to R.J. and said bluntly, "That's what they were going to do to us if Holly Overton hadn't walked in."

"Are you going to tell me about that?"

"About him walking in? I don't know. I suspect my mother may have had something to do with it. I mentioned something to her about us coming to Washington . . . and about the Navy. I have to learn to keep my mouth shut. On the other hand, maybe it's best that I didn't."

"I meant the whole story . . . the real story," R.J. said.

"That is the real story. Hollis R. Overton, currently the senior senator from Oklahoma. You heard him . . . he's been around here since 1946. I guess when you're in this town that long you know your way around the buildings and who's where. And obviously when you say something, people jump."

"I meant the story about Porter Townsend," R.J. persisted. "I've never heard you mention him."

"John Portner Townsend . . . don't forget the 'n'," Jack finally said. "He was my father. He was a Wall Street lawyer and sometime lobbyist. Well, that was his cover story." He looked at R.J. with a wry smile and added, "He really was what our British friends might call an 'Ambassador without Portfolio.' The 'without portfolio' part drove my mother nuts."

"What did he do, exactly?"

"Everything," Jack replied. "Whenever and wherever our Government needed something done . . . something officially unofficial . . . something they could deny if need be . . . Portner Townsend would show up as the attorney for some lofty but obscure client . . . Consolidated Amalgamated

Industries or some such thing. He'd work out an arrangement between his client . . . that was us, of course . . . and whoever was on the other side . . . to do what our Government wanted done. Then he would fly home to New York and never talk about it."

"Are you serious?" R.J. said.

"Remember the 'ping-pong diplomacy' that took place about ten years ago?"

"When the Chinese broke the ice with the Americans by playing table tennis against us, and eventually got recognized by the U.N.? Your father did that?"

"I don't know for sure . . . I doubt if few people other than Holly Overton know the details . . . but at that time my father was the lawyer for the 'Cultural Exchange Table Tennis Foundation,' and he flew to China a lot. After the big ping-pong match, the politicians took over and things began to move pretty quickly."

"It sounds exciting," R.J. observed.

"I'm sure it was," Jack said. "The excitement killed him. He died of a heart attack before he turned sixty."

"God, that's terrible."

"My mother didn't help. She was always bugging him about not getting enough credit for what he did. I guess she wanted the title 'Mrs. Ambassador,' but he was happier working behind the scenes."

"You blamed her?" R.J. asked quietly.

"Yes, I did, when I was younger. It was one of the things that drove us apart." Jack put his head down and continued walking, "But when I got older I learned . . . the hard way . . . the very hard way . . . that things don't have to be anybody's fault. Sometimes things happen for reasons we don't understand . . . and maybe we can't understand. My father's death was one of those things." He stopped walking and said, "It was nobody's fault, Rob. It was just . . . I don't know . . . it was just meant to be, I guess. Let's take a cab the rest of the way."

"And what was that stuff about the 'mills of the gods' supposed to mean?" R.J. asked when they were settled into the back seat.

"It was just a way of letting her know I recognized the rather obscure insignia on her uniform sleeve. It gave us a little 'brothers-in-blood' attachment."

"So, what was it?"

"It's a line from the Classics . . . Greek, I think. 'The mills of the gods grind slowly, but they grind exceedingly fine.' When the Navy JAG Corps was created not too many years ago, some classical scholar decided that instead of the usual scales of justice, the legal insignia should be what's called a 'millrind' . . . It's supposed to symbolize that although justice may be slow, it's thorough."

"Let's hope the justice isn't slow in this case," R.J. observed, stretching back in the seat. "So . . . what's that business about the other thing people call it?"

"It was her way of letting me know that she knew the inside joke: kind of a 'brothers-in-blood' countersign." You can look up for yourself back at the office."

R.J. shook his head. "Jack, where do you come up with this stuff?"

"Latin and Greek? That's from prep school."

CHAPTER 29

Morning found Erlene Rodgers checking out the construction area on the first floor of the main building where Jennifer was huddled in a meeting with Tim Gorman, her construction supervisor. "No problem," Tim was saying. "We'll need to ramp up the electrical service for the lights. And I'm not real sure about that control booth under the stairs. Maybe that should be the rest rooms."

"Keep the rest rooms in the bar area, Tim," Jennifer said. "If anybody has to pee during our live shows, they can go to the bar."

"Hello? C'n I come in?" Erlene called from the doorway.

"Oh, hi, Erlene," Jennifer said. "Come on in. Just be careful, okay?"

"I was j'st wonderin' how the gift shop was comin' along," Erlene said as she stepped carefully through the construction debris.

"The gift shop?" That idea had completely slipped Jennifer's mind in the excitement of the television studio. "Oh, well . . . we'll have to talk about that, Erlene."

"See, me an' Eddie's gettin' all set f'r it. We're figurin' ideas all th' time."

"Gosh, Erlene, I think Eddie Miles is going to have his hands full with another project."

The Gas Girl's face clouded. "Really? He didn't say nothin' ta' me about that."

"It came up pretty quickly, I'm afraid. I know he's been quite busy," Jennifer said.

"We're still goin' ahead with th' gift shop, ain't we? I mean, I'd sure like ta' get off the gas dock . . . and you did kinda promise . . . an' everythin'."

"A promise is a promise, Erlene. We are definitely going to have a gift shop. Tim Gorman and I are just going over the plans right now, figuring out where it will be."

"That's good," the Gas Girl's face suddenly brightened into a full smile. "'cause it's about time ta' get me some air conditionin'." She looked at Jennifer and if she might have said something wrong. "I mean, I'll still handle that gas dock too. I'd never let ya'll down, ya' know!"

"We would never let you down either, Erlene. Just give Tim and me some time with these plans, okay?"

"Sure. An' I guess I'd better be lookin' around f'r a new gift shop helper. Do ya' think Nancy Neblett would be interested?"

"Well, why don't you go ask her, okay?"

"I reckon I'll do just that. Bye now."

Tim Gorman kept his mouth firmly shut during the discussion, but after Erlene was safely out of earshot, he turned to Jennifer and said, "Please don't tell me you're thinking about adding another floor to the building!"

Lunch time in Washington, D.C., found Jack and R.J. at a table for two in the hotel restaurant. Jack decided he would have one—only one—Scotch, well, maybe two—while R.J. drummed his figures on the table and looked like he was about to jump up and begin pacing around the room.

"Drumming your fingers isn't going to make the call come any sooner," Jack said.

"Drinking Scotch won't make it come any sooner either," R.J. shot back.

Jack smiled. Obviously, his young partner had not waited out as many jury verdicts as he had. "No, but me drinking Scotch shouldn't bother you, and your finger drumming is bothering the hell out of me."

"Oh, I'm sorry . . ."

"Come on, I'm just pulling your leg!"

"How can you be so calm?"

"We laid out our case, Rob. We gave every single fact we had to the Department of the Navy, and we may have had some help thanks to Portner Townsend and the Chairman of the Armed Services Committee. And let me remind you of something: that Chairman . . . Senator Hollis Overton by name . . . told us not to leave Washington until we got a call," Jack reminded him. "So now we wait for the verdict."

"A call from who . . . from whom?" R.J. corrected his English usage.

"I don't know. But you have that damn pager you insisted on buying . . . and the desk clerk knows the number. We can either sit here and I'll drink Scotch until I'm plastered and you can beat your fingers until you need a manicure, or we can check out the Smithsonian. When the call comes, you'll get it."

"Maybe we should just wait right here . . . in our rooms or the lobby or something," R.J. suggested.

"Maybe we can find a courtroom somewhere and pitch pennies against the jury box. That worked for me back in my Assistant State Attorney days," Jack said.

"Let's go to the Smithsonian," R.J. groused.

❧ ❧ ❧

Sibby Maggio paced the parking lot as he looked at his knock-off fancy watch and waited for his wife Babe and their two daughters to drive in. He was dressed in a new polo shirt, new khakis—in fact, new everything—right down to his new Topsiders. The only thing he refused to wear was socks. He wasn't about to go that far, even though he promised to take the family out for a real nice dress-up dinner.

Babe's car finally rolled in with Kathy and Clissy in the back seat.

"Hey, Dad! You look great!" Kathy called out.

"Look, a collared shirt and everything!" Clissy added.

"What? Dinner with the family? No jeans?" his wife said with a smile through her open window. "You hit the lottery or something?"

"No, I didn't hit the lottery; I just got lucky on some stuff, that's all," he explained. "Come on, let's go," he added as he got into the passenger seat.

"We wanna see your boat first!" Clissy shouted from the back seat.

"Yeah, we wanna see it," Kathy added.

"We don't have time to look at the boat," Sibby said. "Come on, let's go."

"Please, Dadddyyy?" It was Clissy, the younger of the two. She always got to him with the way she said 'daddy.'

"Okay, okay, we'll just drive up to it and look at the outside, okay? She ain't much. She's pretty old and needs paint and . . . cleaning up . . . and . . ." Before he could finish talking Babe had the car rolling forward. "It's this way, isn't it?"

"Yeah, yeah this is the way. But we're not getting out, okay?"

The minute the car stopped both back doors opened, and the girls looked like circus performers who had been shot out of a cannon.

"Girls! I said we're not getting out!" Sibby demanded.

"Let them have fun, Sib! What's the matter, you got some 'chippie' stashed in there?" his wife said with a wink.

"Come on, Babe, I don't want them going in there. The place is a dump. You know, I haven't kept it real clean . . . or anything."

"What? And we're gonna be shocked?" she said as she opened her door.

"Babe, come on, let's just have a nice quiet dinner."

"Okay, girls, let's go see where your Dad hangs up his clothes . . . if he knows how to hang them up!" his wife said as she helped the two girls on board.

"Ugh, this is really scuzzy," Kathy said as she walked into the main cabin.

"Yeah, but it's neat," Clissy added. "Look at this couch. It would be a great place to watch TV or something."

"Come on . . . everybody out. Come on, seriously, okay?" Sibby protested.

"Kathy, come here! Up in the front! There's these two really neat beds that meet at the foot part! What a neat way to keep your feet warm!" Clissy shouted.

"Yuck! Is this where you go to the bathroom?" Kathy said as looked into the forward head.

"Sibby, really, I don't mean to nag, but . . . this sink!" his wife reminded him in the galley.

Before he could say anything, the girls were rushing past them heading for the aft cabin.

"Wow, look at this!" they heard Clissy shout. "There's two whole beds back here!"

"Eeeyue! You sleep back here, Dad?" Kathy said.

"Okay, okay, I didn't invite you guys here to criticize my life, okay?"

"So why did you invite us here, Sib?"

He pulled an envelope out of his brand-new khaki pants and handed it to her. "I wanted to give you this. But I wanted to do it at a nice, upscale, quiet place, okay?"

The girls were still exploring the boat, with Clissy proclaiming what a great place it was and Kathy telling her not to touch anything. Babe Maggio opened the envelope and gasped.

"Don't bother to count it," Sibby said. "That's a thousand bucks cash. Spend it, 'cause there's gonna be more where that came from."

They were jammed up close to each other in the confines of the galley while the girls ran back and forth between the cabins.

"I'd sleep here in a minute!" Clissy proclaimed.

Babe looked at him and said, "So what did ya' do? Hold up a gas station?"

"No more gas stations, Babe. That's your share of the first payment received by Maggio Marine Services."

"Now you're selling stock in fake companies?"

"It's my company . . . okay, it can be our company if you want it to be. Commodore Townsend set up a corporation for me, and he says there's no problem with financing. He's even got people lined up to do the bookkeeping."

"What's the matter with me?" Babe Maggio demanded. "I did a damn good job of keeping our books when we had the garage." She turned for a moment and shouted, "Girls, settle down, okay?" Her voice had always been the law in the Maggio household.

"You have a job," Sibby reminded her. "You have a nice place. I didn't want to screw that up."

"Girls, settle down!" she said, before she turned to him and added, "You're right, I do have a job and I have the girls and we have a nice place . . . but we don't have you, Sibby."

"Let's go out to dinner, okay?" he said. "I made a reservation at the Bonita Prime Steakhouse."

"Bonita Steakhouse? Isn't that the place with the four dollar bill signs in the Gusto section of the paper?"

"What do you care?" he laughed. "You got your half. The dinner's on me."

❧ ❧ ❧

What should have been an interesting and relaxing couple of days at one of America's greatest tourist destinations wasn't relaxing for R.J. who kept checking his 'beeper' every few minutes to make sure it was working and looking around for telephones to return 'the call' as soon as he received a message. As for 'interesting' sites, the only thing he was interested in was a call from Senator Overton or Lt. Qayona, or both. The call didn't come and, given Overton's stern warning not to leave Washington until it did, R.J. had pretty much resigned himself to another restaurant dinner and a night of watching television in his lonely hotel room.

"Give them time," Jack kept assuring him as they checked out every monument and museum that interested him. "Holly Overton said to stay in town until we got word, and that's what we're going to do." He clapped the younger man on a shoulder and said, "Buckle up, man! The jury's out and now our job is to wait."

"Yeah, well, what if your so-called 'jury' comes up empty?"

"There's always the United States District Court, Rob."

"And newspapers and reporters, and a lot of very hurtful publicity," R.J. added.

"I thought you didn't care about Westenbok?"

"You know, I've been thinking about that poor bastard ever since we left Arizona. What's that line in the Bible about 'tried in the balance and found wanting'?"

"What? Robert! You're quoting the Bible? You're the one who said I shouldn't have made him any promises, remember?" Jack said.

"Yes, and I also remember what you said . . . about him going to meet the final Judge. That stuck with me."

"We'll all get there sooner or later, Rob."

"You didn't say that, but that idea stuck with me too," R.J. added. "We only get one chance, right?

"No, we get many chances; we get as many chances as it takes to get it right. We just have to get it right, before . . . you know . . . the 'Final Process Server' comes with that ultimate summons."

"Let's not get that summons for a long time, okay?" R.J. asked

"I'm glad to hear you've softened a bit, Robert J. Meacham. Maybe when I get up there I'll get couple of points for being your mentor. Now forget about that damn beeper. When we've had our fill of museums and monuments, we'll take a cab back to the hotel. Our call will come when it comes."

Their call did come. It didn't come while they were at Arlington, nor did it come when they were in the taxicab. In fact, R.J.'s pager went off when they were walking through the hotel lobby and he bolted for the front desk.

"I'm Robert Meacham, he told the desk clerk. Do you have a call for me?"

"Yes, Mr. Meacham, I was just paging you."

"I know you were just paging me. I was standing right over there!" he almost shouted as he gestured in Jack's direction. "When did this call come in?"

"Just a few . . . just a few minutes ago, sir," the desk clerk reported.

"A few minutes ago? It's almost six o'clock!"

"Yes sir, I can assure you that call came in a few minutes ago. We were all told it was very important and we were to page you immediately."

"Where's the phone? Give me the phone, quick!" R.J. dialed the number.

"Monica Qayona speaking," the voice on the other end of the line said.

"Lieutenant Qayona, this is Robert Meacham. I was just notified of your call."

"Yes, thank you, Mr. Meacham," the Assistant to the Undersecretary said, "I wonder if you and your partner might come over to my office this evening?"

"This evening? You mean like right now? What news do you have for us, Lt. Qayona?" R.J. asked.

"I'd prefer to discuss that with the two of you in person . . . and in private," the Legal Assistant to the Undersecretary said.

"We'll be there in fifteen minutes . . . depending on Washington traffic, of course."

"I'll be here when you get here, Mr. Meacham, regardless of the traffic."

R.J. ran back to his partner. "Come on, Jack, we have to go," he said.

"Go? Go where?"

"Lt. Qayona's office. She's waiting for us. She's there and she's waiting for us, Jack. It's the jury verdict, remember?"

Jack turned to the desk clerk and told him they might be checking out tonight.

"I'm sorry, sir, but there are no refunds this late in the day."

"Of course not," Jack replied, "nor would we expect any. I'm only giving you what's called a 'heads up.' We may very well be flying home tonight."

CHAPTER 30

Washington traffic wasn't merely bad; it was horrible. It was after 6:30 when they finally arrived at Monica Qayona's office. The young woman, prim and proper as always, horn-rimmed glasses and all, was sitting at her desk doing paperwork, and R.J. immediately began to apologize.

"No need to apologize, Mr. Meacham," she said as she stood up to shake their hands. "I'm working late again tonight. In spite of what many people believe, we do that a lot around here. Please, have a seat."

The woman opened a folder that was lying on her desk. "It seems we made a very bad mistake," she began. "Forty years ago, in . . . I guess what you might call 'in the heat of battle' . . . we sent an innocent man to prison." She handed Jack the folder. "I said we couldn't do anything until we ran our own investigation, Mr. Townsend. We did that, and it confirmed everything the two of you brought to us. And, as the saying goes . . . 'just for the record'. . . the only special consideration this case received was 'fast track' treatment . . . and that was because our witness . . . the only person left who knows the whole story is . . . well, you know . . . he's dying."

Jack paged through the file and handed the documents to R.J. one at a time.

"What I mean to say is this: no elected official had anything to do with the outcome of this case. The only thing Senator Overton was responsible for was bringing it to our attention."

"We understand," R.J. nodded. "We would never suggest to anyone that he influenced your decision."

She looked directly at Jack. "Mr. Townsend . . . may I call you 'Jack'?"

Jack Townsend nodded, "Frankly, I would much prefer it."

"Jack . . . you once said you had a client with enormous damages, and it's true . . . you do. You represent a man who spent ten years confined for a crime he didn't commit. How he lived during those years, and under a cloud for all the years after that, I can only imagine. You could get a hell of a big judgment against us, Mr. Townsend . . . Jack."

"We didn't come here for that, Monica," Jack said. "We came here to see justice done."

"We're not interested in hurting anyone," R.J. added.

"It would be a real show of good faith on your client's part if he would sign a general release."

"I can pretty much guarantee that, Monica," Jack said quietly.

"And I can guarantee that he will receive a rather large appropriation for 'general service' rendered to the United States Navy."

"No newspapers, no reporters," R.J. added.

"None, but I'll be able to close the file, and at least the three of us will know we served the cause of justice . . . Robert . . . or is it 'Rob'?"

R.J. smiled. "Either one is fine; I'm not fussy."

Lt. Qayona stood up, and again offered her hand. "Well," she said, "at least in this case the 'mills of the gods' ground things out properly."

"May we at least take you out to dinner or something?" R.J. asked as he shook her hand.

The prim and proper Lt. Qayona smiled. "Rob, I have at least another hour before I get out of here. And if I accept your offer I'd have to spend more time after that filling out the required ethics forms. So, thank you for the offer, but the answer has to be, 'no.' Besides, if you leave now you might be able to catch a late flight back home. Oh, and don't forget this." She handed Jack a tan mailing envelope. He opened the clasp and glanced inside. It contained only one document, but it was an important one. It was the one Les Leslie had been dreaming about for forty years.

"Thank you, Lt. Qayona . . . Monica," Jack said, shaking her hand. "And if you ever decide to practice law in Florida, please keep us in mind."

The Maggio family settled into a quiet booth in the Bonita Prime Steakhouse. The lady from the front desk handed them their enormous menus—almost too big to open all at once—and a server came around to pour water.

"I'll have a Big Mac and fries," Clissy said when he came around.

"Yes, Miss, your server will be here in a few minutes to take your order."

"Clissy!" Babe Maggio whispered, "this isn't the kind of place where you order a Big Mac and fries."

"But I like a Big Mac and fries! Can't we do what we usually do?" the eight-year-old asked.

"Just be quiet, okay?" her older sister warned.

The server came around to take drink orders. Clissy almost said "Big Mac," but Kathy kicked her under the table. "I want a Shirley Temple," she said. "And my sister wants one too."

Sibby ordered a Manhattan, and with a huge wink asked that an appetizer of escargot be brought out early; his wife ordered white wine. "What do you know about a "Shirley Temple?" she demanded of their daughter after the server left.

"I seen it in a magazine, okay?" Kathy replied. "There's no alcohol so we can have it, okay?"

"You 'saw' it," her mother corrected her.

"What's es-car-go?" Clissy asked.

"Snails," her father answered with a deadpan expression.

"Eewe! Are we gonna eat snails?" Kathy demanded.

"I'll eat one if Daddy eats one first!" Clissy shouted.

"Clarissa! Inside voice!" her mother reminded the younger girl.

The growing insurrection was quashed by the server who brought the drinks and asked if they were ready to order.

"I'll have fill-et mig-non," Kathy announced, "and I want it . . . let's see . . . medium rare, I guess."

"Yeah, me too," Clissy added."

"No, you're not both having fillet mignon," their mother insisted.

"Oh, come on, Babe, let the girls have fun. Don't we deserve to live it up once in a while?"

"We have bills to pay, Sibby!"

"I gave you money for the bills. Let them have fun."

"I want the fill- et mig-non," Kathy insisted.

"Yeah, me too," Clissy repeated.

"Okay," Babe conceded as she turned to the server. "They'll have one fillet mignon dinner spilt between the two of them!" She looked at Sibby and added, "Is that okay with you, Daddy?"

The server smiled and said, "Yes, Ma'am, and for you?"

"Well, why should I be left out? I'll have the same," Babe Maggio said.

"And for you, sir?"

"We're one big happy family here," Sibby added, "Make it the same all around. "And bring my wife another glass of wine."

"And you?"

"What the hell, I'm not driving! Bring it on!"

Dinner was an educational experience as well as a treat. Kathy learned how to pronounce 'fillet mignon' and found out that in addition to being expensive it really was good. Clissy watched her father—and her mother!—share snails; they looked like creepy things someone found in a swamp, and she refused to eat them. Both girls tried Shirley Temples for the first time and liked them well enough to order seconds instead of colas. Babe Maggio learned that when they were put to the test, the girls knew how to behave properly, and Sibby learned—remembered, rather—how much fun it was to be with all of them. By the time the dessert cart came around—"Oh, yeah," Clissy said by way of greeting it—and the parents were relaxing over coffee laced with Amaretto, they were finding it hard to keep happy tears out of their eyes.

"You know what I wish?" Clissy said as she dug into a double-chocolate fudge cake topped with ice cream, "I wish we could always be like this."

"Places like this are a special treat, Honey," her mother reminded her. "Even rich people don't come here every night."

"Not here every night," Clissy said, licking her spoon. "But why can't we be together like this every night?"

Babe looked at her husband who simply shrugged. "Sweetie, Daddy and I had some problems about . . . getting along . . . and we thought it would be best if we were apart for a while."

"I know. You were always fighting about money. Kathy and I heard you when you thought we were asleep. But it looks like Daddy's got money now, so why can't we all be together again?"

"Cliss, your Mom has a very small apartment . . ." Sibby began.

"So why can't we all live on your boat?" the eight-year-old shot back. "You got two bedrooms and even two bathrooms, and a kitchen sink, and . . ."

"Eewe! Who would want to live in that crummy place?" her older sister protested.

"We could clean it up, Kath! It would be really neat if it we cleaned it up!"

"It's a dump," Kathy protested.

"We have Summer Vacation coming up pretty soon. We could go down to the boatyard and make a project out of it. I'll bet we could even get a couple of our friends to help us."

Kathy thought for a minute and said, "Hmm. That would solve my problem of writing an essay about what I did during Summer Vacation." She looked at her sister and added, "And I'd have something to say when that little snot Margie starts telling everybody about skiing in Aspen." She pointed her nose in the air and said, "Well, we were busy doing stuff on our Dad's yacht."

"Girls, wait a minute," Babe Maggio protested. "I have to go to work, and I already made arrangements for day camp."

"I'm not going to another stupid day camp," Kathy said, raising her voice. "Those things are horrible."

"Well, you can't stay in the boatyard alone," her mother reminded her.

"Who's gonna be alone?" Clissy asked. "Daddy lives down there, and I guess he works down there or something. And there are other people around, aren't there, Dad?"

Babe turned to her husband. "Are you hearing this? Aren't you going to say anything?"

Sibby looked at her with the smile of the fabled Cheshire Cat and shrugged. "Hey, I'm just listening."

"Sibby, who's gonna watch them all day? You?"

"I'm a responsible adult." He brushed off the front of his new shirt and said, "See, I wore a clean shirt and everything."

"You're gonna be out making one of your crazy deals, looking for treasure or something!" his wife shouted.

"Bridget! Inside voice!" Sibby teased, using his wife's full name and pretending to be shocked. "Besides, I'm gonna be working on the *Margaret*, it's right across the marina from us. And at fifty bucks an hour, I can afford to take a couple of hours off to supervise them and take them out for a burger at lunchtime."

"See? Pleaseeee, Mom?" Clissy begged.

"Yeah, I think we should do it," Kathy agreed, rubbing her chin.

"What, you too? I thought you were the sensible one? Okay, but you better watch them, Sibby. Make sure they don't get hurt." She turned to the two girls and added, "And don't get into any kind of trouble."

"They'll have plenty of supervisors at Cap'n Kelly's," Sibby assured her. "And if they're really going to clean up that old tub, they won't have time to get into trouble."

❧ ❧ ❧

Jack and R.J. were finally on their flight home from Washington. Getting to the airport had been a nightmare, and they might not have made it if Jack had not told the cab to wait at the hotel while they threw their clothes into suitcases and bolted out the door. They got there just in time to learn the flight had been delayed, but there was one bright spot—if you could call it that—at least they had time for a quick dinner—if you could call it that—before they boarded the plane.

R.J. got to the Magnolia Avenue house after 2:00 a.m., and expected to see the place totally dark. He was wrong. Jennifer was in the kitchen with her sketch pad and a pot of coffee.

"Jen?" he called as he opened the front door.

"Honey! You're home!" she shouted and rushed from the kitchen table to greet him with a few delightful kisses.

"Jen, what are you doing up so late?"

"I'm just working on some ideas," she said, as she poured him a cup of coffee and refilled her own.

"Jen, it's after two o'clock in the morning. You shouldn't be drinking coffee this late."

"I'm so upset, R.J.," she countered as she replaced the pot. "I really screwed up. I got so wrapped up in that television thing that I forgot the purpose of our lives here."

"Jen, I just got home . . . aren't you going to ask me how it went?"

"Oh, yes, I'm sorry. How did it go, R.J.?" she asked, not looking up from her sketch pad.

"It went very, very well, Jennifer. We really got a . . . we really won . . ."

"You know, there's more to this thing than just fixing up some old buildings" she said. "People! People are our real mission here, R.J. Never mind the buildings and the clean-up, paint-up thing and even the *Sposafesta* festival. Our real job is to take care of the people around here. That's what Grandma would have done."

"Jennifer, don't you care about what happened in Washington?"

"Yes, I care. I care about you. I love you. But you can't tell me what you did, right?" she asked, not looking up.

"No, I really can't. But I can tell you we won," he repeated.

"That's wonderful, R.J.," she said. "Of course you won; you were probably doing something to help someone who really needed help, and you were meant to win." She looked up from her sketch, and kissed him. "And you're also brilliant; which helps a lot, too."

"But . . . don't you care about me?"

"I care about you, R.J. I said I love you. I love you right now, and I also love you every day, and every week and every month of the year. You must be very tired. Why don't you go to bed? I'll be up in a minute."

"Aren't you going to join me?

"I will in a minute," she repeated. "I just want to sketch in a few details."

"Jennifer, are you ignoring me?

"I love you R.J., very much," She replied. "But right now I have an idea, and I have to get it down on paper while I'm thinking about it, okay?" She kissed him gently. "Please, go to bed. I'll be up in a minute."

R.J. was too tired to argue, and from the look of the sketch pad and Jennifer's intense expression and the nearby coffee pot, he concluded her kiss was about the only welcome he would receive. It didn't matter. He was much too tired for more, he thought, as he trudged up the stairs with his suitcase.

CHAPTER 31

The next morning R.J. woke up only to find the bed deserted. Jennifer was already at the construction site huddling with Tim Gorman as they reviewed her latest sketches.

"That's a big job, Jennifer," he protested, "and you're not giving me enough time."

"It was kind of your idea, Tim," she countered. "You said that I shouldn't tell you to add an extra floor to the building to make room for a gift shop and offices. Well, this isn't an extra floor!"

"It's not an extra floor, Jennifer, it's an extra building!"

"It's not an extra building! It's an attachment to the building we already have. It's only three walls, and it's on the ground! Come on! How much time will it take to get a cement truck in here to pour a slab?"

"Jennifer, there's a little more to this than pouring a slab."

"Okay, so you get a crew in here and they throw up some cement blocks! It's only a one-story room . . . a little addition, for cryin' out loud!"

"Right," he countered. "One story next to . . . excuse me . . . attached to a two-story building that has a mansard roof and a wrought-iron balcony."

"So we continue the mansard roof look on the one-story addition; make it slightly smaller . . . move the walls in a little . . . and *voila*!"

"And *voila*, when the people on that second-floor balcony look down, what are they going to see? They're going to see black roofing material, and additional air conditioning units, and a few pipes and stacks. It won't be a pretty sight."

"Hmm, I hadn't thought of that," she said. There was a long pause while she tapped her pencil on the drawing. "I've got it!" she said. "How tall does this addition have to be?"

"As tall as you want it to be; you're the one paying for it," he joked. "You and your architect decide that. I just build it."

"Okay, okay. So we make the roof come up to the level of the balcony; we extend the wrought-iron railing all around the top of the addition, and we make that roof into a big outdoor patio!"

"And the utilities?"

"Outside on the ground, concealed by bushes or something. This will really be great Tim, and it was all your idea."

"I suppose you want this finished, when? Tomorrow?"

"September 6 would be perfect; just in time for *Sposafesta*!"

"And that includes the television studio on the first floor, right?"

"Of course! We can't let that go. It has to be ready for the festival!"

Tim Gorman sighed. "Jen, I'll have to hire another crew . . ."

". . . okay, hire them," she said quickly.

"We need to get permits, and permits means plans . . . not just your sketches . . . real plans. And plans mean architects who are willing to drop everything . . ."

"Hire them, too," she said. "Just get it done, okay?"

"And the interior is going to be . . . what?"

"Entry . . . I don't know . . . from the parking lot, through the gift shop; the offices with widows facing the marina just like they used to be in the old building, and maybe a lavatory . . . yes, a unisex lav for the office staff."

"With a small kitchen?"

"Forget the kitchen; we have a restaurant. Well, okay, maybe a break room. But I'd like to use any extra space for another office or two. I'm sure we'll be expanding our operations."

Tim sighed again. "Okay, listen Jennifer, I'm reasonably sure I can deliver on the foundation, and the outside walls and the rooftop patio. I seriously doubt we can get the interior finished in what . . . sixteen weeks?"

"Eighteen, if you include the first five days of September," she corrected him. "And if the interior isn't completely finished, that's no problem. We'll move in temporary tables for the gift shop and put up 'pardon our dust' signs. The mob of people going into the studio and up to the restaurant will want to come back at holiday time to see the finished product. Tell me you'll do it, Tim."

He looked at her and smiled; she was the same old Jennifer: a bundle of ideas and energy, with a wrapper of charm. "Okay, we'll do it. You can count on me. Does Marilyn know about this?

"No . . . you know, she's having a baby and everything. I don't want to get her excited. Let's just keep this a secret for now."

"That's gonna be tough when the extra men show up and the concrete trucks start pouring the slab."

"I'll tell her it's just an outdoor seating area."

"And when they deliver the blocks?"

"I'll break the news to her in pieces. She'll handle it better that way."

❧ ❧ ❧

'Come Into My Kitchen' was taping its seventh episode of the thirteen Jennifer had promised, and Chef Dupré's audience had grown considerably. As yet there was no studio, so Jim Lacey was making do with what he had: the still-unopened second floor restaurant, and the portable bar they had used for the Townsend rehearsal dinner. For the time being the bar would have to be their set—the place where Chef Dupré would announce his plans for the day's meal and invite the audience to 'come into' his kitchen. Only two things were real—the kitchen, of course—and the audience, which had grown. The original audience of Victoria Townsend, Erlene Rodgers and Jim Lacey, had been joined by Jennifer Calkins, Eddie Miles, Dr. Tom and Nancy Neblett, Countess Elena Russo, Arlo Woodbrace, Les Leslie and a few more tables filled with Tim Gorman and his entire crew. There was no longer any reason to plan careful camera angles to make it 'look like a crowd,' for television purposes it was a crowd, and Jim Lacey was ready to try something new. He set one of the two cameramen at the back of the audience and another closer to the front.

"Okay, Henri, we're going to try something a little different," he told his star.

"Different? But why, Lacey? It is going so well . . ."

"It's going to be better, Henri. You trust me, don't you?"

"Yes, but . . ."

"I want to see you walking in among the tables and greeting the audience as you make your way to the set, okay?

Once you get up there, you stand behind the counter, and tell us what you are going to create today. Got it? That's the only change. Oh, and one more thing . . ."

"No, nothing more. Please, no more . . ."

"Your toque will be on the counter. After you invite the audience to come into your kitchen . . . just like always . . . you'll put on the toque and lead them inside."

Dupré nodded. "This I could do."

Jim Lacey turned to the people at the tables. "Okay, folks, please listen up for a minute. There are enough of you here for us to show the Chef coming into the set through the audience. When I give the order to roll the tape, Eddie will make the usual introduction from right here."

He turned to his life partner and said, "Don't worry, about the sound, Eddie; we'll re-record your voice later in the studio. For the moment, I'm just using your intro for timing purposes. When you're finished, I'll call 'Action!' and that will be Chef Dupé's cue to walk in."

Jim Lacey put his arm around Henri. "You got that, Henri? You'll be in the back of the room and when Eddie finishes his introduction, I'll say 'Action!' and you'll start walking in." Chef Dupré nodded sagely.

Now he turned to the audience again. "Okay, now, everybody, when I say 'Action!' and the Chef starts walking in, I want all of you to go crazy with applause, and of course, turn around and look for him. Remember, this is supposed to be a big room. It's filled with people back there, and you don't know where the Chef is coming from . . . and when you see him, shake his hand, pat him on the back . . . Erlene, take out a notebook, hand him a pen and ask for an autograph. The rest of you, while that's happening, keep clapping, keep applauding, until Chef Dupré steps behind the counter, and asks for quiet so he can announce the menu for today. The food is in the kitchen; it's ready to be prepared and I guarantee there's plenty for everybody."

"There's just one thing," Jim added. "The title of our show is 'Come Into My Kitchen,' but, obviously, we can't fit everybody in the kitchen. So I'd like the people at this table . . ." he pointed to the one where Jennifer Calkins, Victoria Townsend and Elena Russo were seated . . . "and these people" . . . he pointed to Doc and Nancy Neblett and Arlo Woodbrace . . . "to actually come into the kitchen. Everybody else will have to wait out here, but don't worry, we have complimentary beverages for you, and we'll take in different groups for each of our future shows."

Finally, Jim turned to the two cameramen. "I'm counting on you fellows to make this look like a very big crowd. Get one or two long shots of the Chef walking between the tables, and then lots of close-ups of him shaking hands, and signing Erlene's autograph book, and things like that. Close ups, okay?"

"Okay, all set?" Jim asked. "Places, everybody. Chef Dupré back of the room, please. Let's roll tape. Eddie, go!" Eddie Miles made the announcement, Jim called for 'Action!' Henri took a step or two and the audience went wild. As Jim expected, the applause was the best narcotic his star performer could have, and his personality instantly exploded. He even added his own ad-lib, when he stopped and kissed a very startled-looking Victoria Townsend on his way to the makeshift stage where he bowed a few times and asked for silence.

"*Merci, merci, mes amis*," Chef Dupré said as though he had done this a thousand times. "You are too kind. But, you know, kindness is a gift from God, and He rewards you for showing it. *Alors*, if you would care to show more of your kindness to me, I will be happy to receive it so you will gain even more favor from Him," he added, pointing a finger upward to heaven. The remark brought more laughter and more applause; obviously the audience was into the spirit of the thing as well.

"Today, *mes amis*, we will prepare *Ris de Veau a'la Financiere*, what the English call 'sweetbreads' in a special *Financiere* sauce, that is one of two sauces you can smell even now as they simmer in my kitchen."

One of Tim's crewmen leaned over to him and said, "My grandma made sweetbreads when I was a kid. Lemme tell ya', they ain't bread an' they ain't sweet. I wonder if I can sneak out?"

"Have no fear, *mes amis*," the Chef said. "This is not English cooking, this is French *cuisine*. Pay no attention to what goes into the pot. Remember, you taste with your tongue, not with your eyes. *Alors*, allow me to demonstrate: Come into my kitchen."

With that he picked up the nearby toque, placed it carefully on his head and sauntered into the kitchen where he was joined by the cameramen and the people Jim Lacey had selected. The remaining guests in the audience were served wine, although Tim decreed the crewmen were limited to one each. In a few minutes the scent of meat being sautéed in butter and spices wafted into the room, along with some kind of simmering sauces that obviously contained more wine, more butter, and more spices.

Chef Dupré did his usual masterful display in the kitchen, but he had warned Jim that regardless of how much advance preparation he had done on the sauces, the final preparation would take at least 30 minutes. That was no problem for the people in the kitchen—they were being entertained—but how about the rest of the audience? Jim had a sudden inspiration: he took one of the cameramen out of the kitchen, and brought him into the main room where he began doing impromptu interviews of the people who remained at the tables—beginning with the fellow who complained about his 'grandma' making sweetbreads. The audience was completely unrehearsed, and so was Jim for that matter, and the whole thing had a sense of on-scene reality that made it as interesting as any news program. The walk-in entrance and the live audience interviews would thereafter become a regular part of 'Come Into My Kitchen.'

Late afternoon found Les Leslie at the walnut door with gold letters that proclaimed the offices of Townsend & Meacham. He didn't like being there. Not that he had anything against Commodore Townsend and Mister R.J., of course. They were fine, upstanding fellas and he would do anything . . . risk his life if he had to . . . for either one of them. But the whole "Law Office" thing bothered him right down to his socks. It made him feel almost like . . . almost like the fellas on the ship used to say how they felt when they began to feel seasick. Les never had a problem with the sea—never. Come a gale, come a storm, he was always able and willing to do his trick, and take another when he had to; he would have stood watch in a hurricane if need be. The only thing that got him in the pit of his stomach was the law. But the Commodore had phoned him and told him to report at sixteen hundred, so at 3:30 sharp he left the party that always followed one of Frenchy Dupré's successful TV tapings, and he got himself across the bridge to Bonita. That was the easy part. Now he had to open that door and walk in.

"Hello, Mr. Leslie," the girl behind the window said, "go right in to Mr. Townsend's office. They're both waiting for you in there."

Both! Waiting for him! That didn't sound good; it couldn't be good. He opened the office door.

"Come on in, Les," Jack said from behind his desk. R.J. was in one of the side chairs. They both stood up and shook his hand before they sat down again. He would have preferred to remain standing. That's how you took it in the Navy . . . and at Leavenworth. If you were about to be keelhauled, you stood and took the news like a man. But they told him to sit and he so did.

"Les, I'll get right to the point," Jack began. "We flew down to Arizona and spoke to Guthrie Westenbok; we tracked down the lawyer who represented you and we spent quite of bit of time in Washington." He took a large brown envelope off his desk and handed it across. "Here's the result," Jack said.

It wasn't gonna be good news, that was sure. Les ripped open the flap, and slid out a single sheet of paper. When he saw the writing on it, he gasped and his hands began to tremble. The paper fell to the floor; Les dropped his head to his hands gasped twice more and began to sob, weeping uncontrollably. The paper on the floor . . . the one right there between his feet . . . was something he had dreamed of for almost half a century: a Certificate of Honorable Discharge.

Jack came around the desk and knelt down on one knee next to him and patted him on the back. "It's over, Les. You are where you should have been."

R.J. was on the other side, consoling him as well. "We shouldn't have sprung the news to you like this, Les. I apologize . . . we both apologize."

Les took a large handkerchief out of his back pocket, wiped his face and blew his nose. "I don't know what you fellas did," he said with a voice still punctured with gasps. "I don't know how much time it took or what it cost. But whatever it is, I'm gonna pay it; I'll pay every dime if I gotta work every day f'r the rest of my life."

"I'm glad you brought that up," Jack said. "The fact is, Rob did most of the work here. He did the really hard stuff, I just came in at the end. He'll have to set our fee."

"Do you happen to have a dollar bill on you, Les?" R.J. asked, "I need to look at one."

"Huh? Yeah, sure, I guess." He took a bill out of his pocket and handed it to R.J. who went over to a plaque on Jack's wall.

"No, I'm sorry, this won't do," the young lawyer said. "Do you have a bill that's older? Something that's a little more worn-out and scruffy looking?"

Les wondered what kind of game they were playing, but he was in no position to argue. He took out a handful of bills and handed R.J. the oldest and most worn looking one of the bunch. Once again the lawyer took it over to a plaque on Jack's wall. "Yeah, this one's okay. What do you think, Jack?"

"It's up to you. It's going on your wall," Townsend replied.

"Okay, that's it. I'd like the plaque to say, *'The mills of the gods grind exceedly fine.'* What do you think, Jack?

"It's going in your office," Jack reminded him.

R.J. looked at their bewildered client as he put the rumpled bill in his pocket. "Okay, thanks, Les. Your fee is paid."

Les looked back and forth between the two men. "What are ya' talkin' about? What's goin' on here?"

"It's pure jealousy, Les," Jack explained with a smile. "Rob has always admired the dollar bill we got for representing our first innocent client. Even though he got his half, ever since we started our partnership he's been jealous of the fact that Marilyn grabbed the actual bill, had it mounted on a plaque and hung it on my wall. He's always wanted one of own. Now he gets to have it."

"I come in here and look at that one every day, Les," R.J. said, pointing to the wall. "It reminds me that our real job is to do justice, not to make money. Now I'll give yours to Jennifer and she can have a plaque made for me, too."

"Don't forget my half!" Jack laughed.

"I have it right here," R.J. replied, slamming a coin down on his desk. "Marilyn can mount it in a paperweight or something."

"What? You mean I don't get it on the end of a gold watch chain?"

"If you want a gold watch chain, I'm sure Marilyn knows where to find a jeweler in Bonita," R.J. teased.

"But . . . but what about payin' ya'?" Les protested. "What about the money you guys are supposed ta' charge me f'r all the flyin' around, an' hotels, an' . . ."

"My partner just told you: that dollar is our fee," Jack said. "You got the family discount. Now if you don't mind, sign this release form, and take off. Rob needs to get back to work on a very large Trust, and I would like to finish my second novel. We'd really love to have you hang around and chat, but, you know, we're pretty busy here."

"I owe you guys my life, ya' know that don'cha?" he said as he sniffed and scribbled his name on the paper lying on Jack's desk.

"Now that you mention that, it seems the Government owes you some money." R.J. said as he shook the man's hand. "The JAG officer we met in Washington is taking care of that. She's a fine young lady and I'm sure she'll do justice, too. When you get the check, you can take us out for coffee."

Les turned back to Jack. "Commodore," he said, taking his hand, "I'll never be able to repay ya' f'r this. Ya' know that."

"Don't worry about it, Les," Jack said. "Things have a way of working out."

CHAPTER 32

The summer heat was already beginning to close in as Nancy Neblett walked her very spoiled Cavapoo dog along the seawall and encouraged him to "do his business" so they could both return to the air-conditioned comfort of *Doc's Aboard*, the 45-foot Matthews yacht she shared with her husband Tom. Nancy, a retired registered nurse, was married to "Doctor Tom" who had retired from the stress of general practice. Nancy was professional and impatient, but Teddy was no ordinary canine. Half Cavalier King Charles Spaniel and half Poodle; he was intelligent, friendly and outgoing. He also had a high sense of propriety and could not be rushed. He sniffed here and sniffed there, never quite sure of which precious spot was worthy of receiving his morning oblation. "Just pee anywhere, dammit!" Nancy shouted, at her wit's end with her pet's performance. That did it, of course. Teddy looked at her with distain and began walking along the seawall, looking neither here nor there. His owner had broken the spell; he was no longer in the mood. They would have to try again later. The walk abruptly ended when they reached the usually-vacant, battered Trojan tri-cabin that was known as the 'roach of the marina.' The vessel wasn't vacant this morning; in fact, two young ladies appeared to be hard at work. A freckled redhead and a smaller blonde were hauling buckets of soapy water aboard along with rags and scrub brushes. Teddy, who had by now forgotten the purpose of his morning walk, barked furiously.

"Does he bite?" the redheaded girl asked.

"Teddy? No of course not," Nancy Neblett replied. "He's just telling me that something unusual is happening here."

"It's not unusual," the blonde girl shouted, "we're just cleaning our Dad's boat. We're gonna live here!"

"You are?" Nancy replied, "Well, that's unusual, isn't it? And it's exciting, too!"

"Can I pet him?" the redheaded girl asked.

"Of course," Nancy laughed. "He won't bite, but he'll probably lick you a lot."

It was all the encouragement the girls needed. The buckets, rags and brushes were left behind and in a minute they were on the seawall petting Teddy, and, as Nancy Neblett had warned, being 'licked a lot' amid squeals of laughter.

"He looks like a Teddy Bear," Clissy squealed. "What's his name?"

"His real name is Theodore Bear. We call him 'Teddy' for short."

"Really? I have a real name too. It's Clarissa, but I hate it and everyone calls me 'Clissy'."

"But Clarissa is beautiful name," Nancy Neblett explained. "It means you are bright or clear or famous."

"Really?" the wide-eyed little girl asked.

"My real name is Kathleen," the girl with the curly red hair and freckles announced. "People call me 'Kathy'."

"That's a beautiful name, too," Nancy assured her. "It's an Irish name that means you are 'pure of heart'."

"What's your name?" Clissy asked while she continued to pet Teddy.

"My name is Nancy Neblett. You should call me Mrs. Neblett because I'm older than you are, but now that we're friends, you can call me Aunt Nancy, okay? And I live right over there," she pointed to the large white boat in the dock just to the Trojan's stern. "I live there with my husband, Doctor Tom Neblett."

"Is he really a doctor?" Kathy demanded.

"Yes, he's really a doctor. But he retired from active practice and now he just takes care of people here in the marina . . . as a friend."

"Wow! You mean the people here have their own doctor and everything?" Kathy asked.

"We have a lot of interesting people living here," Nancy replied. "We even have a real Italian countess. She doesn't live here yet, because her boat isn't ready, but she will someday I'm sure. Meanwhile she just spends a lot of time here with her friend Mrs. Townsend. In fact, Mrs. Townsend's grandfather was the Governor of New York."

"Double wow!" Kathy exclaimed.

"Now, how about telling me who you are and what you're doing here."

"We're gonna fix up this boat so we can live here with our Dad . . . and Mom. We'll be your neighbors!" Clissy shouted, using her 'outside' voice.

"That's a wonderful idea!" Nancy Neblett explained. "But it's a pretty big job. Do you have any help?

"Not so far," Kathy reported. "We kind of thought some of our friends from school would help us, but . . . well, you know, it's pretty hot."

"How about your Mom?"

"She's got a job in Bonita," Kathy answered.

"And your Dad?"

"Dad is the new owner of Maggio Marine something," Clissy shouted. "He's working on the *Margaret* . . . that's the boat over there . . . but he's gonna get lots more jobs pretty soon an' then we'll be rich!"

"And what about your lunch? Did your Dad think about that?"

"Yeah, he said he'd come over here and take us out for 'burgers," Clissy answered. "I'm gonna get a Big Mac."

"Well, I have a better idea," Nancy Neblett suggested. "It's going to be pretty hot and dirty around here. When you get tired, why don't you come over to our boat? We have air conditioning and a TV, and I'm sure Doctor Neblett would love to meet you. And you can help me out a lot by taking Teddy out for a walk, okay?"

"But who's gonna do all this work?" Kathy demanded.

"Oh, don't worry about that," Nancy assured her. "People around here have a way of helping out. By the way, I make much better 'burgers than Big Mac's and we have homemade cookies and fresh lemonade made from real lemons too. And I'll bet there's even some ice cream in the freezer. So, what do you say?"

Kathy looked at her younger sister. She thought for a moment and then nodded. "Okay, but we have to do some stuff around here first," she said.

"Well, whenever you're ready, just come alongside and ask for 'permission to come aboard.' You have to say that. It's the way things work around here."

"'Permission to come aboard,' got it," Clissy said. "We'll see you in a little while, okay?"

~

Elena Russo, the Countess *Falconara*, did not need permission to open the door to the offices of Townsend &

Meacham; nevertheless, she hesitated. She was outfitted as one should be for an important visit. She wore a lady's smart, business attire; with her white blouse and matching beige skirt and jacket, she might be mistaken for one of the many lawyers in the building. Only one thing set her apart: her white gloves. The salesclerk in Bonita had assured her that such things were no longer worn, but Elena insisted, and it had taken some time for the manager to find that, indeed, the store did carry white gloves.

The Countess knew she was on a fool's errand. Although the men behind that door might know the answer to her question, the rules of their brotherhood would not allow them to reveal it. Still, they were her only hope. She opened the door.

"Good afternoon, *Contessa,*" the young woman behind the window greeted her. "Please, have a seat. Mr. Townsend will be right with you."

In less than a minute Jack Townsend appeared in full business attire: jacket, necktie and all. He greeted her and ushered her into his office where R.J. was waiting, similarly attired. She wondered if their offices were always this formal, or if they had dressed up for her.

Jack seated her in one of the guest chairs, and took his place behind his walnut desk. R.J. occupied the other guest chair. 'Now, *Contessa,*" Jack said, "how may we help you?"

"First, *Avvocato,* we can do away with the titles, no?" she responded.

"Sometimes titles are better for everyone," Jack responded. "They remind us of our jobs."

"As you wish. Then, *Avvocato . . . avvocati . . .*" she added, turning to R.J., "I come to you with a most unusual problem."

Neither lawyer responded, and she continued.

"These past few days, *Cecile* has become a new man. He is happy . . . vibrant. He has become much like the young man I knew in Licata many years ago . . ." she looked down and added, ". . . like the young man I fell in love with, in those days."

"Those same feelings have arisen in me now, *avvocati*, and . . . I believe in *Cecile* as well." The Contessa smiled and added, "Once or twice I felt he was about to ask for my hand in marriage, and . . . the truth is, I would be happy to accept his proposal. But it seems he is waiting for something more to happen . . ."

She looked back and forth at the lawyers and added, "Of course, you know such a marriage would be a huge scandal in my town. But what do I care? All my life I lived under the scornful eyes of others. I have my own life now; it is time for my happiness. If he asks me, I will live with *Cecile* even at the marina in that boat of his . . . of ours . . ." She smiled and added, ". . . but only when it is in the water, of course. Does that shock you?"

"My wife and I live there, *Contessa*; aboard a boat that is in the water," Jack assured her, "as do many other very fine people."

The Countess smiled. "Yes, I know your wife . . . and her mother. They are my good friends." Then she went on with her story. "This great change came over *Cecile* very suddenly, soon after you returned from Washington. Yes, I know about that, too, *Avvocati,*" she said, glancing from one of the men to the other. "This place is much like my town in Italy. There are very few secrets when one lives in such a small place."

"And when one is the best friend of the *avvocato's* mother," Jack added.

"Friendships can sometimes be very helpful," the Countess agreed. "Tell me now, did your visit have something to do with *Cecile?*"

Jack's jaw tightened; it appeared the Countess had linked up their visit to Wasthington with Les Leslie's almost-obsessive desire for secrecy.

"I'm sorry, *Contessa*," he said, "but there is no way either of us can answer that question. The things we do are confidential. They have to be."

"*Va bene*," she said, "I knew that would be your answer. But I think . . . I pray . . . that your visit to the American capital had something to do with restoring the honor and good name of a man who I believe was terribly wronged by a man . . . a Sicilian man . . . a Sicilian man who I am sorry to say was my father."

Jack remained silent, but he nodded slightly–involuntarily, in fact–and his movement was not lost on the perceptive lady who was watching him.

"There, you see, *Avvocato*?" she said. "You did not have to say one word. Your eyes spoke to me. They told me everything I need to know. Now, if you will permit me another moment of your time, I would like to tell you a story.

"My late husband, the Count *Falconara*, had two sisters. The girls were *gemelli* . . . twins . . . and, I am sorry to say, they were very jealous of each other. If one had something, the other had to have the same thing . . . only better. The jealousy continued all their lives; if one was courted by a professional man, the other needed a man with a title; and then the first would have to find someone who was higher than that.

"When the girls came of age, their father, who was then the Count *Falconara*, had two *ricordi* . . . How do you say it? Mementos . . . souvenirs . . . made for them. Of course, these things had to be exactly alike. The years went by, and, sad to say, the jealousy of the *gemelli* prevented either of them from marrying. They left no children, and, so, these things came into my husband's hands . . . and, later, into mine.

"Before I left Licata, I went to the church of Saint Anthony to make a prayer for a safe voyage. While I was there, it came into my mind that I should take these things with me to America. At that time, I did not know the reason, but I obeyed the voice. Now I know why."

The Countess reached into her purse and took out two leather cases. She opened them and displayed two matching gold filagree bracelets, each of which was centered with the crest of the *Falconara* family enameled on a gold shield surrounded by the colors of Italy in diamonds, rubies and emeralds. "I believe your wives should have these things, for they are more sisters than the *gemelli* ever were."

"Thank you, *Contessa,*" Jack said, "but I'm afraid if we were to accept your generosity it would create questions which we could not possibly answer. If you truly wish for Marilyn and Jennifer to have these very special gifts, I think it would be best if you presented them yourself."

"*Va bene, Avvocato,*" the Countess agreed. "Then, with your permission, I will give them to your wives, one to celebrate the birth of her first child." She turned to R.J. and added, "And to yours, to celebrate her marriage. Perhaps it can be the 'something old' she needs to wear on her wedding day."

The Countess stood up, and, of course, the lawyers did the same. "And I leave you both, *Avvocati,* with the undying love and respect of *la famiglia Falconara* for as long as the *castello* stands. Thank you for your time," she said, bowing slightly to Jack and then to R.J. "It has been a most instructive afternoon."

CHAPTER 33

"Are you sure you're not mad at me?" Jennifer asked for what seemed like the hundredth time. She had officially received her Master's degree from Bonita College—"Thank God it's over" was her only comment at the large celebration dinner Marilyn arranged at the Bonita Key Yacht Club. But now, with no classes to occupy her time she spent all of her time hanging around the marina. Everyone knew Jennifer really didn't have a 'job' in the usual sense; she was just 'in charge' of everything. And so, without a formal job or a title, she spent a lot of time hanging around in Marilyn's temporary office in the double-wide trailer.

"No, I'm not mad at you," Marilyn replied again. She looked up, smiled and added, "And I'm not angry with you either."

"I didn't major in English, okay?" the younger woman protested. "Besides, I just didn't want you to get upset about . . . you know, that extra room and everything."

"Jen, when you changed the downstairs plan from a lounge to a television studio, and when you moved the bar into the area where our offices were supposed to be . . ."

"We'll get zillions of dollars' worth of free publicity. Jim Lacey has already talked to the TV station about his idea of having a local talent night broadcast live right from here." As usual, Jennifer could not keep her enthusiasm in check.

". . . and when I saw you walking around the place for two weeks with your sketch pad and huddling with Tim Gorman . . ." Marilyn continued.

"Tim said it's really not that big of a deal," she explained.

". . . and when an extra crew came in and began laying out forms for a foundation . . . Let's just say it didn't take a Sherlock Holmes to figure out you were expanding the building," Marilyn concluded.

"The main work will be finished in time for *Sposafesta.* Tim promised me. So don't be upset, okay? It's not good for the baby."

"Jennifer, so far all of your crazy dreams have worked beautifully in this world that you and Grandma created. Why would I be upset now? And the baby is just fine, thank you very much. Now, who is Jim going to get to host his talent show?"

"Eddie Miles, of course," Jennifer responded, as if it was the silliest question she had ever heard. "He's a trained announcer, you know."

"Jen, he studied that in college a long time ago, but I don't think he ever graduated . . ."

Marilyn's objection was cut off by the sudden appearance of Jim Lacey, the director of programing (or should it be, 'Director of Programming?') at Dupré's Restaurant.

". . . and speaking of crazy dreams," Marilyn said.

"Excuse me? Am I interrupting something?"

"Not at all, Jim," Jennifer assured him. "We were just talking about how a lot of dreams are coming true around here."

"Well, I'm afraid mine is coming true a little too quickly," Jim responded. "The station wants at least six more episodes and they'd like to have them pronto!"

"More? But didn't you already give them thirteen?" Marilyn said.

"Yes, thirteen," Jim confirmed. "They were supposed to broadcast them once a week and carry us through right up to *Sposafesta!*"

"So what happened?" Jennifer demanded.

"People began calling in, sending letters, postcards, wanting more; a few even sent telegrams. It seems they can't get enough of the French Chef."

"My father, the TV star. It had to happen," Marilyn said as she tilted back her chair, closed her eyes and settled her hands over her growing tummy.

"They can't continue the current format beyond *Sposafesta!*, Jim," Jennifer protested. "The new shows will have to be live from our studio. I'm not backing down on that!"

"I told them you wouldn't, but that's not the problem. The thing is, to satisfy their audience, they're going to put us on twice a week, and they need at least six more episodes . . . maybe seven or eight . . . just to get us to *Sposafesta!*. After that, our studio will be finished . . . I hope . . . and we can go live, or maybe even live on tape. I'll have to work with them on that."

"My father, the TV star," Marilyn moaned again. "What's next?"

"So what's the big deal? Do what you did before. Why is that a problem?" Jennifer demanded.

"If this is going to look right, we need to expand the audience for the new programs, to show how our audience is building. We'll need to take over as much of the second floor as we can," Jim explained.

"Do it. The second floor is finished; everything is in place up there," Jennifer shot back.

"People, Jennifer. We need people to fill those tables. I can't have my star walking into an empty room."

"'My star,' no less!" Marilyn whispered again.

"Okay, Jim. No problem. I'll round up everybody in the marina. And we'll get as many of Tim's crew as he can spare. I'll tell him to give them half a day off if he has to; I'll pay them. When can we start shooting?"

"We need to jump on it, Jennifer. It'll probably take me a couple of weeks or more to get my crew back together and make the necessary adjustments to the set. We'll need some extra lighting and some additional sound. Let's plan on shooting in three . . . maybe four weeks. We can do a couple of episodes a day if we have to, and we can have everything in the can within a week after that."

"I'll tell Arlo to put out the word. You'll have your audience. You just need to worry about your star . . . and your crew."

"Now it's 'in the can.' And my father is a star," Marilyn said softly with her eyes closed as she shook her head and patted her belly.

❧ ❧ ❧

They didn't need to bother Arlo, and they didn't have to worry about an audience, either. Calkins Harbor and the 'big city' of Bonita over on the mainland were pretty small communities in 1986, and word spread quickly, especially after people began calling the public television station and the receptionist gave them the phone number for Cap'n Kelly's Marina for "reservations and tickets to the show." Reservations? Tickets? Uncle Doug suddenly had a real job and, because it was related to his favorite subject–TV–he launched into it with uncharacteristic gusto.

His first problem was to nail down Jim Lacey about dates. "Our fans are expecting dates, Jim," he said seriously. "I promised to call them back, but I'm already up to three pages!" And, once the dates were established, he had to have tickets printed because–after all, he told Marilyn–studio audiences expect to get tickets and save them as souvenirs. "Sometimes they even ask the stars to sign them," he assured her as she pictured her father, signing his name with a Gallic flourish while he basked in the glow of his adoring fans. Whatever it was that was about to happen at Cap'n Kelly's, it would be nothing like the tumble-down backwater that greeted her on her first day which was—was it really only a year ago? She smiled and calmed Uncle Doug down by assuring him that she would be happy to sit at his planned "Welcome Table" and take his planned ticket stubs.

Everything was running smoothly; in fact, it was perfect until construction foreman Tim Gorman stormed into the office in early June.

"Jennifer!" he shouted. "This is a construction site. I've got two crews working at the same time and I'm trying to keep them out of each other's way so nobody gets killed! What's this I hear about civilians walking around here for your television show?"

"It's our television audience," Uncle Doug protested.

"Your television audience?" Tim demanded. "How many people is 'your television audience'?"

Uncle Doug began to retreat into his normal, comfortable shell. "Well, the room will easily hold a hundred," he said, trying not to answer the question.

"A hundred!" Tim shouted. "You're going to have a hundred people walking through my construction site while I have two crews working?"

"All right, all right," Jennifer said quickly as she motioned for quiet. "Everybody simmer down. Let's work this out, okay? Uncle Doug, have you actually distributed tickets to anyone yet?"

"Well, no . . . I'm still waiting to get the dates from Jim Lacey so I can call Southern Printing and have them printed."

"Okay," Jennifer said quickly, "and these tickets are going to be numbered, right?"

"Well, I hadn't thought about that . . ."

"They're going to be numbered," Jennifer said firmly, which settled the question. "Now, Tim, would you be okay with twenty-five, maybe thirty people, trooping up to the second floor for, say, an hour or two every day . . . for a week?"

"I wouldn't be okay with it even if it was five people."

"Okay, but you'll tolerate thirty, won't you?" She looked at him with her clear blue eyes and added, "For me?"

Tim Gorman nodded his surrender.

Jennifer took a calendar off the wall. The charm vanished. "Uncle Doug, tell Jim Lacey he has to be ready to go by the last week of June. He can film every day with an audience of no more than twenty-five people, and end with a big bash on the Fourth of July, when he can pack the place to the rafters."

"Jennifer, that's two weeks," Tim Gorman protested. "You said a week!"

"Tim, the Fourth is on a Friday. You're not going to have a crew here on Friday, the Fourth of July," she assured him. "And everybody knows nothing serious gets done the day before a three-day weekend. So you're giving Uncle Doug and me an three extra days of audience time: Monday, Tuesday and Wednesday. Live with that, okay?"

"What about the big bash?" Uncle Doug asked.

"Pack the place," Jennifer answered. "What will the room hold? A hundred and twenty?"

"That would really pack them in," he assured her.

"Great! SRO! Standing Room Only! Tell your audience you'll do your best, but they'll be lucky to a ticket for the big event."

"What will the big show be?" Uncle Doug protested.

"That's up to Mister Lacey and his Star," Jennifer said grandly. "They have four weeks to come up with something." She turned to Tim Gorman and said, "Tim, I promise; after that, no more television, no taping, no civilians. The place will be all yours and you'll have nine weeks to give me at least exterior walls for my gift shop, my rooftop patio, and my completed first floor for Dupré's. You can do that can't you?" The charm returned and she added, "Please say 'yes.'"

Tim Gorman nodded again. "Okay, we'll do it," he assured her. "I'm not sure how, exactly, but we'll get it done."

"Now let's all shake hands and get to work, okay? And let's not have any more disagreements in front of Marilyn. She's having a baby."

Marilyn had been watching the scene with quiet amazement. Cap'n Kelly's wasn't the only thing that had changed in the previous year. The shy, blonde college girl who played the piano for her grandmother had taken on the older lady's mantle after her death. She may have been a little more forceful than Grandma would have been today, but the "For me?" and "Please say 'yes,'" were right out of the Margaret Calkins playbook. Yes, Marilyn thought, Jennifer hadn't yet been crowned with her planned *'Sposafesta!'* event, but she was already on her way to becoming the Queen of Calkins Harbor.

CHAPTER 34

News of re-starting the filming Chef Dupré's "Come Into My Kitchen" and its planned Big Event–whatever it was going to be–flashed through the marina and became part of the daily conversation on *Doc's Aboard* where Kathy and Clissy Maggio were by now regular lunchtime guests.

"Nobody knows what the Big Event is," Nancy Neblett reported as she ladled out homemade vegetable soup. "It's a deep, dark secret."

"The Fourth of July is my birthday," Clissy said, unable to hold her voice to an 'inside' level in spite of Aunt Nancy's gentle reminder.

"Well, Uncle Doc," Aunt Nancy said, addressing her husband–she had settled on his new pet name because it sounded better than 'Uncle Tom'–"do you think you can use your influence and get us tickets for the Big Event?" she asked with a wink.

"I don't know," Tom Neblett replied, trying to look as serious as possible. "I hear they're going pretty fast."

"Please, Uncle Doc," Kathy pleaded. "You can do it if anybody can."

"And can you get some for Mom and Dad too? Please?" Clissy added.

"I'll tell you what," Doctor Tom said gravely, "let's finish Aunt Nancy's soup and her delicious grilled cheese sandwiches, and then I'll go over to the office and tell them that the law requires them to have a doctor present for big events like the one they're planning."

"Is that true?" Kathy said, shaking her red curls.

"It sure sounds good, doesn't it? Doctor Tom chuckled. "Let's eat up, and then you two can walk Teddy and I'll go over to the office and try it out."

The fact that two little girls were attempting to clean up the 'Roach of the Marina' and make it into a home for themselves and their parents had not been lost on the other denizens, especially Countess Elena who had a soft spot in her heart for young girls in general and for those willing to tote buckets of soapy water and scrub brushes in particular. She and Victoria Townsend happened to be visiting Marilyn when Tom Neblett came in to reserve six "Big Event" tickets and repeated Clissy's lunchtime stories about cleaning up and moving in, and her wish that the whole family could be together for her birthday.

Elena suddenly got dreamy–in fact, almost tearful. "Vicki," she said to her best friend, "it will be *la picciridda's compleanno* . . . the little girl's birthday," she explained, startled by the long-forgotten Sicilian word that unconsciously popped out of her mouth. "We must do something special for her . . . for all of them."

"What did you have in mind, Elena?" Victoria asked.

"It hurts me to see such beautiful children work so hard," the Countess said, "Especially when we are blessed with so much and they have so little. We must do what we are called to do."

"I'm sorry, but I never learned how to use scrub brushes and tote buckets of filthy water," Victoria protested.

Elena's expression grew firm. "I did," she replied. "And now I can save these two beauties from the lessons that were forced on me."

"You can't save the whole world, Elena," Victoria reminded her.

"The world, no," the Countess replied. "But these two, yes."

"Ah . . . excuse me. I'm afraid I'm going to have to report this conversation to my wife," Doctor Tom interjected. "Whatever you're planning, you better count her in."

"And Jennifer and me, too," Marilyn added from her desk.

"*Va bene*, we are five strong women together," Countess Elena said with a satisfied smile. "More than enough for a small *miracolo*."

❧ ❧ ❧

Jim Lacey was sure he would need a miracle, and a big one, to complete his task. He was wrong. The new episodes of 'Come Into My Kitchen' played to an audience that was primed and ready, and they responded to each of his new ideas with appropriate enthusiasm. The first of those new ideas was to turn over the on-camera-audience-interview-segment to his life partner, Eddie Miles–who at first rebelled at the idea.

"But that's what you wanted years ago! When we were in college, Edward! Remember?" Jim insisted.

"That was radio, James!" Eddie pleaded. "I was a voice. Nobody saw me."

"Don't be silly! You're a handsome guy, and you have a great personality. Just try it, okay?"

After a lot of coaxing, pleading and many more compliments, Eddie Miles agreed to give it a shot, "but only for these two weeks," he insisted. As might be expected, his first couple of days were, well, rough. On camera Eddie did not have the smooth professionalism that his voice projected. But by Wednesday–the third day of that first week–something clicked, and Eddie Miles, dressed in a floral shirt that was to become his trademark, began joking with members of the audience, getting them to open up on camera while Chef Dupré worked his magic in the kitchen. By Friday of that week, Jim made another change in format: instead of Eddie's voice announcing the title, the show would open with him on-camera, in one of those ghastly floral shirts, holding a live microphone (something else that was to become his trademark) and announcing that Chef Dupré was inviting his audience to 'Come Into My Kitchen.'

The weekend following that show found Eddie and Henri Dupré spending a lot of time together, banging around "their" kitchen, kibitzing and comparing recipes. When the Monday show opened, the bantering continued and the audience ate it up. If it went on like this, Jim Lacey thought from his makeshift control booth at the back of the room, Henri Dupré and Eddie Miles could become the Johnny Carson and Ed McMahon of afternoon public television on Florida's southwest coast. The only problem might be Eddie's floral shirts: if he insisted on a different one every day–and, knowing Eddie, that could very well happen–they would have to apply for an additional grant from the Calkins Foundation–and warehouse space for costumes!

But the floral shirt problem–surely a happy one if it happened–was a problem for another day. As the second week of their two-week filming got underway, the Director of Programing, who happened to be a budding amateur by the name of 'James Lacey' dove into his work with no idea of what the 'Big Fourth of July Event' would be–which is why, with Monday out of the way and 'in the can', he drove directly to the doublewide trailer that served as the headquarters of the growing Jennifer Calkins empire.

She wasn't prowling the grounds with her sketch pad and Tim Gorman in tow, nor was she in Marilyn Townsend's office, which was her usual informal hangout. Instead, both Jennifer and Marilyn were huddled in the small kitchen/break room with three other women. He recognized two of them, Countess Elena Falconara, and Victoria Townsend, the lady who had become her constant companion. The third woman was a mystery. Like Jennifer, she was a blue-eyed blonde, but her hair was pushed back in a rather formal style, and when they were introduced, she spoke with a noticeable British accent.

Her name was Barbara Bradley, and she had just opened what she called an 'interior design studio' in what he suggested was an unusual place: 'downtown' Calkins Harbor.

"Yes, well, I have rather a good feeling about this town, Mr. Lacey," she had assured him. "I believe it has good bones, and I predict wonderful things are about to happen here."

He wasn't about to argue, and instead turned his attention to Jennifer. "Jen," he reminded her, "we are now officially three days away from our final taping."

"Four days, Jim," Jennifer corrected him.

"Three, Jen: tomorrow is Tuesday, then there's Wednesday and after that, Thursday. We shoot on Friday. And I still don't have any idea of what the Big Event is, or how many people to expect."

"The Big Event is settled, Mr. Lacey," Barbara Bradley informed him. "We are going to draw tickets for a door prize, and one lucky person will win my services for complete makeover of his or her home . . . up to a maximum 2,500 square feet of course. That should cover most Florida homes, don't you think?"

"But . . . how are you going to advertise . . .?"

Jennifer had the answer of course. "Eddie Miles will keep reminding people to tune in Friday for the Big Event . . ."

"Jen, these shows are on tape. We don't know when they'll be aired!" Jim protested.

"Okay, tell Eddie to leave out the name of the day. Just say, stayed tuned for the Calkins Big Event brought to you by Dupré's . . . Golly, Jim, do I have to come up with everything?"

"Okay, all right," he replied. "Now let's talk numbers. Jennifer, my star performer is talking about something really special; an actual afternoon dinner."

"What's wrong with that?"

"Up until now, the audience has been getting a small portion of this or that . . . he tells them it's a *lagniappe.* It's a New Orleans thing . . . a little taste. This Big Event thing of yours must have gotten to him because he's talking about a full-blown meal."

"Go with it," Jennifer said quickly.

"We can't just 'go with it,'" Jim protested. "You told me to pack the place. There's no way he can turn out a banquet for 100 or more people with our current staff!"

"Okay, what can you do?"

"Forty."

"Make it fifty."

"We're going to need extra people in the kitchen . . . and more servers."

"Hire them. You still have your list, don't you?"

"There's one other thing, Jen . . . Henri says we need to end the program with a champagne toast."

“Great idea. I know we have plenty of glasses up there, and we have lots of refrigeration space. Heck, Jim, we’re a restaurant! Go for it!”

The day of the Big Event arrived quickly. Jim had gone over the details of lighting and arranged for additional staff. The audience was up to 60 because Jennifer couldn’t resist issuing a few spur–of–the–moment ‘y’all come’s’. No problem there: as always Uncle Doug took the precaution of ordering additional numbered tickets. The sound crew set up a separate wireless microphone for Barbara Bradley and another young woman, who were seated at a special table with Victoria Townsend and Countess Elena, along with Jennifer Calkins, her fiancé R.J. Meacham, and his law partner, Commodore Jack Townsend who would be joined by his wife Marilyn as soon as she finished checking people in and depositing their ticket stubs in a glass bowl.

“Let’s see . . . Neblett, party of six,” she said as Doctor Tom and Nancy arrived with the Maggio family. Marilyn carefully wrote their names on each numbered ticket, as she counted them off: “Dr. Tomas Neblett; Mrs. Nancy Neblett; Mr. Sebastian Maggio; Mrs. Bridget Maggio; Ms. Katherine Maggio and Ms. Clarissa Maggio.”

“This is kind a’ formal, isn’t it?” Sibby protested.

“There’s a very expensive door prize involved, Sibby,” Marilyn explained. “We don’t want any slip-ups.”

“Expensive? Is it a car?” Clissy couldn’t contain her excitement.

“No, it’s not a car,” Marilyn told her. “But it’s something very special. Now tear off your ticket stubs, put them in this bowl and go find your table.”

Finally, the audience was in place, and Marilyn was relieved of her duty. She barely had time to join her family and hand the precious bowl to Victoria Townsend who placed it under her chair for safekeeping. Suddenly the room lit up and Eddie Miles in the most flowery of all floral shirts he could find was on camera and announcing that Chef Henri Dupré was inviting the television audience to 'Come Into My Kitchen!'

The chef entered from the back of the room to wild applause, and, as was his habit, stopped at Victoria Townsend's table. But this time instead of giving her a little peck on the lips, he stood her up and kissed her passionately–and, it seemed, Victoria kissed him back! When they broke and the cheering stopped, she picked up a nearby microphone and introduced her new friend, Barbara.

"*Enchanté, Madame,*" Henri said as he bowed and kissed the stranger's hand. "Please tell us why one so beautiful as you has consented to join us."

"Thank you, Chef," the lady began in her clipped British accent. "My name is Barbara Bradley, and this is my assistant, Samantha Thomas."

The Chef bowed to the young blonde and said, "*Enchanté, Mademoiselle,*" while Samantha blushed crimson.

"We are opening an interior design studio here in this lovely community," Barbara Bradley continued. "Today is big event for Dupré's, and our opening will be a Big Event for our company as well. To celebrate moving here to Calkins Harbor, we are going to do a complete makeover of some lucky person's home. We will spare no expense. When we're finished, that person's home truly will be a castle."

The room erupted in applause.

Victoria Townsned handed Samantha the the bowl with the ticket stubs, and Barbara continued, "Please find your tickets while my assistant and I bring the bowl to the Chef's stage where he will draw the winning number."

Confusion erupted as people began checking pockets and purses, while Barbara Bradley and Henri Dupré made their way to the front of the room.

"And now, Chef Dupré, will you do us the honor of pulling one ticket stub and reading the number?" Barbara said theatrically.

Well, of course, the Star of the Show could only do that with his own brand of Gallic *élan* and he reached into the bowl, grabbed one small piece of cardboard and held it high above his head.

"And the number is?" Barbara asked.

Henri Dupré brought the stub down, peered at it gravely and said, "The number in my hand is *vingt-sept* . . . twenty-seven."

"That's me! I won! I won!" Clissy Maggio was using her 'outside voice' before anybody could stop her.

"All right," Barbara Bradley said calmly, "bring your ticket up here so we can confirm it."

Clissy bounded up to the front of the room shouting, "I won, I won!" all the way there while Samantha Thomas discretely picked up the bowl with the remaining tickets and scurried back to Victoria Townsend.

"Now calm down, young lady, and hand me your ticket," Barbara insisted. She looked it over carefully. "This says your name is Clarissa Maggio. Is your name 'Clarissa'?"

"Well, yeah, but see . . . Clissy is my fun name. But Clarissa is my real name. Honest! Right Dad?" she shouted to someone in the audience.

"Wait a moment. I want someone to confirm that your ticket, Clarissa, and this stub have the same number." She turned to a member of the audience. "Can you please confirm that, Sir?"

"That's the number all right, twenty-seven."

"I won, I won, I won," Clissy kept saying as she jumped up and down, her long blonde hair keeping time with her movements.

"Now, Clarissa, where to you live? I would like get started right away."

"Me and my sister and my Mom and Dad almost live on a boat right here at Cap'n Kelly's," Clissy said as she continued to bounce.

"I see. Well perhaps we should bring the entire family up here. Mum and Dad and Sis, would you please join us?"

In short order the rest of the Maggio family was introduced, and after Barbara admitted she had never decorated a boat, she asked whether they were currently living aboard.

"No, not at all," Babe Maggio assured her.

"Wait a minute," Sibby said, "I'm kind of living there."

"He's only staying there . . . temporarily . . . while he's doing a big job on another boat," Babe interrupted.

"Well, Dad," Barbara Bradlley informed him, "I'm afraid you'll have to return to the world of commuters with the rest of us. You won't be able to stay on board while my crew is working."

"That's no problem," Babe Maggio said. "He hates getting stuck in traffic on the bridge, but it'll just be for a little while until we can all move on the boat, right Sibby?

The female Maggio's made a date to meet Barbara at her studio the following Monday for design ideas, and fabrics and countertops and colors and . . . and . . . and Sibby realized it would be best for him to go back home, finish up work on the *Margaret*, then take on Doc Neblett's diesel job and stay the hell out of the way for the foreseeable future.

The show got underway with Henri Dupré describing how they would soon feast on a New Orleans treat: beef tenderloin stuffed with pecans. Six tenderloins had been in the oven for almost 3 hours, he explained, and a lucky few members of the audience would accompany him into his kitchen to observe him put on the finishing touches with a sauce made of wine, Worcestershire sauce and caramelized onions.

Back at the Townsend table, Commodore Jack Townsend sipped an Old Fashioned and smiled at his mother. "That was a nice trick, Mother," he said, smiling, "Did you get the 'switching the bowls' idea from one of my old magic magazines?"

"John! How dare you say such a thing! This was perfectly legitimate and you know it."

"May I see the rest of the ticket stubs in that bowl?"

"Certainly not! And I am offended that you would even ask!"

"I'm not objecting. I think it was handled very well. I would just like to know if you've taken up one of my long-ago hobbies, and if we'll be seeing you performing at a convention of the International Brotherhood of Magicians anytime soon."

Countess Elena stepped in. *"Avvocato,"* she assured him, "miracles happen every day. Sometimes we see them, but many times we do not. They all happen because of His will," she said, pointing upwards. "But you know," she added thoughtfully, "God is a very busy man. He has many problems that require His attention, and sometimes it is best for us to help Him a little . . . with small, human things . . . to do what He would do, if He had the time. Now, is that wrong?"

"No," Jack said quietly, "that is very right. And I am proud of all of you, including Samantha."

"And Mrs. Bradley's services come quite reasonably priced," Victoria assured him, "as you and your partner will soon see."

"Don't tell me you charged it to our law firm!"

"We sought the advice of counsel who assured us that it could be written off as a 'community service.' Isn't that right, Dear?" she added as she looked at Marilyn.

"Don't tell me you were in on this too!" Jack protested.

"I was asked for a legal opinion, and I gave it. I'm a lawyer just like you are and I can do that, the same as you can. And, by the way, I have . . ."

"I know, I know. You have a Master's Degree in Taxation, and I don't have one. Okay?"

"Now may we please relax and enjoy Henri's repast?" Victoria asked as the servers brought around artistic platters of the Chef's creations.

"Well, no, there's something else," Jack said quietly. "Marilyn and I thought the Big Event might be the right time to take care of it. Our home on Magnolia Avenue will be finished soon, and we'll be moving there . . . 'hard aground' as they say."

"And?" his mother prompted him.

"You know, in a way boats are living things. We don't want *Marilyn* to be left alone." He pushed a set of keys across the table. "We want you and Henri to have her."

His mother was speechless, and she felt tears welling up in her eyes.

"John, I'm shocked. I . . . I don't know what to say." She looked at Marilyn and added, "Are you sure you won't be upset about us living in sin?"

"Victoria," Marilyn smiled, "living in sin aboard *Marilyn* is a family tradition."

"We'll see about that," the older Mrs. Townsend replied. She turned to her son and added, "But what will you do without a boat? You've had one almost all your life."

"Don't worry about it," Jack replied. "The little contretemps with Howard Garner left us with an additional share of the marina, and Doc Neblett has located a 56 foot Matthews with crews' quarters so we'll be able to travel with a . . ." He suddenly stopped, afraid of the word he was about to use.

"With a 'nanny'?" his mother asked.

"A babysitter," he insisted.

"A nanny," she replied.

"Okay, a nanny. Does that make you happy?

"John," she said quietly, taking his hand, "it's not a sin to be rich. The sin lies in not properly using what has been entrusted to us."

That life lesson was interrupted by Henri Dupré, who came to the table and took Victoria's hand. "*Ma Chère*, it is time," he whispered.

"Excuse me, we have a rather important announcement," she said as she accompanied him to the front of the room.

"*Mesdames et Messieurs,*" he began grandly, today is special for many reasons. It is the day this great Nation declared its independence and then won its freedom . . . with the help of the French of course."

The crowd laughed politely as the servers continued to pour champagne.

"And today, it is my pleasure to give up my own freedom for I have found here the love of my life, and she has consented to be my wife." He took Victoria's hand and added, "I present to you the future *Madame* Victoria Dupré, and I ask you to join me in a toast to the bride"

The room erupted in cheers and shouts of well-wishes as the newly engaged couple kissed again. Marilyn was speechless, as was Jennifer who was sitting beside her. As always, Jack had his own view of things.

"Well, that takes care of another big problem around here," he observed.

"What . . . what problem?" Jennifer asked.

"When people call here asking for 'Mrs. Townsend,' we won't have to ask which one."

CHAPTER 35

Jennifer's very own Big Event came exactly two months and two days later: on Saturday, September 6, 1986, a date long remembered in Calkins Harbor as both the day of her wedding and the very first '*Sposafesta!*'

The weather was ideal, with temperature in the low 80's, a few puffy white clouds set in an azure sky, absolutely no chance of rain and a refreshing breeze blowing in off the water. Construction genius Tim Gorman somehow came through for his Boss Lady: the 'extra room' and rooftop patio were structurally complete and ready for use. For the moment at least, Erlene's gift shop consisted of folding banquet tables filled with hastily ordered gee-gaws, a few "Pardon our Dust" signs and Erlene's endless assurances that the shop soon would have a lot more classy stuff come the Holidays.

The Maggio family was settling into their new home. They had moved aboard their newly-decorated Trojan tri-cabin several days earlier, and Saturday morning found the four of them along with Uncle Doc Neblett and Aunt Nancy gathered around the salon table enjoying an early breakfast.

"This is really beautiful," Nancy exclaimed, giving her seal of approval to the color scheme, the carpeting, the furniture and even the granite countertop in the galley. "And Barbara Bradley even painted the outside!"

"No, that was my crew," Sibby explained. "I hired them to paint the *Margaret*, and . . . as long as they were here, and Doc insisted on paying me in advance for your engine overhaul, I told them to just keep working. The color is Larchmont Blue. I hope you like it."

"Sibby, it was the best investment I've ever made," Dr. Neblett said. "Now when we sit out on our deck sharing our evening wine and looking aft, we see this beauty instead of the Roach of the Marina."

"And we see two beautiful young ladies, too," Nancy added. "On the whole, I give this place four stars."

Clissy jumped out of her seat. "Hey that's a great name," she said, as her 'outside voice' kicked into gear. "We need a name, don't we? And there's four of us, and we're kind of stars now, sort of. Let's call our boat *Four Stars*!

"I kind of like that," her mother, 'Babe' Maggio agreed.

"Yeah, me too. Great idea, Cliss!" Kathy agreed. "Please, Dad?"

"What can I say when I'm outvoted by three beautiful women?" Sibby laughed. "We'll pick up a bottle of champagne from Dupré's and christen her this afternoon. But right now, we need to get a move on. We have to be at the dock before the *Margaret* arrives with Jennifer and her bridesmaids. She has some really interesting ideas about her wedding."

"Just give me a minute," Babe Maggio said. "I have a little surprise for my stars." She went down to the aft cabin and came back with a sealed cardboard box. "Girls," she said, "I think you should do the honors."

Kathy and Clissy were tearing at the box in a flash. It contained four nautical three-quarter length windbreakers, with a foul anchor and the words 'Maggio Marine Services' embroidered on the left breast and–of course–the name of each individual Maggio in script on the other side.

'We'll have *Four Stars* embroidered under your names next week."

"This is great," Kathy said as she put on the jacket and stroked her arms. "Dad, is this really the color they use at that fancy yacht club up North?"

"That's why they call it 'Larchmont Blue,' Kitten," he assured her.

"Wait 'till I tell that snobby Margie that we live on a yacht that's the same color as the fancy ones up North. I can't wait to wear this when I go back to school."

"Can we wear them right now?" Clissy demanded.

"No," their mother replied. "You're both going to wear those pretty green dresses Aunt Jennifer picked out for you. You're her flower girls, remember? And you have to get dressed right away because we're supposed to be waiting on the dock when she gets here aboard the *Margaret*. Now come on, hop to it."

"Then when can we wear our new jackets?" Kathy demanded.

"After the ceremony there's a luncheon, and then Aunt Jennifer and Uncle R.J. will go off to have wedding pictures taken and everybody will go home to change into their casual clothes. And while that's happening, we can come back here with Aunt Nancy and Uncle Doc and we'll all put on our jackets and officially christen *Four Stars*. And you can wear your jackets for the rest of the night. Okay? Now get busy."

There was no time to waste. Les Leslie and Arlo Woodbrace had taken *Margaret* up to the Bonita Key Yacht Club the previous day and left her there overnight. Early

Saturday, Jennifer and her bridesmaids arrived at the Club and were shown into a room that had been set aside for their use. While professional stylists put finishing touches on their hair and makeup and helped them into their gowns, Les and Arlo returned in the short-sleeve white uniforms Jennifer had ordered for them and took command of the *Margaret.* Two members of the yacht club staff volunteered to be additional crew for the short voyage around the island to Calkins Harbor.

It went perfectly. Sibby Maggio's workmen had removed Margaret's old, rusted trawler rigging and covered her with a new coat of gleaming white paint, highlighted by a red stripe along her freeboard and a green deckhouse. When he protested that green wasn't really a nautical color, Jennifer told him she didn't want 'nautical colors'–she wanted the colors of '*Sposafesta!*'

The *Margaret* arrived at the Calkins dock shortly before noon. Arlo and the volunteer crew from the yacht club made the vessel's lines fast to the dock and helped Jennifer's three bridesmaids down the gangway where they took the arms of the young men who would be their escorts for the day. 'Captain' Les then stepped out of the pilothouse door resplendent in his white uniform with four gold stripes on each shoulder and gold oak leaves on the visor of his white cap, all of which contrasted splendidly with the green of the deckhouse–just as Jennifer had imagined it would. Captain Leslie held the door open and the Bride herself emerged. The bright Florida sun reflected off her elegant white dress and her golden hair, so perfect against the 'non-nautical' green of the deckhouse. She stood there for a few moments and surveyed her creation. "It's perfect," she whispered to herself. Countess *Elena* was standing first in the reception line, wearing a pale yellow mid-length dress with a red, white and green sash held in place by a diamond broach featuring the *Falconara* coat-of-arms. Marilyn was next to her, seated in a throne-like chair wearing a gown that tried–unsuccessfully–to hide her 8-month 'baby-bump'; Jack was next to her in his formal yacht club uniform: tropical white pants and shoes, and a black double-breasted jacket covered with the braid and silver stars that marked a former commodore. Next to him stood R.J., looking so young. His uniform coat was decorated with far less braid, which, she thought, was as it should be. After all, young princes had to earn their stripes, and she was sure that R.J. would be up to that task in the coming years.

With everything in place, she gave her arm to Captain Les Leslie, and they proceeded down the gangway. He presented her first to Elena and Marilyn, and Jennifer curtsied before them. They both nodded regally, and Commodore Townsend and Lieutenant Meacham, snapped perfect military salutes to Jennifer in return. It was the script that Jennifer had worked out in her head: the legend of '*Sposafesta!*': every year a new princess would be brought to the Island; she would be presented, and curtsey to the retiring princess, after which the new princess would be crowned and rule for one year. Then, the following year, she, in her turn, would be replaced by another. Other people may have seen this day as Jennifer's wedding, but Jennifer saw it as the first day of a long, wonderful tradition.

Following her recognition of the royalty waiting ashore, Captian Les Leslie gave Jennifer's hand to her very own prince, R.J. Meacham, who kissed it, and whispered "I love you."

"I love you, too," she whispered. "You're my Prince Charming, and this is the perfect day for us. Let's get married!"

Captain Les moved back to take his place with the Countess, and Jennifer's bridesmaids/ladies-in-waiting and their escorts began the procession to the tent, and Kathy and Clissy Maggio, fell into line ahead of the Bride, with baskets full of rose petals and green leaves that they would begin to scatter as soon as they reached the white runner at the entrance to the tent—a tent that had once had been rented to sell junk, but in Jennifer's eyes had become a royal pavilion where she and her prince would be joined forever as husband and wife.

The 'intimate luncheon' following the brief ceremony was supposed to be for '50 or so close friends,' but Jim Lacey and the staff of Dupré's had grown used to Jennifer's informal 'y'all' come invitations and set up 12 tables of eight–96 people in all. The tent was full to overflowing, but at least all of the guests had seats, and with Henri and his helpers in the kitchen, food was never a problem. The only problem–and it was a good one–was that each one of the 100 or so intimate friends wanted to congratulate the bride and groom personally and take one or two (or three) pictures with them. R.J. got to drink one glass of champagne when Jack Townsend proposed the traditional Toast to the Bride, but Jennifer didn't even get that because Marilyn had warned her the strict rules of protocol demanded that "one does not drink a toast to oneself." At least Jennifer did get to eat a piece of the wedding cake, but that was only because it was traditional and staged for the photographers: both their own and one from the *Bonita Journal.* Needless to say, there was none of that cake-in-the-face nonsense at <u>this</u> wedding; she and R.J. did 'feed' cake to each other (the photographers insisted on the 'shot') but they did it with silver forks off china plates. Then, after a brief dance on a very small dance floor, they escaped with Jack and Marilyn to the quiet coolness of the *Marilyn.*

"Do you mind if we take a nap in your room?" Jennifer asked quietly.

"Honey, we changed the sheets this morning, and the room is yours. Do whatever you like," Marilyn assured her.

"Yeah, but we're both so worn out, all we probably will do is sleep," Jennifer groused.

"You're the one who planned this tea party, Princess," Marilyn reminded her. "Don't say I didn't warn you."

Jennifer's eyes lit up. "Yes, but isn't it just perfect?" she said. "Can't you see the bones of a wonderful tradition?"

"I'll be seeing your bones if you don't get something to eat. Go get changed while Jack and I make you grilled cheese sandwiches. And don't worry . . . I'll knock before I bring them in." She pulled Jennifer close, kissed her forehead and added, "Now go get some rest. You have a long evening ahead."

By 4:00 p.m. a ground crew under the supervision of Tim Gorman had rolled up the sides of the Royal Pavilion, put together a temporary wooden dance floor and moved in chairs for musicians who were arriving with sound equipment. The extra staff hired by Jim Lacey set up outdoor tables and chairs, and covered them with tablecloths, candles and menus from Dupré's, while a local rental company brought in picnic tables and benches for '*Sposafesta!*' participants who brought their own treats or purchased items from food trucks. Over Marilyn's objection, Jennifer had invited vendors to set up those trucks along with carnival games and Uncle Doug took on the job of telling them where to set up.

People began arriving and joining those who lived at the marina and the guests who had not left. When Jennifer, R.J., Marilyn and Jack left the sanctuary of the *Marilyn* at 7:00 p.m., the entire grounds had been transformed into a real '*Sposafesta!*' with clowns and jugglers and magicians who wandered through the crowd.

"This is fabulous!" Jennifer gushed. "This is just what I wanted! This is my dream! This will become the place to be in Southwest Florida in September! And it's all thanks to you, Marilyn" she added, hugging her.

"Me? I didn't do any of this. If anything, I was opposed to most of it, remember?"

"Of course, you had to be. You're the practical one; that's your job. But you let me go ahead with it, and now it's finally happened."

"Well, Your Highness, Jack and I are going to sit on comfortable chairs at one of those Dupré tables and order something from our restaurant menu. Think of us when you're out wandering among your loyal subjects."

Jennifer laughed, kissed her sister on both cheeks, then took R.J.'s hand and said, "Come on, Prince Charming, it's time for us to meet our people."

Marilyn and Jack retreated to a quiet table–well, a table that was as quiet as possible during '*Sposafesta!*'–and were elated when they were greeted by a young man wearing a polo shirt with a Dupré's monogram. "May I get you something from the bar?" he asked.

"Yes, please," Jack answered. "An Old Fashioned. If Marty's the bartender, please tell him it's for Commodore Townsend."

"Yes, sir," the young fellow answered. The name obviously meant nothing to him.

"May we order, please?" Marilyn said. "I'm starving."

"Would you like a minute to study the menu?"

"I know the menu well," she told him. "The chef is my father."

"Are you Mrs. Dupré?"

"I used to be Miss Dupré, but now I'm Mrs. Townsend. And please tell Papa that his unborn grandchild would like Oysters Rockefeller . . . ASAP!"

"Yes, Ma'am, I'll run up and get those and that drink right away, and then I'll come back for your real order, okay?" the young man said as he scooted away without waiting for an answer.

"Oysters Rockefeller?" Jack said, looking at his very pregnant wife. "Are you sure that's a good idea when things are this far along?"

"Jack, I need something special, okay? Just this once." They were both quiet for a minute before she added, "So, have you thought of a name yet?"

"I thought you didn't want to know the baby's sex in advance? You're the one who refused to get one of those sonogram things, remember?"

"Take my word for it, he's a boy," she said.

"How do you know that? You can't be sure," the unborn baby's father replied.

"Jack, I've been carrying him around for eight months; I know what he is. Besides, I talk to him all the time."

"You do? Well, what do you call him?"

"John, of course," the mother-to-be replied. "'John DeWitt Townsend, Jr.' I think it's a very nice name."

"Ouch! No way! I haven't had much luck with juniors. I certainly don't want to create one."

"Well, do you have a better suggestion?"

"As a matter of fact, I do," Jack replied. "I've been thinking about 'John Dupré Townsend.' Then we would have the same initials and he could use all of my monogramed stuff when he gets older, but, technically, he won't be a 'junior'."

Marilyn smiled at the idea. "Of course you know Papa will be over the moon about that name."

"Yes, I thought about that, too. But I'm sure he'll eventually come back to earth."

"Won't your mother be upset about leaving out her famous grandfather's name?"

"You mean the future Madame Dupré? I think she'll be fine with the idea."

Their conversation was interrupted by the server who brought Jack's drink and Marilyn's oysters. "Would you care to order now, or wait a bit?" he asked.

"Give us a minute," Jack said. "We're working on a name for Chef Dupré's grandson and we almost have it."

"Of course," the young man said with a laugh. "I'll be watching you carefully, so just let me know when you're ready."

"Well, shall we settle it with a toast?" Marilyn suggested after the server left. Jack held up his Old Fashioned and Marilyn was about to meet it with her glass of water.

"No, no! Don't do that!" Jack warned. "There's an old saying that if you toast with water someone will die from drowning within a year."

"Well, I'm not going to drink alcohol until after Johnny arrives," she said. "So what do you suggest?"

"How about one of those oysters?" Jack suggested. "Can you pick up one of the shells?"

"Jack, you can't toast with oysters!"

"Says who? It's called 'toast', isn't it? Maybe you can even do it with bread."

"Okay." She picked up an oyster shell and touched it to his glass. "As of this moment, our son's name is 'John Dupré Townsend.' Now drink up because I can't wait to get to these oysters."

Jack barely took a sip of his drink before someone yelled, "Fire!" and people were pointing toward the *Margaret*. "Fire on the *Margaret*," someone else shouted as they watched the figure of a man holding a torch and setting fire to the deckhouse.

"What is it? What's happening?" Marilyn demanded.

"It must be Junior Calkins," Jack guessed. "He's here to wreck Jennifer's wedding and Margaret's plan." He took off his jacket and said, "I'll be right back."

"Jack, no!" she screamed. "Don't go over there. Call the police. Call somebody."

"He's not going to wreck this, Marilyn. I won't let him. Stay here. I'll be right back."

"Jack! No!" she screamed after him; the turned to the crowd that had gathered, "Somebody stop him! Somebody stop that man! Please! Call the police! Call the fire department. Just stop that man!"

Jack didn't hear her and wouldn't have stopped if he did. His mind was on only one thing: stop Junior. The crowd was frozen into inaction, and Marilyn's cries for help seemed to freeze them even more. She watched in horror–almost slow motion–as Jack jumped aboard the deck of the Margaret and began chasing Junior.

The scene aboard the boat was crazed violence. "Oh, look! It's the lawyer-funny-man," Junior taunted when he caught sight of Jack. "Here, want some fire, Mr. Lawyer-funny-man?" Jack grabbed a nearby fire extinguisher and tried to douse the flames around him. "Go ahead and try, Mr. Lawyer-funny-man. I'll be up front when you're finished." Junior ran forward, touching his torch to the newly-painted pilothouse and to anything else that looked like it would burn. Back on shore, R.J. and Jennifer suddenly appeared at Marilyn's side.

"What the hell's going on?" R.J. demanded.

"It's Junior. He's setting fire to the *Margaret*! Jack has gone after him!"

R.J. took off at a run, but Sibby Maggio –who, it turned out, had been a high school track star–sprinted after him and tackled him to the ground before he reached his goal.

"Sibby, are you crazy? Let me go! I've got to get Jack out of there."

"Listen to me," Sibby shouted. "Those tanks are loaded with gasoline! That baby could blow up any minute!"

"Then we've got to get Jack out of there!" R.J. shouted again.

"You gotta stay out of there, man," Sibby shouted in reply. "We can't afford to lose both of you. Jack can jump for it!"

Back aboard the *Margaret*, Junior had run to the farthest point of the bow, and, with nowhere else to go and the flames spreading, he turned to face his pursuer. Jack suddenly realized that he was in serious trouble. He was alone, unarmed and facing a madman who held a burning torch.

"You want some of my fire, Mr. Lawyer-funny-man? You want to burn too?" Junior advanced on him and Jack began backing up.

"Junior, listen," he shouted. "Whatever problems you have here, we can settle them. You don't have to do this."

"No, I have to do this, Mr. Lawyer-pain-in-my-ass-man," Junior retorted. "I have to get rid of that old bitch's memory, and my daughter's fancy ideas, too." He took another vicious swipe at Jack with the torch. "And if I get rid of you at the same time, that's what I call a trifecta."

Junior took another step forward with the torch. Jack took another step backwards, slipped and fell against a stanchion. He tried to get up, but Junior was right in front of him, smiling viciously and poking at him with the torch. "Have some fire, Mr. Law . . ." And then suddenly Junior was gone. And then the *Margaret* was gone. And Jack was flying though the cool night air.

The thought instantly flashed through Jack's mind that he was dead; that he was floating above the scene of his own death, and he was supposed to go toward the light. Only there wasn't any light; there was nothing ahead of him but darkness. And in another instant, he felt the soul of his unborn son rushing past him in the opposite direction, on his way to his mother, Jack thought. And then . . .

All his thoughts ended in a splash of cold, dark water. He was fully awake now, and he was sinking, but he was unable to control his arms and legs. All he could do was sink farther, and that's when he was sure that although he wasn't dead yet, he was going to die.

He had almost given himself up to that idea when a strong arm wrapped itself around his neck and he was brought, struggling, to the surface. "Relax, I gotcha," a familiar voice said. "I gotcha, Commodore. Just relax and let me do the work."

Back at their table, Marilyn suddenly doubled over in pain. "It's the baby!" Jennifer shouted.

"No, it can't be!" Marilyn replied. "I have another month! The doctor said so!"

"Somebody get one of those rescue squad guys. She's having her baby right here."

"No, this can't be happening!" Marilyn protested as Erlene Rodgers ran toward one of the trucks with flashing lights that had arrived on the scene.

"Quick! The lady's havin' a baby!" she shouted to one of the crews who rushed to follow her.

"Relax, Ma'am," one of the EMT's told her. We've done this before."

"Well I haven't!" Marilyn screamed.

On the other side of the marina, Les Leslie, was swimming toward the seawall with the powerful strokes he learned in the Navy and practiced throughout his career as a merchant seaman. The people standing on the dock pulled Jack up and Arlo helped Les scramble up a nearby ladder. Les took command instantly. "Leave 'im alone; I got this," he yelled as he turned Jack over onto his stomach and began pressing down on his back, forcing water out of lungs.

"Come on, breathe! Breathe, God damn it! Breathe!"

Through a dark haze Jack thought he recognized Les' voice, but it could not have been Les. He never used language like that. Jack was about to say something to that effect, but his voice was cut off by foul-smelling, oily seawater that gushed out of his nose and mouth as Les continued to press on his lungs.

"Sir? Sir? We can take over now." It was the member of another EMT crew, and he was patting Les on the shoulder. "We handle cases like this all the time. We know what to do."

"Yeah, give 'im air. Oxygen if ya' got it. He'll be all right."

"Yes, sir, you did great job. You saved the man's life."

"Well . . . I owed 'im. He saved mine," Les said as he sat on the ground and began to cry.

Suddenly, Elena was next to him, sitting on the ground in her "holey jeans" and hugging him. "You are a brave man, *Cecile*; you are a brave, strong, beautiful man. One day you will teach me to be as brave as you are. Come, now, let us go home to our little *Elena* and rest."

Two ambulance units pulled away from Cap'n Kelly's and headed for Bonita Gardens Hospital while fire crews stayed behind and fought the fires on what was left of the *Margaret.* It was the end of Jennifer's '*Sposafesta!*'

CHAPTER 36

It was well after dawn the next morning when Jack woke up to the feel of clean, crisp hospital sheets and saw Jennifer standing next to him while R.J. dozed in a nearby chair.

"R.J.! R.J.! He's waking up."

His young partner was suddenly by his side. "Hey, partner, you gave me a hell of a scare. Who was I going to rely on for advice in my next assigned counsel case?"

"What happened?" Jack croaked, still struggling with his voice. "Is Marilyn okay? Did Junior get away?"

"Your wife is just fine," Jennifer assured him. "As far as that other person goes, no one has seen him. And I hope we never will."

Jack reached up and touched her face. "You poor kid. We ruined everything for you, didn't we?"

"What do you mean?" She turned to R.J. and said, "Maybe it's the concussion talking."

"Your '*Sposafesta!*' idea was ruined."

"Yep, it's the concussion all right," she said as she ran her cool hand over his forehead.

R.J. laughed. "Jennifer's been up all night, drawing ideas on hospital placemats. It'll take her a week to paste them into her sketch pad."

"See," she suddenly said to Jack, moving closer to his bed with a handful of drawings. "From now on, every year '*Sposafesta!*' will end with a gigantic fireworks display to commemorate the burning of the *Margaret.* We won't tell people how she burned, of course. It was an accident caused by Grandpa being so stingy and buying gasoline engines. In a couple of years, people will forget what happened last night and just know about the fireworks."

Jack looked at her and said, "There's a lot of your grandmother in you, you know that?"

Jennifer's excited expression softened, and she put on her best movie-star Southern accent: "Whay, C'mmodore Townsend, that is th' naicest thaing any Yankee genl'man has ever said ta' me." She kissed him on the forehead and said, "So, are you ready to meet your son?"

"My son?"

"Oh, didn't we tell you? Last night while you were taking a swim with Les Leslie, Marilyn was doing something more important."

"Is she okay?"

"Yes, she's fine. And he's fine, too."

"He's 'John Dupré Townsend,' with an *accent aigu* over the 'e'. She kept saying it the whole time she was in labor. It was almost funny," R.J. added with something of a laugh.

"Like the 'n' in 'Portner', right, Rob?" Jack joked as his voice cracked.

"Okay, R.J. can help you get dressed. I'll get a nurse with a wheelchair and we can all go down the hall and visit her," Jennifer said as she left the room.

A few minutes later the nurse returned, and helped Jack out of bed. "We'll take him from here," Jennifer assured her.

"Well, I'm supposed to remain . . ."

"No problem. We'll just wheel him down the hall," R.J. confirmed.

"If you say so." It seemed the Calkins name had a certain caché even on the mainland in Bonita.

Marilyn was dozing when they walked in but woke instantly.

"Hi. How are you feeling?" Jack asked weakly.

"How are you feeling?" she demanded. "You're the one in the wheelchair."

He stood up and said, "You're the one who gave birth."

"Women give birth every day," she reminded him. "But most people don't chase after crazy people who have burning torches!" She would have shouted it, but she was too tired.

"Okay, no more crazy people with torches," he assured her. "How is John Dupré?"

"John Dupré is just fine. Papa would say he's a little 'underdone,' but the doctor gave him a 10 Apgar score, and the nurse says he never does that for anyone, especially not for preemies."

He took her hand. "Are you sure you're okay?"

"Yes, I'm fine. Really."

He was standing next to the bed, holding her hand when the Sheriff walked in. Only he wasn't the usual "Bear Harper" in a casual polo shirt and khaki pants. Sheriff Beverly Harper was in full dress, white shirt with gold stars and a gold badge, green pants with a gold stripe, and topped off by a green straw Stetson hat with gold cord, which he removed. "Jack, Ah'd like ta' talk to you alone for a minute, if you please."

"I'll go with you," R.J. said. "I'm his lawyer."

"He don't need a lawyer at the moment, Counsellah. Ah'd just like ta' get a few facts straight before Ah speak with th' State Attorney."

Jack turned to his partner. "Why don't you take Jennifer home?" he said. "You've both had enough excitement for one day."

"Come on, R.J., let's go," Jennifer whispered as she took his arm.

It was clear that R.J. was leaving under duress. "Call me. Right?" he said. Jack nodded his head in response.

"Would you care to step outside?" Bear asked after they were gone.

"We can talk right here in the room, Bear," Jack suggested. "After all, my wife is a lawyer too."

Bear Harper sat down heavily and toyed with his Stetson. "Ah'd like ya' ta' tell me what happened on that boat last night," he began.

"I'm sure you know most of it. I saw a guy running around with a torch of some kind; it was clear he was trying to set fire to the *Margaret*. I knew instantly it was Junior."

"And?"

"And I ran over there to stop him."

"Did you have a weapon of any kind? A gun, a knife or . . . anything?"

"No, of course not. I don't have that stuff; never did, even when I was in the State Attorney's Office and authorized to 'carry.'"

"So what was your intention when you ran over to the boat?" the Sheriff asked.

"Aren't you supposed to read my rights now, Bear?" Jack replied.

"Jack, you know 's well 's Ah do that 'rights' thang only applies if you're a suspect. At the moment all I suspect you of is not havin' the common sense that God gave a goat.

You're tellin' me you chased after a crazy man with a burnin' torch an' you were barehanded?"

"It was a real torch, then?"

"We found it floatin' in the marina this mornin': a two by four with a whole bunch of kerosene-soaked rags tied around one end. Junior fixed himself up with plenty a' fuel."

"He was going nuts when I got alongside the boat. The deckhouse had already started to burn. I jumped aboard, grabbed a fire extinguisher and put it out. By then Junior was on his way forward, torching the side of the pilot house and anything else that he saw."

"What did you do?" Bear asked.

"I followed him up there, of course."

"Alone? With no weapon?"

"I wasn't thinking clearly," Jack admitted.

"Ah'll say ya' weren't. Go on."

"He was running away from me, and I ran after him. I guess I thought I could tackle him. The chase ended when he got right up to the bow. I had him cornered, so he turned around started to come at me . . . coming at me, swinging that damn torch back and forth. That's when it occurred to me that I was in trouble."

"You were in trouble, all right," Bear agreed. "So what did ya' do?"

"I started backing up to get away from him. I tried to reason with him . . . told him we could work out any problems . . . but he just kept coming at me, with an ugly sneer on his face and waving that torch back and forth. That's when I slipped and fell backwards against some kind of stanchion or something. And a couple of seconds later, Junior just disappeared. It was like, 'poof!' he was gone." And a second or two after that there was a big 'whomp' sound, and I was flying through the air. And then Les Leslie was pulling me out of the drink."

Marilyn twisted the bedsheet and tried to control herself as she thought of her reaction when the boat exploded. At that moment she had been sure Jack was dead; she would never see him again in this life.

"Yeah," Bear Harper agreed, "Ah know all about that. But let's go back to Junior disappearin'. Do ya' remember anything else? Anything at all?"

"Well, now that you mention it . . . but it's kind of silly . . ."

"This is a possible homicide; there's nothin' silly about it, Jack."

"Okay, well . . . this is really strange . . . but just before Junior disappeared . . . like half a second before . . . that sneer left his face and he looked . . . surprised. It was a surprised expression . . . and then 'poof' he was gone."

"Yeah, that fits," Bear said as he leaned forward and toyed with his Stetson again.

"Fits? What do you mean, 'fits'?"

"Junior violated a primary rule of walkin' around a foredeck. You're always supposed ta' know where your feet are. Junior was standin' on the anchor chain. And the thing you fell against wasn't a stanchion; it was the lever that released the winch. I reckin' that surprised look you saw was when he realized the chain had snatched him. We found his body this mornin' with the chain still wrapped around his foot, in eight feet of water directly under what was left of the *Margaret*."

"Oh, Dear God," Marilyn whispered as she crossed herself.

Bear looked at Jack and said, "It's somethin' ain't it Jack? Casey always said that one day he was gonna wrap that boy in anchor chain an' tho' him overboard. I reckon he finally got around ta' doin' it."

Jack smiled and said, "That was a private joke, Bear. How do you know that Casey said it?"

Bear smiled back. "Ah'm the Sheriff, Jack. This is mah county. Ah know everythin'." He looked at his watch and stood up quickly. "Good night, look at th' tahme. I best be gettin' ta' the State Attorney and make my report."

"What are you going to tell him about Junior?" Jack asked.

"Accidental death." Bear shook his head sadly. "It's no use dragin' Casey's family through ahny moah mud. How's this for a Press Release?"

"Mr. Kelly Calkins, Jr., was attendin' his daughter's weddin' reception at the *'Sposafesta!'* celebration when he noticed that fahr had broken out aboard the family's boat, the *Margaret.* Mr. Calkins quickly boahded the vessel and was seen runnin' around the deck attemptin' to put out the flames with a fire extinguisher, but he was too late. The *Margaret* exploded, killing him and injuring John D. Townsend, a local lawyah and formah commodore of the Bonita Key Yacht Club who was nearby and attemptin' to help Mr. Calkins extinguish the flames.

"A memorial service will be scheduled by the family at a later date. The cause of the fahr is undah investigation."

"How's that, Counsellah?"

"I'm sure Casey would be pleased," Jack said.

"But Ah'm gonna mark mah personal file 'N.K.' . . . 'Needed Killin'."

"I'm sure Casey would be pleased about that, too," Jack agreed.

"Well, Ah'd best be goin'," Bear said as he headed for the door. He stopped, turned to Marilyn and said, "Ma'am," in soft voice that carried a somewhat heavier-than-usual Southern drawl, "Ah'd 'preciate it if you would do me a small courtesy."

"Anything, Sheriff," Marilyn replied just as softly.

"Ah wish you'd keep your husband from gettin' inta' anymore faghts in mah county. Somebody needs ta' explain ta' him that he's a lover, not a fighter."

"Ah'll see ta' that, Sheriff," she replied in drawl that matched his.

"Thank ya' Ma'am. Ah'm much obliged."

"We're much obliged to y'all, Sheriff," Marilyn said in their suddenly shared language.

Bear put on his hat and touched the brim with his thumb and two fingers, bowed his head slightly and said, "Ma'am."

As he turned for the door, a nurse walked in pushing a portable incubator, and Bear peered at the baby inside.

"That's a fahn lookin' son ya' got there, Jack. I shore hope he's got more sense than his Daddy."

When the door closed the nurse announced, "Breakfast time, Mommy. This little guy is hungry."

"You're telling me? I'm about to burst!" Marilyn said as she pushed down the covers and began unfastening the nursing bra.

"Wait a minute!" Jack protested. "You're not going to do that with me here, are you?"

She looked at him as she exposed her breast. "Jack, you've seen my boobs before," she reminded him.

"Well . . . yes, but . . . never . . . never in actual use . . . as it were."

The nurse tried to suppress a laugh as she handed Marilyn the baby.

"Good Lord what is it about you men and women's breasts? Is it some kind of unresolved Oedipal complex?" She took their son in her arms and added, "Come here, Johnny. Come here, Honey." In an instant the baby was attached to her breast and suckling greedily.

"Enjoy yourself, Sweetie," she said to the baby. "And don't pay any attention to your Daddy." She looked at her husband with eyes that promised a thousand future delights, smiled wickedly and added, "He's just jealous!"

Jack looked at their son, enjoying the comfort of his mother and he said quietly, "You're a lucky boy, John Dupré Townsend; you're a lucky, lucky little boy."

The End . . . For Now

ABOUT THE AUTHOR

Joseph A. Tringali has been admitted to the practice of law in both Florida and New York, and served as an Assistant Attorney General for the State of Florida, where he regularly appeared in all federal and state courts. He is a member of the United States Supreme Court bar, a former Mayor of North Palm Beach, Florida, and was elected to three terms on the Village Counsel. He has served as Assistant Corporation Counsel for the City of Buffalo, Assistant District Attorney of Erie County, New York, and Assistant State Attorney for the Fifteenth Judicial Circuit of Florida.

While living in Florida Mr. Tringali served as president of the Guild of Catholic Lawyers of Palm Beach County, and he and his wife served for three years as president and secretary of the Friends of Fisher House of West Palm Beach, a local group dedicated to providing free lodging for families of Veterans being treated at the regional Veterans Administration Hospital.

Mr. Tringali is an active alumnus of the University at Buffalo Law School, and a loyal member of Phi Alpha Delta Law Fraternity where he served both on the International Tribunal and as District Justice for New York, Massachusetts and Connecticut. He is a lifelong boating enthusiast and longtime member of Buffalo Yacht Club (New York). He has served as Commodore of North Palm Beach Yacht Club and Commodore of Palm Beach Sailing Club. He is a Life Member of United States Power Squadrons and holds the grade of Senior Navigator, having successfully completed all of the advanced grade and elective courses in the Squadron's educational program. He is a Past National Rear Commander of USPS, where he was Chair of the National Flag and Etiquette Committee.

As a Major in the Civil Air Patrol, Mr. Tringali commanded the Western New York TAK Squadron which was recognized as "Squadron of the Year" by the Niagara Frontier Group, CAP. In his spare time, he enjoys the study of magic and has received the Order of Merlin with Shield from the International Brotherhood of Magicians.

In addition to *Harbor of Dreams*, Mr. Tringali wrote *Harbor of Refuge*, a novel that introduces some of characters found in this book. He also wrote *I Was That Baby,* his personal story of growing up adopted and finding his birth family at 56 years old; *A Quiet Family Murder,* a story based on a case in which he represented the State of Florida on appeal; and *Yachting Customs and Courtesies*, a two-volume set of over 1,000 pages that has become a resource for yacht clubs around the world.

Mr. Tringali insists his novels are "pure fiction" although some members of the Palm Beach County Bar swear they see certain resemblances to colorful but long-deceased local characters. He has also written articles for numerous periodicals including The Florida Bar Journal, Lakeland Boating and Fate magazine.

Mr. Tringali lives in North Palm Beach, Florida, with his wife, the former Mary Lou Privitera, who is a graduate of D'Youville College, and holds a master's degree in public administration from Florida Atlantic University and a doctorate in management from the University of Phoenix. They have two children: Lt. Col. John A. Tringali USAF (Ret.), a pilot for Delta Air Lines, and Elizabeth A. Tringali, PA-C, the owner of Tringali Vibrant Health, a medical practice specializing in wellness and anti-aging in Palm Beach County.

Made in United States
Orlando, FL
15 November 2021

10436137R00226